Air and Ashes

Margaret Mantor

Book Cover by Damonza

Illustrations by Margaret Mantor

Hardcover ISBN 979-8-9909389-0-8

Paperback ISBN 979-8-9909389-1-5

First Edition: 2024

MM INK

To Will.
Or as you named yourself in my phone "Best Husband Ever."
You make me smile and laugh every day, especially when you ask to be a character in my book. But the truth is you inspire every hero I write.
Love you.

1

Someone can be right while also being wrong. I just wish I'd realized that on the day I found out everything had been a lie.

I glared down at the list—or lack of one—displayed on my screen and resisted the urge to throw my laptop across the coffee shop. All the while, the blinking insertion point timed me. Evaluated me. Who knew a little blinking line could be so judgy?

I would have much rather been drawing in my sketchbook or out running, but this midday college research session took priority.

"You look like you're trying to solve global warming."

I looked up from my screen. Claire Baker had been my best friend since eighth grade. Sitting across the coffee-stained table, she looked completely composed with her strategically tousled red curls, flawless fair skin, and photo-ready cherry matte lips. Like a social media motif in real life, all her study materials were perfectly coordinated with her hint-of-rose-gold outfit.

"Everyone needs a hobby." I shrugged, pushing up the sleeves of my loose-knit sweater that I paired with jean shorts. Unlike Claire, I'd never had the ability or energy to stay on trend, so I just did my own thing.

"You're making this *waaay* more difficult than it needs to be." Claire grinned, her eyes still focused on her latest fruit-logoed laptop.

"True." I propped my chin on my palm, looking anywhere except where I needed to.

The little coffee shop buzzed with the Saturday lunch rush. It was mostly tourists passing through on their way to the beaches around Drakes Bay or to hike to Tomales Point. The rest were locals of Point Reyes Station, like Claire. And me—well, at least for the past four years.

From the time I was eight years old, my Aunt Viv and I had bounced around various small towns in Northern California, never staying in one place for more than a year or two because of Aunt Viv's consulting job. That was, until we moved here. And the serene sandy beaches and cozy no-streetlight town had convinced Aunt Viv to stay. So, bright side?

"Which part of the college checklist are you stuck on?" Claire asked.

"Potential majors." I said as my screen went dark from inactivity. A slightly rounded face framed by wavy shoulder-length hair took center stage. The early afternoon sun highlighted my high cheekbones.

My dirty blonde hair and bone structure were all thanks to my mom, while my light amber skin and blue-flecked hazel eyes were from my dad—or at least that was my theory. But the anxiety shining in their depths? That was all mine. A common side effect when trying to decide your entire future—or maybe that was just me.

"Wait." Claire frowned, her pink highlighter pausing over her notes. "I thought you were working on a list of colleges and safety schools."

"I was, but I wasn't getting anywhere, so I switched." I swiped my fingers across the touchpad, wiping away my apprehensive reflection. "And then I switched again."

Claire's face scrunched with disapproval.

"Plus, why not start with the career I want?" I fidgeted with the simple gold sun charm on my necklace. "Then match that against where I want to go."

"Good point." Claire grinned. "What majors do you have so far?"

"The thing to focus on is not the ones listed, but all the ones I eliminated." Pre-med. Computer science. Poli sci.

"*Sooo* translation: You have nothing?"

"I wouldn't say nothing."

"Then what do you have?"

"A title and some bullet points." Which was something.

"*Emma Cross*." Claire pointed her pink highlighter like a judge's gavel. "How do you have nothing? We've been here for two hours."

"I know, I know. But it's a massive life decision." I tucked back a rebellious wave of hair. "Not everyone knew what they wanted to be since the age of five."

"It was more like nine."

I arched my brows at her.

"Point taken." Claire waved a dismissive hand. "But you're forgetting my momentary lapse of sanity when I thought about switching from pre-med to pharmacology."

"Oh, the horror," I teased her.

"But thank heavens I did my research and, of course, that article I found. Who wants the headache of dealing with the shady drug underworld or the unethical experimentation black market? Do you know who doesn't look like drug dealer material?" Claire pointed a polished nail at herself. "This girl."

I grinned, even as a spark of jealousy flared. I couldn't help it; it happened every time I thought of Claire's goals. She knew where she fit in and what she wanted to be. I've never had that kind of clarity. More like a dense fog obscuring every possibility in sight. Hell, until Point Reyes I'd never been in one place long enough to really take my future seriously. Maybe that was why I couldn't imagine leaving now.

My phone dinged with a notification, and I reached into my backpack to dig it out. The screen showed a missed call and a voicemail. When did it ring?

"I still don't know how you do it." Claire's face pinched with disgust.

I snapped open the phone. "It's not that bad."

"It's a flip phone," she said, like it personally offended her. "And not the new fun kind."

I shook my head as my fingers flew across the vintage keys, the ancient technology struggling to keep up as the battery light flashed red.

Nice.

Hitting play on the message, I put the phone to my ear just as Aunt Viv's enthusiastic voice came through the speaker.

"Hey. Hey. Hope you and Claire are making me proud by nerding it up today." She chuckled at her own corny joke, making me smile. "This project is taking longer than expected so it looks like I won't make it to the store. Would you mind stopping by on your way home? We just need a few things." I snagged my pen and flipped to a blank page in my sketchbook, scribbling down the list of items. "And remember, not everything has to be healthy. Throw some junk food in there. Go crazy. I'll see you when you get home. Love you, Emma-bug."

Aunt Viv might be a technological wizard—or Spunky-Tech-Guru, as I'd fondly dubbed her—but the whole parenting thing? Not really her strong suit. But she definitely got an A-for-effort. A participation trophy. An attendance sticker.

I'd never admit it out loud, but a part of me would always wonder how Mom would've raised me or helped me find my path in life if she were still here...

I shook myself, the turn in my thoughts not surprising. Especially around this time of year. And maybe especially *this* year, what with it being my senior year and my eighteenth birthday only five months away.

"Tell me again"—Claire's highlighter was back in action—"why your aunt makes you use that thing?"

"That thing has a name." I placed a hand over my heart. "And Flipper is a sensitive soul."

"Uh-huh."

"As for Flipper's purpose—"

"Punishment," Claire corrected.

"Aunt Viv said it's about building character and not letting technology rule my life." I shrugged. "Which is—"

"Ironic coming from her?" Claire offered.

"A bit." I lifted my cup of tea only to find it empty.

"Although, she might have a point. Considering you're close to finishing your GED and it's only the beginning of September." Claire tapped her highlighter against her chin. "Who knew homeschooling would have such benefits? Think of all the extra time you'll have to plan out your college strategy. Super jealous."

One person's seclusion was another's oasis. Or something like that.

With Point Reyes being such a small town, there was only an elementary and middle school within its limits. So, when it had come time to start high school, instead of busing me off to another neighboring town like Claire, Aunt Viv had enrolled me in a virtual education program. Which, yes, had its benefits, but also definitely its drawbacks—*cough*, social outcast, *cough*.

"I guess, but it's funny." I picked at my cup sleeve. "Aunt Viv has always encouraged me to boost my education, but lately she's been acting really weird."

"How so?"

"The whole college thing. Anytime I bring it up, she gets super jumpy." I waved a hand at our table. "I didn't even tell her we were researching colleges today, only that we were studying. Just to avoid the drama."

"Really?"

I nodded. "I don't get it. I figured she'd be fully on board the college train. But maybe she thinks I'll just be wasting my time and money." Without a clear goal, that was entirely possible.

"Or maybe," Claire fake sniffled. "She's realizing her baby bird is leaving the nest."

I snorted, though I had to admit the idea of Aunt Viv on her own was terrifying. Technically she was a full-grown adult, but if the past nine years were any indication, the outcome didn't look promising.

"Hey, no judgment toward Auntie V." Claire rested her chin on her fist. "My mom's going to bawl her eyes out when I leave for college."

My heart constricted as I gripped my sun charm. Would Mom have cried if I left for college? Or been the one encouraging me to get out there and discover my place in the world?

Mom always had this way of creating a safe harbor in the storm—a *home*. Whether it was her paint-covered studio or her vanilla candles and optimistic smiles, she always created a place where I belonged. Even on her worst days when her disease reared its ugly head...

"I'm sorry." Claire broke into my thoughts as I tried to figure out why she was apologizing. "The mom comment. I didn't think."

I squeezed her hand. "You did nothing wrong."

"Still, I should have read the timing." Claire fidgeted with her highlighter.

"Honestly, with all the talk about colleges and the future, my mind would've gone there regardless." I swallowed hard. "Especially since Aunt Viv keeps bugging me about a graduation present, but I've been thinking about making a donation instead, maybe even getting an inscription added to my mom's memorial plaque—you know, as a way of including her in the moment."

"That's a great idea." Claire smiled. "Where did she get treatments? Maybe my parents know someone there, and they could investigate the options for you."

"That'd be amazing. But I..." I hesitated, trying to remember back. "I never actually went to the treatment center. My mom didn't want me seeing all that, especially at the end."

"Understandable." Claire grimaced. "All the chemo bags and needles are enough to scare anyone."

A shiver cascaded over me. The IVs and home treatments during the last year were enough to achieve that. Even almost nine years later, I still couldn't look at medical equipment without feeling lightheaded.

"I do remember they have a digital version of the memorial wall." Aunt Viv had shown it to me when Mom's dedication was first unveiled. We'd already moved by then and couldn't be there in person, but we'd held a candlelight vigil next to the computer screen to honor the moment, and then we went and got my mom's favorite treat—doughnuts. We did that every year after her passing. But my heart pinched as I realized I couldn't remember the last time we'd done that...

Determination coursed through me as I promised myself to do whatever it took to make sure it happened this year.

"And I remember the treatment center's logo, but not the name." My brows pinched in concentration. "*Ugh*. How can I remember the sketchy mountains and trees but not the name?"

"Don't worry." Claire waved her hand. "It'll come to you."

The sinking feeling in my chest told me otherwise, but I plastered on a hopefully reassuring smile. "Yeah, I'm sure it will."

An awkward silence settled over our table as the tip-of-the-tongue sensation nagged at me.

"Refills?" Claire held up her cup, her smile tentative. "Then we can talk about shopping for our homecoming dresses."

"Yes, please." I dug out my wallet, feeling giddy. This would be my first high school dance, and by some miracle I'd convinced Aunt Viv to let me go, so I was so on board for that.

"Perfect. I'll order this round." Claire scooted out of the booth and grabbed the cash I offered. "Seriously, you need to get on board with digital currency already. You make me feel like a hooker with these onesies."

"*Aww*. It's sweet that you think I could afford you."

"Not with your budget." Claire wiggled her eyebrows before sauntering away.

I tried to imagine what kind of dress I'd wear. But just as I thought about searching for options, it occurred to me. *Searching*. That was how I'd find the treatment center name.

My fingers sprinted across the keys. I didn't know exactly where to start my search, but that's why Google existed. I plugged a few keywords into the search bar and sifted through the results until I found a promising site—a cancer treatment center just north of Carnelian Bay.

Nestled on the North Shore of Lake Tahoe, Carnelian Bay was where the little cottage the three of us had called home resided. It hadn't been much, but it was the first home I'd ever known. It made sense that Mom's treatment center would be as close as possible to where we'd lived. Feeling confident, I clicked the link and immediately my path was blocked.

Crap.

Aunt Viv's firewall was working hard, even on a Saturday. My aunt had blockers on basically everything, lecturing me over and over about the dangers of the dark underbelly of the digital world. And sure, she had way more experience with this stuff than I did, but I was willing to roll the dice this one time.

It also helped that I'd learned the administrative passcode a few months ago. I'd always had a thing for patterns. I was weird like that. It was one reason I was so good at puzzles or how I could draw various sequences so well. And that's what this passcode was—another pattern. One that would lead me to answers.

My fingers hesitated on the keys. Aunt Viv's warnings returned with a vengeance. Her words were so ingrained in me that it felt like a betrayal to ignore them. If she ever found out, she'd be so disappointed. Would she ground me? Take away my computer privileges? Or worse, not let me go to Claire's homecoming dance? Was I really willing to risk that?

On the other hand, there was a chance Aunt Viv would never know, and it wasn't like this was the first time I'd bent the rules. Plus, if this was the right site, then technically I'd already been there, done that.

Heart pounding, I tapped the proper keys, each one blazing through my vision like they were backlit. But I refused to focus on the faintly glowing sequence of keys that no one else could see. This time they were helping me—like with learning the administrative passcode—not distracting me or highlighting the weird way my brain worked.

I hit *enter* and held my breath, waiting to be denied—or for Aunt Viv to pop up out of nowhere. But the passcode worked, and a professional and inviting website with an achingly familiar logo appeared on my screen—score. The site was easy enough to navigate and with a couple of clicks I located the Donations & Memorials page, plugged in Mom's name and hit *enter*.

Zero matches.

2

How were there zero matches?

I double-checked the spelling and found nothing out of place. Not panicking yet, I entered the date instead. But again, no matches. What the hell?

The date was correct. I knew it was. September thirteenth would always be seared into my memory. Was it the wrong treatment center? That seemed unlikely. The logo was right, and Aunt Viv had shown me Mom's memorial page several times before. It had looked exactly like these.

Breathing deep, I consulted the mighty Google once more, this time plugging *Annalyse Cross* straight into the search engine. There had to be a direct link to the memorial page or an obituary at least.

Nothing.

How was there nothing? There wasn't even a photo of her. How was that possible?

Heart thundering, my hands grew clammy as the herbal tea and banana nut muffin from earlier contemplated a revolt. But before I could truly lose it—in so many ways—Claire headed back over.

I cleared my screen, wiping away all evidence of my search before closing my laptop. Not that I didn't trust her or think she wouldn't bust into full detective mode if I needed her to. But I didn't particularly want an audience for that potential freakout. Plus, what if I was blowing this out of proportion?

I couldn't allow a full mental meltdown until I talked to my aunt and she explained the logical reason behind all this. Because there had to be one...

"One steamy cup of dirty water." Claire set my tea in front of me before scooting into her side of the booth. "So next Saturday, want to do our shopping spree?"

"I need to check with Aunt Viv first, but that should work." I grabbed my laptop and sketchbook. "But hey listen, I need to go."

Claire looked up from her over-sugared coffee. "What? We still have another hour."

"I know." I loaded up my bag. "But I need to get home."

Claire sighed, snagging her laptop and highlighters. "*Fiiine*. I should go, too. I need to finish up some chores before my mom gets home from the hospital anyways."

Packing up, we grabbed our stuff before I hurried toward the door, a light breeze lifting my hair as we exited the coffee shop.

"What's the rush?" Claire scrambled to catch up.

"Sorry." I slowed my pace while navigating the meandering tourists and shoppers. "I just need to..." Crap. *The groceries*. "I need to get to the store before all the good produce is gone."

As much as I wanted to race home and confront Aunt Viv, I couldn't abandon all responsibilities. Especially if I was blowing this all out of proportion, which I really hoped I was.

"You're so weird," she teased me.

That was me—the health-obsessed, medical-weary, pattern-loving outcast. But hey, everyone had their quirks.

I stuck my tongue out at her before switching my tea to the other hand and checking my phone to make sure Aunt Viv hadn't sent any last-minute additions to the grocery list.

"Damn."

"Did you kill Flipper again?" Claire adjusted her backpack on her shoulder.

"I didn't kill him." I dropped my phone back into my bag. "Only potentially, slightly, entirely drained him."

"It's honestly impressive how often your battery dies."

"I have a gift," I said dryly.

"More like the curse of ancient technology. Have you told Auntie V about this?"

"No way. She'd trash Flipper if she knew." And just give me another antique. So, what was the point? Plus, Flipper was configured just the way I liked—despite all its flaws.

"Would that be the worst thing?" Claire hip-bumped me. "You realize this is why you don't have a boyfriend, right?"

"Is not."

"Uh-huh."

"There are like five guys in this town." As if that was explanation enough—small town, small pool and all that.

"And the ones from my high school?"

"We didn't connect." Which was true, just not in the way Claire was talking about.

"Yeah, because it's like trying to communicate in the Stone Age with that thing." Claire snagged her keys with a jingle. "Although, even with a new phone I still think you'd friend zone them anyways."

"Would not." I tightened my grip on my bag. "But even if I did, it'd only be to avoid getting attached before going off to college. No one wants that road to heartache."

"Uh-huh, sure." Claire stopped next to her sporty SUV.

"What?" I sent her a pointed look.

"You keep saying you want to create ties and belong somewhere, but you're always running away from stuff like that." Claire shrugged before returning my pointed look. "And I'm not just talking about dating."

My stomach plummeted. Was she right?

Not the point right now. "Well, I do love to run," I teased.

"I mean, I get it. You can't control the choices forced on you." Claire bit her lip. "You've moved around a lot, and then losing your mom like you did, it makes sense..." Her words faded out before she waved her hand around. "Never mind. Forget I said anything."

"No, no. We're good." I squeezed her arm.

Claire nodded as she fidgeted with her keys.

"I'll call you later, okay?" I gave her one last squeeze before backing away. "We can figure out plans for next Saturday and whatever fashion nightmare you envision me wearing."

"One day you'll appreciate my fashion sense." Claire gave me a sassy smile. "And of course, this all depends on if your phone hasn't given out on you."

"Funny." I returned her smile.

"But seriously, ask your aunt about getting a new phone for graduation." Claire shouted after me. "It's time you joined the real world."

Wasn't that the truth? Just not necessarily about that. It was time. Time to ask questions. Time for answers.

"Don't worry." I waved goodbye. "I plan to."

***

I clenched the steering wheel of my beat-up clunker as the wheels crunched down the long gravel driveway. Tall blue oaks lined either side. The still-green leaves fluttered in the breeze while the late afternoon sun reflected off the windows and metal roof of the small farmhouse up ahead.

Home.

Knots twisted my stomach. I had used the time grocery shopping to organize my thoughts, rehearsing my questions so they were clear and concise. I just hoped they stayed that way when the time came.

Bypassing the front circle loop, Aunt Viv's SUV was parked out front—not by the detached garage where it belonged. I shook my head. She was always leaving things scattered about. I parked in the correct spot, grabbed my backpack and the bags of groceries, and climbed the porch stairs.

From the outside, the small house might look a little worse for wear, but Aunt Viv was always testing out new security systems and top-of-the-line tech. I punched the code into the keypad lock at the side door, and the numbers lit up in my mind like dim beacons.

Crap.

The pattern-tracking was getting worse. What had started as a whispering disturbance was growing into a full-on shouting distraction. Just one more thing keeping me from fitting in. Which was why I hadn't told anyone about it yet. For one, it was *waaay* too embarrassing and weird for anyone to believe. And for another, I was kind of hoping it would just go away... But I couldn't focus on that right now.

The door creaked open and the coastal spices of Aunt Viv's favorite fragrance greeted me like a comforting hug. I shuffled inside with my wide load, pausing only long enough to reset the alarm.

"Hey. I'm home," I called out, proceeding past the mudroom into the kitchen. "Be proud. I got mangoes. Which I know technically isn't junk food, but they're surprisingly high in sugar, so there's that."

I set the bags on the island and started unpacking the groceries. Sunlight streamed into the living room beyond, illuminating the coffee table and cream couches. But there was no sign of the Spunky-Tech-Guru.

She must not have heard me. With her multiple screens and endless lines of code, she often got so absorbed in her work that the rest of the world disappeared.

Nervous energy zipped through me. I'd rushed through the grocery store and back home precisely to speak to her, but now that I was here... *Stop.* I could do this. I knew I could. No backing out now—

A loud crash reverberated through the floorboards above. I dropped the basil back into the bag. My heart rate picked up as I imagined broken mugs and lamps. When Aunt Viv was in the zone, she wasn't the most observant.

I left the groceries on the counter and headed up the stairs, the wood creaking under my feet as I hustled upstairs. I probably should've grabbed the vacuum, but I might as well assess the damage first. I poked my head into Aunt Viv's office, but it was empty and all four of her computer screens were asleep.

Weird.

I continued down the carpeted hallway to the only other room up here besides the bathroom: my bedroom. As I drew closer, I heard rustling and ground to a halt in the doorway, trying to process what I was seeing. The room that had been clean and organized this morning now looked like a tsunami had struck. What the hell?

My closet doors were thrown open. Clothes hung haphazardly off hangers or in piles on the floor while shoes created a trail branching out from their cubbies like ants searching for a picnic. Pens and sketchbooks littered my desk, though my course books and binders were nowhere to be seen. And they weren't the only items missing. The pictures I had strung up across the wall were now nothing more than a network of strings and clothespins. And standing confidently in the center of it all was Aunt Viv.

Her elegant features were set in concentration. Her long blonde hair was in a high ponytail and she wore black skinny jeans and her favorite *Saved by the Dell* T-shirt. Despite her overall geekiness, she was a total knockout—tall, lean, and toned even after years of hauling down junk food, which drove me crazy. Considering Mom's health issues, you'd think she would take better care of herself.

And *my* things.

"What are you doing?" I asked as Aunt Viv yanked shirt after shirt out of my dresser and then shoved them into my canvas duffle.

"I tried to pack all your favorite things," she said without even slowing down. "Grab anything you wouldn't want to leave behind."

Leave behind? I stepped farther into the disaster zone. "What's going on?"

"Only what's important." Aunt Viv waved her hand around the room before zipping the overstuffed duffle and setting it on top of my sunflower bedspread.

"Aunt Viv!"

Anxious eyes met mine, finally acknowledging my presence. "I tried calling you."

"My phone died." I looked around at my new Saturday night plans. "What's going on?"

"Emma-bug, I need you to listen to me." Aunt Viv gripped my shoulders. "We don't have much time."

Confusion flooded me. "Why?"

"I'll explain things in the car." She squeezed and released my shoulders with a little push. "But for now, I need you to do exactly what I tell you and grab your stuff. We need to hit the road."

A powerful wave of déjà vu hit me, sending tingles down my spine. Where the crazy sensation came from, I had no clue. If I had ever been in a similar situation, I definitely would've remembered it, right?

I grabbed my aunt's arm. "But—"

"Emma, *please*," she pleaded, her voice dire. "We don't have time for this. They've found us."

My blood froze. Who found us?

A second later, glass shattered as a loud crash echoed from downstairs.

3

F ear froze me in place. What the—

A shrilling chorus of beeps sounded throughout the house, and Aunt Viv's smartwatch lit up like the Fourth of July. I covered my ears as red notifications from the security system flashed across the tiny screen. Was someone breaking in? Was this part of the "they" my aunt had mentioned?

In an instant, the lights went out and the piercing alarm shut off, the house going eerily quiet. The power had been cut... but not by either of us.

Someone was in the house.

Pressure seized my lungs as I strained to hear any additional noises, swallowing back a gasp when a hand latched onto my arm.

Aunt Viv placed a finger over her lips and whispered, "Keep quiet, but I need you to grab your stuff and stay close." She squeezed my arm. "Do you remember your training?"

I nodded as my pulse raced. Years ago, Aunt Viv had started training me in self-defense. According to her, there were an untold number of creeps in the world and I needed to be able to protect myself. But waking up this morning, I'd never imagined I'd have to call upon those lessons today.

"Good. Don't hesitate to use it." Aunt Viv crept to the open doorway and peered into the hall.

I grabbed my favorite sketchbook off my bedside table and stuffed it into a side pocket of my duffle. There was no time to grab anything else. Throwing the strap over my shoulder, I raced back to Aunt Viv's side, the heavy bag thumping off my thigh. The hallway was dim as I trailed behind my aunt, the high window in the foyer beyond glowing like a soft beacon.

The house was silent as we crept across the carpet, but there was an intruder in the house—potentially more than one. Were they robbing us? Or were they after Aunt Viv because of a top-secret project she was working on?

At the top of the stairs, Aunt Viv halted with me not far behind. My fingers dug into the strap of my bag as I strained to listen. Out of the silence, the hardwood below let out a subtle creak.

Aunt Viv signaled for me to stay put before pulling out a small copper item from her back pocket. It looked like a lighter. What the hell was she going to do with a lighter? Unless... she planned to light the house on fire? If so, I really hoped we were outside first.

Aunt Viv descended the stairs as I lowered my duffle to the floor with a shaky hand. Sweat coated my forehead as I inched toward the wood railing and peered down into the foyer.

At first, I saw nothing. Then a dark figure stepped into view. A man, dressed in black and decked out in full-blown tactical gear—the kind I imagined a SWAT team wore. But what captured my full attention was the gun in the soldier's hand.

Holy shit. Were they here to kill us?

Chest constricting, I couldn't seem to get enough air. This couldn't be happening. How could this be happening?

All at once, Aunt Viv and the soldier locked eyes. He reached for the communicator on his shoulder, but Aunt Viv moved lightning fast. One second she was on the last step, and the next she grabbed and twisted the soldier's arm, disarming him. Then, using his own body weight against him, she had him down on the ground and his weapon pointed back at him.

My grip on the railing tightened. Aunt Viv was a badass. I already knew that from training with her, but seeing it in action was a whole different thing.

With a suppressed flash, Aunt Viv discharged the gun twice, the silencer keeping the noise contained as the soldier went limp. My wild gaze scanned the downed soldier, expecting to find two bloody holes. Instead two tiny, purple-tipped darts protruded from his torso. What the—

Without warning, an arm banded around me and ripped me backward as a hand clamped over my mouth, stifling my gasp of surprise.

No, no, no.

Panic clawed deep as air lodged in my throat. This had to be a nightmare. *Please let this be a nightmare.*

"Don't even think about igniting," a deep voice commanded from behind me.

Igniting? Like I was some kind of candle or firework?

After years of practice, I forced myself to relax and allowed instinctual maneuvers to take over. I slammed my heel down on the soldier's foot as I threw my head back. A wet crunch and grunt of pain sounded out as the arms around me loosened. Breaking the hold, I started forward.

"Oh, no you don't." The handsy soldier snagged my arm.

I stumbled sideways, knocking into the corner balustrade. Pain lit up my system, but the soldier with an iron grip around my arm claimed more of my attention. He was a terrifying copy of the one Aunt Viv had just taken down—SWAT gear and all. Except on this one, I was close enough to make out the royal purple accents that lined his gear and helmet.

"Don't even think about it." The soldier wrenched me forward as he reached for his tactical belt.

Not good.

Utilizing the momentum, I thrust my palm up, striking his already wounded nose. A curse greeted me as I twisted away, but his hold remained strong, knocking us both off balance. My knees crashed into the carpet while the soldier flew forward, smashing into the corner balustrade. The wood groaned from the impact as he released his grip and tipped sideways, careening down the stairs in slow motion. A symphony of bone-chilling noises sounded out as different body parts cracked off the wood steps like a human Slinky before ending in a fleshy thud.

Frozen in place, I swallowed down the bile climbing up my throat while I waited for the soldier to get up.

He never did.

A dark pool spread out from around his head. I knew what that meant. Knew he would never get back up, because his chest wasn't moving and I had... I had been protecting myself. And I would do it again, without question, but that didn't mean I wanted this.

A knot clogged my throat, threatening to suffocate me. But I couldn't think of that right now. Instinct roared at me to get up. Get moving. There could be more soldiers getting in upstairs.

Down below, Aunt Viv was busy taking down a third soldier. With another double tap of the purple-tipped darts, he buckled like a sack of flour. I rose on shaky legs as I snagged my duffle. The journey downstairs felt more like traversing a cliff than a path I took every day. As I cleared the last step, I kept my eyes trained on Aunt Viv and not the motionless soldier—or the expanding dark puddle.

Skirting the wall, I moved to her side, the once immaculate foyer now looking more like a war zone. This was insane. Had Aunt Viv stolen some top-secret technology or something?

A heartbeat later, another massive soldier plowed into us like a bulldozer. With the duffle's weight, I was thrown back against the wall as he and Aunt Viv crashed to the floor. Metal clattered against wood and the tranquilizer gun was knocked from my aunt's grip before sliding across the floor.

Rooted to the wall, I watched, paralyzed, as they scuffled and rolled. *What do I do? What do I do?* I looked frantically in every direction.

The tranq gun.

I spied the weapon only a few feet from me as nausea twisted my stomach. I'd never fired a gun before. Never even handled one. Could I really do it now? What if I missed? I might accidentally hit Aunt Viv—

The discharge of a different firearm whipped my head back around.

No, no, no. Please, no.

To my relief, Aunt Viv was very much alive and kicking—literally. She hit the fourth soldier where it counted before rolling away and grabbing the discarded tranq gun. In a fluid motion, she raised the weapon and double-tapped him with two darts, the soldier going down in a heap. The *click-click* that followed, however, was less encouraging as she tossed the emptied weapon to the floor and stood.

I hauled in one deep breath before four more soldiers appeared. Two in the archway from the living room and two from the doorway beside the stairs. With their firearms at the ready, they formed a semicircle, trapping us as tiny red dots landed on our chests.

My heart stopped as I pressed back against the wall.

This was it.

I was going to die. Before I'd even had the chance to figure out where I belonged in life.

"Hold!" one soldier commanded. "Orders are to take the assets alive. No deviations."

The three other soldiers halted, looking uncertain. Aunt Viv took advantage of their hesitation, pulling out the copper lighter from earlier.

The little wheel clicked as she moved her other hand toward the portable fire starter. What the—

Flames burst into the air like a blowtorch on steroids.

Jerking back, I fell onto my butt as the raging inferno fanned out across the foyer, striking the soldiers before they could even react. Screams of agony split my ears as heat singed the air. In seconds, the blazing fire engulfed the four soldiers. Then it consumed their screams, leaving only silence.

And corpses.

4

The bodies were charred beyond recognition as wisps of smoke rose like tendrils in search of the sun. And the smell... My stomach churned at the sickly smell of roasted flesh.

I should look away. Give my retinas a break from all the carnage, but it was like a train wreck—unstoppable. It all felt surreal. Had that really just happened? Aunt Viv had shot flames out of her hand. At a bunch of soldiers who'd broken into our house.

I squeezed my eyes shut. For what could've been seconds or minutes, I couldn't move. The scenes from earlier were on constant replay as I waited to be woken up from this nightmare. Only the cringe-worthy sound of metal scraping against wood pulled me from the endless loop. Opening my eyes, I found Aunt Viv returning from the back hall. In one arm she had a load of electronics, while in the other she dragged the large metal basin from the mudroom.

Stopping in the middle of all the wreckage, she lowered the basin and then dropped her remaining load in with a symphony of bangs. There were hard drives, an old camera, her smartphone and smartwatch, and *my laptop.*

I peeled myself off the floor. "What are you doing?"

There was no answer as Aunt Viv kept dumping electronics into the basin.

I felt like I was viewing the world from underwater—everything distorted and fuzzy. "We should call the police."

"The police can't help us." She discarded the last item.

"What?" I shook my head. We'd just been attacked. That's what the police were for.

"I need your phone." Aunt Viv walked over to me, extending a hand.

I stared at it. "What?" Apparently, that was the only word I knew right now.

"Your phone." She curled her fingers in a gimme motion.

"It-it's in my backpack."

Pivoting without another word, she disappeared into the back, only to reappear moments later with my backpack. She removed the phone in question, along with my wallet, before handing me my bag.

"We can't call on my phone, the battery is—"

Clang.

I winced, helpless to save Flipper from its free fall into the basin. Or my wallet which followed shortly. Aunt Viv pulled out her lighter again, flipping it open in one swift flick.

I leaped forward. "Don't—"

Too late.

For the second time today, flames exploded from her palm, incinerating everything in the basin. The odor of burnt plastic infused the room.

"How?" I coughed, covering my mouth and nose. It was one of a hundred questions flooding my brain. Was Aunt Viv a dragon or something?

Holy crap.

Were dragons real—*stop*. I needed to get a grip. I knew I wasn't thinking straight, but right now nothing made sense.

Aunt Viv smoothed back her disheveled hair before pointing to my discarded duffle. "Get your stuff."

"Your arm," I blurted as blood dripped down her bicep.

She looked at the wound. "I did get clipped."

Clipped? She'd been shot. It must've happened when the bulldozing soldier had taken her to the floor. When I'd simply stood there.

"It's not too deep. It'll be okay," she reassured me. "Now, grab your stuff. My car's out front. I'll be right behind you."

"I don't understand." I struggled to get enough oxygen. "What's going on? Who were those people? And how did you do that thing with the fire?"

"Emma, calm down and look at me." Aunt Viv grabbed my arms, her hands shockingly cool as her eyes drilled into mine. "I know you have questions and I'll try to answer them, but first I need you to go to the car. We're still not safe here."

I shook my head. "But—"

"*Please*, Emma." She squeezed my arms. "It'll be okay. I promise." She pressed a quick kiss to my forehead. Then she walked off.

I didn't believe her. Not for one second. How could it be okay after everything that had just happened? And even if there weren't charred corpses littering the floor, how could fleeing like a couple of criminals possibly mean things would be okay?

I moved as if encased in fog, nothing fully registering as I slung my backpack over one shoulder and my duffle over the other.

In the living room, Aunt Viv was prying up a floorboard. My steps faltered as her hand disappeared between the boards and then she pulled out a Ziplock bag. I had so many questions, but Aunt Viv's words—*We're still not safe here*—raced through my mind. I stepped out the front door and headed for her SUV. The sunshine that hit my face felt out of place. I half expected to exit out into the dead of night, surrounded by an eerie fog and gnarled trees.

I added my backpack and duffle to the pile of bags already in the back before moving to the passenger side door. The farmhouse showed no external signs of the chaos within. I stood there for a moment, memorizing the place. The porch swing in front where I loved to spend lazy days reading. The dining room beyond where I studied amongst the knick-knacks and artwork. My bedroom above where the pale blue walls and countless sketchbooks held all my secrets.

This had been my first real home since Carnelian Bay. And sure, I'd never really fit in here, but I hated the idea of leaving it all behind.

Aunt Viv rushed out with one last load of items, beelining it for the front of the car with a white bandage wrapped around her arm. She ducked behind the hood before a shower of sparks flew like something was being welded.

As she dashed to the back of the car, I walked around the front. Where a California license plate had once been, a Colorado plate now hung in its place. What the hell?

I stumbled back and climbed into the car, Aunt Viv not far behind me. The clicks of our seatbelts filled the silence as the mysterious Ziplock bag somehow landed in my lap. Next came the roar of the engine, followed shortly by Aunt Viv steering us down the driveway.

As our small farmhouse grew smaller in the rearview mirror, I couldn't fight the sickening feeling that I'd never see it again.

But I couldn't go there right now. I had to stay positive. Otherwise, I'd fall apart.

I glanced down at the bag resting in my lap and tensed. Inside there were several rolls of cash—legit rolls. Two passports. A black billfold. And a sea-green wristlet I recognized. Popping the seal, I pulled out the small wallet from my childhood, the worn leather an unexpected comfort against my skin as I opened it. My driver's license photo smiled back at me—the same one Aunt Viv had just toasted like a marshmallow in the metal basin. Except unlike the photo, the name on this license was different.

"Who's Emily Crawford?" My wild gaze darted to my aunt. "You need to tell me what the hell is going on right now."

With one hand on the wheel, Aunt Viv snatched the Ziplock bag and old wristlet from me, shoving them in the center console and out of sight.

I twisted in my seat, the seatbelt biting into my shoulder. "You promised me answers in the car. Well, here we are. *In the car.*" I waved my hand around for emphasis. "Who were those people? And why did they attack us?" I swallowed hard as the image of burnt bodies flashed before my eyes. "What are you?"

"Emma, I..." Aunt Viv's words faded out.

I stared at the person I trusted most in this world. "Answer me."

Aunt Viv released a heavy breath. "Those people were Recall Agents. They were part of what's called a Recall Team. They were sent to detain..." Her knuckles turned white as she clenched the wheel.

"You?" I asked, needing her to keep going—needing answers.

"I want to make one thing perfectly clear." Aunt Viv glanced over at me. "I still am and will always be your aunt." Her eyes turned glossy. "And I would never harm you."

Guilt rushed over me. "I know."

She nodded, clearing her throat. "As you obviously noticed, I'm not quite like you."

"The flames shooting from your hands were kind of a giveaway."

"Don't be ridiculous," she said. "They didn't shoot from my hands."

My fingers dug into the leather seat. "I just witnessed you burn four people to ash. And you want to argue that flames didn't shoot from your hands?"

"That's not what I'm saying. The flames didn't just manifest out of nowhere. It doesn't work like that. They were created by manipulating the combustible materials and molecules in the surrounding environment. I can't just make them appear out of thin air. A source is always required."

It took a hot second for that to sink in. "The lighter?"

"Yes." Aunt Viv stared out at the road ahead. "Only the most skilled Elementums can operate without a substantial source. Which goes to show how out of practice I am."

"Ele-what?"

"Elementum." Aunt Viv placed a hand on her chest. "That's what I am. Specifically, I'm an Igniter Elementum. Igniter for short."

I couldn't believe what I was hearing. If it wasn't for the whole *seeing is believing* thing, I definitely wouldn't believe any of this.

"H-how?" I struggled to find words. "How is that possible? How are you..."

"Possible?" Aunt Viv finished for me, her words tinted with sadness. "When I was younger, I was genetically engineered into an Elementum. It's how I can manipulate one of the four primary elements."

"Genetically engineered? By who?" My brain desperately tried to keep up.

"No, it's my turn now." Her tone brokered no argument. "You were studying with Claire today, right?"

My brows furrowed at the extreme U-turn in subject. "Yes."

"What exactly did you study?"

"We were researching colleges." I waited for the usual college discussion weirdness to emerge—it never did.

Instead, Aunt Viv pushed for further information. "What specifically did you research? Anything out of the ordinary? I need you to really think."

Unease grew like a toxic weed as I started to shake my head when my search for Mom's memorial came crashing back to me.

"What is it, Emma?"

I hesitated, sliding my sun charm along its chain. I had planned to discuss this with Aunt Viv anyway, right? Well, *here goes everything.*

The floodgates opened as I recapped the whole research session. The discussion about leaving for college, my idea for a graduation gift, and not being able to remember the treatment center's name.

I stalled out at the next part, taking a deep breath. But I already had the shovel in hand, I might as well finish digging the grave. "I wanted to see Mom's memorial page, since I hadn't in a while. But to access it, I…" I cringed, shoulders tensing. "I had to override the firewall."

Aunt Viv slammed her hand against the steering wheel, causing me to jump. "How could you be so foolish?"

Heat climbed up my throat. "I'm sorry."

"Did it ever occur to you that I put those firewalls there for your protection?" Aunt Viv glared at the road straight ahead. "But *nooo.* Heaven forbid you allow me to keep you safe or prevent you from making stupid mistakes. And now I have this mess to deal with."

I shrank back in my seat. I'd never seen Aunt Viv this upset before. Was this all really happening because I'd overridden a firewall to view Mom's memorial…

No. No way.

Dots connected as I clasped my sun charm, a prickly sensation crawling up my throat. I struggled to form the words to the question I wanted to ask—*needed* to ask. Even if I wasn't ready to hear the answer.

"Mom didn't die from cancer, did she?" My voice cracked a little.

Seconds ticked by as my thundering heart drowned out the sounds of the road.

"*Did she.*" My throat felt raw.

Aunt Viv exhaled heavily. "No, she didn't."

5

It had been a lie. *Everything* had been a lie.

All I could do was stare at my aunt. It felt like I'd been going about my normal life only to find out that the set and scenery weren't real.

"I'm so sorry, Emma-bug." Aunt Viv's voice turned hoarse. "I never wanted this day to come."

Nausea twisted my stomach. "You know what really happened to her, don't you?"

Aunt Viv glanced at me, her eyes watery. "Yes."

"How did it happen?" I struggled to intake enough air.

She closed her eyes briefly. "Emma, it's complicated—"

"*How?*" The last few years of Mom's life flashed before my eyes. "Because she was sick. I remember her being sick. I'm not imagining that, right?"

"You weren't imagining that. She was sick." Aunt Viv tightened her grip on the wheel. "But that's not what ultimately got her."

An icy blast invaded my chest. "Was it a group like the one that attacked us? A Recall Team?"

After a heart-stopping moment, Aunt Viv nodded. "Yes."

"Why?" I twisted in my seat again, brain spinning. "Because she was like you? An Elementum? An Igniter?"

"Yes." She nodded again. "But it's a long, complicated story. Do you remember when I moved in with you both? You were about four years old."

I shook my head, feeling unglued.

"Well, before that, you and your mother were in hiding," Aunt Viv switched lanes. "Anna managed to evade detection by keeping a low profile and not staying in one place for more than a few months. But she knew that wasn't sustainable. That's why she contacted me. Hoping I could help keep us all hidden."

The three of us had been in hiding, and I'd never known. Not a clue. And sure, we'd moved around a lot after Mom was gone, but I always thought it was because of Aunt Viv's consulting job.

"And it worked," she continued. "For a while, anyway. But eventually we were discovered. Thankfully I got you out in time, but they'd..." She swallowed hard. "They'd already found Anna."

My heart tripped over itself. I was still trying to process the fact that my mom—my free-spirited, warm, and loving mom—had been in hiding *while hiding all of this from me*. Only to end up being hunted down like some animal...

"Anna always knew it could happen." Aunt Viv's voice filled with sorrow. "That's why we had plans in place and took every precaution we could. But it was difficult when we were trying to keep things as normal as possible for you, and then Anna started declining so fast. It made it harder to cover our tracks."

"Why lie, then?" I asked, my chest burning. "Why not tell me?"

"You know your mom. She was a dreamer." Aunt Viv's lips tipped up in a heartbroken grin. "Her head was always up in the clouds thinking about a better and brighter world. And she wanted that for you. She wanted a different life for you."

You're my spark. Promise me you'll always be a spark in the darkness, okay?

As Mom's words came rushing back to me, I clutched my precious sun charm. Those were the same words she'd said when she'd placed the necklace around my neck. Back then, the promise had felt like an installation of trust and faith. And now each word felt like a stab to the chest. How could I ever fulfill that promise when they'd intentionally blinded me all along?

Bile climbed up my throat. "So, you thought a life of lies was better?"

"That's not what I'm saying." Aunt Viv shook her head. "It's hard to understand."

"Then explain it."

"It wasn't an easy decision. And believe me, we didn't make it lightly. But Anna didn't want you dragged into all this."

"But why?" I was shouting now.

"Because this isn't your fight," she shouted back, "and Anna never wanted it to be."

I jerked back at the conviction in her words. The car went silent as I attempted to keep my tear ducts from leaking.

"I'm sorry for yelling. That wasn't fair of me." Aunt Viv released a heavy breath. "I know this is all an enormous shock, but please try to understand. Your mother wanted you to have a normal life."

"And lying to me was the only way to achieve that? Leaving me to be blindsided? All because you two were genetically engineered, and I..." My brain got hung up on something that probably should have occurred to me before now. "If Mom was an Igniter, then doesn't that mean I'm one?"

"You never developed any abilities."

That made sense. If I had, I surely would've noticed, right? Accidentally singeing the curtains would be hard to miss. Not to mention an inconvenience. I kept focused on that, instead of the sprouting disappointment in my chest that this had somehow been the piece I was missing.

"It was the one saving grace your father ever bestowed upon you."
Aunt Viv shook her head, focusing on the white lines and asphalt ahead.

"My father?" I never knew my aunt had any knowledge of my father.
I mean, obviously I had one—cause *duh*—but Mom never talked about
him. Or at least not to me.

"Yes, but before you ask, that's the only thing Anna ever told me
about the bastard. She refused to talk about him." Aunt Viv bristled at
having been kept in the dark. "Whether that was to protect his stupid ass
or what, I'll never understand."

"Funny, I know how that feels."

It was childish, I fully acknowledged that, but it was hard not to lash
out when I was being treated like one.

Aunt Viv tensed behind the wheel. "I know you're upset and you
have every right to be, but you're human, Emma. That—"

"And you're not?" I said hysterically.

"Okay, I phrased that wrong. I am very much human. The big
difference is I would've come in real handy back in the dark ages." Aunt
Viv chuckled at her own joke.

Normally her corny jokes were a bright spot in my day. But not today.

Aunt Viv's face grew serious. "The point I'm trying to make is that
your normalcy is a gift. You don't understand how much of a gift it is."

"Exactly!" I threw up my hands in frustration, the seatbelt biting into
my shoulder.

"Emma, I don't have the energy to argue with you right now. It's
already been a long day, and I probably shouldn't say any more."

I opened my mouth to protest but Aunt Viv cut me off. "It's for your
own protection." Then she turned on the radio, filling the silence—a
not-so-subtle hint that our conversation was over.

But that was probably for the best. My vocal cords and ear canals were
past functioning anyway. A wave of exhaustion cascaded over me as I
leaned my head against the window, the tree-covered hills whizzing by.

I could understand Mom and Aunt Viv wanting to protect me, especially after everything I'd experienced today. But I couldn't fight this feeling that there was more to it. More to be uncovered.

My search for answers wasn't over, even if Aunt Viv didn't know it.

6

"Are you sure this is a good idea?" I focused my gaze out the windshield as we sped down the highway.

Ever since we'd crossed the Colorado-Wyoming border early this morning, the mountains lining the western horizon kept drawing my attention. That, and the approaching skyline. The glass and steel skyscrapers rivaled the jagged peaks as they rose from the surrounding plains like beacons in the late morning sunshine.

"Yes." Aunt Viv rolled her shoulders while keeping one hand on the wheel, her olive fleece successfully covering the bandage underneath. "They can help us."

As the city of Denver took shape, I wondered for the millionth time why we were traveling three states away to get help. And who were these "friends" Aunt Viv wanted to meet up with?

"Are they Elementums, too?" I asked, stomach flip-flopping. Would they be upset that I knew their secret? What would they do when they found out? A fire hydrant of flames popped into my mind.

"They are Elementums, but you don't have to worry. I've known them since I was a teenager. They'll definitely help us," Aunt Viv said before quietly adding, "I hope."

Well, didn't that just install monumental confidence. I wanted to trust her—truly—but after yesterday, that portion of my brain was temporarily out of order.

The five-lane highway was clogged with weekend commuters as Aunt Viv guided us toward a spaghetti-tangle of overpass bridges. Taking one of the noodles, we exited the highway and made our way through the northern edge of the city.

A rainbow of colors snagged my attention. The impressive mural spanned the entire side of a building while the vibrant patterns of paint zig-zagged in and around the windows and doors, making me itch to grab my sketchbook.

A wave of helplessness washed over me as I realized I didn't know the next time I'd be able to sketch again... But I couldn't go there. Nothing good would come from going down that road, so I shoved those dark thoughts aside.

Old warehouses and brick buildings made up the majority of the city blocks—many of which had artwork somewhere on their facades—with a few taller and more modern buildings interlaced. We passed an assortment of shops, restaurants, and bars, all buzzing with people.

When we stopped at a red light, Aunt Viv pointed to an old brick building on the corner that extended over half a block.

"There it is," she said, relief coating her voice.

A coffee shop anchored the corner of the building and a cidery took up the rest. Toward the back, an elegant combination of brick, glass, and steel rose up from behind. It looked like an apartment complex that blended the old with the new.

Getting the green for go, we turned onto the side street and I discovered another colorful mural. The triangular shapes and angular lines intertwined across the brick exterior to create a geometric backdrop for the sleek metal letters spelling out: *THE BREAKPOINT.*

Aunt Viv steered us into the parking garage entrance at the end of the building. A sudden influx of nerves overwhelmed me as bright red "no trespassing" signs littered the alcove and a sturdy metal gate blocked our path.

Super comforting.

What if these "friends" didn't want to help us? Would they even let us in? Or just not *me*? After all, I wasn't one of them.

At the security checkpoint, Aunt Viv rolled down her window and hit the button. A chime-like ring echoed off the concrete walls as we waited.

On the third ring, a spunky female voice crackled through the speaker. "This is private parking. Read the signs."

"Nova." Aunt Viv took off her sunglasses and look at the camera. "It's Viv."

After a brief pause, there was a shocked whisper. "Viv?"

"I know I owe you an explanation, and you'll get one. But first I need you to let me in." Aunt Viv's grip tightened on the wheel. "*Please.*"

Silence.

Then a surprising groan of metal sounded through the alcove as we received clipped instructions on where to park.

After twenty hours straight of driving, I relished the chance to stretch my legs as I noted the few other vehicles parked nearby. At first the parking garage seemed like any other with its unique blend of exhaust, oil, and concrete. Then I noticed the large, reinforced door in the corner. A bank vault door like that was only used to keep something out. Or worse, *in*.

My stomach plummeted. "What is this place?"

"The general population believes it's an apartment building that never has any vacancies." Aunt Viv stretched her arms.

"But what is it, really?"

Aunt Viv hesitated. "It's an outpost for one of Arcadius's compounds."

My brows pinched. "Arcadius?"

"Arc for short. It's a secret network of safe havens where Elementums could feel protected and carve out a place for themselves."

Not missing the plural on safe havens and compounds, I wondered how big Arcadius really was. And who they needed protection from. Maybe whoever had sent the Recall Team after us?

"Who—"

"For now, that's all I can say for your own protection." Aunt Viv cut me off. "But don't worry, we can trust my friends here. Everything will be okay, I promise."

There it was again, the promise that everything would be okay. And again, I struggled to believe her. We were three states away from okay.

I nodded even though it felt hollow.

A metallic groan sounded out as the Defcon One door cranked open, revealing a punk goddess. She was a good six inches taller than Aunt Viv but appeared to be around the same age. Maybe younger? And she had the coolest hairstyle ever. The ends of her pin-straight dark hair looked as if they'd been dipped in turquoise paint, creating an amazing ombre effect.

The Punk-Goddess walked over to Aunt Viv as the almond hued planes of her face set in displeasure. With her worn-out Avril Lavigne T-shirt and multiple piercings, she gave off an edgy vibe. Was this Nova?

"You have some nerve." The Punk-Goddess crossed her arms over her lean form, solely focused on my aunt.

"Nova, I—"

But before Aunt Viv could finish her sentence, Nova launched herself at my aunt.

My heart sprinted as I stepped forward. To do what exactly? I had no clue. But I wasn't going to just stand there and do nothing. Not again.

But just when I feared the worst, Nova wrapped Aunt Viv in a stage-five-clinger hug. *What the what?*

"This is for being alive," Nova muffled into Aunt Viv's olive fleece. Then she performed a catch-and-release, pushing Aunt Viv away. Only to be followed shortly by a smack.

"Ow." Aunt Viv rubbed her arm.

"That's for disappearing on me," Nova said, throwing out her arms. "What the hell were you thinking? We all thought you were dead. *Or worse.* How dare you ghost me like some bad Tinder date. How could you do that to me? To *me*? So much for being tight techies for life."

The sheer amount of words per second that spilled out of her mouth was impressive, but also concerning when you considered the whole air intake requirement. It was exhausting just witnessing it.

"So, where've you been? What've you been doing? I must know all." Nova practically bounced on the tips of her toes.

Aunt Viv grinned. "Glad to see some things haven't changed, Supernova."

"You ain't seen nothing yet. I—*Oh*, hi," Nova said, finally noticing me. Then her wide eyes swung back to Aunt Viv. "Good lord, did you have a kid?"

A harsh laugh punched out of Aunt Viv. "Of course not. Don't be ridiculous."

My cheeks heated as I tried not to take offense.

"Ridiculous? She looks just like you." Nova gave me a once over. "Although, to be honest she's a dead ringer for..." She whipped her head back to Aunt Viv. "*No.* It can't be."

"Nova, I'd like you to meet my niece, Emma." Aunt Viv gestured in my direction.

I plastered on a hopefully convincing smile and lifted a hand.

"You're Annalyse's kid," Nova said in awe.

Not a question. She had known my mom. But how?

"Oh my god." Nova turned her stunned expression on Aunt Viv. "You found her."

Aunt Viv nodded solemnly, and I remembered her comment from yesterday about us being in hiding. Apparently, we'd been hiding from both sides of this secret world.

"I have so many questions." Nova waved an arm in my direction. "Like, is she—"

"No," Aunt Viv jumped in. "Emma never developed any abilities, and she's never been involved with the fight."

Nova's beautiful face pinched like it was in overdrive. "Even more questions."

"Listen, I know there's a lot to explain." Aunt Viv rubbed her face. "But I need to speak with whoever the Commander is here."

Commander? That made it sound like Arcadius was part of some secret government facility. Area 51 came to mind.

"You've been gone a long time, Viv." Nova stared hard at her. "A lot has changed."

I deflated at the tone in her voice. Now that she knew I wasn't one of them, would she force us to leave? Where would we go now?

"Come on." Nova headed back to the bomb shelter door.

Wait. Punk-Goddess says what?

Nova opened things up with a swipe of her key fob. "Let's make like a GPS and update our location."

7

"How did you find us?" Nova asked as we followed her down a hallway of white walls and brick columns. There was a faint chemical aroma coming from farther down the hallway. It reminded me of a pool.

"Luck." Aunt Viv grinned. "I figured you guys had relocated since I was last in Denver. Protocols and all that. But before I left, I knew about the potential relocation sites for the Breakpoint and took a shot at the most likely one."

"Wow. One-shot wonder." Nova chuckled before stopping in front of an elevator and hitting the call button.

"No kidding." She nudged Nova with her elbow. "Saved me a lot of time driving around."

The elevator arrived with a ding, and I posted up in the back corner as Nova swiped her fob to start our ascent. I was betting you couldn't get anywhere in this place without one of those nifty little babies.

As we climbed, Aunt Viv and Nova continued chatting—most of it going completely over my head—but it was clear they went way back on the friend scale. Which is why I tried to ignore the glances Nova kept sending my way. I knew I looked like a hot mess after being stuck in a car all night. But come on, it had been a rough twenty-four hours.

Thankfully, I was saved by the ding. The elevator doors opened two floors up, revealing another hallway that split in two directions. In one stood a set of closed double doors, while in the other, a hallway lined with doors stretched out into what looked like a construction site.

"Excuse the mess." Nova headed toward the assortment of ladders, tools, and construction plastic. "It's only been a few months since the relocation, and we're currently upgrading all the security systems."

Upgrading? Didn't that just send a shiver of unease down your spine. This place already felt more like a fortress than a haven.

"You weren't kidding about things changing." Aunt Viv glanced around. "This place is much nicer than the last facility."

"All the bells and whistles." Nova wiggled her eyebrows as a pining glow filled Aunt Viv's eyes—the same look I got on the pen aisle of an art store. "I'll show you all the new toys later."

Passing a split in the corridor, I trailed behind as we continued to the end before turning onto a loop of offices and conference rooms. The nameplates on the doors gave no clues away, specifying either a certain meeting space or an unknown name. Well, except one that listed another military title of Captain.

In front of our group, a different door swung open and a mountain of a man stepped out. With his plaid flannel and scruffy beard, I imagined he'd fit in perfectly in a granola or REI ad. All he needed was a Yeti cooler and some hiking gear to seal the deal.

"Well, look who's still breathing." The man's voice boomed down the hallway.

"Captain Herrera." Aunt Viv smiled as he pulled her into a bear hug.

"That's Commander Herrera to you now." He stepped back and crossed his arms over his barrel chest, the rolled-up sleeves revealing a large section of scarred and uneven tawny skin on his forearm—a burn mark. "When Nova informed me who just showed up on our doorstep, I couldn't quite believe it. Where have you been all this time, Firebird?"

"Firebird?" I blurted as the image of charred ashes flashed in my mind.

Keen eyes shifted to me, and I suddenly felt like I was under a microscope. The Commander title made sense now. This man could make anyone fall in line with just one look.

"Antonio, I'd like you to meet my niece, Emma." Aunt Viv shared a look with the Commander. If he was shocked to find out who I was, he hid it much better than Nova had. Or maybe, unlike her, he hadn't known my mom.

Nerves swamped me. I'd never met a military leader before. Should I salute?

Thankfully, Commander Herrera solved that dilemma by extending his hand. "Welcome, Emma. It's nice to meet you."

"Nice to meet you too, uh, Commander." I clasped my much smaller hand with his.

A warm smile graced his time-worn face. "Please, just call me Herrera. Everyone here does." Then he faced Aunt Viv and Nova, running a hand through his salt-and-pepper crew cut. "I see we have a lot to catch up on. Let's step into my office, shall we?"

"Stay here, okay?" Aunt Viv pointed to one of the benches lining the hallway. "We won't be long."

Before I could even protest, I found myself alone, studying the wood grain of a closed door. What the hell?

I released a breath and headed over to the bench. Putting butt to cushion, I ran a hand through my hair, only to cringe at the oiliness. I needed a shower and an entire bottle of body wash. Also, a change of clothes wouldn't hurt. I was still in the loose-knit sweater and jean shorts from the coffee shop. Funny how only yesterday my biggest concerns had been scraping together a list of colleges and finding a homecoming dress... I guess I wasn't going to the dance now.

It was a silly thing to focus on—all things considered—but that still didn't stop the sinking feeling that coursed through me. And what about college? With us on the run and the changed identities, would I still be able to go? Or, like my old ID, had that bridge been burned?

I didn't know which rattled me more: that I truly had no clue what the future held or that I really wasn't going home. Everything felt out of control, a tailspin with no brakes.

Too antsy to sit still, I went in search of a much-needed refresher. With all these offices around, common sense said there had to be a break room with a water source close by.

Checking around the loop, I found more offices or rooms without sidelights. Almost all the doors were locked—requiring a fob or keypad code—but the few that weren't ended up only being supply closets.

The floor was like a ghost town, which I attributed to the construction zone. But that worked in my favor, keeping the chances of running into someone low—or at least that was my theory.

Heading in the other direction, I noted the polished concrete floors, exposed ceilings, brick columns, and art-lined walls. This place looked more warehouse-chic than military facility. But maybe that was the point. Hidden in plain sight.

To my relief, the double doors past the elevators didn't require a fob, but there was definitely something strange about the frame. It had an embedded track on the ceiling and floor, but the walls gave no clue to its purpose—if there even was one.

Weird.

On the other side, I expected to find more offices but instead was transported to some sort of industrial spa where the air smelled like eucalyptus and citrus. A fully equipped command center was to my right while a waiting area with plush chairs and even a wick-your-worries-away water feature was to my left.

The hallway continued to another set of double doors. There were treatment rooms on either side and a few splits in the corridor but I stuck to the main route until I came across a larger room at the end that looked promising. As my eyes adjusted to the darkened room, I found what could only be described as a medical bay. Patient beds, medical equipment, and supply cabinets lined the far wall, and the smell of disinfectant made my head flutter and my muscles go weak. Definitely not a spa.

Shh-shh, shh-shh.

The rustling sound was faint, almost like an air vent had kicked on but not. If I hadn't been relatively still, I would've missed it.

I stepped back out into the hallway but found nothing. I mean, I was already on the hunt. What could it hurt to look a little farther? Especially if it meant getting away from that medical nightmare behind me.

With that solid theory, I headed for the second set of double doors with the same weird frame. Checking the vision panel, I found the coast was clear and placed my hands on the push bar, only to hesitate. Should I be doing this?

I wasn't exactly snooping—*snooping* was a strong word—but I didn't imagine Aunt Viv would be happy if she found me *exploring* like this. Also, what would Commander Herrera or Nova think? Would they deny us help if I was discovered?

Then, the little voice in my head—the spirited one that always shouted *jump*—chimed in with a *where has naïve bliss ever landed you?* And it wasn't like Aunt Viv was offering a lot of explanations. If I wanted answers, it was obvious I'd have to get them myself.

Squaring my shoulders, I pushed to the other side and was greeted with the mingled aromas of rubber, air freshener, and an undertone of sweat. The hallway extended in another stretch of doors and construction equipment.

Shh-shh, shh-shh.

A tingle of awareness ran down my spine as the sound repeated, but louder this time and it was accompanied by a... splashing faucet?

I pressed on, passing an Olympian-worthy weight room, various training rooms, and what appeared to be a yoga studio. I zeroed in on the sounds, stopping just short of an open doorway. Palms sweaty and pulse racing, I peeked inside. It was another training room with sleek metal storage containers on the sides and a large black padded mat in the center. But that's not what captured my attention. No, it was what was on the mat that held my gaze—or rather *who*.

Two guys faced off in the center. Both were dressed in training gear and looked well acquainted with their gym memberships. They appeared to be around my age or slightly older, although the taller of the two had his back to me, making it harder to tell. The one facing me had a leaner build with sandy blond hair rocking a man-bun. Concentration consumed his boyish face as he lifted a pale arm.

Shh-shh, shh-shh.

A stream of soil rose like a snake, the rocks within rustling past each other as the soil-serpent weaved its way around the sandy blond's arm.

Holy sh—

Yanked backward, my head and back slammed into the wall as a forearm pressed securely to my throat, efficiently blocking air from my lungs.

"How did you get in here?"

It took me a moment to focus on the demanding source. As I followed the inky lines on the arm pinning me to the wall *up, up, up,* I found myself staring at a UFC fighter. With dark slicked-back hair and a five o'clock shadow only slightly lighter than the tattoos on his arms, he leered down at me with harsh green eyes.

"Well?" the fighter asked, his tone eager for a fight.

Responding wasn't really an option; the forearm pressing against my windpipe made sure of that. I struggled to get enough oxygen as all of my defense training vanished. But just as things got fuzzy, the pressure suddenly relented. I gulped down air as my legs took a timeout, sliding down the wall until my butt hit concrete.

Fingers snapped near my face, startling me as I finally registered the solid body crouching down in front of me. The new guy rested his arm on his thigh, matching the position of his other arm which had a metal and silicone prosthesis from the forearm down. Shifting my gaze up, I discovered a different definition of being struck silly, which I fully blamed on being slammed into a wall—no other reason. *Nope.* Not at all.

The striking face in front of me had a strong jawline with three scarred slashes cutting across his bronze skin that most would find detracting, but apparently not me. The scars started on the left side of his neck and then sliced upward like claw marks before ending just below his cheekbones. His hair was cut to an ultra-short fade on the sides, while the top was left longer, allowing the dark waves that reminded me of a raven's wing to topple forward onto his forehead.

When his lips moved, I tried to catch what he was saying, but at the moment my brain couldn't track—never stood a chance. And I was staring. I should look away—look anywhere else—but it was like I was under a spell, ensnared by his blue eyes. They reminded me of the warm waters off Hawaii, making me wonder what it would be like to bask under them.

Wow. Okay, that was a fast dive into the gutter. I needed to get it together. Sure, the guy was good-looking but seriously that should be the last thing on my mind right now.

"You all right?" His voice was deep and commanding.

"Looks like a power outage," the fighter said, shaking off the hold of the sandy blond from earlier. "But maybe if she stares hard enough at Kaden, the lights will click back on."

Heat flooded my face. Did he really just say that?

"Whatever, Decker," the one known as Kaden said, but his lips tipped up in a smirk, making his scars stand out.

I turned to the fighter named Decker, a surge of anger outweighing the humiliation. "For your information, Ink-Wad, my cognitive functioning is just fine and I'm not the one with the problem." I circled my hand between us. "I'm not the one slamming strangers into walls." Then I turned my fury on Kaden. "Can you back off so I can stand?"

Undeterred, Kaden and his infuriating smirk didn't budge. "She speaks."

"Come on, guys. We should help her up," the sandy blond said, looking concerned.

"More like she bites," Decker said, ignoring the push for decency. "And here I am without my rabies shot."

My cheeks blazed hotter, but I refused to admit how much they were getting to me. Or to just sit here and take it. As I pushed to my feet, a wave of dizziness tipped me sideways. But before I could swan dive back into the wall, Kaden caught me and steadied me, causing the distance between us to evaporate.

Man, he was tall. Not as tall as Ink-Wad over there but still at least a head taller than me.

"Decker, go find Herrera." Kaden's voice radiated authority—a shocking contrast to his gentle but sturdy hold.

Decker did not look like a happy camper, but to my surprise he turned without a word and disappeared down the hall.

I breathed deep and caught the intoxicating scent of pine with a hint of mint over the unique gym blend. Was that Kaden?

Okay, it was official. I'd lost it. Or maybe it was the impact of making besties with the wall. Or possibly a brain aneurysm. Choices, choices.

"You're probably right about your cognitive functioning, but just to be safe, let's take a seat, all right?" Kaden steered me to one of the wooden benches lining the hallway, making me feel like a kindergartener with an owie—*real attractive.*

The sandy blond scrambled forward, moving a plastic sheet and box of tools out of the way. Then he lifted one hand in greeting. "I'm Reed Wilson, by the way, and next to you is Kaden Hale."

I lifted my hand in response. "Emma Cross."

Or was it *Emily Crawford* now? Man, my life was a mess.

"Nice to meet you." Reed smiled, but his warm brown eyes still looked concerned. "And I'm sorry about Decker. He really shouldn't have gone all mega Terra on you."

Confusion engulfed me as I let fly a curse-inciting question. "What's a Terra?"

8

"Let's not make a big deal out of this," I said, still perched on the wooden bench. "Honestly, I'm fine."

"I think you only bruised it." Reed prodded the back of my head as he politely ignored me. There was a lot of that going around lately. Ever since friendship-bracelet-ing the wall, both he and Kaden were conveniently ignoring my questions.

Then again, I was successfully avoiding theirs. Two could play at that game and all that.

"It will be tender for a while, so I'd take it easy." Reed added, his athletic shirt stretching as he finished examining the back of my head.

With my lungs full of oxygen and my head safely away from any walls, I was able to study Reed and Kaden's workout gear. They were made of similar material, but the styles and colors were different—Kaden's shades of black versus Reed's black with patches of gray. And there was a silver-threaded band wrapping Kaden's right sleeve while Reed's had none.

"I'd also recommend not smacking your head against anything else." Kaden leaned back against the wall across from me, adjusting his prosthetic arm.

My gaze narrowed. "Duly noted."

A deep chuckle sounded in response. It would've been a nice sound, but I was pretty sure it was of the I'm-laughing-at-you-not-with-you variety.

"Not exactly how I would've put it, but yes that would be recommended." Reed hitched his thumb over his shoulder. "I'm going to grab you some water, but it'd be good to stay seated for a little longer. Just to be sure."

In other words, enough time for Decker to get Herrera and confirm I was allowed to be here. That's when memories of bone-chilling cracks and spreading dark pools filled my mind. Had Decker assumed I was a Recall Agent when he'd found me sneaking around? In the heat of the moment it had been easy to judge—not that I condoned jumping to violence—but after yesterday, could I really blame him for his reaction?

Yes. No. Maybe?

Reed disappeared back into the training room just as the door to the medical spa burst open and Aunt Viv raced toward me.

"Emma-bug, are you okay?" She crouched down in front of me, concern etching her face.

My cheeks heated. "I'm fine."

Next, Herrera joined our group, followed shortly by Decker, and even Reed reappeared just in time for them to form a loose semi-circle around me. My face blazed hotter as all eyes shifted to me. I'd somehow become the nucleus of this little sideshow attraction.

Fantastic.

"What happened?" Aunt Viv gave me a once-over, but it was Decker's glare that I felt like the strength of the sun—and here I was without sunscreen.

"It was just a misunderstanding." I waved a dismissive hand as the power of the sun dimmed and a stunned expression took its place. Extending an olive branch to Decker, I hoped to create, well, *friendship* wasn't the right word. *Acquaintances who were civil* sounded more accurate—maybe.

"Would this misunderstanding have anything to do with why you're not in the administrative wing?" Aunt Viv pressed.

"It was nothing," I repeated before looking over at Herrera—not wanting to get Aunt Viv into any more hot water with her friends. "And it's not like I really saw anything."

Decker balled his fists and whirled on Herrera. "You let a bunch of *Newts* in here?"

Snap went that olive branch. Did he really just call us amphibians?

"Watch your tone, son." Herrera crossed his arms. Decker might have had the slight height advantage, but the Commander was in a different weight class. "You don't know what you're talking about, and this decision is above your pay grade."

After that epic shutdown, Decker closed his mouth and leaned against the wall next to Kaden, looking about as friendly as a rattlesnake.

Herrera looked at Aunt Viv. "We need to finish our conversation, Firebird." Then he turned to his crew, causing them all—but especially Decker—to stiffen. "Due to our unexpected visitors and unforeseen circumstances, all extracurricular activities will be halted for the time being. Do I make myself clear?"

Kaden straightened. "What?"

"Do I make myself clear?" Herrera repeated, his tone leaving no room for argument.

"Yes, sir," Reed, Decker, and Kaden said in unison, reminding me of a military unit.

"Good." Herrera nodded before looking at Decker and Kaden. "Now, Mills and Hale, don't you two have assignments to take care of?"

"Come on, Deck. Let's go." Kaden prowled toward the exit.

Herrera followed them down the hall, shouting after them. "And if you see Avelino, tell him I need to speak with him."

With that, Kaden, Decker, and Herrera disappeared through the double doors, mercifully reducing my audience to two: Aunt Viv and Reed.

"They're allowing us to stay here tonight," Aunt Viv informed me quietly.

My eyes widened at that news.

"I know we still need to talk, but first it's important that I finish my conversation with Herrera."

I nodded. Talking would be good. Maybe then I wouldn't be put into chokeholds quite so often.

"I didn't mean to overhear." Reed handed me a much-needed bottle of water. "But I'd be happy to show Emma to the guest rooms while you finish your conversation."

My eyes narrowed as red flags went up. Was this some kind of trick? Or a ploy to lure me into Decker's evil lair? Then again, that didn't seem to be Reed's motive. And after the wall encounter, he had looked genuinely concerned while offering to help. So, he got points for that.

Aunt Viv hesitated, the stress basically leaking from her pores. I'd never seen her like this, and I didn't want to pile even more on.

"Thanks, Reed. That'd be great." I pasted on a smile.

"Yes, thank you. That's very kind of you," she said before squeezing my arm. "I'll come find you in a bit, okay?" Then she headed down the hallway and threw over her shoulder, "Make good choices."

My grip on the water bottle tightened, the plastic crinkling under my fingers. Good to know her sense of humor was still intact.

"*Sooo.*" Reed shifted from foot to foot. "Why did you cover for Decker?"

"Cause snitches get stitches." I opened the bottle, taking a swig.

Doubt crossed Reed's boyish face, but he didn't push it.

On the other hand, how else did I expect to get answers? Changing my tactics, I hoped I could trade an answer for an answer. "You obviously picked up on the fact that I don't know what's going on."

Reed's blond brows rose. "You don't say."

"Funny." I sent him a pointed look. "Well, I'm just trying not to ruffle any more feathers, especially after facing a Recall Team yesterday."

"You faced a Recall Team?" Reed froze. "How? Why?"

"Thanks for the vote of confidence." Although, after witnessing Aunt Viv's fan-of-flames and Reed's soil-serpents, I had to admit it was a valid question. "And I believe it had to do with my Aunt Viv being an Igniter."

Reed's brows pinched. "Then why did you ask what a Terra was?"

"Because until yesterday I had no clue what an Igniter was."

"Oh." Reed blinked.

"Yeah." I looked away. My mind went over all the secrets and lies I'd uncovered since yesterday, and I asked myself for the hundredth time how I could've missed it all.

"Earth," Reed said, surprising me.

"What?"

"The element a Terra controls is earth."

My heart jumped. But this was good. It was an olive branch. "So, they're another type of Elementum."

Reed nodded. "There are four primary elements: water, earth, fire, and air." He raised a finger to indicate each. "And the four different Elementums who control them: Hydro, Terra, Igniter, and Aero." He ticked off the same order on his raised fingers.

"So you would be a Terra Elementum?" I asked, thinking of his soil-serpents.

Reed's eyes widened.

"I saw you earlier with the soil."

"Right," Reed said, excusing me basically spying on him. "And just Terra works."

"So, calling Decker a mega Terra, that's not an actual classification, right?"

A laugh burst from Reed. "He might be classified as a mega-ass or mega-douche, but no, that's not a technical term."

I smiled, happy to know I wasn't alone. "Dude is mega-scary."

"Is that why you covered for him? You were scared he'd retaliate?"

I bit my lower lip. Could I really trust Reed? It would be nice if that were true, especially since I was running low in the friend department right now. I had no way of contacting Claire anymore, and even if I still had Flipper, I wouldn't risk it. I didn't want a Recall Team coming after her. Aunt Viv had reassured me she would be left alone as long as we cut all ties.

So, here I was. I guess it was time to leap into the trust pool.

"First, let me say I don't agree with his method of slamming strangers into walls. But after surviving the Recall Team, I wanted to believe that he was only trying to protect everyone here." I shrugged. "Plus, my mom used to say honey attracts more bees than vinegar. And I figured I should avoid being on the wrong side of Decker if I can help it."

Reed grimaced. "I've only known him a short time, but I can attest to that. He would do anything to defend this place. It's all he has."

All he has?

"But the real question is," he continued, "are you sure you want to attract *that* bee?"

"Good point." I snorted. "I'll try to stick clear of *that* bee while I'm here."

"Safe plan." Reed smiled before hitching his thumb toward the opposite end of the hallway. "Shall we head to the guest rooms?"

"Sure." I returned his smile.

He started to turn when he halted. "Just be careful, Emma." He grew serious, sending an icy chill down my spine. "You'll find most Elementums view the world through a broken lens. They won't hesitate to defend what we've created, sometimes mercilessly. And there are grave reasons for that."

9

The sensation of mint and bristles against my teeth was a relief after spending all night driving. It also helped that I had washed my hair twice and scrubbed myself head to toe with basically a whole bottle of body wash.

The guest dorm assigned to me looked like a swanky hotel room—clean and efficient. With a mixture of white paint, brick walls, and simple furniture, the room lacked any sense of permanence. No sketchbooks littered the desk. No sunflower bedspread to brighten the room. And no personalized pictures strung across the wall. Which, *okay*, fine, would've been weird if there had been, but I hated to think those things were gone.

At least the bathroom had every travel product I could ever need. So, bright side?

I rinsed out my toothbrush as my wet hair dripped onto my shoulders, soaking the straps of my fresh tank top I had paired with leggings. Unlike home with its chilly ocean breeze, it was hotter here and too warm for sweater weather—not that I ever wanted to see that sweater again.

Toweling off my hair, I tried to ignore the dark circles forming under my eyes. I really needed a good night's sleep. Or like six. That's if the nightmares of shrouded soldiers and expanding dark puddles didn't keep finding me. Another stark reminder of the total one-eighty my life had taken. Which begged the question, if yesterday had never happened, would Aunt Viv have ever told me about all this?

It all felt like some cosmic joke. If I just hadn't unblocked that stupid firewall, I would still be at home. Squeezing my eyes closed, I could almost imagine it. Imagine I was in my own bathroom, where my biggest worries were deciding on a college and finishing my GED. Except when I opened my eyes, the bumps and bruises littering my body shattered that illusion.

But come on, like living in an unshattered illusion would be any better? *No.* No, it wouldn't.

Sure, I missed home. But the thought of going back to a life filled with secrets and lies made me want to vomit. I couldn't go back to that. Wouldn't go back. *This* was my new reality—a reality I needed to learn more about. Especially about my mom and if I wanted to survive. If I could do that, then maybe I could figure out why she'd hidden this all from me. Because there had to be a stronger reason than just "gifting me with a normal life." I knew there was. I could feel it in my bones.

Heart resolved, I left my guest dorm and headed down the fourth-floor hallway lined with doors. The Breakpoint consisted of five levels plus a basement, which included the parking garage and an aquatic center, solving the chlorine mystery from earlier. Not exactly the puzzle I wanted to solve, but you know, baby steps.

On the ground floor was the coffee shop and cidery I had spotted while driving in. The second floor was divided into three wings: the administrative, medical, and training wings. And on the upper two floors were the guest dorms and common areas on this level and the apartments for those stationed here on the floor above.

There was no mention of the third floor or what was located there. And when I tried to ask, Reed only said it was classified. Obviously, the sharing-is-caring only went so far.

Entering the common area, it was a spacious two-story room where the industrial-chic theme was still going strong. A large steel staircase and a luxurious kitchen with a center island that could seat at least ten people took up one half. While the other was filled with various games like Skee-Ball and ping pong lining the perimeter and a section of comfy couches and a huge TV with a news report from Times Square occupying the center. I zeroed in on the sitting area when I noticed someone sitting next to Reed.

The girl's form-fitting training clothes showed off her lean frame, reminding me of a dancer in combat boots. Her long, dark braids were tipped with orangish-red hair coloring—similar to Nova's—as they cascaded around the tablet she was focused on. But even despite the downward angle, the screen illuminated her beautiful bone structure and light black skin.

"Do you think the Clinic's movements have something to do with it?"

"What's the Clinic?" I asked, stopping behind one of the couches.

The Combat-Ballerina looked over as eyes the color of whiskey scrutinized me from head to toe. "Oh, Reed, you've been making friends."

"It happens occasionally." Reed shrugged with a grin.

She placed a hand over her heart. "Without me."

Reed mirrored her stance. "It was a difficult journey, but I had to go this one alone."

Amusement shined in their shared grins, making me miss Claire. Would I ever see her again? Would she think I'd just vanished?

"Emma Cross, this is Saylor Campbell." Reed introduced us.

"Hey." I gave her a little wave.

She looked at Reed. "You sure about this?"

I tensed as Reed's warning returned with a vengeance. Was I facing down yet another defensive Elementum so soon?

"She's cool," he said, only slightly decreasing her frown. Then he winked at me. "And she took on a Recall Team."

"What?" Saylor straightened and leaned to the edge of her seat. "Oh, spill. Tell us everything."

Reed smiled like he'd just helped me pass some unknown test into the club.

"You came here with your aunt, right?" she continued. "Nova never said, but how did you guys even know about this place? And what—"

"Calm your waters, Saylor." Reed interrupted the frenzy. "Let her sit down first."

"Oh, *fiiine*." Saylor waved a dismissive hand at him, the multiple rings she wore glinting in the light. They looked like gear parts from some sort of machinery.

I joined the Dynamic-Duo over on the couches. "Calm your waters?"

Saylor smiled, extending a tense hand over the orange water bottle on the coffee table. My breath stalled out as a thin stream of water rose from the opening, rippling and surging upward like a vine seeking the sunlight.

Holy crap.

"I'm a Hydro." Saylor wiggled her eyebrows. The liquid rope collapsed back into the bottle as water droplets splashed the table. "Although, someone recently thought I was an Aero for whatever reason."

Reed snorted. "That's probably because of your obsession with Nova and her wind-wonderfulness."

"*Is not*." Saylor stuck her tongue out at him before turning to me. "So, did you really take on a Recall Team?"

I didn't know if it was the kindness they had extended or the sheer exhaustion blanketing me—or both—but I ended up telling them the entire story. Living in Point Reyes with my aunt. How only yesterday I'd been researching colleges, which was how I found out they were seniors too and were only stationed at the outpost for a month-long field training session. Then I explained what happened with the Recall Team and finding out Aunt Viv was an Igniter. And last, fleeing our home and coming to the Breakpoint. The only part I left out was the bombshell about my mom's death. Since I was still grappling with it myself, I just wasn't ready to share that yet.

"You really had no idea." Saylor's stunned expression matched Reed's.

"No." I studied the geometric patterns on the rug.

"Don't be too hard on yourself." Reed leaned forward on his elbows. "It sounds like your aunt hid everything really well. Plus, all of this must be a little—"

"Crazy town?" Saylor volunteered. "Wacky world? Kooky-listic?"

"I was going to say hard to believe." Reed coughed a laugh. "But don't worry, you'll get used to all this."

Would I? Aunt Viv hadn't exactly divulged her next steps for us. But it wasn't like I had anywhere else to go. I didn't know this city. And if another Recall Team found me, I had no clue what I would do.

Saylor frowned. "If your mom was an Igniter, then aren't you one as well?"

"No, my father wasn't an Elementum." I slid my sun charm along its chain. "And even though I've never met him, I guess I must take after him because I never developed any abilities."

Reed straightened. "So, you're a Halfbreed."

"Oh my god, you totally are." Saylor's voice filled with awe.

But I couldn't understand why. I wasn't the one with the super nifty abilities. I was just... me.

I shifted in my seat as I glanced around. "Is this place always this empty on the weekends?"

"Oh, no. We just started our two-week fall break." Saylor tucked her sunset-tipped braids back. "We run on a year-round schedule with intermittent breaks, and they basically evacuated everyone for the security upgrades..." Her words faded out with a look from Reed. "*Aaand* I should not have said that."

"So, is this some kind of military facility?" I asked as images of a CIA covert program churning out soldiers flashed inside my head.

"Sorry," Saylor mouthed to Reed as she fidgeted with her rings.

A pang of guilt hit me. I didn't want to get them into trouble, especially since they were being so nice. But how else was I going to figure things out?

"Listen, we can totally relate to wanting answers," Reed said.

"Preach." Saylor threw up her arms.

"But you haven't been cleared yet, so we're only allowed to give you the basics," he continued. "And I believe you can understand why."

The sensation of a forearm being pressed against my throat rushed back to me. If Reed and Kaden hadn't been there to pull Decker off of me, would he have stopped?

I swallowed hard, probably not wanting to know that answer. "I understand."

"But I can tell you the military and government don't even know we exist," Reed added in a lighter tone. It was another olive branch. "And we'd like to keep it that way. As history has shown, people don't always react well to things they consider different."

Man, wasn't that the truth. And manipulating elements definitely qualified as different.

Saylor nodded. "Arc's goal is to keep us off the radar as much as possible."

"Is that also from the Clinic you mentioned earlier?" I asked, my pulse accelerating as visions of needles and tourniquets haunted me.

"You mean the vortex of evil," Saylor said, each word laced with venom.

At my confused expression, Reed explained, "The Clinic is a dangerous organization that was founded back in the late sixties by a group of scientists and geneticists. They're the ones responsible for the Recall Teams."

Ice cascaded down my spine. That meant the Clinic was also responsible for my mom's death.

"They're the main threat against everyone here at Arc," Saylor added. "And are the ones who created Elementums in the first place."

"Why?" I asked, the question completely bypassing my filter as the color drained from Saylor's face. "Wait, that didn't come out right."

Crap. I'd basically just asked why they existed.

"It's okay." Saylor's smile didn't quite reach her eyes. "I know what you meant."

Thankfully, Reed jumped in. "The world's always been in an arms race, and the creation of Elementums was no different."

"Weapons," I breathed.

Reed nodded solemnly. "Elementums were genetically engineered to be stronger and faster, with enhanced gifts. Perfect as super soldiers. Even if it didn't start that way."

I frowned. "What do you mean?"

"Supposedly the Clinic's original mission was to advance treatments for genetic disorders and cancers," Reed said, making my heart constrict, "with the hope of one day discovering a cure."

"Experimentation for the greater good and all that," Saylor sneered.

"And Elementums do heal faster," Reed shrugged. "We also rarely get sick thanks to all that research and development, but there are other costs."

Rarely, but not impossible obviously...

"How is this all secret?" My mind spun as I tried to process it all.

"Cover-ups. Payoffs. Blackmail." Saylor's face twisted in disgust. "Money and influence can get you far in this world and keep many people silent."

"The Clinic is made up of a continuous supply of fraudulent shell corporations." Reed leaned back against the cushions. "Too many that Arc can't keep track of them all. For every one that is dissolved, several more are established in its place."

"It's like trying to pin down constantly moving shadows." Saylor sighed.

So, there could be an unlimited number of Clinic companies out there just lurking in the shadows.

Reed's phone dinged, and he dug it out, wiggling the screen at Saylor. "My reminder to work on our paper."

"You've got to be kidding me." Saylor threw up her arms. "Over our fall break?"

"While we have time," Reed reasoned with a smile.

I sat back, my brain on overload as a tidal wave of exhaustion cascaded over me.

"Oh, no. I know that look." Saylor pointed an accusing finger. "No way. Not happening. What you're asking for is *beyond* tragic."

As their tennis match of words went back and forth, I curled up against the cozy cushions in the spectator section. Eventually my eyelids lost the fight to stay open. Then, my switch to consciousness flipped off.

Lights out.

***

Sometime later, a gentle shake on my shoulder coaxed me awake, the heavy cobwebs of sleep slow to dissipate. Blinking away the dense fog, I realized I was still curled up in the common area. How long had I been out?

"Sorry to wake you." Aunt Viv crouched down in front of me, still in the olive fleece and black skinny jeans from earlier.

"No, no. It's fine." I sat up, rubbing my face. "What's going on?"

"I hate to do this, Emma-bug," Aunt Viv said, concern lining her face. "But I need to leave with Herrera and Nova."

"Okay. When do we—" I paused. "Wait. I'm not coming with you?"

Aunt Viv shook her head. "You don't have clearance to go to the compound, but this is the fastest way to get information and hopefully the help of the Arc Council."

The next person who mentioned clearance levels to me had a high chance of getting dropkicked. But after yesterday, I couldn't deny that we needed help. And if this Arc Council was the fastest way of getting it, then I'd pull on my big-girl pants and stay behind.

I squeezed her hands. "I understand."

"You'll be safe here at the Breakpoint. I wouldn't leave you if that weren't the case," she said before giving me a knowing look. "But stay out of trouble, okay?"

Heavy footfalls announced someone's approach.

"You ready?" Commander Herrera stopped next to the coffee table.

Shock rippled through me. "You're leaving now?"

"Yes, I'm sorry." Aunt Viv exhaled harshly. "I feel like I'm on a never-ending loop of apologies lately, but we need to leave tonight. These council decisions take time so we might be gone for a few days, but once I get back, we'll get everything straightened out, okay?"

"You promise?" I asked, the big unfinished conversations still looming between us. "We'll talk and there'll be no more secrets?"

"No more secrets." Aunt Viv placed a hand over her chest. "Only the truth from now on, I promise."

I nodded, wanting to believe her. But how could I? If I really thought about it, Aunt Viv had been lying to me for *years*. For most of my life, actually. How could I ever fully believe her again?

"So, a little birdie told me that you have a bit of self-defense training," Herrera said. "But Viv and I thought it might be good for you to have a refresher while we're gone. And I have the perfect trainer for you."

Or in other words, a babysitter. But I kept that to myself.

"It's a very generous offer," Aunt Viv encouraged, squeezing my shoulder. "And honestly, it couldn't hurt."

Herrera nodded. "But it's completely your choice."

Over the past twenty-four hours, I had been grabbed from behind twice and basically tossed around like a rag doll. And even though I didn't technically belong here, I still felt like I was being dragged along the fringes. Exposed to all the dangers, but not truly invited into the haven—because I wasn't one of them. But then, what was I to this hidden world?

Hindrance. Clueless. Burden.

No, I wouldn't accept that. Not if I could help it. I needed to protect myself in this world, and I wasn't going to be the cause of someone else getting hurt.

"So, how about it?" Herrera prompted. "You want to train?"

I locked eyes with him. "Yes, I'll train."

10

The city noises made it difficult to sleep. As I lay in bed, the glowing red numbers of the alarm clock announced the late hour. It also didn't help that I'd basically hibernated the day away, making sleep virtually impossible. But truly those weren't the two problems plaguing me now.

My stomach grumbled. For one, I had opted for sleep over dinner earlier, and now I was paying the price. And the second problem had wings and enjoyed swarming like a tropical storm. The moment I had agreed to training, the nervous butterflies had broken free of their cocoons. And sure, I was anxious about not making a fool of myself, but it was more than that. Training felt different this time—more serious. Probably because I'd faced actual threats.

Releasing a heavy sigh, I tossed back the covers, threw on my favorite fleece sweatshirt, and grabbed the limited-access fob that had been gifted to me. I was determined to find a solution for at least one of my problems as I crept out into the silent hallway and down to the delightfully vacant common area. Zeroing in on the monster fridge, I scoured the fully stocked shelves, avoiding the stuff already labeled and claimed. But despite how hungry I was, nothing appealed.

That's when one of the labeled containers caught my eye, and a horrible thought occurred to me. Herrera had never mentioned *who* my trainer was, only that I had one and they would meet me in Training Room A at eight o'clock tomorrow morning. What if it was Decker? What a cruel joke that would be.

I shoved the fridge door shut on that nightmare scenario as I turned away, spotting a fruit basket on the island. With all the butterflies raging in my gut, a lighter snack seemed the better way to go. I grabbed an apple and managed to find a jar of peanut butter, a cutting board, and an actual knife—score. Then I organized my chop station on the back counter and got to work cutting and heavily slathering my slices.

"Would you like some apple with your peanut butter?"

Zoned out, I jumped at the familiar deep voice behind me, resulting in a rather embarrassing squeak.

"Crap." I dropped my supplies as blood oozed from the tip of my finger.

A cool, soft-rubbery material captured my wrist as Kaden gently guided me with his prosthetic hand over to the sink. And still reeling from his stealthy arrival, I didn't fight him as I took in his black shirt, light gray shorts, and bare feet.

My finger found its way under the rushing spray, the sting from the cold water clearing away some of the shock. The hand-like prosthetic that held my wrist was a combination of metal, plastic tubing and a black silicone covering. But the most captivating part was how it flexed and moved like a flesh-and-blood hand. How was that possible?

I glanced up at Kaden only to find his face set in an icy mask. Surprised by the intensity, I snapped my focus back to the running water. What the hell was he so pissed about? Wasn't like I cut his finger.

"I got this." I tugged my hand, but it wouldn't budge.

A deep chuckle responded. "You really don't like being helped, do you?"

"Only when I don't actually *need* help." I pulled harder, shifting our hands. But somewhere in between slicing my finger and being treated with kid gloves, I'd forgotten I was dealing with an Elementum. The stream of water fluidly curved at an angle to continue washing over my finger.

Holy Hydro.

The gasp I released must've made him realize what he'd done, because in the next instance he released my wrist and the water fell straight. Thrown off balance by the sudden lack of resistance, I teetered sideways. But before I could successfully kiss the concrete, strong arms shot out lighting fast and caught me.

"Careful there, Firefly. We can't have you hitting your head again."

I tensed. "What did you call me?"

Kaden ignored my question as he effortlessly pulled me back to vertical, where I found myself against a very warm, very hard chest. Like, rock hard—which I only confirmed because somehow my traitorous hands had found their way onto it.

I yanked my hands away and stepped back as my face heated. "I don't want to get blood on your shirt."

Kaden smirked as he pulled out a first aid kit from under the sink. "Honestly, I never thought this would get any use. All the medical supplies must be aflutter with you around."

More like I was, but he didn't need to know that as I snagged a paper towel to staunch the bleeding.

"Well, it would be wholly unfair of me if I didn't give them all a shot." I gave him a saucy smile, determined not to let him or my medical apprehension get the best of me.

Kaden's brows raised before he opened the plastic tub and sorted through the supplies.

That's right, buddy. My auntie raised no fool.

"Let me see." He waved me closer.

"I know how to work a Band-Aid." I extended my open palm for the supplies.

"And miss witnessing you swipe right on one of these little guys?" Kaden grinned as he jiggled the box of adhesive strips. "Not likely."

I fought the pull at my lips as I studied him, a challenge lighting his sea-blue eyes. He appeared dead set on bandage duty, and was I really going to duke it out over some silly Band-Aid?

I relinquished my finger, bringing him close once again. Not pec-in-hand close, but close enough to catch his minty-pine cologne—which I healthily ignored.

"So, no magical healing powers with the water?" I asked to distract myself.

"Unfortunately not." Kaden removed the paper towel around my finger. "Although that would be convenient."

That made sense. Otherwise, why would they need a high-tech medical wing?

"I imagine so would not requiring a source," I joked as he inspected my cut. "Do you just carry water around with you all the time?"

"Some Hydros carry water around with them." Kaden tapped his unique prosthetic, drawing attention to the clear plastic tubing lining his bionic hand that was filled with water. So that was how he could move it like a normal appendage. He was manipulating the water within it.

"But usually that depends on their skill level," he continued while grabbing the antiseptic spray, the sting to my finger barely noticeable. "As we gain experience, we learn to pull our sources from the surrounding environment, even when it's in short supply."

"How does that work? Do you *see* the water around you?" I asked, thinking of a certain pattern-tracking problem.

Dark brows rose in question.

My cheeks heated, looking away. Clearly, *not* how it worked. Which meant what for me and my weird brain?

"It's more like sensing the water vapors in the air." Kaden extended his hand. "Then drawing them together."

My mouth parted on a soft inhale as tiny pellets of ice formed in his upturned palm. Then in a seamless motion circled his hand—talk about a targeted Hale-Storm. The control was beyond impressive, which should have scared me. I waited for it to scare me...

"It also doesn't hurt that seventy-one percent of the Earth's surface consists of water." Kaden shrugged. The pelts thawed and evaporated out of sight.

I had roughly known that, but suddenly it took on a whole new meaning. If he could control the oceans, where did that leave me? Up by the life jacket rentals or drifting out to sea with no harbor in sight? Choices, choices.

As Kaden grabbed the box of Band-Aids and started opening one, his jaw was locked in concentration. I traced with my eyes the uneven skin cutting across his chiseled features. It only made him appear more rugged and matched his stormy persona. But I bet his scars and maybe even his prosthetic hadn't come from training, which was crazy since he couldn't be more than a year older than me.

I averted my gaze as his nimble fingers—both flesh and bionic—wrapped the Band-Aid around my cut. "So, could you move a river? Or stop the rain?"

Kaden paused, a heart-stopping grin shaping his face. "I think the better question is why would you want to stop the rain? What did it ever do to you, Firefly?"

My eyes narrowed. "Why are you calling me that? Is it another inside joke like the Newt thing?"

He released my finger, his face locking down, as if suddenly he'd remembered who he was talking to. After packing away the supplies, he returned the first aid kit back home.

"You're lucky the cut wasn't deeper." Kaden crossed his arms, propping a hip against the counter. "Especially considering how high you jumped. Makes me wonder if you really survived a Recall Team."

I stiffened. How... *No*, it was better if I didn't focus on him talking behind my back. It wouldn't do my ego any favors.

Kaden tilted his head. "Or was that rumor wrong?"

I took a page from his playbook, ignoring that Q&A section. "I only jumped because you snuck up behind me."

"I believe it's pronounced *walked*." Kaden's grin hitched higher. "I *walked* up behind you."

I threw up my arms. "How's that any better?"

"Intention." Kaden shrugged, no heat behind the word.

Well, crap. Wasn't that the truth?

But unfortunately, I had a short fuse after everything. "Did you intend to walk like a ninja? Stalking up behind a preoccupied person?"

Kaden leaned toward me. "Maybe you should be more observant."

"Or maybe someone should put a bell on you." I leaned forward too.

Kaden chuckled. "I think that would be a little counterproductive."

"To what? Your craft?" I shot back.

"Everyone needs a hobby," Kaden said in a rough voice.

Suddenly my mind revisited the gutter from earlier, plummeting right back into it. I could only imagine what his craft and hobbies entailed—oh, the possibilities.

My heart thundered. With us both leaning into the argument, there wasn't much space separating us now as I felt the heat rolling off his body. Too close. We were *way* too close.

"And I should probably add hiding sharp objects to my hobby list. You know, for your own safety," Kaden said, amusement shining in his eyes. "Also, maybe strap a first aid kit to you before I go."

"I'm not that accident prone." I stepped back, afraid I might hit him—or do something even more foolish.

He gestured toward my bandaged finger. "You sure about that, Firefly?"

"Why do you keep calling me that?" I bit out. "Did I somehow offend your family crest? Insult your brother or something?"

In an instant, the icy mask was back as Kaden stepped forward. All the space I had gained vanished. "I would've thought it was obvious, *Emma-bug*."

I tensed as recognition flared.

"Despite your spirited spark, we don't need you buzzing around here, messing things up." Then he turned on his heel and stalked off without another word.

My tear ducts prickled, but I refused to cry. Refused to give Hale-Storm that kind of power over me. I mean, I figured my stay at the Breakpoint had upset some people. But clearly his irritation with me went way deeper than that.

But why? He didn't even know me.

Snack forgotten, I walked back to my room on numb legs, Kaden's words leaving me frozen to the core.

11

The training wing consisted of multiple fitness spaces, a cardio center, a yoga studio, and a large two-story gym. Training Room A ended up being next to the impressive weight room I'd seen yesterday. The room was a continuation of the Breakpoint's warehouse-chic theme—concrete, brick, steel, and greenery—but I could still see the dings and scuff marks from all the lives that had passed through.

A large, black padded mat took center stage, while the perimeter of the room was lined with a water station, towel hamper, four sleek metal storage containers, and wooden benches. The brick walls were bare save for two fire extinguishers and a first aid kit, its red cross basically taunting me about what went down last night. But I refused to give it headspace.

The nervous butterflies swirled back into action as I messed with one of the zippers on my newly borrowed tactical pants. They kind of looked like a pair of leggings and moto pants had a love child. I'd paired them with the matching athletic top and my running shoes. Unlike the Clinic's blatant tactical gear I'd seen the Recall Team wear, Arc's gear was retrofitted for blending in. Each set was styled and colored in different variations to disguise the fact that they belonged to the same group. The only constant was the threaded bands on certain individual's sleeves—not including mine. But the gear still made me feel like a badass.

I only hoped the feeling persisted after my trainer walked through that door. I wasn't sure which option would be worse: dealing with Ink-Wad after his near asphyxiation attempt or facing Hale-Storm after his frosty warning.

I gripped my necklace and walked over to the metal bins, noticing a small symbol on the top corner of all of them. Each was different but they were definitely a set.

The symbols reminded me of the geometric mural I'd seen outside, but simpler—less chaos and color. As I traced a finger along one of the triangular designs, the embossed edges lit up like a neon sign.

My pulse skyrocketed. Well, that was new. I'd never seen it glow so bright before. It had to be all the stress from the past two days—definitely nothing more. *Nope*. Not at all.

To distract myself, I peeked over the rim to see what kind of equipment was inside. Images of nun chucks and throwing stars ran wild. *Water*. Liquid H2O filled the first container. The second was divided into three sections of soil, sand, and rocks. A fan occupied the third. And the last held a perforated metal ring attached to a... small propane tank?

Right. Elementums.

Each bin contained one of the four elements to train with. It wasn't like I'd forgotten where I was or the situation I was in. The nightmares last night proved as much. My brain had simply taken a vacation. To the Bermuda Triangle. For like a hot second. Which did not bode well for—

"You must be the trainee."

At the detached male voice, I whipped around to find a guy who appeared to be in his mid-twenties and was built like a Navy SEAL. With his crew cut black hair and razor-sharp dark eyes, he looked as if the word *fun* wasn't in his vocabulary.

"My name is Clay Avelino. I'll be your trainer for the next few days." He set his bag down on one of the benches as the olive skin around his face tightened into hard lines. Apparently, someone wasn't too thrilled to be here, turning this into more of a glass-half-empty situation.

Fantastic.

But I refused to let anyone make me quit. I was determined to follow this through, even if I had to fill the glass myself.

I stepped forward with a smile. "I'm Emma Cross. I'm—"

"My punishment, I know." Clay pinched the bridge of his nose.

It had sounded more like a statement to himself, but still that seemed harsh. Since entering the Breakpoint, I'd somehow gained three new members to the Cross-Decontamination-Fan-Club: Ink-Wad, Hale-Storm, and now Major-Hard-Ass.

So much for not ruffling any more feathers.

"Let's start with the protocols. Then we'll warm up and review what you know." Clay stepped onto the mat. "Protocol one. Burn this room's location into your brain. We'll be practicing here every morning for the foreseeable future."

I blinked. Every morning?

"Two. Warm up starts promptly at eight, so don't be late." Clay's plain white T-shirt stretched as he placed his hands on the hips of his dark joggers. "Three. From eight till eleven, your focus will be solely on training. No silly distractions. If we're stuck together on this, then we're going to do it right."

That one was easy considering I didn't have a phone anymore—R.I.P. Flipper.

"Four. Respect everyone on the mats."

A snort came out before I could stop it, thinking of a certain Ink-Wad. "Does that apply to everyone?"

"Yes," Clay said with authority. "I don't care if you're an Elementum or not. As long as you're on these mats, you'll be given that courtesy."

Stunned, a small kernel of admiration grew for Major-Hard-Ass.

"But I won't sugarcoat it. There might be some animosity thrown your way." Clay's features sharpened. "You see, this is an unusual case and granting you access to the Breakpoint has sent some waves through the ranks. My advice to you: Keep your head down and stick to training."

Knots twisted in my stomach. Funny how also in this world I was the unusual case—the misfit Halfbreed. "Don't worry, I've gotten used to this transient lifestyle."

Clay frowned before shaking it off. "Protocol five. Under no circumstance are you to leave the Breakpoint without permission or a chaperone."

Wait. Major-Hard-Ass says what? How had I gone from basically being an independent young adult to *this*? And what if I needed to leave to find answers about my mom?

As I opened my mouth, Clay lifted a finger. "When you agreed to stay here, you also agreed to follow the terms of being under our protection. To allow you to leave with knowledge of this place, however limited it may be, would be foolish. For us and for you." His serious gaze held mine. "Make no mistake, our enemies will go to extremes to extract that information from you."

I swallowed hard as the fear of being surrounded by shrouded soldiers rushed back to me.

"We're a team here." Clay gestured around him. "What one person does can have untold consequences for everyone else. It's important that you understand that and know that the rules are not only for your protection but also for everyone else here."

We don't need you buzzing around here messing things up.

"I understand." I slid my sun charm back and forth as Kaden's words crashed into me like a tidal wave.

Clay appeared surprised, almost like he expected a fight. "This isn't a prison." His tone lightened. "Just ask someone beforehand and think of them more as a guide, all right?" Then he jerked his chin toward the center mat. "Now, let's begin."

***

According to Clay, my previous self-defense training had been fairly basic. Adequate enough if an untrained person tried a snatch-and-grab. But with a trained Recall Agent, I was less likely to be effective. And a fully trained Elementum? I could forget about it.

"It's commendable that you actually took down a Recall Agent." Clay stood on the mat, arms crossed. "But based on the accounts I heard, you still hesitated and panicked."

I sat cross-legged on a bench, head leaned back against the wall.

"Those first few moments of an attack are critical and can decide the entire outcome. So, on top of defense tactics, that's where we'll be focusing. But make no mistake, if you find yourself facing another Recall Agent, your goal is to survive the initial attack and then escape. And I won't even attempt to train you against an Enforcer. With our limited timeframe, it would be pointless."

"Enforcer?"

"See, pointless." Clay released a heavy breath. "Enforcers are Elementums who fight for the Clinic."

My spine straightened. "Why would an Elementum ever fight for the Clinic? Aren't they a vortex of evil?"

Clay raised his brows. "I see Campbell has been running her mouth as usual."

I sealed mine shut like a vault.

"The first three lessons will take place off the mats." Clay tapped his temple. "Self-defense training—any training, really—starts in your head."

The image of a cartoon brain lifting dumbbells popped into my mind—*not helpful*.

"Lesson one: Be aware," Clay said. "Sounds simple, but being completely present is something most people struggle with, especially these days. Distractions prevent you from observing your surroundings and allow others to get the jump on you."

Made sense.

"Lesson two: Mark your physical boundaries. This is the personal space around you." Clay indicated a circle around himself. "Nothing and nobody should enter this space without you being aware of it."

Again, made sense.

"Lesson three: Breath control." Clay patted his chest. "The more you can achieve discipline over your breathing, the stronger your chances will be of fighting off the hesitation and panic." He inclined his head. "Remember those three lessons; they'll be the foundation of our training. Understand?"

I nodded, but I had a feeling it would be harder than it sounded.

Clay jacked his thumb toward the center mat. "Onto drills."

For the next two hours, we focused on various defensive moves and blocking techniques, repeating each one until I got it down. Then we worked on linking them together in a series of combinations.

Despite our rocky start, Clay was nothing but professional—intense, but professional. He even explained why he made each correction, including me fully in the training. Which sounded silly but actually made a huge difference.

By the third hour, we hit the core and abdominal portion of the training session. With my butt securely on the cushy mat, I was busy knocking out sit-ups.

"Strong core muscles are fundamental in improving your balance and stability," Clay said as I finished with my up-and-down routine. "They're the key to transitioning and holding your stances."

On the last upward rise, I groaned before collapsing back onto the mat.

"Let's go, Cross," Clay barked. "Plank position."

I squeezed my eyes shut before rolling over and lifting myself into place. I was all for working out and staying healthy, but whoever invented the plank could go to hell. Not even ten seconds in and my arms were shaking like a seismic wave. How did anyone—

Thwack.

I lost my plank, landing on the mat with a thud.

"What the hell?" I rubbed my shoulder as I picked up the quarter-sized sphere that had landed next to me. It was coarse to the touch, and ended up being a compressed ball of sand. "So, you're a Terra."

Clay rolled another sand projectile between his fingers. "Does it matter?"

I shook my head. "No—"

Thwack.

"Hey!" My other shoulder stung as I glared daggers up at him.

"You let your guard down," Major-Hard-Ass said. Clearly his personal info was off limits.

"What did you expect? I was planking as requested. You could've at least given me a heads-up."

"You think a Recall Agent will give you a heads-up?"

My nose wrinkled. "Well, no."

"You forgot the first two lessons." Clay tilted his head. "Not to mention you panicked and lost your positioning."

Well, crap. He was right.

"You need to find a balance of staying focused but keeping aware. And *this*"—Clay held up the coarse little orb—"will act as your reminder."

Was he insane? How was I supposed to block a tiny sand missile? It was impossible. And I was ninety-nine percent sure Major-Hard-Ass was just doing it for funsies.

"Back in plank position, Cross."

The next thirty minutes continued like that, one core exercise after the next with intermittent sand missiles bombarding me. None of which I could block, let alone even anticipate.

I finished my last set of flutter kicks, letting my head fall back against the mats. Man, I was going to hurt tomorrow. Hell, the ache-train would roll into the station later today.

"We'll stop here for today." Clay tossed his latest sand bomb back into the bin.

I sent my gratitude heavenward as I somehow mustered the strength to lift myself back to vertical, draping my arms around my bent legs.

"It'll get easier." Clay crouched down next to me. "I'd recommend hydrating and also repeating your stretches again later to help with the soreness. But overall, good job today, Cross."

"Thanks." A burst of pride warmed my chest.

As if realizing he had—insert gasp—paid me an actual compliment, Clay straightened and grabbed his bag. "You seem to have some natural talent, no doubt from your lineage. But you still have a long way to go if you want to be effective against a Recall Agent."

Well, wasn't that inspiring.

"Can I ask you something?" I looked up at him. "Did you know my mom or aunt from their time in Arc?"

Clay stared at me, no doubt from the out-of-nowhere question. "No. We never crossed paths."

"Oh." I tried to hide my disappointment. "So, you know nothing about them?"

"No. I'm sorry, I don't."

I nodded as my hope sank at the thought of finding answers.

"I'll see you tomorrow at eight sharp," Clay added in a softer tone.

"Yes, sir." I gave him a mock salute.

His gaze narrowed at me before two bodies crowded the doorway and snagged our attention. "I see the Troublesome-Two have come to spirit you away. Until tomorrow, Cross." He strode toward the exit, nodding to Reed and Saylor as he passed. "Wilson. Campbell."

Then he was gone.

"Hey." I waved them over, contemplating how difficult standing would be, but thankfully, a helping hand entered my eye line. Placing my hand in Reed's, I noticed the dirt smudges along his forearms and clothes as he hoisted me to my feet.

Both of them were dressed in their different variations of black and gray training gear. Unlike Clay. I hadn't noticed it before, but he hadn't been wearing actual gear. Was it because it was fall break? Or was it because the training sessions with me weren't official?

"Thanks." I dusted off my pants.

Reed smiled. "Who am I to deny a damsel in distress?"

"I would've thought a dude in distress was more accurate." Saylor wiggled her eyebrows.

Reed nudged her. "It's a good thing I love you."

"And you're stuck with me." Saylor smiled, undeterred.

"Like a rash."

"New profile description." Saylor framed her hands. "Cute, lovable, and *infectious*."

Reed shook his head, strands of sandy blond hair escaping his man-bun.

"Also, top story." Saylor bounced over to me. "I can't believe you didn't tell us Clay is your trainer. How did it go?"

I grabbed my water bottle, instantly regretting moving. "Besides feeling like I took on a bulldozer, it went decently well. Or at least according to Major-Hard-Ass, it did."

"More like Captain-Hard-Ass." Saylor twisted her sunset-tipped braids around.

"What?"

"Clay is Captain of the Breakpoint," Reed said before frowning. "Which makes this training situation rather odd. He usually only teaches more experienced fighters—if he trains anyone at all."

That shed a new light on Clay's punishment comment from earlier.

"Very odd." Saylor shared a look with Reed. Then she clapped like a happy seal. "And here I thought fall break would be boring."

Reed looked skyward. "It's supposed to be relaxing."

"Same thing." Saylor looped her arm through mine, pulling me toward the door. "All this excitement has made me hungry."

"Breaking Grounds?" Reed suggested.

Saylor nodded eagerly.

I looked between them. "Breaking what?"

"It's the café out front," Reed explained.

I pulled up short, remembering the protocols from earlier. "Clay said I can't leave without permission or a chaperone." Saying it out loud made me feel like I couldn't cross the street by myself—oh, how the independent had fallen.

"Permission granted. Chaperones acquired." Saylor gestured between herself and Reed. "Plus, it's just downstairs. As Nova would say, *technically* we're not leaving the building."

I hesitated as Clay's stern face flashed before me. Was I really going to risk crossing Captain-Hard-Ass so soon? But another part of me—*cough*, the nervous-new-kid part, *cough*—wanted Saylor and Reed to like me.

I smiled. "All right, I'm in."

"*Woo.*" Saylor threw up her free arm as we strolled out the door.

Heading for the elevators, we weaved our way through the groups of jumpsuited workmen and assorted tools, the security upgrades in full swing for the day.

As we approached the double doors to the administrative wing, I pointed to the strange embedded track. "What's up with these frames? A lot of the doors have tracks to nowhere."

Saylor tilted her head. "Oh, you mean the shield doors?"

"Shield doors? As in…" I stalled out as Reed pressed what appeared to be a smudge on the wall, but in reality was a discreet button.

Swoosh.

Small, hidden slats retracted on both sides of the door as a solid panel protruded out of a pocket in the wall. Reed gripped the sturdy handle, hauling the imposing door out a few feet.

"As in *shield doors*." He knocked the military-grade panel with his knuckle. "There's one on each side of this doorway and at other junction points throughout the building. They allow us to seal off portions of the Breakpoint, if necessary."

I shuddered to think of when that would be necessary.

"And man oh man, once you latch these babies shut, it's case closed. No getting through them," Saylor said before shrugging. "Well, without an impressive amount of force, that is."

"But they've never been used." Reed slid the panel home again. "And we plan to keep it that way."

12

The smell of heaven surrounded me. Heaven and the fresh batch of raspberry muffins that Reed was currently snagging for all three of us to split.

Breaking Grounds was a lively place with an industrial but cozy vibe. Configured in an L-shape, the main counter wrapped the inner perimeter while a large community table and booths lined the outer brick walls.

As I sipped my tea and snuggled deeper into the comfy booth, I thought of what Saylor and Reed had told me earlier. Apparently Breaking Grounds, the Two-Points Cidery next door, and the Breakpoint were all connected, with the café and cidery acting as fronts so the outpost could operate without detection. The fact that Arc needed fronts wasn't exactly comforting—organized crime rings came to mind—but if they wanted to stay off the Clinic's radar, it made sense.

"I figured you'd be an iced vanilla, three pumps sugar-cookie coffee kind of girl." Saylor looked up from checking to see if Nova had sent any more updates. All I knew was Aunt Viv's group had made it to the compound safely, and they'd be in meetings for the next few days. Other than that, I was in the dark. Which seemed highly unfair, considering these meetings affected the next steps in *my* life.

I pursed my lips. "That sounds hostile and extremely unhealthy."

"A real sugared-up nightmare." Saylor's face scrunched in disgust. "But isn't that what all you Cali girls drink?"

"Sorry to disappoint. Plus, that's more likely trending in SoCal. I'm certified NorCal." I flashed the two-finger salute. "Peace and love, man."

Saylor burst out laughing. "Oh, you'll do just fine here. It's all granola wishes and mountain dreams."

I snorted and took another sip of my tea.

"What's California like? I have the image of surfer boys and sandy beaches for days." Saylor twirled her finger over her own simple latte, swirling the foamy surface. Thankfully, all the adjacent tables and booths had already cleared out, so there was no one around to witness her water-wielding abilities.

"Depends on where you go." I watched the hypnotic coffee. "Some parts are like that, near L.A. for instance, but the northern coast is a lot colder. Typically, only crazy wet-suited people actually get in the water." I smiled, remembering Aunt Viv's impressive squeal at her first encounter with the arctic waves. "I've heard the Atlantic is much warmer."

"That's on my list as well." Saylor dropped her arm and stared out the window.

"You've never been to either coast?" Her comment caught me off guard. With her spontaneous spirit, I had pictured her jet-setting wherever inspiration took her, but maybe she was more stuck than I'd imagined.

Saylor's gaze was fixed on the street. "I was actually born in New York but only caught a glimpse of the ocean before I was relocated here. I was ten. That's when I met Reed and his mom. They took me in."

As in... she had nobody else?

"Reed's like a brother to me." Saylor fidgeted with her rings. "He was there for me the most after the Clinic killed my parents."

Holy mother—

"Muffins." Reed set a plate down in front of us. "Fresh from the oven and full of raspberry goodness."

Saylor pepped up. "Always a good day when your berries are razzed."

The change in her was startling. I wanted to ask more questions, but I got the feeling the door to that conversation was firmly shut. No wonder the discussion about the Clinic yesterday had been so touchy.

"*Saylor.*" Reed slid into the booth beside me. "No ruining muffin Monday."

"What?" Saylor asked innocently. "No razzing your berries? Assessing your apples?" She gave him a wicked smile. "Oh, what about licking your lemons?"

"Why would you kids be licking lemons?" asked a new voice with an accent, the *would you* coming out more like *woodyuh*. New York? Maybe Boston? I wasn't sure exactly, but definitely East Coast.

At the end of our booth, Grandma-Moxie stood with her bob of auburn hair and short, rounded frame. I had no clue if she was actually a grandma, but she looked capable of a mean hug.

"For making lemonade, of course," Saylor said quickly. "Right, Reed?"

Reed cleared his throat, his face flushing red. "Of course."

Behind the rims of her glasses, Grandma-Moxie's concerned eyes shifted between the Dynamic-Duo before landing on me. Her eyes widened.

Oh, goodie. Had I added another member to my fan club already?

Reed mercifully piped in. "Mrs. Herrera, this is Emma."

"I've told you, dear, just call me Cathleen. Makes me feel young." Grandma-Moxie gave me a warm smile. "You must be the one causing all the talk around the Breakpoint." The *talk* sounding more like *tawlk*. "Toni said you might stop by."

"That's me." I smiled awkwardly, tucking back a loose strand of hair.

"Mrs. Herr—" Reed halted after one sharp look from Grandma-Moxie. "I mean, Cathleen is the Commander's wife, and she runs both the café and cidery."

"Like a boss." Saylor hoisted a muffin in salute.

"It's nothing, dear." Cathleen swatted away the compliment as she sat next to Saylor, pushing up the sleeves of her flowy blouse. "Toni definitely has the more challenging task of running the Breakpoint and keeping track of these two troublemakers."

"Hey," Saylor said around a mouthful of muffin.

Reed grinned as he snagged two muffins off the plate, giving me one and keeping the other for himself. "I think everyone would agree that the Breakpoint wouldn't run nearly as efficiently without you."

A long silence followed.

As I peeked up from my muffin, Cathleen's stare glowed with what appeared to be wonder and... anguish?

"I apologize for staring." She took a heavy breath. "I know how overwhelming all this must be, but I didn't think this would hit me so hard. You're the spitting image of Anna."

I sat back, muffin forgotten. "You knew my mom?"

Cathleen nodded, bringing a hand to her throat. "I'm so sorry for your loss. It was heartbreaking to hear of her passing."

Murder, I mentally corrected as the vice around my heart squeezed tight.

"Both her and Viv trained under my husband as blooming Igniters." Cathleen's gaze became lost in memories. "Viv was such a spitfire, always so fierce and determined. I swear she was born with liquid fire in her veins." She grinned, making the laugh lines around her face crinkle. "Well, honestly both of them were. The Phoenix and the Firebird."

I straightened in my seat as Saylor and Reed's faces scrunched.

"The Phoenix?" I'd never heard that reference for my mom before. Then again, why would I have?

"Yes. Anna was a force all her own." Cathleen nodded, her short hair flicking forward with the motion. "Actually, out of the two, Anna was the one with natural talent. Of course, Viv made up for it through hard work and sheer will. But even at a young age, Anna could perform highly advanced techniques that fully grown Igniters struggled with."

I gripped my sun charm. The admiration radiating from her voice made me wish I could've seen that part of my mom.

"As one of Toni's first students here, Anna was something special." Cathleen smiled fondly. "A true spark in this world."

You're my spark. My heart pinched. Had my mom's words been an Igniter thing all along? A thing she never wanted me to be a part of...

"When did Commander Herrera start training her?" I asked, desperate for answers. And sure, Aunt Viv had promised we'd talk when she got back, but I wasn't so sure it would happen. And even if it did, could I really trust her answers?

"Let's see, I guess Anna was only thirteen at the time." Cathleen adjusted her glasses. "Although Toni wasn't a Commander back then. He had only been promoted to a Breaker Captain the previous year before he was transferred to Colorado to help implement the new training protocols—which is how he met Anna."

I hung on every word.

"And naturally, there were the Riff-Raffs," she continued. "Viv and Nova were inseparable. Viv followed Anna around everywhere, and Nova was always in tow. They were all so young back then." She chuckled. "They all trained together, until the summer when Anna... She must've been eighteen I believe... Yes, she was because she was under consideration to become a Breaker when she went missing."

Missing? A cold sweat engulfed my body. Was this when my mom went into hiding? But if she was already a part of Arc, that made no sense. Maybe something more sinister had happened—like the Clinic. Or maybe my mom had met someone. With my father not being an

Elementum, that would make sense. Had she seen her opportunity for a normal life and taken it? I wondered if my father had even known about the Elementum world or that she was an Igniter. And come to think of it, I wondered if he'd even known about me.

My heart sank. I couldn't decide which was worse: him not knowing I existed or him knowing about my weird Halfbreed genetics and not sticking around.

"Anna's disappearance hit Viv the hardest. She was a complete wreck." Cathleen's features clouded with sadness. "I'm just so glad they reconnected before..."

Before the end, I finished for her. My chest ached fiercely. Because even after almost nine years, I still had a hard time unlocking that grief-case. But it was worth it to keep my mom's memory alive. Worth it to keep my promise and do whatever it took to honor the day of her passing in four days. Too bad they didn't sell doughnuts here at Breaking Grounds.

I filed that bittersweet task away to figure out later as I refocused on Cathleen. "How—"

The urgent shout and symphony of smashing plateware from the back had everyone's head on a swivel.

Cathleen cursed under her breath before rising from the booth with an apologetic smile. "I'm afraid I'll have to cut our conversation short, but hopefully we can chat again soon."

"Yes, please." I resisted the urge to lunge across the table to make her stay.

With that, Cathleen pivoted and disappeared into the back, leaving me with a head swirling with questions. Questions that reminded me just how little I knew about my mom and this world. It felt like I'd woken up in a foreign country where I didn't speak the language.

"Why didn't you tell us your mother was almost a Breaker?" Saylor asked in awe.

Reed looked skyward. "Seriously? That's what you took away from all that?"

Saylor shot him a quizzical look.

"A breaker of what?" I asked. Codes? Bones? Kit-Kat bars? The options were endless.

"Just Breaker." Reed turned to me. "They're a high-ranking division within Arc and are considered the very best among us. Trained to handle only the toughest missions."

"Think Black Ops or SEAL Team Six," Saylor said, starry-eyed. "I'd do bad, bad things to become a Breaker."

And my mom had been under consideration to be one. My vanilla-candle-loving, always-covered-in-paint, constantly-optimistic-even-in-sickness mother. How was that possible?

In the words of Aunt Viv, it just didn't compute.

Saylor looked at Reed. "Another clue?"

"Clue to what?" I glanced between them, nervous energy zipping through me.

Reed double-checked that our area was still clear before lowering his voice. "We noticed it about two weeks ago. Mainly when Saylor was stalking Nova—"

"*Hanging out,*" Saylor corrected him with a glare.

"Uh-huh, sure." Reed pinned her with a look. "Well, supposedly Nova's been working on a top-secret project for Commander Herrera. We didn't know much, only stuff that Saylor either overheard or glimpsed. But then—"

"You guys showed up," Saylor whisper-yelled. "And I overheard Herrera telling Nova that this recent development involving the Phoenix could be the key to changing the course of the war."

I jolted in my seat.

"We didn't realize they were talking about your mother until Cathleen mentioned the nickname just now." Reed braced his arms on the table. "And after what Saylor overheard, it all feels like too big of a coincidence."

Yeah, it did. Especially if this secret project somehow involved my mom.

"There's something bigger going on. We just know it." Saylor practically bounced in the booth. "And now you're part of the investigation squad, too."

Was I? Did I want that? Just because it felt good to be included didn't mean I actually belonged here. Or change the fact that diving deeper into the Elementum world felt like a betrayal of my mom and Aunt Viv, and everything they had sacrificed to protect me from it.

"That's if you want to be?" Reed asked.

The only thing I wanted for sure was answers, and this could be a direct path to finding them.

I squared my shoulders. "Count me in."

13

Breath control was a bitch. A stone-cold, pant-inducing bitch.

In theory? Sounded doable.

In reality? Brutal—especially at altitude.

I collapsed onto the mat. It had been like this all morning. Well, the past two days actually. My second training session yesterday had been just as brutal, if not more. And the late-night strategy sessions with the Dynamic-Duo weren't exactly helping my energy levels.

After our lunch at Breaking Grounds, the three of us met up every day and night to go over strategies for how to find more information on this secret project. But so far, none of our ideas had any merit, what with the Commander's group being away at the compound and none of us having high enough clearance in the computer system.

But we weren't giving up yet. And I wasn't giving up on talking with Cathleen again, however every time I looked for her at Breaking Grounds, she wasn't there.

"Up, Cross," Clay ordered, the sting on my right shoulder signaling his impatience to start the next round of drills.

"Cheater," I bit out, hating Captain-Hard-Ass's impeccable aim with a fiery passion. "Isn't it against some code to use your Terra trickery for evil?"

"Who said I'm using it?" Clay rolled another sand bomb in his hand. "Are you done lying around?"

"Are you done using me as your own personal dartboard?" I rolled over, glaring up at him. "Do you really expect me to catch one of those?"

"I never asked you to catch one." Clay crossed his arms, his plain white T-shirt stretching. "I'm simply asking you to be aware of them. Aware of me." He pointed to himself. "If you can mark where I am, then you already know where the attack is coming from."

I sat up. "But you can launch those things from anywhere."

"True, mostly." Clay inclined his head. "However, that would be cruel and futile. If I expect you to learn a skill, the exercise must first be achievable. Thus, I've modified these vicinity drills to accommodate your particular skill level." *Or lack of abilities.* "Every single sand pellet I've thrown has come directly from my hand."

"Oh," I finished lamely, draping my arms around my bent knees. Why hadn't I picked up on that? That was a much bigger and easier target to track.

"Remember, the key is to keep aware but focused. We're not only trying to improve your defensive tactics with this training but also to raise your awareness of your surroundings." Clay indicated the area around him. "You see, the sooner you can pinpoint a threat, the better your chances are between life and death." The muscle along his jaw tightened. "Or worse, capture."

"Capture is worse?" Ice crawled down my spine. If that was true, what did that mean for me? A Halfbreed misfit. Would the Clinic even deem me worthy of capture or was I just collateral damage to them?

"It's better than being tortured for research and analysis." Clay sent me a hard look.

"That makes Elementums sound like lab rats." A disturbing image of rows and rows of human-sized metal cages flashed in my mind.

Clay shrugged. "To the Clinic, that's what we are. A valuable invention, but a proprietary product all the same."

My stomach hollowed. "That's... I don't even have words for it. What kind of sick person allows that?"

"It's astounding what someone is capable of when they believe they're on the right side of things." Clay's jaw tightened.

As I gripped my sun charm, it really sank in why everyone was so tightly guarded around here. I mean, if it was between that or a trip to the little-lab-of-horrors, I knew where my vote would be.

"Were you ever held by the Clinic?" I asked before I could help it.

"Enough chitchat." Clay set off toward the medicine balls. "We came here to work."

Too personal for Captain-Hard-Ass—shocking.

"O Captain, my Captain." I gave him a mock salute as I got to my feet.

"Knock it off, Cross." Clay tossed a medicine ball at me, and I caught it with a grunt. "Strength training, let's go."

And go we did. The last forty minutes of training continued on with more of the same: sweat sparkles, silent swearing, and putting in the hustle for that muscle. By the time I hit the plyo-box section, I was riding high on a wave of exhaustion. But through the mental fog and rhythmic ups and downs, I started noticing... something. A sequence—if I could even call it that.

I stepped up on the box, then stepped down on the floor.

Was there a sequence to Clay's sand bombs? I was pretty sure there was. Had there been one all along?

I stepped up on the box. If I could just track—

"How's circus training going, Clay?"

Startled by Decker's venom-coated question, I faltered while stepping down and clipped the edge of the box. I flung my arms out to catch my balance like some sort of deranged pigeon. But too late. It was a total tushy takedown as I landed with a groan.

"I give her an eight for enthusiasm, but a two for the landing," Kaden said, causing heat to blast across my face.

Fan-freaking-tastic. The whole Cross-Decontamination-Fan-Club was present and accounted for. Clay looked down at me with arched brows, which was probably the closest thing to concern I could expect.

"Don't mind me. Just performing a gravity check over here." I debated if I lay here long enough, maybe the mats would swallow me like quicksand.

"Mills. Hale." Clay addressed Decker and Kaden in a detached voice. "You're early."

"Decker didn't believe you were in session." Kaden shrugged. Both Hale-Storm and Ink-Wad had traded in their training gear for street clothes today.

"Still don't." Decker crossed his tattooed arms and leaned against the wall.

Well, Ink-Wad was certainly in top fighting form today. I sat up and rubbed my lower back. If the insults weren't being directed point-blank at me, I honestly would've respected his ferocity to protect the Breakpoint and everyone in it. But here I was in his line of fire.

However, before I could respond to his circus training comment, Kaden stopped next to Clay and lowered his voice. "Did you get the text about the project from Nova?"

"Herrera said it was halted for the time being." Clay pulled Kaden over to the bench with his bag. He grabbed his phone as they continued chatting out of earshot. As he plugged in his four-digit code, I tracked the side-to-side and diagonal movements.

My pulse accelerated. Could they be talking about the secret project—the one Nova was working on that somehow involved my mom?

"I still can't believe Herrera has Clay wasting his time teaching circus tricks," Decker sneered from his lean against the wall.

Excuse him? I climbed to my feet, too exhausted to put up with his crap. "You know what, Ink-Wad?"

"I know lots of things, little Newt," Decker said. "Like you shouldn't call someone names if you have nothing to back it up with."

"I might not." I clenched my fists, never wanting to throat punch someone so hard in my life. "But that still doesn't give you the right to call me a circus act."

"You're right. That would be demeaning to the whole circus profession." Decker sent me a smirk. "You can't even balance on a box."

"Here, let me try again. But this time with an upgrade." I jumped on top of the plyo-box before operating the invisible crank connected to a certain central finger.

"Wow. Nice one." Decker stepped forward, widening his stance. "Did your aunt have you housebroken, as well? I hear that's very important for circus animals."

Screw this. "At least I have someone to house-train me." I remembered Reed's comment about this place being all he had. "I'm not some bitter loner who's as hostile as the Clinic."

Instant regret. Shame and guilt engulfed me as I desperately wished for a magic eraser.

The atmosphere shifted in a flash. A threatening silence spread through the room like an aftershock. Decker's face became devoid of all emotion, and soil lifted from the metal bin along the perimeter.

Holy Dirt-Wad.

If I'd thought Decker was dangerous before, I was severely mistaken as I eyed the growing grave cover. *Not good.* Breathing deep, I willed my body into a defensive stance like Clay had instructed me. My chances of blocking a wall of earth were slim, but I was the one who'd poked the fault line and now I'd be the one to dig myself out—possibly literally.

All at once, a vortex of water encircled my box and then froze solid like an icy shield. The chilly chest-high armor sent goosebumps racing across my skin as the soil surged toward me. But then suddenly it liquefied and rained down on the floor in sludgy splats.

I exhaled in an icy puff. At that moment, it dawned on me how completely out of my depth I was here.

As quick as it all had appeared, the icy shield thawed and drained away, followed shortly by the muddy mass snaking its way back home, leaving only an earthy residue and aroma in its wake.

"That's a write-up, Mills." Clay's tone held no give.

"What? How am I in trouble when she's causing disruptions and intruding in places she doesn't belong?" Decker scowled at Clay. "I can't be the only one who finds the timing of their arrival a little too convenient."

What was he talking about?

"That doesn't mean you can nuke the Newt." Kaden sent him a pointed look, his midnight waves falling forward. "What a mess that would've been."

I stiffened.

"Enough." Clay crossed his arms. "You know my rule of respecting everyone on the mats. I expected more from you, Mills." He pointed toward the door. "My office. Now."

"Fine," Decker bit out, heading for the exit with Clay not far behind.

"Oh, come on, Decker." Kaden grinned, following them out into the hall. "We can't just disappear people like the Clinic."

Once all three of them were gone, I collapsed onto the plyo-box, clutching the edges for support. I tried not to think of how close I'd come to an actual dirt nap. But as scary as Decker's burial attempt had been, I realized this was my chance.

I darted over to the black gym bag, checking over my shoulder as I went. I reached for the zipper, only to stall out. Was I really going to do this? Betray Clay's trust and rifle through his things? He wasn't the friendliest guy, and we'd gotten off to a rocky start, but after that he'd treated me with nothing but respect.

But where did that leave me? Sitting and waiting for answers that may never come.

I unzipped the bag, revealing a pile of dark clothes, a towel, and—miraculously—Clay's phone. When I tapped the screen, an image of a sandy desert glowed to life. But that wasn't the only thing that glowed. Creating an upside-down triangle, the lower four digits on the lock screen blazed through my vision like a string of lights.

Crap.

My heart thundered at the increased brightness, but there was no time to focus on that now. I repeated Clay's movements from earlier, relieved to see the home screen pop up after hitting the last number—score. Locating the messages app, I pulled up the latest text string from Nova and found one message that had been sent this morning.

An address.

Why would they be interested in an address? What was located there? Definitely something worth checking out. I glanced over my shoulder again before committing the string of numbers and letters to memory, then I put Clay's phone back in the same position and zipped the bag shut.

"I know Decker is highly skilled at getting a rise out of anyone, but you shouldn't push his buttons," Clay said from behind me.

I snatched up my water bottle and turned around. "Yeah, that was foolish." I tried to play it cool. There was no way he could tell I'd just ransacked his stuff. Absolutely no way, right? "Thank you for stepping in. I would've been in real trouble if you hadn't."

Clay grunted as he walked over, running a hand over his crew cut.

"But you know whatever Decker thinks about our arrival, he's wrong," I said, for some reason needing him to understand. "We only came here for help."

"I know." Clay's face softened. "Let's cool down and get out of here."

"Is what Kaden said true? Can the Clinic make someone disappear without a trace?" Just rip them from their everyday life. Was that what they'd done to my mom when she went missing from the Breakpoint?

Clay's expression turned grim. "Yes, they can."

14

"Oh, it looks like some sort of business." Saylor tilted her head, the light from her laptop screen reflecting on her orange crop top and puffy bomber jacket. "Maybe an office?"

"And you're sure this has something to do with the secret project?" Reed asked as we huddled around the kitchen island.

"Pretty sure." I adjusted my fleece sweatshirt as I perched on a stool with my history book in front of me. It was a convenient alibi if anyone came along and asked what we were doing. After training that morning, I'd rushed off to tell the Dynamic-Duo what I'd learned. We decided to investigate the address later that night, which was how we ended up here—*studying*.

"I still can't believe that Clay and Kaden are in on this, too." Reed shook his head. "Although I guess that means more potential sources of information."

And more opportunities for frostbite.

"There's no telling what this place is." Saylor rotated the street view displayed on the protected browser so it couldn't be tracked. "There's no identification pin or signage anywhere that I can see."

The building on the screen was nondescript, with beige bricks and tinted ribbon windows. There was a parking lot on the left, while a gated service yard took up the right. But as Saylor said, there were no signs or markers to note what the place was.

"I've been thinking about what Herrera said about changing the course of the war." Reed pushed up the sleeves of his green flannel. "What if we misunderstood the term 'secret project'?"

Saylor's fingers froze on her touchpad. "You think they meant a Clinic project?"

Reed shrugged. "It's possible."

"Clinic project?" I asked, my mind revisiting the little-lab-of-horrors from earlier.

"The Clinic conducts various research projects," Reed explained. "Each one has its own goals, but all of them are usually tied back to one of four main projects."

"What are those?"

Reed tensed a hand over one of the potted succulents on the island and a stream of soil funneled out, blanketing the counter. With a flick of his wrist, the soil shifted until it formed four designs.

"The Hydrus, Terraris, Aerius, and Ignis projects." Reed pointed to each of the designs. "Each project has a correlating emblem and I think you can connect the dots on their goals."

Dots definitely connected. The projects represented the creation of the Hydros, Terras, Aeros, and Igniters.

Saylor leaned forward. "It's one of the few things the Arc founders adopted from the Clinic."

"What?" I was sure I'd heard her wrong.

Reed extended his hand again and the soil created a second line of designs. Or more accurately, replicas of the geometric symbols etched into the top corners of the metal bins in the training room.

"Each type of Elementum has their own symbol within Arc," Reed said as I associated them with the specific element each column represented from left to right—water, earth, air, and fire. "Although, as you can imagine, Arc's symbols don't relate to any experiments or projects."

"So, how do we figure out what this place is"—I pointed at the screen—"and if it's connected to a secret Clinic project?"

And how it involved my mom? If my suspicions were correct about why she went missing, then this might shed some light on why she never returned to Arc—and why she'd hidden all this from me.

"That could take some time." Reed returned the soil back to its planter.

Time wasn't a luxury I had right now. I only had a couple days to work with. What would I do now?

"I know an easier way." Saylor had a wicked glint in her eyes. "Storm the barricades."

"Not funny." Reed sent her a pointed look. "That would be suicide."

"What would be suicide?"

The critical voice sent an icy wave down my spine. I mistakenly thought I'd hit my Dirt-Wad quota for the day. But no, there Decker stood at the far side of the island, all spruced up with his dark hair slicked back as if he'd just gotten out of the shower. Honestly, I would've considered him good-looking if not for the dark-alley vibe he gave off. And his stupid mouth.

"None of your concern." Saylor cleared her screen. "Especially after how you treated my friend."

My heart warmed at her fierce defense as I pulled my decoy textbook closer.

"I wouldn't get too attached to the Newt, Saylor." Decker crossed his inked-up arms. "If we're lucky, this will be a catch-and-release situation."

The edges of my textbook bit into my palms, but I managed to keep my mouth shut—*barely*.

"Knock it off, Decker." Saylor gave him a hard look. "If you weren't so busy being an ass, you'd find out us lowlings aren't as annoying as you think."

"Well, Saylor is," Reed teased. "But that's a lovable given."

"To know me is to adore me." Saylor sent him a vulgar gesture, making Dirt-Wad's lips twitch.

"Something like that." Reed pretended to catch the one-fingered salute and held it to his heart. "Now, can't we all just hug it out?"

"Careful, Decker is allergic to physical contact and emotions." Kaden appeared at my end of the island. "Can't have him breaking out in hives right before we head out."

Oh, goodie. The Hale-Storm had rolled in too.

Kaden was similarly freshened up, his dark jeans, navy shirt, and black jacket only enhancing his commanding charisma. The cultured pirate stealing hearts to Decker's harsh hellion wreaking havoc.

But I refused to focus on that. Instead, I noted the dark, slim-banded device around his wrist. And Decker had one too. They reminded me of fitness trackers, but something told me that wasn't what they were.

Weird.

"How tragic that would be." Saylor made a face, opening a document on her laptop.

"Devastating," I seconded.

Decker easily brushed off our remarks as he debated with Reed about all the potential dangers he faced if he were to "hug it out" with Saylor. All of which I was fine with, but I kept that to myself.

Kaden tilted his head, his midnight hair toppling forward. "What's with the doodles?"

I looked down at the margins of my history book. "Nothing, just couldn't concentrate."

"Not a history buff?"

"Not even close."

"Shame." He grinned. "The doodles are pretty though, almost like snowflakes."

"They're only aimless patterns." I resisted covering them with my hand. "Nothing special, like..." I caught myself before telling him about my sketchbooks—not that they were super special either, but they were private. And even though he'd helped me earlier, I knew he didn't want me *buzzing around here,* so he didn't deserve to know about them.

He frowned. "Like what?"

"Kaden, we should go," Decker called from across the island.

Kaden tugged a piece of my hair and lowered his voice so only I could hear. "See you around, Firefly."

My heart rate doubled. But before I could smack his hand away, Kaden straightened and moved toward Decker.

As the pair of good-looking bad-life-choices headed for the exit, Decker tossed over his shoulder, "Have fun, kiddies."

"Give my best to the randoms," Saylor yelled back as they disappeared. "Hope they have all their shots."

Silence fell over the kitchen. No one enjoyed being called a kid, especially when you were on the brink of adulthood. We were old enough to know better but still too young to be taken seriously.

"They think they're *sooo* high and mighty just because they're out of training. Well, guess what, jackasses?" Saylor shouted at the vacant hall. "You're still only Rookies!"

"You tell that empty space." Reed grinned.

So, Dirt-Wad and Hale-Storm were also at the bottom of the Arcadius food chain. Something about that was very satisfying. "If they're only Rookies, how do the Arc rankings work?"

"Everyone starts out as a Trainee in the Academies, like Saylor and me." Reed gestured between them. "Then after testing and graduation, we can choose from whichever of the six sectors we qualify for. Those are the Command, Tech Ops, Med Unit, PR, Academies, or Arc Council."

"But naturally, most choose the Command route." Saylor rested her chin on a fist.

"Naturally," Reed playfully echoed, grinning at me.

"Which starts as a Rookie?" I asked.

"You got it." Saylor nodded. "One silver band. That's their rank."

Reed tapped his sleeve. "The more bands you have, the higher your rank."

"Like stars in the military," I said, thankful they didn't seem to believe in negative bands, because as a Halfbreed misfit I'm pretty sure I'd land somewhere in that category.

"Exactly," Reed continued. "After a year, a Rookie typically gets promoted to one of three paths." He held up three fingers. "A Striker, who specializes in offense. A Shield, who specializes in defense. Or a Breaker, who specializes—"

"In everything." Saylor grinned as I remembered the high-ranking division that my mom had been considered for.

Reed shook his head. "Then above that you have the Captains, Commanders, and at the very top the Command General."

"The Command General is the big gun, and directly leads the Breakers." Saylor leaned forward enthusiastically. "We've never met him, but the stories about him are legendary."

Calling this place a network of safe havens was like calling the army a local neighborhood watch. And I had a feeling I was barely scratching the surface.

"But even the Command General has to answer to the Arc Council," Reed added before disappearing into the pantry.

And me apparently. I thought of the latest update from Aunt Viv's group. Supposedly, meetings with the Arc Council were taking longer than expected and I'd be staying here for few more days. But to my surprise I was okay with that because, despite its drawbacks—*cough*, the Cross-Decontamination-Fan-Club, *cough*—I was growing to like it at the Breakpoint.

In the short time I'd been here, it had begun to feel like a safe harbor of sorts. But that could all change when Aunt Viv got back. Would we head somewhere else or stay? Although, I guess the more accurate question was would we be allowed to stay? Or rather, would *I* be allowed to stay?

I glanced at Saylor. I was envious of her and Reed. Not of their abilities. Well... okay, *fine*, that was a lie. But come on, who wouldn't be a little jealous? No, what I envied most was their purpose within Arc. They knew exactly where they belonged, while I merely watched from the harbor dock, waiting for the next storm to toss me adrift. Helpless to stop it.

Saylor sighed, pulling up the street view from earlier. "I'd still take the power of the Command General. Then I could figure out what this place is."

One silver lining with staying here a few extra days? I had more time to search for answers. I nudged Saylor's arm and pointed at the screen. "How would you scout this place?"

15

Sweat glided down my face as I pumped my arms and legs. The brick buildings and modernized warehouses of the River North Arts District—or RiNo as it was known—were cast in golden tones from the last rays of sunlight as I jogged away. Nervous energy zipped through me, making me feel like I was running faster than I ever had before.

I entered a more industrial area and slowed down, looking for the markers I had memorized last night. I knew I'd get in trouble for sneaking out. It was something right out of the bad-idea-database. But my limited time made it unavoidable.

I had to know how my mom was involved in all this.

Soon I stopped and pulled off the main path into a group of trees. Under the glow of the just-woken-up streetlights, I spotted a familiar, nondescript building with beige bricks and tinted ribbon windows across the street.

Thanks to Saylor's intel last night, I knew the urban Clinic sites were temporary locations that were continually rotated on random schedules. Meaning the main security and safeguards for the site were kept inside of the building—because that's where the goods were and it was also impractical to have them going off for every squirrel that went by. So, if I stuck to the exterior, I had a chance of finding clues and staying alive—or at least that was my theory.

"You have some nerve."

I whipped around as Saylor stopped next to me. The Combat-Ballerina looked pissed with her hands braced on the hips of her training leggings and the chest of her black athletic crop top pumping hard from chasing me down.

"Plying me for information last night," she continued, "then sneaking out with the construction crew just now—genius move by the way—and the cherry on top? Stealing my Arc-Jammer. But you missed one thing."

"What?" I lifted the hem of my tank top, checking that the green light was still present on the small black device at the hip of my black running shorts.

"*Me.*" Saylor pointed at herself, and my gaze snagged on the slim device around her wrist. "You're just lucky I had time to gear up and grab my Arc-Armor."

"Arc-Armor?" I pointed to the mystery accessory. It was the same kind that Kaden and Decker had on last night.

"Oh, this little baby helps prevent detection by disrupting my Power Signature. It only intercepts the Clinic's detectors for a few minutes, but for a trained Elementum that's enough."

"Power Signature?"

Saylor pointed at her chest. "All Elementums have one, and there are even some Elementums with the high-level ability of Tracing them. But that also means the Clinic can too. Thus, the armor." She shrugged. "Although, honestly I wish I didn't have to wear one. It always makes me feel off. But worth it to survey this place."

"Well, actually," I shifted on my feet. "I came to do a little more than that. You can stay here. I'll be right back."

She gaped at me. "What—"

But before she could stop me, I left caution at the curb and dashed across the street, heading toward the gated service yard.

Saylor caught up to me just as I closed in on an intimidating metal barricade. "*Emma*. Are you insane?"

"Your Arc-Jammer is set on high and will disable any cameras in the vicinity, right?" I patted the green-lighted device at my hip. "If we hurry, no one will even know we were here. Don't you want to know what this place is?" I focused on the locked gate in front of me, grabbing the bars to start my climb.

"Oh, fine. I do." Saylor stopped me before shifting closer to the gate. "Here. This will be quicker."

She bent down and opened the slender canister strapped to her thigh. A thin stream of water rose with the movement of her hand before surging toward the secured keyhole. Then soon enough a metallic click sounded out and the gate inched open.

I seized the opportunity and slipped through to the trespassing side, hugging the brick wall with Saylor not far behind. I crossed patches of asphalt and dirt, skirting dumpsters and all sorts of equipment—loading jacks, electrical boxes, and water meters. Thankfully, the service yard wasn't well lit in the darkening evening, keeping us better concealed.

I halted near a loading dock entrance and crouched down next to three pallets, all of which contained boxes that looked promising.

"They're only empty boxes," Saylor said in a low voice behind me.

"But they still have the shipping labels." I tapped the white sticker, thinking of what Aunt Viv taught me. "There is tons of information and potential leads on these if you know what to do with them."

"Brillant." She pulled out her phone and started snapping pictures of the labels, saving me from physically carrying them off.

"What do you think was in them?" I whispered, swiveling my head in all directions.

"Clinic supplies of some kind." Saylor tossed her ponytail of braids over her shoulder as she continued her photoshoot. "I think this place is a Supply Site."

"How do you think this connects to the secret project?"

"Not sure yet." She put her phone away.

"What are you two doing?"

16

Wheeling around, for once in my life I was happy to see Decker's harsh face. Dressed in all black—shirt, jeans, ink—he looked like a dark knight about to grant either rescue or retribution. And based on his expression, he must have been leaning toward the latter.

"What are *you* doing?" Saylor asked. "Did you follow me?"

"Of all the foolish things." Decker crouched down next to her. "Why would you break into a random building's service yard?"

"It's not random." Saylor tapped the boxes next to her, side-stepping the fact that this was my plan. "And here's the proof."

"You think this place is tied to the Clinic?" Decker scrubbed a hand down his face. "I know it's difficult, Saylor. But sometimes the greatest harm can come from not following the instructions you're given."

Her cheeks tinted pink as they looked at each other, and suddenly I felt a kinship with a third wheel.

"Come on." He shook his head as if to clear away the attempt at emotion. "We need to get out of here bef—"

Heavy metal doors clanged shut in the distance, and we all froze. Even my own breathing sounded too loud. Then another round of hefty metal opening and closing at a closer range had Decker cursing under his breath.

In a frenzy, we turned and rushed away from the pallets. The gate seemed leagues away, every step only gaining us an inch as a door on the far side of the barricade of boxes clanged open.

Too late.

We'd be spotted before we reached the exit. But I couldn't let that happen—couldn't let them go down for my plan.

I snagged Saylor and Decker's arms, pulling them between two dumpsters. I took the lead and aimed for the crawl space between the receptacle and the wall. I wasn't sure we'd fit, but we had to try. I channeled my inner octopus and squeezed into the tight space, scraping my knee on the metal and my elbow against the brick.

A plethora of pungent odors engulfed my nostrils, and I refused to think about the mysterious liquid my foot was currently marinating in as Saylor squeezed in behind me. I looked back for Decker, realizing there was no way he would fit. Where would he hide?

Wide shoulders blocked out the streetlights as he posted up outside the opening, the alcove between the dumpsters providing him with some coverage. But it didn't seem like it would be enough.

Then a jittery wall rose from the ground. No, not a wall... A *shield*. Made up of particles of dirt and dust.

As Dirt-Wad's shield pulsed silently into place, I imagined the alcove now looked like any other dirty spot in the service yard—or at least that was what I hoped. I peeked out the opposite side of the crawl space and spied the pallets and loading dock in the dim lighting. Then the clap of an exterior door shutting rang out like thunder.

My heart pulsed somewhere in my throat as the grit and grind of approaching footsteps paralyzed me in place. One pitfall of hiding? We were now trapped. Cornered. Snared.

"Yeah, yeah. The cameras look intact." An annoyed male voice echoed off the brick as a short, heavyset man stepped into view. He had a pinched face and graying brown hair, and wore a blue security uniform, but otherwise he looked like anyone off the street. Had we been wrong about the address being connected to the Clinic?

"Has to be a glitch. Just call the technician," the security guard said into his earpiece as he walked around the pallets. "Yeah, yeah. I'll do a lap while I wait."

Crap.

The security guard proceeded in the other direction and out of view, but it wouldn't take long before his lap reached our area. What if he saw through Decker's shield? What would we do then?

In no time at all, the security guard's heavy footsteps signaled that he was heading this way. As he closed in on our alcove, I wondered how I ever thought hide-and-seek was fun as a kid.

Please don't look here, pleasedon'tlookhere, pleasedon'tlookhere.

I sent up the silent prayer as the security guard circled the gated area and dumpsters, passing our little hidey-hole on the loop back when his boots paused.

No, no, no.

"It's all clear," the security guard announced from the opposite side of our dumpster. "What'd the technician—"

The groan of a metal gate opening cut off the security guard's words, and then headlights streamed across the service yard. A sleek black passenger van with tinted windows approached the loading dock, parking in front of the pallets we had been inspecting and giving me a clear view of the driver's side.

"Pickup's here," the security guard said into his earpiece. "Yeah, yeah. I'll grab it." He waved the occupants of the van inside before disappearing with a clang of the exterior door.

The driver's side door opened and a man in his mid-thirties stepped out, a black tactical outfit encasing his built frame. But it was the familiar royal purple accents on his gear that sent a shiver of dread down my spine—the Clinic.

Not good.

The driver hit a vertical panel along the frame of the back door and a digital keypad lit up. He plugged in a five-digit code as I followed his movements: two repetitive keys down low and a downward procession of three near the top.

A click sounded out as the back door slid along its rails, revealing another tactical-suited nightmare. As black boots hit the ground, a tall, lean guy with spiked icy blond hair that somehow made his fair skin appear warm in comparison exited the van. He looked to be around Kaden or Decker's age and seemed every bit as confident that he could handle himself.

"Let's move," the driver said, his face set in hard lines. "The package is inside."

The other soldier hesitated, glancing inside the van.

That's when I saw him.

Illuminated under the van's overhead light, a young boy was strapped in on the other side of the van. His dark hair was shaved tight to his skull while the black planes of his innocent face appeared relaxed, as if he were asleep. But based on the way he was secured to his seat, I knew that wasn't the case.

"The kid's fine." The driver hit the lowest button on the keypad, triggering the side door to slide shut and lock with a flash of the headlights. "He's not going anywhere." He turned before looking back. "And Griffin?"

The icy blond soldier straightened.

"No funny business," the driver warned. "You might be on loan to me from Agent Todd, but you know the consequences for insubordination."

Griffin's jaw hardened, but he nodded.

"Good. Let's move." The driver stalked toward the service entrance with Griffin in tow, the exterior door announcing their departure with a thunderclap.

I launched myself from the crawl space and dashed toward the van. I knew it was a risk going after the kid rather than escaping. Hell, if I wasn't fast enough, all of us could end up strapped to a seat in that van. But I couldn't just leave him there.

My feet slid to a crunchy halt as I tapped the digital keypad along the door panel, the red numbers blinking to life. A wave of relief washed over me as I noted the four digits that blazed brighter than the others. *Thank you.* Never thought I would think that as I punched in the code I'd seen the driver use. The resounding click and slide of the van door was music to my ears.

I leaped inside and hastily worked to undo the straps securing the kid to the seat. His slender frame was wrapped in a white jumpsuit with red stitching, making him appear like an inmate. But as concerning as that was, it was the black band wrapping his thin neck that ultimately drew my attention. I had one theory of what it was, but it made my stomach turn.

I loosened another buckle, and the kid flinched away. The groggy groan he released broke something inside me as his dark brown eyes met mine.

"It's okay," I promised. "I won't hurt you. I'm here to help you, okay?"

After a tense moment, the kid nodded and I released the last strap.

"What the hell are you doing?" Decker demanded from behind me. "How did you even get in here?"

"What's happening…" Saylor's voice faded in shock before returning with conviction. "We need to help her."

Decker looked at her. "We need to get out while we have the chance."

"We can't leave him." Saylor stood her ground.

"You don't know what you're asking for." Decker exhaled heavily before entering the van. "Move."

I shifted between the seats so that he could get in. He grasped the kid's arms and draped him over his shoulders like some messed-up piggyback ride. Then he hoofed it toward the exit with Saylor and me right in his wake. But just as we reached the gate, there was a shout from behind us and a blast of air hit the fence, rattling the metal rungs.

I looked over my shoulder, spying Griffin halfway between the van and us. A shiver of recognition crawled over me as he released another blast of air just as Saylor pulled me out of the way.

Aero.

In a flash, Decker retaliated with a tidal wave of dust and dirt, knocking into Griffin and carrying him back toward the still-open van door. A rope of water shot across the service yard, latching onto the door handle and whipping it shut. The lock secured into place with a click.

But no time to celebrate now.

With a quick up-down of the gate latch, all four of us slid through to the other side. Once we were across the street, a heart-stopping explosion sounded out as a gust of wind rushed out in all directions.

Holy crap.

If the other agents didn't know the kid was gone before, they definitely knew now. Not waiting another second, Decker led us deeper into the darkened streets of the surrounding neighborhood. I really hoped he knew where he was going, because I was completely turned around. But honestly, I was just happy to be moving again. I'd run all across Denver if it meant I wasn't trapped behind that dumpster anymore.

A couple of blocks later, we turned onto another street and stopped next to a dark SUV with a blue-starred logo. The kid groaned like he was in pain, but I hadn't noticed any injuries.

Decker opened the rear door, being careful not to jostle the kid too much. "Grab the extraction kit from the trunk. We're getting too far out of range. We need to neutralize the Collar before it seriously hurts him."

Saylor nodded before darting to the back.

Decker shifted the kid off his back but struggled with the squirming body. The kid tilted sideways as a result. Scrambling forward, I grabbed his shoulder before he could become acquainted with the sidewalk.

"Thanks," Decker grunted, adjusting his grip so we each held a side of the kid. "Let's get him into the backseat."

Decker backed through the open door, jamming himself into the far corner as I scrunched in against the back of the passenger seat. "Just be careful of—"

I cried out, wrenching back as a searing pain lit up along my neckline where the kid's hand had somehow landed in the shuffle.

"...the kid's hands." Decker exhaled harshly, shoving his dark hair back. "They must've Boosted him recently. Otherwise his abilities would be contained by the Control Collar."

That's when I noticed Decker's arms. The skin above his tattoos was severely inflamed and blistering... in the shape of two five-finger silhouettes.

"The kid did that?" I touched the side of my neck. Thankfully, my shirt had caught the brunt of it.

Decker sent me a pointed look.

Right. Elementums.

Talk about pyro prints. Man, the kid looked so small and harmless. Then again, in nature some of the smallest creatures could inflict the greatest harm.

"Here's the kit." Saylor stuck her head through the open door, handing over a hard plastic case to Decker.

I squeezed out of the car to give him space to neutralize the Control Collar. It reminded me of shock collar for a dog. If this was how the Clinic kept its assets in line, had my mom had one at some point?

I gently touched my sun charm, relief washing through me at finding it still there. I knew there were more important things to worry about—like the kid squirming in pain in the backseat—but the sentimental value of the necklace still won out.

"That must've been a Holding Site," Saylor said on the curb next to me. "Or else they stopped at that Supply Site before transferring him to one of the Detainment Hubs. I've never..." Her words faded out as I noted her rattled expression. "I've never seen someone extracted directly from the Clinic. You hear about it, but you don't truly understand what it means when the Clinic strips you of all your choices, control... of everything."

I understood her shock at the whole thing. I was definitely more attuned to what we just witnessed after being denied the truth and the choice to be part of the Elementum world. But I still had no comprehension of what that kid possibly went through.

Decker stuck his head out the open door, presenting a set of keys to Saylor. "I need you to drive us back, but keep it casual. No speeding. No drawing attention."

Saylor took the keys with a nod and raced around to the driver's side as I started for the passenger seat.

"So idiotic," Decker said to me in a low voice. "You have no idea what you've done."

17

Pure chaos. The medical bay looked like a tornado had hit it. Gauze rolls and medical supplies were littered everywhere while the kid's jumpsuit was balled up in a corner.

Cemented to the wall, I stayed out of the way as the mayhem unfolded. Saylor stood next to me after helping bandage Decker's injured arms. Clay fiddled with a mysterious contraption. And Reed had donned welding gloves to assess the new addition to the Breakpoint.

Lying on one of the patient beds, the kid was wrapped in an oversized medical gown. Reed's gift of sedation had finally calmed his groans. With the Breakpoint shut down for the security upgrades, the Med Unit had been cleared out since all missions were supposed to be postponed. That left us to rely on Reed's basic medical training.

"How did this happen?" Clay looked between the three of us. "I want answers now."

I hesitated, not knowing what to say without throwing Saylor and me completely under the bus. We were so screwed.

"I was scouting out a potential Supply Site," Decker said, "but I wasn't aware these two were following me."

Wait. Dirt-Wad says what? Was Decker actually covering for us? Was the world ending? Although I felt positive Saylor was the only reason behind this burst of kindness.

"What the hell were you thinking, Decker?" Clay asked. "Infiltrating a potential Supply Site by yourself is bad enough, but to let a Trainee and a Neutral follow you into a dangerous field situation is inexcusable."

Holy crap.

Neut equaled *Neutral*. So, it hadn't been an insult after all—well, mostly. I was pretty sure Decker had intended it as one.

"How did you even find that site?" Clay fumed as I shared a look with Saylor. "And that isn't even the worst offense on the list. You know the potential complications of extracting an Elementum at this kid's age. You better pray that—"

"That wasn't him." I stepped forward as Clay turned his fierce stare on me. "Decker had nothing to do with going after the kid. That was all me."

Back at the Supply Site, rescuing the kid had seemed so cut and dry, but ever since we arrived at the Breakpoint everyone was acting like it wasn't. How could saving him from the Clinic be a bad thing?

Clay looked back at Decker. "Is that true?"

Decker nodded.

After a tense moment, Clay shook his head. "That doesn't excuse the mess we're in, and I still want to know how you two snuck out." He looked at Saylor. "I'm betting its thanks to the Troublesome-Trainee over there, and after the incident a few weeks ago, Saylor how could you be so reckless? I should just send all of you back to the compound."

Saylor stiffened.

As I opened my mouth to intervene, Clay sliced the hand holding the mysterious instrument through the air. "Actually, save it. Anything you two say right now will only be rocks to the mudslide." He exhaled roughly. "First things first, we need to get the kid taken care of and settled. Then we'll talk about the details and consequences."

Not waiting for a response, Clay turned away and focused on the kid.

"What incident?" I whispered to Saylor.

"Oh, it happened before we arrived for our second field-training session." Saylor leaned toward me. "But apparently an experienced Striker and his son were only a few blocks away from the Breakpoint when they were attacked by a Recall Team. The Striker ended up dying from his injuries, and the kid was captured."

Decker's comment rushed back to me. *I can't be the only one who finds the timing of her and her aunt's arrival a little too convenient.* "No wonder Decker and Kaden have been so on edge about our arrival."

"Try not to take it too personally." Saylor said in a low voice. "It's brought up a lot of emotions for both of them."

"What do you mean?"

"Decker was only extracted from the Clinic about a year ago." Saylor fidgeted with her gear rings. "And I mean, most Elementums don't talk about their time in the Clinic, but I believe he must've lost someone either when he went in or while he was on the inside."

A tidal wave of remorse engulfed me for the comment I'd made yesterday.

"Which definitely explains his, um, rough personality," she said. "As for Kaden, I don't know much, but I heard he lost someone to the Clinic about two years ago. That's why he's so driven—like he's always training. So, he can put an end to the Clinic."

My heart sank for both of them as I gripped my sun charm. I understood the agonizing pain of loss. And only recently finding out I had someone to blame...

"But Kaden can get edgy when things upset that drive," Saylor said, then quickly amended. "*Not* that that's your fault. You guys only showed up to get help."

But it was my fault.

Yes, we were only seeking help. But it all led back to that damn firewall. And even though I didn't want to take it back, it was still my choice that had sent ripples of upheaval through the Breakpoint. Just like today's mess.

"I want to remove the tracker first." Reed shifted the wand of what looked like a portable ultrasound over the kid's forearm, and a dark oblong mass came into view.

I frowned. "Is that a GPS tracking implant?"

Saylor nodded. "The Clinic embeds them in all their subjects. But don't worry, Arc has signal jammers installed everywhere. It won't last indefinitely, but it'll give us enough time to remove and deactivate it."

"You can handle this, right?" Clay asked as he clicked another part of the mysterious metal instrument into place. On closer inspection, it resembled what I imagined the lovechild of a futuristic blaster and a syringe looked like. With a long metal trigger and a sturdy looped handle, the main body of the device was tipped with a plunger at one end and a broad hollow needle at the other that made my knees go weak.

"I've seen Raine do it." Reed swallowed hard. "Once."

"Don't think about it like that." Clay softened his voice. "Just remember, this kid is out and you're doing your best." Then he handed over the instrument to Reed.

"Right." Reed twisted the needle-of-nightmares into place and positioned it over the kid's forearm.

Not trusting myself to stay calm, I slipped out into the hall. Using the wall for support, I squeezed my eyes shut and breathed in the eucalyptus and citrus scent to help settle my racing mind.

What kind of monster did that to a kid? Tagging and tracking him like some kind of wild animal. I hated to think of how close we'd come to sharing a similar fate. That could easily have been one of us lying in there—*or worse*. Because if that's what the Clinic did to someone they considered a valuable asset, then what would they have done to me?

Cannon fodder sounded accurate.

A clatter of plastic meeting concrete drew my attention down the hall. Before I knew what I was doing, my feet were moving. The room next door was empty, and it wasn't until three doors later that I found the source of the noise.

The door was ajar, and the light was on. I peeked inside the treatment room, and then my brain sort of short-circuited. Sometime during all the disarray of getting the kid into the medical bay, Kaden had vanished. But I found him now. However, that's not what halted me in my tracks.

No, it was the full display of bronze skin.

18

Holy Hale-Storm was right. Kaden was hazardous in so many ways.

Focused on the mountain of supplies on the exam table, his back was to the door—his shirtless, sculpted back. A tattoo was etched down his ribs. The details were intricate and yet captivatingly simple. Four major leaders spanned out in the cardinal directions while the center was being devoured by an icy tidal wave that splintered outward, creating a fractured compass. The only orienting line not coated in ice was the one pointing to his chest. What did it mean to him?

I should look away. Give him privacy. But as Kaden twisted at the waist and reached for an item, I shamelessly watched the cords of muscles flex and contract—muscles genetically engineered to shift tides. Then my gaze snagged on the inflamed injury marking his shoulder blade. He must have gotten burned when he helped carry the kid up to the medical bay.

Guilt formed knots in my stomach as he straightened and arced his arm over his shoulder. He struggled to reach the inflamed area with a small wet towel.

"Here. Let me help." I snagged the towel from Kaden's grip and banned my eyes from staring straight at his frontal view. Good thing my peripheral vision worked just fine. Damn, Kaden was ripped—all honed power and chiseled strength from his shoulders down to the little indents just above his tactical pants. I was exhausted just thinking about the workouts required to get those.

"Find something intriguing, Firefly?"

Without realizing it, my traitorous body had turned toward him. My cheeks heated as I looked away.

A knowing grin lit his face. "I'm sure you were just checking me over for purely medical reasons."

"Absolutely." I said sweetly before grabbing a stool. The rattle of the plastic wheels filled the room. "And since you helped me swipe right on that Band-Aid a few nights ago, I figured I'd return the favor and see which of these lovely supplies is the one for you."

A hard laugh burst from Kaden, causing his stomach muscles to do fascinating things. "Well, when you put it that way, who am I to deny you?"

"Noble choice." I grinned, pointing to the stool. "Now, sit."

"If I'm a good boy, do I get a treat?" he asked, a challenging glint in his sea-blue eyes.

"Depends on how fast you learn to listen." I smiled demurely.

"Good thing I'm a quick study then." Kaden lowered himself onto the stool and spun around so his back was to me. "Although, I'd be intrigued to see what you'd do with a bad boy."

I knew he was messing with me, but that didn't stop the blush from hitting my face. "A whack on the nose has a nice ring to it."

That earned a deep chuckle.

"All right, let's get you patched up." I leaned in for a closer inspection, his minty-pine cologne surrounding me.

"You know, this is when a personal first aid kit would've come in real handy," Kaden said. "Missed your chance at having one a few days ago."

I glared at his back. "Not funny."

I refocused on the mountain of medical supplies, contemplating where to start. But the longer I stared at the pile, the stronger the tingles and shortness of breath became.

I wanted to bolt. Leave the medical wing and never look back. But just like I couldn't leave the kid back at that service yard, I couldn't leave Kaden here to patch up the mess I'd caused. I took a deep breath. I just needed to take one step at a time, then maybe I could do this... and possibly avoid rocking in a corner somewhere.

"You'll need to cool the burn first," Kaden said over his shoulder.

"Right." I snapped to attention, folding the damp towel in my hand.

Kaden sent me a quizzical look. "You okay back there?"

"Yeah." I circled a hand around. "I'm just not a big fan of medical stuff." I pressed the wet towel to his scalded skin and he winced.

"Sorry." I adjusted the fabric gently.

"I'm sorry, too," he said softly. "For what I said to you the first night. That wasn't fair."

Stunned, my heart warmed at the sincerity in his voice. "After you shielded me from Decker's dirt nap yesterday, consider it forgiven."

Kaden nodded with a half-hearted smile before staring down at his hands.

As the silence stretched out, the anxious fluttering in my head and throat increased. "So, what does your tattoo mean?" I asked to distract myself.

"Noticed that, did you?" Kaden chuckled. "How about a trade? I'll tell you, if you tell me why you're not a medical fan."

"That's not a fair trade."

"How so? It's an answer for an answer."

"The level of information being traded isn't equal. Your tattoo is more on the level of my favorite color or something."

"Always the intrigue." Kaden tilted his head, his dark waves falling forward. "All right. Favorite color, then. Mine's maroon by the way."

"No, I didn't mean…" I stumbled, but talking was better than facing the anxiety. "Fine, it's blue. Like a sea-glass blue. Most think it's because Point Reyes is by the ocean, but it's actually from my days at Lake Tahoe. In parts of the lake, the water is so clear you can see all the way to the bottom and the shallows are this stunning array of blues."

Kaden's face softened. "Sounds beautiful."

"It is." I smiled wistfully. "I've tried to recreate it in drawings, but it's never the same."

"One can only imagine what else you enjoy drawing, Firefly."

"I'll give you ten free trades if you stop calling me that."

"Not even close to what it's worth." Kaden gave me a heart-stopping smile. "My turn."

We continued like that for a while, trading questions and answers for this game we somehow ended up playing. It was interesting to see this side of Kaden—more candid and carefree—and it was a nice distraction for me.

I snorted. "Seriously?"

"What? Most people don't know that ninety percent of volcanic activity happens in the ocean." Kaden grinned. "Always thought that was interesting."

I shook my head as I removed the towel from his back. "I think this is cooled enough. What's next?"

Kaden handed over a small tub with a dark blue lid. "Slather this on the area."

I removed two fingers' worth of the cool jelly and gently brushed my fingers over his burnt skin.

Kaden's back straightened at the contact. "So, do you miss Point Reyes or the ocean?"

My chest pinched as I thought of the cozy, no-streetlight town. The sea air that filled my lungs when I ran along the coastline. The warm sun that kissed my skin as I sketched on the porch swing. And the laughter that filled our house when I goofed off with Aunt Viv or Claire.

"Yeah." I swallowed hard. "After I'd moved around so much, it was the first place that felt like home since Carnelian Bay. I guess that's why it was so hard to leave it all behind."

Kaden ran his bionic hand through his messy hair. "Does that mean you left someone special behind?"

Someone special? As in... My pulse sped up. "Trade?"

Kaden nodded.

"Uh, friends. My best friend Claire, specifically, but no one else." I repeated the dunk-and-slather routine. "What about you? You have anyone special?"

Kaden shrugged. "Not specifically."

"Not big into relationships and labels?" I used the damp towel to wipe my hand.

He handed over a bundle of bandages and tape. "Never had time for that type of distraction."

Man, Saylor hadn't been joking about him being driven. It was a merciful reminder that I wasn't here to play with getting frostbite. I needed to get answers about the secret project—about my mom.

"Decker said the kid must've been Boosted recently. What does that mean?" I asked as I started taping the bandages into place.

Kaden glanced over his shoulder. "It's a serum the Clinic uses to strengthen an Elementum's abilities. They typically reserve it for their Enforcers, but they've been known to Boost more experimental assets too."

I swallowed hard, recalling Griffin's explosive but thankfully contained burst of power back at the service yard. If the Clinic had something like that, what else did they have at their disposal?

"The Clinic likes to test some of their projects to the extreme," he continued. "Pushing Elementums to their limits and pumping them full of highly experimental serums." He pushed to his full height, gingerly testing out the stretch of the bandages. "Always striving to create the perfect soldier."

Maybe that was how the secret project was connected to that Supply Site—and possibly the kid. Maybe the Clinic was holding an experimental serum there, one being tested on Igniters. Was that how my mom was connected to all this?

Kaden faced me and then frowned. "What happened to your neck?"

"What?" I reached up, finding the singed collar of my shirt. "Oh, it was an accident."

"Here, let me see." Kaden stepped closer and brushed a few loose strands of my hair aside, the soft contact causing my stupid heart to flutter. His calloused thumb slid along my skin before gently pulling back the collar of my shirt. The pop was subtle, barely audible. I felt the release more than anything as the delicate chain around my neck fell forward.

My hand shot up, trapping the priceless keepsake in the folds of my shirt. I pulled the necklace out, careful to keep the sun charm from falling off.

Kaden cursed. "I'm sorry. I didn't think I pulled that hard."

"You didn't." I adjusted the necklace in my hand for a more secure grip. "The chain must've gotten damaged when the kid's hand burned my shirt."

He didn't appear to believe me. "Well, your neck looks fine. It seems he only grazed you."

"So, why that kid?" I asked to alleviate his remorseful stare. "As opposed to another?"

Kaden leaned back against the exam table and crossed his arms. "He's likely someone who wouldn't be missed. A runaway, homeless, immigrant. Although some people do it for the quick money."

My stomach hollowed. "You mean people volunteer?"

"Or are volunteered. There's a reason child services will always be around. But yeah, some people choose to do this."

"Why would anyone subject themselves to that?"

Kaden's jaw flexed, making his scars stand out. "You've never been to an Outreach Center. They promise things. Miracle treatments, clinical trials."

My grip tightened on my broken necklace. Back when my mom was sick, it had been excruciating to watch her fight to live every day, knowing there was nothing I could do... If given an opportunity like that, could I really deny I wouldn't have jumped at the chance to save her?

The sinking feeling in my chest told me I already knew that answer. "So, the Clinic preys on people's desperations?"

"When faced with the outcome of a deadly disease or watching a loved one suffer from one with no other options," Kaden said in a rough voice, "people tend to do some pretty desperate things."

19

The two-story gym at the end of the training wing was impressive. I sat with Saylor watching an intense soil-to-soil sparring match between Decker and Reed unfolded across the way while Kaden prepared for our next training drill.

After the interrogation sessions with Clay this morning, he reassigned me to train with Saylor and Kaden this afternoon. I was pretty sure this was just a convenient way for Clay to keep track of both Saylor and me until he decided our punishments for last night's accidental extraction. I just hoped he didn't send everyone back to the compound like he threatened. I didn't know how I would find answers if he did.

But with that threat looming and everything else, would I allow that to stop me from doing what I needed to do today?

"I think there's a chance Asher is connected to the secret project," I said in a low voice.

"The kid?" Saylor grabbed her orange water bottle. "How do you figure?"

I laid out my theory—with a little help from Kaden—about why the kid had been Boosted, why he'd been taken to the Supply Site, and the possibility of an experimental serum being held there. "If this somehow involves my mom, then it makes sense that they're testing the experimental serum on Igniters."

Because if there *was* a secret serum, then it could be the key that Herrera had mentioned to changing the entire course of the war. But more importantly, it could also be the reason my mom had gone missing from the Breakpoint so long ago. She might have been captured by the Clinic and then subjected to this experimental serum. The theory fit with all the puzzle pieces we'd discovered so far, but it was still hard to process. It seemed so at odds with the upbeat, warm, and loving woman I'd always known. Were there any signs of her captivity I'd missed? There must've been...

A growing conflict rose inside me. On one side, I wanted to keep everything that happened to my mom a mystery—afraid that the truth would somehow tarnish my precious memories of her. On the other, I needed to know what happened to her.

"Experimental serum. That makes sense." Saylor eagerly patted my arm before she frowned. "But even if that's true, the Clinic would've already shut that Supply Site down and moved everything after our break-in."

"What about the photos you took yesterday? Did you find anything from the labels?" I caught my hand halfway to my neck. I felt off balance with my neckline so empty now.

"Unfortunately not." Saylor's braids swung as she shook her head. "Stupid clearance levels. But when I sent Nova the encrypted data from the Control Collar last night, I included the photos. Covertly of course." She wiggled her eyebrows. "Hopefully she'll find something. Until then, I say we focus on what Asher can tell us."

If his memory returned. Since being extracted, he'd been experiencing some severe memory loss due to all the trauma, but so far we knew he was twelve and an Igniter with budding abilities I'd experienced firsthand—but that wasn't the only thing I'd experienced.

Across the gym, I watched the hazardous Hale-Storm set up our next training drill. During our little patch-up session, I'd seen a different side of Kaden. One that was even more dangerous than his typical stormy persona. Because after last night I realized I could see myself liking him.

"You're staring."

I jumped at Saylor's voice. "Was not."

"Uh-huh, sure." Saylor sent me a knowing look. "Can I give you some advice? About Kaden."

My cheeks heated. "That obvious?"

Saylor's sympathetic look made me twitchy. "I don't really know him except through my field training and he's so not my type, but just be careful, Emma. Don't go down that road unless you're only looking for something fun or temporary."

Well, temporary did seem to be my motto in life. But I'd never done the casual thing before. I'd dated some, including two ex-boyfriends. So, I had experience—however limited it was—but I wasn't sure I could do the whole friends with benefits thing. *Not* that that was even on the table.

"It's your call." Saylor squeezed my arm. "No judgment either way."

I waved a dismissive hand. "There's no call to make."

"Campbell. Cross," Kaden shouted. "Let's go."

I clambered to my feet before dizziness made me falter mid-step.

Saylor grabbed my arm to steady me. "You okay?"

"Yeah, just stood up too fast," I said, even though I'd been feeling off kilter all morning. I blamed it on last night's drama and the nightmares that kept chasing me awake. But nothing that some sweat sparkles couldn't fix. "Come on."

We crossed the varnished wood floor to where Kaden awaited us, wearing a navy athletic shirt and tactical pants. To his credit, for every drill we did, he performed them right alongside us. Even after my protest about his injury, to which he reminded me that Elementums healed faster—fully establishing that his default mode was training.

"On to footwork drills." Kaden pointed to a configuration of short neon-orange cones, foot-high hurdles, and agility ladders. "First, we'll focus on individual drills, and then we'll move on to a group course."

Saylor groaned while I resisted clapping like a seal. I was more than happy to switch to agility training. That was where I thrived.

Kaden demonstrated the footwork techniques for each of the stations before laying out the time requirements. "High intensity for one minute per station, followed by one minute rest, and then switch. And Saylor, your bonus during these drills is sustaining a water pedestal."

"Water pedestal?" I asked, trying to imagine what Hydro move this one was.

A gurgle of water drew my attention to the metal container in the middle. When Kaden raised his bionic hand, the water surged upward before plateauing a few inches above the surface and creating a liquid willow tree. My next breath stalled out. I didn't think I'd ever get over seeing an Elementum in action.

Kaden extracted a small rubber ball from his pocket and placed it in the center of the geyser. "The goal is to keep the ball elevated the whole time."

Saylor opened her mouth to comment when he added with a hard look, "You have your own curiosity to thank for the extra push." He crossed his arms before his sharp eyes zeroed in on me. "And Emma's as well."

Guilt rocked my system. Saylor was only being punished because of me. But I couldn't say anything, otherwise it would blow Decker's cover story and lead to questions about us knowing the Supply Site address—which couldn't happen with our secret project investigation.

Saylor swiveled to me, pointing at the constellation of cones next to us. "I could go for a footwork drill right about now. How about you, Em?"

"How thoughtful. I'd love one." I placed a hand over my heart. "They say a drill a day keeps the curiosity away."

"Best we get to it then." She smiled sweetly as we positioned ourselves at a station.

"Just for that, make it a minute and a half," Kaden ordered, swiftly killing the mood.

We made it through each station twice before moving on to the group course. We ran through the course multiple times, each time with a new leader. The goal was to not get caught by anyone who was behind you, which turned out to be challenging whenever Kaden trailed either of us.

Sprinting through my fifth lap of the hurdles-of-hindrance, I pivoted to the ladders-of-limitations. I bounced on the balls of my feet like the varnished floor was lava, my neck tingling from my competitor closing in.

"Happy feet, Cross," Kaden called out, gaining more ground.

"They are happy." I pushed harder, trying in vain to put more space between us.

"They could be happier. Or are you going to let me lap you?"

"How about I shove my joyful foot up your ass and see who laps who then?"

"If you think you can get it that high," Kaden challenged.

"Jackass." I summoned every ounce of speed I had left, the competitive corner of my brain refusing to let him win.

I completed the last rung of the ladders before taking off, determined to finish the last leg of the course—a literal sprint—before Kaden. I might be a Neut, but I was a tenacious and motivated Neut, and that had to count for something, right?

I pumped my arms and legs for all they were worth, crossing the half-court basketball line for the win. My greedy lungs gulped down air as Kaden reached the finish line only seconds later.

"Who's got happy feet now?" I broke into a happy dance. It was a small win in the bigger scheme of things, but it was mine.

"Yeah, yeah. Dance it up, Firefly." Kaden chuckled hoarsely. "At least I know you can get away if you're ever being chased."

"You two suck." Saylor passed the finish line and collapsed to the floor.

"Not as much as you two." I wiggled like a worm on a hot sidewalk. "Look at me and my happy feet. Uh-huh, uh-huh, uh-huh."

"You realize he let you win, right?" Decker pinned me with a pitying look before turning and tossing over his shoulder to Kaden. "Pathetic, dude. Losing to a Neut, even for other benefits."

Heat splashed my face at his barely veiled implication. Decker was clearly still pissed about yesterday. And even though he'd covered for us, that comment was still way over the line. I clenched my fists, stepping forward.

A band of steel wrapped around my waist, halting the intended smackdown. "Stay in your lane, Firefly," Kaden warned in a low voice, his warm breath tracing across my temple. "Not the smartest idea to mess with Decker today." He released his hold. "But your choice."

I took a deep breath, logic thankfully taking back control. "Fine. But can't you just Hydro-cannon his ass?"

I felt the chuckle roll through him.

"As much as I would truly enjoy being your personal Pokémon, it's against protocol outside of sparing. But don't worry, he'll pay for that comment later." Kaden said, raw power in his tone. "And by the way, I didn't let you win."

Then he strode off as an unwanted flutter went through me.

Crap.

I shook it off and followed Kaden back to the ladders and cones when shouts echoed through the open doors of the gym, halting all activity.

20

I found myself in the medical bay again. Twice in twenty-four hours—that had to be an omen.

Everybody from the gym lined the perimeter of the room as Asher thrashed and groaned on his patient bed, but two new people had arrived. The shorter and curvier of the two was a woman dressed in forest green scrubs who appeared to be in her late twenties. Maybe early thirties? A dark gray hijab covered her head and neck, allowing for a clear view of her soft features as she plugged the ends of a stethoscope past the dark fabric and into her ears.

"Raine, get him on his side," she ordered to the other new addition.

The one called Raine was a tall, lithe young woman who looked to be only a year older. The symmetrical planes of her face were set in concern as she gently rolled Asher onto his side. Even in light green scrubs, the champagne-blonde beauty looked more like she belonged at Coachella than in the medical bay.

Asher squirmed at their touch and let out another delirious groan. He was still wrapped in an oversized medical gown, but the IV attached to his arm was new.

I leaned over to Reed. "What's happening? Why is he in pain again?"

Reed crossed his arms. "It appears he's overdue for his weekly Stabilizer."

"Oh, that makes sense," Saylor said on my other side.

Reed grunted. He also must've been mad at us for our life choices yesterday. And I couldn't blame him for that.

"Weekly?" I asked.

Saylor nodded, sending Reed a sad expression. "Once we hit puberty and start developing our abilities, we require them weekly until the age of sixteen, when it gets pushed out to every three months. Then after we're eighteen, it thankfully gets bumped out to every six months."

I couldn't imagine needing a treatment every six months—let alone on a weekly basis. "What happens if you miss a treatment?"

"Increasing weakness and disorientation," Reed clipped out. "Uncontrollable elemental flare-ups. And if we go long enough, our bodies start attacking themselves, causing severe sickness."

Memories of Mom's delirium spells flashed through my mind. Maybe she'd never had cancer and this had been the cause of all her suffering. It would definitely explain why I'd never been to the treatment center in Tahoe and why Aunt Viv had faked the memorial page. But if that was true, then why not go back to Arc? Why suffer when they knew where to get treatments all along?

I had one theory, but it made me want to cry and also throw sharp objects. Was it because of me? Me and my normal life... And what about Aunt Viv? She must've needed Stabilizers too, so why didn't she get sick?

None of it made any sense.

"But don't worry, the medics will get him treated soon," Saylor assured me.

"That's if the Clinic hasn't altered his genetic makeup too far past the standard Ignis DNA code," Reed added before moving to the other side of Decker.

"Okay, Rookie. What do we do first?" the older medic asked.

Raine hesitated.

"Think, Rookie. Time is ticking, the patient is struggling."

"First, we need to get him sedated before he hurts himself or any of us." Raine lowered Asher carefully onto his back.

"Good. You're learning." The experienced medic popped the cap off a syringe and plunged it into Asher's IV line, causing my muscles to go weak. "Mills, go find Clay for me."

"Yes, Sage." Decker nodded before subtly leaning over to me and lowering his voice so only I could hear. "It would've been a kindness to leave him there." Then he disappeared out the door.

My stomach hollowed. Was he serious? How could leaving him in the hands of the Clinic be better than this?

"Wilson, grab the welding gloves." Sage pointed to a set of supply cabinets next to the oxygen tanks and IV poles. "And get over here to hold him until the sedative kicks in."

Reed scrambled forward.

"Rookie, go grab the Stabilizers. Hale, help her with that," Sage directed before turning her harsh expression on us. "As for the rest of you, show's over. If you're not helping, then you need to get out."

All righty, then. Subsequently dismissed, I followed Saylor out into the hallway. Although it was probably for the best. As soon as more needles came out, there was a good chance I'd find myself hyperventilating in a corner somewhere. So, bright side?

"Were you training today?" Raine asked as she and Kaden filed out of the far door of the medical bay.

Kaden smiled over at her. "I think you know the answer to that."

A slap whipped across the air with a loud smack.

"Hey." Kaden rubbed his arm. "Hitting's not nice."

"Be thankful that's all I did." Rainy-Day braced her hands on her hips. "I told you to take the day off to heal, you idiot."

"Pretty sure name calling is also on the not-nice list."

"Want to find out what else is on that list?"

Kaden chuckled, lifting his hands in surrender. "No."

"Good. Now, tell me everything." Rainy-Day looped a possessive arm through Kaden's before pulling him in the opposite direction, leaving me with a sharp, unpleasant sensation creeping up my chest.

"Sage has some nerve." Saylor rolled her eyes. "Why Reed idolizes her I'll never understand."

I nodded as I considered how to phrase what I wanted to ask next. "*Sooo—*"

"What's the deal with Raine and Kaden?" Saylor suggested.

My face heated. "Not even close to what I was about to say."

"Uh-huh, sure." Saylor grinned.

Cue the crickets.

"Fine." I exhaled. "What's their deal?"

"Knew it." Saylor hip-bumped me. "From what I know, they were in the same grade and trained together as Hydros at the Academy. They've been dating on and off ever since. I'm not really sure where they stand on the dating front now, but they always seem to remain friends even when they're not together, which is rather sweet I must say..."

At that point, my hearing took a T.O. as the hot, ugly sensation increased. As much as I wanted to deny it, I was woman enough to admit—to myself anyway—that I was jealous. And it all stemmed back to what I'd realized earlier: I liked Kaden. Which was dangerous for my heart, especially since his clearly wasn't up for grabs.

"...but her mom is a total control freak," Saylor finished as I zoned back in.

Her last comment made my heart squeeze, but it was a good reminder on what I actually needed to focus on.

"I tried to warn you," Saylor said softly, misinterpreting the shift in my mood—*mostly.*

"I know." I smiled solemnly.

"Campbell," Sage called through the open door, causing both our heads to turn. "Get back in here, we need your help."

"Oh, great," Saylor muttered.

I snagged her arm before she could leave. "Hey, can I borrow your phone?"

"While we're young, Campbell," Sage shouted.

Saylor groaned before extending her phone. "Run. Get out why you can before Sage traps you under her stringent thumb too." Then she squared her shoulders and stalked into the medical bay.

I planned to do just that, even if it wasn't what Saylor had meant. Since training appeared to be over and everyone was now preoccupied, it was time to turn lemons into lemonade and get back to my real priorities.

21

The balmy night air filled my lungs as I exited the pharmacy, shoving the newly purchased lighter and necklace chain into the pocket of my jeans. They fit in next to the small candle I'd smuggled from one of the training bins this afternoon.

I hesitated at the curb. Using Saylor's Arc-Jammer to sneak out again was foolish. Like, no-handing-a-scooter foolish. I was risking a second round of Clay's wrath—a formidable consequence all on its own—and then there was the possibility of getting kicked out of the Breakpoint and losing Arc's help, but this was something I had to do.

Anyone who'd lost someone close to them would understand the importance of honoring the person who'd given them so much. Understand the importance of remembering their smile, their smell, the sound of their voice, when those once-sharp details dulled over time—no matter how hard you tried to stop it. Would understand that even after all the pain and suffering, you would trade anything for one more moment with them.

That's why I couldn't break my promise. Not this year. Not after everything.

I pulled Saylor's phone from the other pocket and reviewed the directions displayed on the screen. Now, all I needed to do was follow—

"Funny finding you here." Kaden's deep voice made me jump.

"Bell." I placed a hand over my racing heart. "Next birthday, I'm gifting you a bell."

"Only if it's musical and makes my eyes sparkle." Kaden grinned as he eyed the map on the screen. "Although, it looks like you won't be sticking around until December. You making a run for it, Firefly?"

"Don't call me that." I glared at him, putting Saylor's phone away. "And I wasn't running for it. I just needed to... *Wait.* I thought you were helping with Asher. Why are you here? Were you following me?"

Kaden chuckled. "I think that line of questioning should offend me."

I sent him an arched expression. "Remove the word *think*."

Kaden placed a bionic hand over his heart. "You wound me, Firefly."

"Hardly. And if you don't want to be wounded, I suggest not stalking people."

"I believe it's pronounced lending a little extra supervision."

Extra supervision? As in... "I don't need a babysitter." I pivoted away, hitting the crosswalk.

"I never said that." Kaden easily caught up to me. "More like a trusted guide. Who knows what troubles await as you wander around out here?"

"I'm not wandering around." I continued down the lit sidewalk as he kept pace. I sighed. "Any chance I can convince you to go home? Or am I stuck with you?"

"Like glue." Kaden smiled, the breeze ruffling his midnight hair.

I pulled up short. "Why aren't you dragging me back to the Breakpoint?"

"Do you want me to?"

My nose scrunched. "Well, no. But—"

"Then, here we are." Kaden shrugged. "Your choice to go, and my choice to follow."

Stunned, all I could do was start walking again as I tried not to read too much into his choices. Especially now. Kaden had never mentioned

Raine. Never mentioned her while he teased and flirted with me or when we'd discussed having someone special.

I cringed, realizing Kaden had never specifically mentioned anyone, had he? Not being big into relationships and labels—or *that type of distraction*. So, why did it matter?

"Is there a destination at the end of this little treasure hunt?" Kaden asked. "It better not be a return trip to a certain Supply Site." He gave me a pointed look. "A site that I know Decker knew nothing about."

Damn, Kaden was sharp.

"There's a destination." I avoided his intense stare. "It's the second star to the right."

Kaden sent me an arched expression. "Do I look like a lost boy to you?"

"You probably don't want me to answer that." I spotted my target up ahead.

The brick building looked like most in the area, the industrial structures having been modernized. The specific shop I was searching for fronted the main street and wrapped the interior edge of a mid-block plaza, where several other businesses lined the common space with sectioned-off patios that were filled at this hour with mid-meal diners and post-work drinkers.

"A coffee shop?" Kaden asked as we reached the main entrance. "You realize we have one of these back at the Breakpoint, right?"

"I know." I paused at the front door.

"A perfectly good one. With no travel time." Kaden leaned in. "And no exposure."

A pit formed in my stomach. It had been fine—*well*, relatively fine—when this mission had only involved me. My decision. My mission. My consequences. Now? Those consequences included him.

I could tell him to go, but I knew it'd be pointless. If his previous actions were any indication, he wasn't one to just walk away and leave someone to fend for themselves. A comforting thought—not going to lie—even though my conscience was currently struggling in the guilt pool.

I should be the one to leave. Head back to the Breakpoint before Clay ever found out I'd left and keep Kaden from exposure. I should... But some things were worth the risk.

"No question, Breaking Grounds is great." I glanced up into his piercing stare. "But they don't have what I'm after."

I pulled open the door and headed for the counter. The scent of freshly brewed coffee enveloped me. At this hour, only one other person was in line while a few others were scattered at various tables. When researching different doughnut places, I'd found a few good options, but this was the only one open late. I just hoped they still had some doughnuts left.

"Always the intrigue." Kaden came up beside me. "What are you after, Firefly?"

Wasn't that a loaded question. And based on his mischievous grin, he knew it, too.

"You'll see." I tucked a loose strand of hair behind my ear.

Kaden studied me before turning to look at the overhead menu.

The café was about half the size of Breaking Grounds, and instead of leaning into the industrial theme, they went for a chic contrast—gold trimmed accents and marble galore.

"Next?" a raspy female voice announced.

I stepped up to the counter. The young woman behind the register looked about college age with a long ponytail of black hair, a Hello Kitty choker, and a blue apron hugging her curvy frame. Her bored expression told me how ecstatic she was to be working at this late hour.

"Can I get an herbal tea and"—I peered over at the display case—"one of the blueberry cake doughnuts, please."

Coffee-Kitty tapped away on her tablet. "Anything else?"

"Plus whatever he's having." I jacked my thumb at Kaden.

In a flash, Coffee-Kitty's entire demeanor changed—flirt-mode activated. "And what may I get you?"

I couldn't blame the barista for her reaction. Kaden was a double-shot of good-looking in anyone's day. But that sharp sensation creeping up my chest again was frustrating—and wholly unnecessary.

"I'll have a large cold brew," Kaden said before sending me a cunning smile. "And two of your lemon cake doughnuts."

Yep, he had definitely caught on to my goal.

"Those are absolutely stellar." Coffee-Kitty smiled sweetly. "You won't be disappointed."

I bit my lip to keep from laughing. Clearly, I had made it into the non-threat category of her competition-or-not glance test. That, or she just had some brass ovaries. I couldn't decide which.

After a few seconds of eyelash-batting, Coffee-Kitty finished ringing us up. I paid before she went to grab our doughy carbo-load.

"My adventure," I said to Kaden. "My treat."

He simply stared at me with a look I couldn't quite decipher, making my smile falter. I couldn't have offended him that much by paying. Come on, he had to have more self-confidence than that, right? Well, sorry, not sorry. Because feminism was here to stay—hear me roar and watch me soar.

A slow smile transformed his features, ensnaring me as he tugged a strand of my hair. "Thanks."

My cheeks flushed as he faced the counter when the barista returned.

"Here you go." Coffee-Kitty leaned forward, sliding the two pastry bags toward him.

Not wanting to witness the counter fail—or something even more damaging—I swiped the bags with a crinkle. "I'll grab a table while you get the drinks."

Pivoting without waiting for an answer, I headed out the patio door and into the balmy night air.

22

A table in the far corner of the patio caught my eye. I selected a seat against the building that allowed me to look out toward the bustling restaurant and brewery surrounding the plaza.

Settling back, I breathed in the fresh air as the slight breeze played with the festival lights strung overhead. If I closed my eyes, I could almost imagine I was back in Point Reyes and Aunt Viv was only moments away with doughnuts from our usual bakery in hand. Even though I was still upset with her, I couldn't help but wish she was here. She would make ridiculous jokes about overloading on sugar and somehow have all the right answers.

But she wasn't here, was she? Wasn't here to give me answers when I needed them most. My throat burned as I thought about launching both pastry bags across the plaza, but thankfully Kaden placed a cup in front of me, saving the doughnuts from a concrete landing pad.

"I've never seen anyone get emotional over a pastry before." Kaden sat next to me. "But I guess there's a first time for everything."

I blinked a few times to clear my blurry vision. What a time to unlock my emotional baggage—*not*.

"You need me to teach these doughnuts a thing or two?" Kaden pulled the brown bags away. "Cause I can always remove the offensive pastries if needed."

"Never," I snorted, halting the doughnut heist.

"Good." Kaden relinquished my bag, scooping up his own and popping a section of sugary bread into his mouth.

I followed suit, and we enjoyed the companionable silence, each of us alternating between our doughnuts and drinks. The steaming tea was a welcomed comfort. As I leaned back in my chair, I noticed he was already one doughnut down.

Kaden paused pre-bite. "What?"

"Low on sugar?"

"I'm feeling rather judged right now."

"Not judging." I two-handed my cup. "More like assessing."

Kaden lounged back. "And what's your assessment, Firefly?"

"Still compiling data," I evaded.

"My sweet tooth is well known around the Breakpoint." Kaden sipped his coffee.

My eyes widened. "Really?"

Kaden grinned. "Is that so hard to believe?"

I circled a hand in his direction. "It's just with your…"

"Oh, please continue." Kaden's eyes sparkled with mischief. "I think I want to hear this."

"I assumed with your, um"—warmth splashed across my cheeks—"*training*, you wouldn't haul down sweets."

"Well, you assumed wrong." Kaden bit into his last doughnut like a hungry, hungry hippo—a very well-built hippo. "So, now that you know I have a sweet tooth, is that worth a trade for why these pastries upset you?"

I shook my head. "Nope."

"Fine." Kaden chuckled. "A sweet tooth, then?"

I shrugged. "Don't have one."

Kaden arched his brows, glancing from me to the doughnut in front of me.

Right. Guess that wasn't exactly true. "Okay, this is an annual exception."

Kaden frowned. "Annual exception?"

I looked down at my sugary treat. "It's complicated."

"Does this have anything to do with why you were teary-eyed earlier?" Kaden tilted his head, his midnight hair falling forward. "Any chance you'd trade for that?"

I took a long sip, debating whether to share. Then again, he had risked a lot by coming here with me. I picked at the edge of my cup sleeve. "What's the trade?"

"Something of equal value, I promise." Kaden's sea-blue eyes locked with mine. No nickname. No jesting. He was asking me to trust him. Giving me the choice to trust him.

"It wasn't the doughnuts that upset me. Well, not entirely."

"I'm leaning toward it having something to do with the reason behind this little reckless escapade." Kaden leaned toward me. "Emma, you've only seen a small portion of what the Clinic is capable of. How can a doughnut be so important to endanger yourself like this?"

As I scanned the plaza, it hit me that I had no clue what someone from the Clinic even looked like in a normal setting. Anyone on the street or in the coffee shop could work for them. Hell, for all I knew, Coffee-Kitty could be one of them.

I squeezed my eyes shut. "I didn't mean to be reckless. I just..."

My words faded out as my vocal cords constricted, not quite believing I was about to grant him access to this emotional rollercoaster.

"When my mom was sick." I swallowed hard as the vice around my heart tightened, realizing he was the first person at the Breakpoint I was sharing this with. "During breaks in treatments, doughnuts were her favorite go-to. Even if they made her sicker later, she'd always get them. She said life was too short to let doughnuts pass you by."

"I couldn't agree more." Kaden smiled softly. "Is that why you came here? Because of your mom?"

"Yeah." I reached absently for my empty neckline, only to stop myself. "After she died, my aunt started this tradition. Every year on the day we lost her, we'd go get doughnuts and light a candle in her honor." My throat tightened as I looked away. "And sure, as I got older and our lives got busier, we missed a few years, but this year I..."

"You didn't want to miss it."

"I owed her that much, especially after all the damage I've caused." The guilt from my Stabilizer theory about my mom threatened to consume me.

As silence fell between us, I envied the moonlit clouds drifting aimlessly by, not a care in the world.

"Guilt is a powerful thing." Kaden's stare was fixed on nothing in particular. "It sticks with us, especially after the lives we've lost—and the ones we've taken."

Taken? What was he talking about?

"After getting extracted from the Clinic, I used to take my little brother for ice cream," Kaden said. "That was our tradition."

My heart stilled. Kaden had been in the Clinic.

"He used to pester me all the time to take him." He chuckled without humor. "Would give me the most innocent face and say *mint chip is life, Kaden* until I gave in."

"Sounds like he knew how to play you." I smiled softly, imagining a younger Kaden with a mini-him in tow.

"Even with him being two years younger than me, he always got the upper hand." He grinned, running a hand through his hair. "He also teased me relentlessly about my favorite flavor and how I wasted my options *on lemon, of all things.*"

I giggled. "Lemon? Really?"

Kaden tossed up a hand. "It's a severely underappreciated flavor."

"Well, I have to side with your brother on this one. He sounds like a smart kid."

Kaden's jaw flexed, making his scars stand out. "He was."

Was. As in past tense...

A knot twisted in my stomach. Saylor mentioned that Kaden had lost someone to the Clinic. That must've been his brother.

"We should get back." Kaden uncoiled himself from his chair and took his empty items to the trash can.

Too stunned for words, I tossed back the rest of my lukewarm tea and rose on stiff legs.

When he returned, the icy mask shrouding his features shot straight to the center of my chest. I knew that pain. I was all too familiar with it.

I fumbled for the right thing to say. "Next time, we should get ice cream with our doughnuts. That way, we can both honor the ones we miss."

The moment those silly words left my mouth I wanted to snatch them back. Like there would be a next time.

Just then, the side door to the coffee shop opened and a determined Coffee-Kitty strode over. No doubt about who she was after.

Fantastic.

Not wanting to witness the oncoming pursuit, I attempted to sidestep out of the way but was impeded by a bionic hand on my waist.

"You have a deal, Firefly," Kaden whispered. "But only if you help me now."

Help him? With what—

"I wanted to check and see if there was anything else I can get you?" Coffee-Kitty's smoky voice intruded on my confused thoughts as a calloused hand curled around the nape of my neck, capturing all my attention.

I felt the heat rolling off Kaden's body as his intoxicating scent enveloped me. His cologne was extra minty today and sent shivers pulsing through me. Without thinking, my eyes fluttered shut as my hand latched onto the silky material of his athletic shirt. Beneath the thin fabric, I felt the hum of restrained power as his nose brushed against my cheek, the soft contact causing my stupid heart to race.

What was he doing? What was *I* doing? There were three states' worth of reasons why I shouldn't let anything happen between us. But mainly, the temporary transplant situation that was my life right now.

Kaden leaned over to my ear. "I'll count this as my treat for being a good boy last night."

My eyes blinked back open, and I dropped my hand.

Kaden turned, a satisfied grin gracing his rugged face. "I'm all good here."

An exasperated huff sounded out, reminding me we had an audience. I watched Coffee-Kitty walk off.

"I think our performance delivered the message." Kaden chuckled, sending ice straight to my chest. "Thanks for helping me out."

Did he really just... I stormed away without looking back.

***

As I hurried down the sporadically lit sidewalk, I knew I shouldn't have stormed off like that. Shouldn't have let our, um, *close encounter* get to me so much. But I couldn't help it. I needed time and space.

Otherwise I was liable to push Kaden. Off the curb. Into traffic.

You know, reasonable impulses after being used for ulterior motives. Not to mention his on-again, off-again non-girlfriend girlfriend whom I'd seen earlier.

I shook myself mentally, struggling to overcome my growing collection of frustrations. But not with Kaden—well, mostly. Mainly with myself. I'd been aware of his reputation, and he'd been very clear about where he stood. And what aggravated me the most?

I'd wanted him to kiss me.

It'd be one thing if it was only about physical attraction—which was present and accounted for. But no, it was his shield-summoning heroics and his stupid lemon-loving personality that were the bigger concern.

And even though I liked Kaden and he seemed to enjoy flirting with me, I reminded myself that nothing *actually* happened between us. And nothing ever could. Especially since I'd probably be who knows where in the next few days. I needed to stop this little crush from getting blown out of proportion before it turned hazardous.

I dashed across the crosswalk. A couple of cars lined the streets with their hazards flashing, either picking up or dropping off their riders. The few other pedestrians that were out were too engrossed with their own drama to pay any attention to me.

I should figure out where I was. After my quick exit to lose Kaden, I had gotten a little turned around. But taking some time to cool off was probably for the best before I made my way back home—*whoa*. I'd meant the Breakpoint, but somehow my mind had autocorrected to home. But that wasn't right. Not even close.

Thankfully, at that moment I spotted a familiar marker—the retail center where I'd bought the lighter earlier—and down the service alley I spied the glowing sign of the pharmacy. From there, I could easily retrace my way back to the Breakpoint—*not home*.

The pungent smell of the dumpsters made my nose wrinkle, but taking the service alley was a hell of a lot shorter than going all the way around. I passed the empty pharmacy drive-thru—no shock there. Anyone seeking meds at this hour wasn't looking for the legal variety.

Up ahead, I spied two people and a delivery van outside the pharmacy loading dock. My heart rate sped up as my steps slowed—until I noticed the scrubs. Clearly they were taking a break, which was supported by the lit cigarette in the man with the light blue scrubs' hand. That or a delivery or pickup was in the works.

I squared my shoulders and resumed my pace as I entered into earshot of their conversation.

"...just need it with the pickup. Come on, it's not a big deal," said a woman in plum scrubs. She gave a flick of her fiery red hair, her voice giving sugar cookies a run for their money.

"All right, all right. But you owe me." Blue-Scrubs extinguished his cancer stick.

"My hero." Plum-Scrubs placed a hand over her heart.

"Yeah, yeah. Be right back." Blue-Scrubs chuckled, disappearing through a door.

I had to give props to Plum-Scrubs; she knew how to use her flirtation skills to her advantage. It was never really an art form I'd comprehended. Sure, I understood the premise, but the execution? Not so much. I'd never been the girl with the world wrapped around her finger. It was usually the other way around—the wrappee, instead of the wrapper. And I was fine with that... truly. But if I had to guess, Raine looked like an experienced wrapper—*nope*. Not going there.

I closed in on the far side of the pharmacy, exchanging a polite smile with Plum-Scrubs. The alarm on her smartwatch went off, reminding me that I should get back to—

Without warning, someone crashed into me, the impact knocking the air from my lungs. Fire radiated along my kneecaps as they slammed into the asphalt, causing my eyes to tear up. There wasn't even time to scream as a hand clamped over my mouth, cutting off my agonized curse. Only the sudden pressure and biting sting at the side of my neck was enough to pull my attention away from the blazing pain. Had I just been injected with something?

I grasped at the forearm of my attacker as panic dug in and a faint sweet taste coated my tongue. I grappled for my self-defense training, but I was having trouble focusing. It was like my brain was trapped under plastic wrap and the layers were only growing thicker. I swung my elbow back, but my limbs felt weighed down with cement.

"That should calm you down," a vaguely familiar voice said. "Can't hide from us."

Horror paralyzed every muscle as Plum-Scrubs's statement connected. But then a heavy wave of dizziness washed over me, obliterating everything until the world faded out and there was nothing.

23

A soft clinking of glass registered from somewhere close by. I inhaled the sharp stench of rubber as I fought to open my eyes, but it was like they were buried under an entire sandbox.

Hazy clips of sugary pastries and teasing smiles flashed through my foggy brain as I struggled to remember what happened. The last thing I remembered was walking down the alley to the pharmacy and...

Plum-Scrubs.

My eyes flew open and I looked around wildly. I wasn't in the alley anymore, that was for sure. The ground—or more accurately the floorboard—I was lying on was moving, which explained the smell of rubber and the clinking.

The darkened interior of the vehicle made it difficult to see, but I could make out racks of rattling boxes. Biohazard warning labels were plastered on each one, along with the same logo I'd seen on the delivery van in the alley—Summit Health & Pharmaceuticals.

Ice blasted my chest as understanding flooded me.

The Clinic.

I'd been taken by the Clinic. I knew it, even if the logo didn't spell it out. And clearly Plum-Scrubs worked for the away team. But how had she known I had any connection with Arc? Had she followed Kaden and me? Had he been snatched too? Or had she recognized me because of the Recall attack back home?

I squeezed my eyes shut as I tried to calm myself down. I needed to keep aware but focused. That's what Clay would instruct me to do, so I could figure out a plan to get out of here.

Careful not to draw too much attention to myself, I shifted my sluggish body to get a better look around, but my hands hit constriction. What the hell?

I glanced down. My hands were freaking *zip-tied*. Causing my chances of escape to plummet.

"I'm on my way in." Plum-Scrubs said from the driver's seat, her silhouette barely visible from my vantage point. "Save it. I have an unexpected gift."

I checked my feet for restraints. Relief coursed through me when I discovered none, counting that as a positive.

"Of course I know, but that changes nothing," Plum-Scrubs said. "I can't risk anyone taking credit for my capture, so prepare for an asset intake. I'm only a few minutes out."

Not good.

I was running out of time. If I arrived wherever Plum-Scrubs intended to transport me, my chances of escaping would be close to zero. I racked my cloudy brain for—

Holy crap.

I twitched my thigh and almost cried at the returned pressure of Saylor's phone. If I could just reach it—*no, wait.* First, I needed to escape the van. Find a populated area. Then call for help.

I peered to the side of the van, noting the small latch on the door. *That* was my goal. Reach the latch and, you know, just jump out of a moving vehicle. It sounded painful. But it was better than sticking around here for the alternative.

I needed to be fast. The fastest I'd ever been. I coiled my muscles in preparation and shifted my hands for better leverage before silently counting down.

One. Two. Thr—

Everything went pitch dark as the vehicle jerked to a stop. I gripped at the floor to keep from sliding but was no match for Newton's law as the floor's rubber lining abraded my skin. The driver's side door slammed shut, followed by a chorus of muffled voices.

Too late. Option tuck-and-roll was no longer a choice. But I couldn't give up.

Think, think, think. Running was still an option. I just had to pick my moment. A moment when Plum-Scrubs believed she still had the upper hand. I went limp as a whoosh of air filled the interior and sliding metal announced the beginning of option play-sedated-and-run.

"The asset is still unconscious." Plum-Scrubs's voice drew closer. "Let Griffin and Dr. Mallory know I've arrived."

"Yes, Agent Todd," said a male voice, followed shortly by a door shutting.

Another positive, assuming that left me and Agent Todd—formerly known as Plum-Scrubs—alone.

Rough hands rolled me onto my back before shoving themselves under my arms. I battled to stay relaxed as I felt myself being pulled from the van. Halfway out, I squinted. We had stopped in another loading dock. While the overhead covering blocked out most the light, it transformed the nearby streetlight into a beacon, showing me the way I needed to run.

My shoes clipped then cleared the lip of the van, free falling. I tucked in my legs to ensure my feet landed flat. Using the momentum to pull the agent forward, I thrust my head back with the stability of my newly planted feet and felt the crunch of skull to nose. The grip on my arms loosened as Agent Todd released an impressive string of curses.

I pushed awkwardly off from the enraged agent, sprinting on heavy legs into the wind toward the beacon. I had no clue where I was and my surroundings were no help. A chain-link fence topped with barbed wire enclosed the shadowy loading dock, but the area beyond was too dark to distinguish anything besides nondescript buildings.

One silver lining? The gate we'd just driven through was still open.

I pumped my legs with everything I had but didn't even make it to the gate when my legs were snagged. The ground rushed at me as the instinct of face over forearm won out. I yelped as I crashed into a heap, pain slicing along my wrist. The world spun, but I didn't feel my attacker anymore. Hoping I'd lost them in the fall and they were also stunned, I used my good wrist to push up.

Within seconds, my ankles were snagged again, my body and head jerked to the side. The pain receptors along my temple and side lit up as the strong breeze whipped my hair every which way. Then I was being dragged. I threw out my bound arms as I struggled to stop the pavement water slide, but it was no use. I looked up at my elevated ankles, expecting to see Agent Todd only to find... no one. What in the *literal* nothing?

I stared at the blank space. The pulling sensation was still present—my nerve endings could attest to that—but there was no physical body at the helm. Had I finally lost it? Or was this all some drug-induced dream and I was still out cold in the back of that van?

I reached for the invisible tether holding my ankles, but a powerful gust knocked me back. The pavement caught me like a bag of flour before my body ground to a halt. I cradled my injured wrist as a shadow blocked out my beacon.

"Well, that was fun," a male voice mocked. "And pointless."

It was the Aero from the Supply Site. The memory of Griffin's tall frame, spiked icy blond hair, and confident demeanor would be seared into my brain for eternity. I only hoped it didn't go both ways, and he wouldn't recognize me.

With a groan, I tried to scoot away from him as some sort of primal alarm went off deep inside me, alerting me to the lethal threat in front of me.

"You're only making it harder on yourself." Griffin sighed like kicking my ass was an extreme annoyance for him.

"Bite me." I continued scooting away, no doubt leaving a bloody trail in my wake.

"Real original, Sweetheart." Griffin gave me a predatory smile.

"You bitch," Agent Todd shrieked, making me flinch. Blood streamed down her face from her swollen nose. "Detain her."

Shit.

I scrambled to get up, but when Griffin lifted his arm, a gale-force wind slammed into me. In a blink, the invisible force pinned me to the ground. This was an Enforcer truly in action. Super soldier, indeed. Immobilizing me had been child's play for him.

"No more miscalculations." Agent Todd knelt down next to me and started patting me down. I gritted my teeth against my pressurized prison as she removed the necklace chain, candle, lighter, Arc-Jammer, and Saylor's phone.

"Typical Arc burner. Probably with a wiping function." Agent Todd handed it over her shoulder to another agent who had appeared out of nowhere. "Destroy it."

My heart sank as the agent with sandy brown hair crushed my only lifeline into pieces. How would I contact the Breakpoint now? Would they even know I'd been taken?

"I thought you neutralized her," Griffin sneered as Agent Todd finished her search.

She glared up at him. "I did."

"I guess your nose spontaneously sprung a leak?" Griffin raised his brows.

"Watch it, Griffin. Your father can't handle another delay in treatments because of your incompetence." Agent Todd warned as the air compressed further. "I miscalculated. I only had one dose on me and I thought a half would do the trick, and"—she shook her head—"I'm your Handler, not the other way around. I don't have to explain myself to you. It's done. I got the resilient little pest here. And she is resilient, I'll give her that." She bent closer to me as she uncapped what looked like an EpiPen. "But not to worry, we'll strip you of that."

Panic flared like a wildfire as I wrenched against my invisible confinement, but it was useless. A familiar sting pricked the side of my neck and the plastic-wrap haze rushed back in.

"That should keep her neutralized." Agent Todd turned to Griffin as the hurricane downgraded and then stopped. "Now, get her inside so Dr. Mallory can start the intake process." With that, the bloodied Agent Todd strode off with the other agent.

For a moment, Griffin merely stared after the departing agents, a muscle twitching along his jaw. Then he released a sigh and prowled toward me. A wave of helplessness washed over me as he slipped his arms under my shoulders and legs, lifting me. My eyes grew heavy, but I fought to keep them open. A nagging sense told me it was important to remember our path, but the dense fog closing in made it impossible to pinpoint the reason why.

"It's easier if you don't fight them," Griffin murmured. At least that's what I thought he'd said, or maybe that was the tongue-sweetening sedative talking.

But then the relevance of it all drifted away. And then I drifted away, blinking out like a faulty lightbulb.

24

For the second time in an unknown amount of time, I dragged myself out of a murky oblivion. The first thing to register was the foam padding underneath me and a heart-fluttering aroma of disinfectant.

Above me there was a stained ceiling, and to my side a glass wall. A row of glass walls in fact, each housing empty hospital beds. I swiveled my head and discovered more glass walls in front and to the other side, forming a glass cage.

Reality, meet worst nightmare.

Bile climbed up my throat. This had to be a Clinic Holding Site. In my cage there was only the bed I was on and an empty side table. At the front, a sliding glass door extended from the scuffed linoleum floor all the way to the dingy ceiling. And to the side of the dented metal frame there was a keypad, while a tinted plastic bubble with a camera dominated the corner overhead.

Across from my enclosure were identical sets of stainless-steel medical cabinets and equipment, each corresponding to one of the cages and all in various stages of being packed in bubble wrap or boxes.

Weird.

Careful to keep my movements subtle, I tested the mobility of my thankfully restraint-free limbs. Dull pain flared along my tender skin and injured wrist. The sedative was still very much in effect, but I was pretty sure I could get myself up and moving when the time came—or at least I hoped.

A hollowness spread through my chest. What would they do when they discovered I wasn't an Elementum? I doubted it would be a catch-and-release situation.

I hated the thought of leaving Aunt Viv alone. Putting her through another loss at the hands of the Clinic. Would she even know what happened to me? Or just find out I disappeared without a trace?

No. I couldn't think like that. My journey would not end here.

Muffled voices drifted closer. But until I had an adequate escape plan, I needed to keep my range of motion to myself. The double doors at the end opened, revealing Griffin and an older gentleman with salt and pepper hair. Overall, the man appeared indistinguishable in his khaki slacks, white button-down, tie, and glasses. But what sent chills down my spine was the white lab coat he had on.

Walking down the row of cages, the older gentleman removed a tablet from the docking station across the way before approaching my glass cage. Punching in a code, the seal broke with a hiss as the door slid open, the muffled voices suddenly becoming coherent.

"...should have been transported to the new facility. This is below my pay grade. What was Agent Todd thinking?" The older gentleman ranted with Griffin in tow as the door shut. The hard clicks of bolts locking made my stomach drop. "Did the entire Enforcement Division forget how to do their jobs? Two undetained assets out west and another one lost this week—the Director is going to have a field day." He shook his head, fiddling with the tablet in his hands.

Griffin posted up in the far corner, the harsh lines of his face making him appear as friendly as a honey badger. Under the bright fluorescent lights, I could pick out the subtle lilac-gray accents running along his tactical gear and the black band wrapping his wrist. It reminded me of the Control Collar that had been around Asher's neck.

The older gentleman moved to my bedside, the ID badge hanging from his pocket confirming him as Dr. Mallory. He propped up his tablet on the side table before shifting through the various tabs that were open. Most flashed by too quickly, but I caught a few things like lab results, a six-pointed star with the label Horizon Project, a patient's chart with a photo of a young boy, and last was a blank form titled *Patient Intake*.

"Let's begin, shall we?" Dr. Mallory said.

"You can't do this." My words were slurred, and my throat was so dry I had trouble swallowing. "I have rights. I—"

"My dear, assets have no rights, only opportunities for improvement. Now, control yourself or I will have to ask the Enforcer over there to do it for you."

My lips pressed into a hard line. As hard as it was to accept, I knew the less Hurricane-Griffin was involved the greater my chances would be of staying mobile.

Dr. Mallory pressed a red button on his tablet. "Intake patient zero-nine-one-three, initial workup. Doctor's notes: Sedative appears to be waning. I believe it is due to the dosage amount and intervals for which it was administered, but time frame should still be adequate."

He clasped two fingers to my thankfully uninjured wrist before studying his shiny gold watch as I struggled not to shove away his hand. "Vitals are slightly elevated, but within normal range." He then pulled a penlight from his pocket, shining a blinding light in my eyes. "Pupils are dilated, but reactive. Besides some surface injuries from detainment, the patient appears healthy."

I'd never felt more like an inanimate object under a microscope. "The patient is right here, you sick bast—"

"Hearing and speech are functional." Dr. Mallory spoke over me as he extracted a small black object from his coat. It looked like a cross between a calculator and a thermometer. "Now, patient typology."

My chest hollowed as a piercing sting pricked my finger. An initial beep echoed off the glass, starting the countdown to my big discovery. What would they do when the disappointing results came back? Would they dispose of me right there and then? Should I make my move now?

Ding.

"Unknown?" Griffin broke the silence. "How's that possible?"

Because I'm not one of you.

"Enforcers are to be seen, not heard," Dr. Mallory said. "Or do you need another write-up?"

Griffin tensed. How did anyone want to be an Enforcer? Especially if you were treated like this.

Dr. Mallory repeated the whole sting-and-double-beep routine on another finger. "Useless. Note to IT: There are still bugs in the system."

Lucky for me the bugs in their system were faultier than they knew.

Dr. Mallory shook his head. "No point in proceeding. Doctor's note: Make sure to run a full panel and workup at the time of patient's arrival to determine typology. In conclusion, after a cursory workup, the patient appears healthy, viable, and stable for transfer."

My stomach twisted like a pretzel. Transfer? To where?

The door slid open and Agent Todd entered, a bloodied tissue clenched in her hand. "What've we got?"

"Unclear." Dr. Mallory closed the tablet before checking his watch. "The software updates didn't clear up the bugs—which wouldn't be an issue if you'd transported her to the new facility as instructed."

Agent Todd ignored the shot at her defiance as she walked to the other side of my hospital bed. "I found a lighter stashed in her pocket when I detained her. Could be an indication she's an Igniter."

"That's where I've seen her." Griffin straightened. "She was at the Supply Site when Asher was taken."

Crap.

"Seen, not heard," Dr. Mallory snapped, glaring at him.

Agent Todd turned her hostile stare on me, making me flinch. "So, you're the reason my golden ticket is missing." Then she gave me a cunning smile. "But not to worry, I'll get him back."

Golden ticket? She talked about Asher like he wasn't even a person, but what really worried me was the confidence in her voice about recapturing him. As if she somehow knew where the Breakpoint was. But if that were true, I was positive the Clinic would've already infiltrated it—so, what did she have up her sleeve?

"You speak as if that unique asset has already been assigned to you." Dr. Mallory scoffed at her. "But you don't even know what he's being utilized for."

Agent Todd's face turned sour. "I know the Horizon Project is the Director's number one priority, and it's something I have to get in on."

"Such a shame, Ms. Todd." Dr. Mallory shook his head. "You're too busy clawing your way up the ladder to realize they would never trust you with such an important project."

"Very high and mighty, coming from a simple Holding Site geneticist," she sneered. "Good to know I have you to keep me company at the bottom."

"Crossbreeding Elementums takes an experienced hand." He lifted his chin in superiority. "Something you obviously know very little about."

For a second, my heart forgot to beat. If they were crossbreeding Elementums, I could only imagine it was to create an even more powerful super soldier with control over more than one element. If they succeeded, it would give the Clinic an untold advantage over Arc.

"Now, if you'll excuse me, I have samples to get to before overseeing the final pieces of this move." Dr. Mallory straightened his tie before heading for the door and punching in a code on the keypad. I strained to see but the keypad was too far away and I couldn't see the movements of his hand.

"Oh, and Agent Todd," he added, "if you would like to avoid another write-up, I'd suggest you go prepare the transport van. The new asset needs to be transferred to the proper facility before the night is up."

Agent Todd stiffened at the low-key threat as the doctor exited my glass enclosure and placed the tablet back in its docking station. Then she gritted her teeth and stalked out the door with Griffin right behind her.

The cage door bolted shut, echoing like a cannon. But even as panic threatened to overwhelm me, one thing became very clear. I could *not* be transferred.

25

It was risky. Depending on my pattern-tracking to work when I hadn't seen the keypad numbers. And sure, it'd been there so far—like a bad infection—but what if this time it didn't work?

I glanced at the tinted security bubble as I discreetly retested my muscles. I needed to be quick. Efficient. And even then, I might not make it past the door. But I'd never know unless I tried.

Determination infused my veins. I might not be an Elementum or trained like those at the Breakpoint, but there was no way I would just lie here and let them transfer me without a fight—or more accurately a *flight*.

I rolled off the hospital bed, landing in a crouch. The world swam a little, but my legs held up. I darted forward, bracing my uninjured arm against the glass for support. Butterflies swarmed my stomach as I reached the keypad, but to my relief four digits and the enter key were illuminated like neon signs. Not only that, each one had a slight variation to their illumination, like a dimmer had been installed, which was new... The enter key glowed the brightest while the other keys dimmed one by one until the number zero. Reversing the order from dimmest to brightest, I devised what I believed was the code: *Zero. Nine. One. Three. Enter.*

My fingers trembled as I focused all the energy in my foggy brain on pressing the correct sequence. I punched the last button and waited for an alarm to announce I'd done it wrong. But no, the bolt retracted and the door hissed open, making my heart sing.

I flung myself out the door, turning toward the double doors before stalling out. I made a quick detour to grab Dr. Mallory's tablet and then sprinted toward the doors. Adrenaline pumped on high, helping suppress the pain, haze, and fear just waiting in the wings.

The hall was blissfully empty. But not knowing which way Griffin had brought me in, I relied on the next best thing: exit signs. I raced toward the red glow, clutching my stolen treasure in a death grip. At a fork in the hall, I peeked around the corner, spotting my next glowing target and mercifully nothing else. I dashed toward it, using the walls like a crutch.

This could really work. I just needed to track my glowing landmarks and keep moving.

"Oh, *Sweethearrrt*." Griffin's voice echoed from behind me. "You're really wrecking my night."

My heart rate skyrocketed. Instead of sounding the alarm, Agent Todd had sent Griffin to recapture me. She must've figured I wouldn't get far under sedation.

I barreled down the hallway, pushing through doors and making various turns. Next thing I knew I had lost track of my landmarks. This place was like a maze—the same scuffed linoleum floors, dreary white walls, and panic-inducing disinfectant smell everywhere I turned.

I raced toward the next set of doors, my hand reaching for the handle when I heard footsteps. They were coming from the other side of the door at a rapid pace, along with another sound I couldn't quite place. Groaning metal?

I was trapped. If I turned back, I risked getting snared by Hurricane-Griffin. If I stayed, I could face another Enforcer. The only thing I had on my side was surprise. I tucked the tablet into the back of my jeans. Then planted myself into position and compelled my breathing to stabilize.

As the pounding footfalls drew closer, the sound of groaning metal intensified, rattling the sprinkler head above. The latch clicked like a gunshot, the door swinging toward me. With an exhale I swung out, aiming for the body coming through.

In a flash, my fist was caught and my back met the wall, a powerful arm pressing against my throat. A broad, black-clad chest blocked my view as a minty cologne surrounded me. The pressure suddenly relented and I stumbled forward into strong but gentle arms.

"That wasn't very nice, Firefly."

"Kaden," I breathed, tingles of relief racing down my spine. I couldn't quite believe he was standing in front of me in his silver-banded tactical gear.

"Always the intrigue. Here I find you needing no saving. But what were you thinking taking off like that?" He shook his head and gave me a once-over. "You okay?"

I nodded. But doubt invaded Kaden's sea-blue eyes as he looked at my cradled wrist.

"Come on, we need to get out of here." I started for the doors he just came through.

He snagged my waist. "I'm all for that, but heading straight for the main security center might be counterproductive."

"What?" I blurted, glancing at the doors I'd been aiming for. If that was true, and he had no reason to lie, I would've been running right back into the Clinic's hands.

"*Sweethearrrt.*" Griffin's voice had both our heads snapping in the opposite direction. "Come out, come out, wherever you are."

Every muscle in my body locked up, causing my wrist to throb.

"Stay behind me." Kaden moved to partially block me.

Oh, crap. *Water*. Where would Kaden find water? He had the small amount in the tubing of his bionic hand, but would that be enough? Also, if Griffin was Boosted, this wouldn't even be a fair matchup. Had I just ensured Kaden's return to the Clinic?

As Griffin appeared at the end of the hall, the groaning metal returned with a vengeance. Was that him? Was he messing with the air ducts?

"Hello, Sweetheart. Aren't you just a big pain in my ass tonight." Griffin's gaze locked on me before turning to Kaden. "And if it isn't the notorious Kaden Hale." He smiled viciously. "This must be my lucky day."

"Aw, Griff. You flatter me." Kaden stepped forward with a lethal calm. "But don't you need to check in with your Handler first? Wouldn't want you getting into trouble for daring to think for yourself."

Raged contorted Griffin's face as he stepped forward, lifting a hand. A blast of air ripped through the hallway like a tropical storm. At the same time, the pipes overhead burst, spilling a torrent of water in front of Kaden. In an instant, the waterfall froze solid, blocking the blast of air. Then, in an impressive display of strength, Kaden splintered the ice wall and sent the frozen projectiles in the opposite direction.

Holy Hale-Storm.

Griffin deflected most of the icy missiles with a swirling buffer of his own, whipping the frozen shards around like a spin cycle before winging them back at Kaden. My heart skipped a beat. I darted forward without thinking, but skidded to a halt when the ice-nado shifted directions toward me.

Not good.

I squeezed my eyes shut and raised my arms, bracing myself to become a frozen pincushion. *This* was going to hurt. In the next second, a powerful body knocked into me, pushing me back against the wall. Stunned, I found myself crammed between the wall and Kaden before he grunted and frigid droplets splashed my face. Bloody frozen shards protruded from his bronze skin. Then, right before my eyes, the ice melted and joined the whirlpool of water now circling us.

"Listening isn't your strong suit, is it?" Kaden asked before twisting toward Griffin and pushing me back.

"How heroic." Griffin widened his stance. "You keep expending your energy like that and this fight will be over before it's started."

My blood ran cold as I flashed back to a similar situation involving nameless mercenaries, me rooted in place, and Aunt Viv getting shot for my floundering.

"Your concern warms me, Griff." Kaden stalked forward, the water shifting to swirl around his arms like liquid sleeves. "In places I didn't even know needed warming." Then he moved lightning fast, snagging Griffin's outstretched arm with a liquid rope before twisting him around and slamming him into the wall. The drywall cracked on impact.

Griffin fell forward, landing in a crouch before popping up and retaliating with an air missile. Kaden used his stream of water to dampen the blow but the plaster on the other wall wasn't so lucky as it fractured against the force.

Kaden sent the stream of water around Griffin's other side, using the liquid weapon as a remote assailant on multiple fronts. Exploiting the distraction, Kaden kicked Griffin behind the knees, causing him to crash to the floor with a grunt. Then Kaden wrenched his arm back and up, up, up. A sickening pop sounded out, making me flinch.

Griffin's scream was deafening. His back bowed as the color drained from his face, and then Hurricane-Griffin released. A blast of air radiated out in all directions. The force was so intense it dented the ceiling, deepened the fractures in the walls, and blew both Kaden and me back. I collided with the door as Kaden hit the floor.

Griffin trembled with rage and agony as he prowled toward an unmoving Kaden. Leaving logic behind, I grabbed the closest thing to me—a baseball-sized piece of ice—and hurled it at Griffin. It shattered against his shoulder before he pivoted with a snarl.

"A chunk of ice? Really?" He strode toward me, lifting his good arm. "Wrong move, Sweetheart."

An invisible lasso wrapped around my legs and ripped my feet out from under me. Stars burst behind my eyes as pain shot down my side. But before the sting diminished, a surge of air brushed me back like a curtain in a wind tunnel. I smacked against the double doors hard enough to elicit a cry.

Pinned in place, I stared up at Griffin. The gale-force current crackled and whistled, consuming all the surrounding oxygen. A bolt of fear spread through me. Clay had been right. I had no chance against a fully trained Elementum—the burning in my lungs proved that. I knew it would only take one more pulse of pressure for him to crush my throat or another vital organ beyond repair.

But just as my vision went fuzzy, a brutal, watery arm swept Griffin back and oxygen returned to the hallway. I toppled sideways, gasping for air as tremors racked my body.

Kaden blocked off my side of the corridor as he faced Griffin, the water receding to circle around his arms again. I needed to get up. Needed to be prepared for anything. With agonizing movements, I shuffled to my feet, using the wall as leverage as my wrist throbbed from all the strain.

"Impressive, Hale." Griffin laughed, the tone sounding all wrong. "But it won't save you or your little friend." He smiled venomously. "Just like it didn't save your brother."

In an instance, everything about Kaden changed. The water circling his arms froze to his skin in glacial bands as waves of cold violence and raw power poured off him. It saturated the air, coating the hall in an icy sheen. The tiny hairs all over my body stood on end.

Without warning, a tidal wave of ice crashed into Griffin, trapping him against the wall and encasing him in ice from the chest down. Kaden stalked toward him with lethal grace. Then he cocked his arm back and punched Griffin in the face.

Griffin spat blood. "Hit a nerve, did I?"

The squeal of ice constricting set my teeth on edge as strained grunts leaked from Griffin's bloody lips. The arctic expression on Kaden's rugged face was a clear indication of how far he intended to take this as Griffin's grunts escalated to moans of pain.

I leaped forward, latching onto Kaden's arm. I couldn't just stand by and let him add another life to his list of lives taken. I couldn't allow this to weigh on his conscience. Not when this was all my fault.

"Kaden, stop. You're killing him." I squeezed his arm. "*Kaden, please!*"

The ice halted as Griffin's head fell limp, but Kaden stayed locked in place, his chest pumping in heavy breaths.

I squeezed his arm again. "I know Enforcers are irredeemable, but he's not worth it."

Kaden paled as warmth flooded back into the hall. But then a blaring alarm ricocheted off the damaged walls, alerting the entire facility to our jailbreak.

Kaden grabbed my elbow. "Time to go."

26

We hustled away from the carnage as the ear-splitting alarm echoed all around us. I allowed Kaden to lead me down the corridor, the glacial bands still tattooing his forearms just above where our hands were joined.

My battered and bruised body limped as fast as it could go, but as we made various turns and passed through multiple doors, I knew I was slowing down our progress.

Eventually the fresh night air filled my lungs as we exited into the same loading dock Agent Todd had first brought me to, the only difference being the glowing taillights from the boxy black SUV idling in front of the kidnap van. My breath hitched at the sight of Reed's sandy blond head peeking out the driver's side window.

"Emma, thank goodness," Reed said.

I smiled at him as Kaden opened the back door. I lifted myself into the SUV and slid across the cool leather, my wrist throbbing with its own heartbeat.

"Where are the others?" Kaden asked.

"Inside." Reed's grip on the steering wheel tightened.

"Still? What's taking so long?" He looked back at the facility just as a metal door flew open.

Saylor, Decker, and Clay burst into view before executing a well-practiced exit drill. Saylor hopped into the passenger seat as Clay slid in next to me. Decker jumped into the back while Kaden climbed in on my other side.

As the last door shut, Reed revved the engine. "Hold on."

We peeled out of the loading dock, swaying with the centrifugal force as Reed took tight turns and steered us through darkened streets I didn't recognize. As the distance between us and the facility grew, my adrenaline levels drained and the hazy sensation rushed back in, blanketing my brain in a sedative-infused fog.

"Calm down, speed racer." Kaden tapped Reed's headrest. "Time to blend in."

Saylor twisted in her seat to look back at me, her eyes filled with concern. She opened her mouth, but then snapped it shut after the look Clay sent her.

"First." Clay turned his glare on me. "Are you all right?"

I nodded, not trusting my voice. My face burned from the intensity of everyone's stares.

Clay's steely eyes filled with doubt. "Sage and Raine can confirm that when we get back."

Fantastic.

Another thing to look forward to. A checkup with Kaden's on-again, off-again non-girlfriend girlfriend.

"Second. What the hell were you thinking?" Clay asked, outrage consuming his tone. "After everything, how could you sneak out from the Breakpoint again? And that *you* would let her." He leaned forward, sending Kaden a hard look. "Don't think I've forgotten about that. You're just extremely lucky that after things went sideways, you had the common sense to ask for help and we could track Saylor's burner phone. Otherwise this would be a *very* different conversation." Then he glared toward the front of the car. "And even though it ended up saving someone tonight, that doesn't excuse the fact that you two broke protocol by tampering with your phones. We'll be revisiting that subject, I can assure you of that."

So, that's how they'd found me, and how Kaden had found me before making it to the coffee shop.

Clay's jaw flexed as he geared up for another round, but before he could lay into anyone else, I jumped in.

"Don't blame Kaden or any of the others." I tried to sound more assertive than I felt in my sedative-haze. "They had nothing to do with my decisions."

"I find that hard to believe, all things considered." Clay said, sarcasm dripping from his tone. I opened my mouth to argue, but he held up a hand to stop me. "Nothing you say can change the fact that I'll be reporting them, so this isn't for you to worry about." I.e. this team isn't your area to interfere. "But regardless of who did what, the consequences are still the same. *Think*, Emma. After everything that went down at the Supply Site and the attack on you and your aunt less than a week ago, how could you go waltzing out into the night like it was nothing?" His hand cut through the air. "And now your decision ended up putting us all at risk."

I flinched.

Clay shook his head. "How is it you just seem to be at the center of all—"

"Enough, Clay." Kaden cut him short. "I'm not saying we don't deserve a stern reprimanding or punishment, but can you hold off on yelling at her until the sedative the Clinic drugged her with wears off?"

With that little announcement, shocked silence filled the car.

Clay cursed as he sat back. "Fine. We'll pick up this conversation later." He exhaled, his anger deflating for the moment. "But I expect a full report when we get back. And Hale, make sure you follow exposure protocol with the plates on your Jeep. Same goes for your burner phone, Campbell."

Both of them nodded but otherwise kept quiet. As the silence stretched out, I squeezed my eyes shut. What a mess. An apology didn't feel like enough after all the trouble I'd caused.

We don't need you buzzing around here messing things up.

My heart sank. Everything Kaden had feared when I'd first arrived was coming true. I had messed things up. Not only had I endangered everyone here, but I'd received a firsthand demonstration of how weak I was. It had been so easy for Griffin to detain me. And sure, I'd managed to escape my glass cage, but if Kaden hadn't shown up, I would've run right back into the Clinic's hands, proving just how little I was cut out for this hidden world.

"You can stop checking the mirrors, Reed," Decker said from the back. "No one is following us."

"He's right," Clay added in an exhausted tone. "The facility was basically empty."

Kaden turned from staring out the window. "Then what took you all so long?"

"Searching for any tech or files left behind," Clay said. "But they'd already cleared everything out."

I reached behind me and removed Dr. Mallory's tablet from its indent in my back. "The screen got cracked and it might've sustained more damage when Griffin attacked us, but maybe this will help."

27

"According to the X-rays, your wrist isn't broken. But it is sprained," Raine said, inputting information to her tablet from her rolling stool. "Looks to be only a grade one, but you'll need to wear a splint for a few weeks."

I glanced down at my tender wrist, grateful for that news. A removable splint was way better than a cast. A long-lasting fiberglass reminder of my mistakes?

Hard pass.

In the past hour, we'd made it back safely to the Breakpoint where I landed in one of the treatment rooms and was examined by a bright-eyed and competent Rainy-Day. The exam had been efficient, professional, and only a little anxiety-inducing.

By the time Raine finished, I was sitting upright on the exam table, breathing in the eucalyptus and citrus scent. The serene space felt so at odds compared to my sterile, Lysol-soaked Holding Site experience. The reasons behind Arc choosing the spa-like interior and tranquil medical equipment taking on a whole new meaning.

"Now, besides the sedative that thankfully appears to be wearing off, are there any other injection sites that you're aware of?" Raine leveled her steady light blue eyes on me.

"No, only my neck." I touched the area in question. What with my torn clothes and trails of blood, I must have looked like I'd gone two rounds with a rabid raccoon—*and lost*. And I shouldn't have cared. I knew I shouldn't. Rise above, and all that. But deep down I did. Who wouldn't?

"Good, and I didn't see anything in my exam, which means they didn't have time to fit you with a tracker." Raine gave me a soft smile and pushed her stylish black-framed glasses back up before finishing her notes. And try as I did to prevent it, my mind wandered to the one thing I had no business knowing—I fully blamed the sedative. Were Raine and Kaden together?

I should just ask her. It was cowardly that I hadn't, I knew that.

"I'll grab that splint for you." Raine closed her tablet, setting it on its docking station before she stood. "Do you mind if I let the others back in? I know Clay would like to get going on his report, and I can bandage your abrasions at the same time."

"Sure." I was completely onboard with getting this over with.

As Raine disappeared to find a splint, Clay strode in with all the venom of a rattlesnake. Kaden followed with his bandaged forearm, looking like he wanted to be anywhere else. Clay stood room central with his arms crossed, the three silver-threaded bands signifying him as Breakpoint Captain catching my eye. If I hadn't already known how serious this situation was, the fact that he was wearing those three bands would have driven it home.

"Don't mind me." Raine walked back in, not at all fazed by the hostility infusing the room. She set a small bundle of black straps and supplies next to me. "Just need to patch her up while you talk."

Clay looked me straight in the eyes. "Can you tell us everything that happened? And in as much detail as you're able. Even the smallest detail can give us intel on the Clinic and maybe tell us why they felt the need to detain you."

An answer I would have very much liked myself. I wasn't an Elementum, and I wasn't part of the Breakpoint team. The only two reasons I could think of were: one, Agent Todd had followed us and nabbed me under the assumption I was one of them. Or two, I'd been recognized from the Recall attack back home. Those were the only options that made any sense.

So, that's where I started when I explained it all to Clay. The exam room was quiet except for my voice and Raine's diligent work cleaning and bandaging my injuries until I reached the Patient Intake part.

"Wait," Kaden said from his lean against the far wall. "You're saying the Typology Detector triggered on you, but the results came back as unknown?"

"Yeah, the doctor blamed it on recent software updates and that's why…" My words faded out as I saw the look on Raine's face. "What?"

Raine's hands were frozen over a piece of gauze. "It's just that even if there was something faulty with the software, and I'm not saying there wasn't"—she glanced at Clay—"but those devices are designed to quickly assess the presence of any Elementum Markers, no matter how limited it may be."

Clay scratched his chin. "You're saying the device wouldn't have triggered if Emma didn't have any Elementum Markers?"

"It would've read as Non-Detect," Raine said. "Although, I guess with Emma being a Halfbreed, her genetic makeup could have enough Markers to be detectable but not enough to develop abilities."

Right. I guess that made sense. Well, *mostly.* If my hunch about my pattern-tracking was right, then I had enough Markers to develop a weird version of abilities—if that was even what it was—but not enough to develop anything of substance. So, I kept that to myself. No need to call any more attention to how I didn't fit in here.

But that also meant Agent Todd hadn't followed or recognized me at all; she had detected me and my Halfbreed-misfit-genes.

"I'd have to do a full blood panel to confirm that." Raine faced me. "I could run one, if you want?"

I hesitated. Did I want to know my genetic makeup? With my brain still fuzzy, I wasn't sure. Also, the idea of letting her near me with a huge needle made me want to run for the hills.

"It wouldn't change anything in terms of you having abilities, but as a Halfbreed there could be so many fascinating indicators that we rarely see." Raine stared off into her own world. "And just think, if the Clinic had figured out what you are, they would've relished the opportunity to study you." Shock splashed her face. "Oh my god. Not that I want to *study*, study you. That came out wrong. What I meant is—"

"It's okay." I gave her a hopefully reassuring smile. "I understood what you meant."

And I did. As long as it was done responsibly and with consent, I completely respected the desire to keep learning and exploring. Aunt Viv had always taught me that knowledge was the cornerstone in expanding your understanding and attitude toward the world. It helped shape you, and it should never stop. So, I had to admire Rainy-Day's badass medic skills and her continued thirst for knowledge.

Well, crap. Now I liked her.

"Okay, good." Raine gave me a soft smile. "And actually, don't answer me right now about the blood panel. Just think about it, and you can let me or Sage know later if you want to go through with it, okay?"

Remembering where the other medic, Sage, currently was, I said, "Oh, Clay. There's something else. Agent Todd mentioned getting Asher back."

"Not a surprise." Clay rubbed the back of his neck. "I'm sure she didn't appreciate us snatching him out from under her Enforcer's nose."

"You've encountered her and Griffin before?" I asked, remembering Griffin's greeting to Kaden earlier.

"Out in the field." Kaden shrugged, not meeting my eyes. "They're one of the main Enforcement teams in Denver. Griffin is considered a relatively powerful Enforcer while Todd was only known as a low-level Handler until she was promoted to being Griffin's Handler."

Clay nodded. "But they're nothing we can't handle."

You're the reason my golden ticket is missing.

My heart dropped as I imagined little Asher at the mercy of that cold-hearted, wasteland of a human being. "No, you don't understand. Agent Todd was adamant that she'd get Asher back. It has to do with the project he was a part of."

Clay's face changed. "What project?"

"She called it the Horizon Project and said it was the Director's number one priority." Suddenly the air in the room changed and everyone grew tense. "What?"

Clay looked at Kaden. "If this is the head of the Clinic's top priority, then we need to do everything to figure out what exactly the Horizon Project is."

"Crossbreeding Elementums," I said.

Three pairs of eyes snapped to me.

"That's what Dr. Mallory said when he shoved the information in Agent Todd's face."

Clay cursed as he paced a few steps. Kaden straightened as he shared a look with Raine, who looked like a nuclear bomb had just been dropped.

"None of this leaves this room, do you understand?" Clay locked eyes with each of us. "At least until we have a better understanding of what we've stumbled into. If this gets out, it could send others into a panic and possibly put an unnecessary spotlight on Asher, and I think we can all agree he's been through enough."

I nodded in sync with Kaden and Raine.

"Good." Clay exhaled roughly. "Let's get some protocols taken care of and then get some rest. Tomorrow's going to be a very long day." He then turned to me. "And Emma, I'll be reporting this to your aunt, and she and Herrera will decide on the penalties you'll face."

I nodded. "I'm sorry. I know that's not enough, but please believe that I am."

"I know you are." Clay held my stare. "But that doesn't change what happened or the danger you put us all in tonight."

My throat burned at the rightful call out.

"The information you just gave me and the stolen tablet will help, at least in Herrera's case," Clay continued, stunning me. "If we're lucky, some good can come out of this mess."

With that, Clay and Kaden exited the room.

I resisted the urge to chase after Kaden to apologize and thank him for what he'd done tonight. But after everything I figured I was the last person he wanted to see right now.

"Is it possible?" I asked Raine. "To crossbreed Elementums, I mean."

She reached for the splint next to me, the hiss of Velcro echoing through the room. "I'd like to tell you no, but the Clinic is capable of a lot of incredibly scary things." She fastened the brace in place before locking eyes with me. "That's why even the toughest of us need protecting."

28

Ice spread from the shadows, creeping along like fog in a valley. The chill seeped into blood and bone as I lay immobilized on a familiar foam padding, the frozen crystals closing in around me.

I exhaled in visible puffs as I tried to lift my arm, my leg, anything from the neck down. But nothing budged. It was like I was anchored in place as I heard the constant sound of dripping in the distance. And I wasn't alone. I don't know how I knew that, but I did.

Sweethearrrt. A voice drifted out of the darkness. *Come out, come out, wherever you are.*

A spike of fear shot through me as the shadowy fog billowed and receded, revealing piles of ice and murky puddles. Puddles too dark to see the bottom, and too dark to simply be water... Then two forms emerged out of the darkness, capturing my attention. Griffin stood strong and confident with a cunning smile directed at the other unveiled body.

Kaden.

Encased in ice from the chest down, Kaden gritted his teeth as his eyes filled with cold violence. But this wasn't right. I'd been here before, but it had been different—hadn't it?

I struggled to sit up, but I was powerless to help. Shrouded soldiers materialized along the periphery like wraiths in the night, creeping closer with every frosty breath.

"I'm so glad you brought your friends, Sweetheart. They fought so valiantly, but in the end, you were the key to their demise." Griffin turned his devious grin on me as the surrounding fog receded further, revealing Aunt Viv and the rest of the Breakpoint Team trapped in ice. "Let's finish this, shall we?"

Griffin lifted his arm toward the frozen prisoners, the air constricting as strong as an undertow, dragging me down until I couldn't escape. Until—

My eyes sprang open, heart thundering. The slow rotating blades of the ceiling fan came into focus as everything rushed back to me. I wiped the chilled sweat from my brow as the residual fear sank in. But I wasn't in that glass cage at the Holding Site; I was in my dorm room at the Breakpoint—safe.

I stared at the ceiling for a while as the events from two nights ago were on constant replay in my head. I had screwed everything up so royally. Aunt Viv's hard work to keep me away from the Clinic had been shot to hell. Saylor's phone had been burned and lost. And on top of all that, everyone at the Breakpoint had been put in jeopardy. I was just checking *all* the boxes lately.

But at least a few positives had emerged from the wreckage. The information about Asher and the Horizon Project, for one. Also, the stolen tablet—hopefully. And my sketch. I glanced over at the bedside table, finding my sketchbook.

I knew the six-pointed star symbol from Dr. Mallory's tablet screen was somehow tied to the Horizon Project, but other than that I had no clue if it would be of any use. But you'd never know unless you tried, or rather showed them, right? Which I planned to do. That's if Clay ever talked to me again.

I sighed heavily and lightly poked my wrist, the deep ache somewhat of an improvement. But the crack-of-dawn red digits on the clock said it was time for more ice and pain meds. I threw off the covers, tossed back two pills, and applied the ointment Raine had given me to speed healing. Then I changed into a long-sleeved shirt and a pair of leggings. Who knew putting on leggings one-handed could be considered an Olympic sport?

After getting my participation ribbon, I looked over at my broken necklace next to the purple-capped jewelry cleaner I used almost weekly. I hated not having it around my neck—like I was missing a part of myself. But with Agent Todd confiscating the replacement chain, I guess I'd have to go without it for a little while longer.

I kicked my stiff and sore body into motion. The kitchen was thankfully empty as I grabbed a cold gel pack from the freezer, my eyes snagging on the Costco-worthy number of them—and I'd wager they weren't there for keeping food cold at a picnic. No one else had been hurt the other night, but that didn't mean there hadn't been close calls or there weren't repercussions still to come. I felt like I'd lit a whole stand of fireworks announcing, *hey, look over here.* Was Kaden back on the Clinic's radar? Or any of the others? I had no clue, and the fact that I didn't was further proof that I didn't know this world or how it worked, and it was terrifying to think how much damage my ignorance had already caused.

I slammed the door shut on that mental spiral.

"You're up early," Reed said, surprising me. He held a bag of gardening tools and looked like he'd been rolling around in the dirt. It wasn't unusual to find him with patches of dirt on his skin or clothes—cause Terra, duh—but this morning it was streaked along his chin, down his gray pullover, and on his dark green joggers. "How are you feeling?"

"I'm okay." I held up the gel pack as if I needed an alibi. "Just needed some ice for my wrist."

"So, in truth, you couldn't sleep?" Reed's warm eyes were lined with concern, a nice change from his previously cold shoulder.

"No." I shivered, recalling what had woken me. "Too much running around my mind."

"I bet. Have you decided on the blood test yet?"

When Reed and Saylor had checked in on me yesterday, I'd filled them in on everything—the secret project investigation winning out over Clay's request to keep it quiet.

I shook my head, not wanting to poke *that* hornet's nest quite yet. "But I feel like I need to apologize again." Clay had suspended both him and Saylor because she'd tampered with their phones—on top of the suspension Saylor and Decker received for the Supply Site break-in.

Reed waved a dismissive hand. "Our punishment was completely fair. Saylor isn't exactly thrilled about being benched, but with how she likes to live on the edge we're just lucky no one ever found out before now."

"Why did Saylor mess with your phones? Not that I'm not grateful." But Arc burners typically couldn't be tracked.

"When we were eleven, Saylor accidentally got separated from my mom and me." Reed's lips turned up in a goofy smile. "It was in the compound and she was never in any danger, but after losing her parents it understandably left a scar. So, when she learned how, she re-engineered our phones so we could always find each other."

"That's sweet." I said with a bittersweet smile, imagining a young Saylor terrified of losing the new family she had only just found.

"Sweet, but risky." Reed ran a hand through his loose, sandy hair.

"Well, I'm sorry I brought it to Clay's attention." I adjusted my grip on the gel pack. "Hopefully he'll be more lenient about everything after I'm gone."

"You know your stay here might not be as temporary as you think." Reed locked eyes with me. "Even if you don't have enough Markers to develop abilities, you still have enough to be detected, which means it's not safe out there for you. Maybe even more so than a full-blooded Elementum, since we at least have our abilities to rely on."

Holy crap.

Why hadn't I considered that? But up until now I'd made it without being detected. Maybe that was why Aunt Viv had always chosen to live in small towns. More seclusion. Less chance of running into anyone from the Clinic. And if someone from the Clinic showed up, they'd stand out. If the Arc Council rejected us, would we move to another one?

"Plus, there are other Neutrals in Arc. Not many, but some," Reed said. "Cathleen is a great example."

My eyes widened. "Cathleen? Really?"

He nodded. "She might be married to an outpost Commander, but she also helps keep everything running smoothly on the public front so the Breakpoint Team can focus on fighting the Clinic."

That made sense. If Cathleen was a Neutral, that would definitely lower the chance of detection. But I wondered how she'd gotten pulled into this world in the first place. Also, had she gone through the same council approval process I currently was?

Reed shrugged. "All I'm saying is don't pack your bags just yet."

He said it like I had any say in the decision. When in reality I was more likely a fleeting detour in their lives. A limited-time series with the credits on the horizon.

"What's with the gardening tools and all the dirt?" I asked to distract myself.

Reed chuckled, looking down at himself. "Just tending to all the plants in the Breakpoint. But now it's time for the exterior ones. You want to join me? It always helps me when I can't sleep."

I hesitated. "I don't think me leaving the Breakpoint right now is the best idea."

"Not a problem." Reed smiled. "Trust me."

I bit my lip as I considered the sincerity in his eyes. I trusted Reed would never intentionally mislead me. "All right. Lead the way."

29

A green oasis. Everywhere I turned, greenery surrounded me. Vines climbed up the brick walls, flowers and leaves rustled in the crisp breeze, and the rich aroma of soil saturated the air. Reed had been right; leaving the Breakpoint hadn't been a problem because *technically* we'd never left. We had simply gone up.

The Breakpoint's rooftop was a plant lover's paradise. Concrete pots and planters of all sizes flanked the dirt-smudged pathways as I followed Reed through the forest and out into an extensive garden area. Low planters were arranged in tidy rows while wire frames rose out of the soil like little skyscrapers. Cushioned benches and patio furniture lined the perimeter. A train sounded in the distance, and the first rays of sunlight glinted off the backdrop of downtown Denver.

"Pretty incredible, right?" Reed nudged me before weaving his way to a far planter.

"I had no clue this was even up here." I wandered after him, my fingertips brushing the dewy leaves.

"It's my secret sanctuary—which really isn't all that secret." Reed smiled, patting the cushioned bench nearest to him. "Here, sit."

The soft padding cushioned my achy body as I sat in a growing patch of sunlight. I unlatched the straps of my brace and wrapped the gel pack around my wrist before cinching the straps again to hold it in place.

Shivers ran through me from the chilly contact, and I still felt a little fuzzy. Was it still from whatever Agent Todd had drugged me with? Or I guess it could be an after effect from all the trauma I'd been through over the past week.

Reed positioned himself in front of a wire trellis, one hand hovering over the intertwining vines. Without him touching them, the vines parted as a jittery stream of soil rose from below, shifting the stems and leaves aside to reveal little pops of red. Keeping one strained hand poised over the soil, he used his other to pick off the tiny cherry tomatoes and place them in a basket.

I sat back. "I see why it's your sanctuary."

"It's cathartic to grow something from a seed in the soil and watch it transform into something entirely new." Reed held up a ripe tomato between his dirt-smudged fingers. "One day, I'd love to have a garden as diverse as the Kew Gardens in London. It'd be a dream to study there."

I smiled at the sparkle in his eyes. "Then why not go? You clearly have a passion for it."

"I wish." Reed laughed without humor. "But I don't like to dwell on the impossible."

"What do you mean?"

"For Elementums it's close to impossible to get out of this life." Reed gazed intently at the tiny tomatoes. "If I left, I'd always be on the run, constantly looking over my shoulder."

Like Aunt Viv and me—only I hadn't been in on the strategy.

"Plus, I wouldn't have the protection of the Tech Ops Team anymore. I'd be completely cut off. No contact with anyone in Arc."

"What?" I jolted in my seat.

"I know that sounds harsh, but it would be too dangerous for them. I could accidentally trigger an alert or unknowingly aid the Clinic in some way, and I'd never forgive myself for that." He swallowed hard. "And

I couldn't do that to my mom or Saylor. Chasing a dream isn't worth leaving behind the people I care about most."

My heart sank at Reed's defeated smile. When I'd first met him, he seemed to have it all put together. But that had just been a well-built façade, hadn't it? In reality, he was as much of a stumbling wreck as Saylor and me. He just hid it better.

"Also, there's the whole Stabilizer thing." Reed shrugged. "If I was cut off, I'd have no way of getting my regular treatments, which would basically be a death sentence."

I unconsciously reached for my empty neckline, only to catch myself. "And there's no other option besides the Stabilizers?"

"No." Reed focused on collecting tomatoes with his soil stream. "I think the Clinic set it up that way to ensure our dependence on them, and roughly that's still true."

"What do you mean?"

"Even though Arc has the Stabilizer formulas for the four main typologies and we try to stay on top of any changes, the more the Clinic alters an Elementum's genetic makeup, the less effective the Stabilizers become and the more the formulas need to be re-engineered or even recreated."

Like with the Horizon Project? I opened my mouth to ask the question when Clay emerged from the dense forest carrying a watering can—as if my thoughts on the secret project had magically summoned him. I snapped my mouth shut, figuring this conversation would be better to carry on later.

Clay stopped next to us, sloshing water onto his dark teal sweatshirt and jeans. "Shouldn't you be resting?"

"Probably." I gave him a tentative smile and fiddled with the straps of my brace. An irrational spark of hope flared that he was speaking to me—although, had I really expected him to straight-up ignore me? Actually, yes. That definitely had been a possibility.

Clay turned to Reed. "I brought up the new bags of soil if you wanted to get started on repotting the seedlings."

"Perfect." Reed stood, brushing off his pants. He stepped around his tomato basket and tools before pausing to look at me.

"I'm good." I said, not wanting to leave my patch of sun with the brisk air and gel pack combo going on. "I have Cap here to keep me company."

"Haven't heard that one before," Clay said dryly. He started watering the low planters as Reed disappeared into the botanical jungle.

As time ticked by, Clay's shoulder grew colder and colder—to the point where I would have preferred a full-on chewing-out session like the one in the car. At least with the scolding, I knew where I stood with him. I had let so many people down the other night, but somehow it felt worse with Clay. Even though he'd never wanted to deal with me in the first place, he had. He'd put in the effort. And just when I thought we were making progress, I went and messed it all up. Was this it for our training sessions? Was he going to throw in the towel and give up on me?

"Here." Clay's deep voice startled me as a dark teal sweatshirt appeared in front of me. "Can't have you turning into a popsicle."

My teeth hummed from the cold. "You sure?"

"Your lips are turning blue right before my eyes."

"Thanks." I slipped on the soft, oversized outerwear and zipped it up, grateful for the warmth.

Clay grunted, turning his attention back to the garden.

As I stuck my numb hands into the front pockets, I hit two solid objects. The first I recognized as Clay's fob; the second I was a little surprised hadn't fallen out when I'd put on the sweatshirt.

"Clay, your phone?" I held up the device.

He glanced over. "You can leave it on the bench. I'll grab it in a minute."

I set it next to me as I thought of Flipper. It was a frivolous thing to miss, all things considered, but that didn't stop the feeling of loss that shot through me. Or that it made me think of Claire and how she was doing. Probably prepping to go all out for the homecoming dance in a few weeks. When she realized I was gone, would she go without me? I wouldn't blame her if she did. I knew life continued on and all that, even if it was hard to accept sometimes.

The cushion vibrated next to me and I looked down. A text from Commander Herrera flashed across the screen. I told myself that I didn't mean to read the message meant for Clay. Really. But...

Don't forget the file I emailed you. Also, when you get the chance, dig deeper into that theory Viv gave us.

What theory? Possibilities raced through my mind, but unfortunately it could've been about anything. The Clinic. My mom. Hell, it could be about the Loch Ness monster for all I knew. As the sounds of the waking city washed over me, I leaned back in frustration and switched my focus to a different spiderweb of theories.

First, there was Herrera overseeing the investigation into a secret project, one that somehow involved my mom and could be the key to changing the course of the war.

Next, there was the address connected to the project that had ended up being a Supply Site where Asher was found—which had led to the belief that an experimental serum was being stored there.

Then, there was the information I'd gained from the Holding Site about Asher and the Horizon Project, which supported my theory that the secret project and the Horizon Project were one and the same. Also, that crossbreeding Elementums was the key to changing the war.

But the unanswered questions I still had were all about my mom. When she'd gone missing from the Breakpoint so long ago, was it because of the Clinic? Had they captured her and then subjected her to the Horizon Project? Was that why she'd gotten sick and Aunt Viv hadn't?

If what Reed had said was true, it made sense. Aunt Viv must've brought Igniter Stabilizers with her when she'd come to stay with us, but because of the alterations the Clinic had made, they would have had little effect on my mom.

I swallowed hard, snuggling deeper into my borrowed sweatshirt. But again, these were only theories. And I could keep working them over and over until my brain went numb, but until I had actual answers that's all they would ever be—*theories*.

Clay started hydrating the planter to my left.

I turned to him and asked, "Do you think the Clinic has really achieved crossbreeding Elementums?"

He stared at me, no doubt stunned by my audacity to bring up the Horizon Project after everything that had happened. He stared so long that I was convinced he would ignore me, but then he walked over.

"Honestly, I'm not sure." He sat down next to me. "It really depends on how far the Clinic has taken its experimentation for the project."

"You mean, how far they took experimenting on Asher."

"Among others, I'm sure. It's unclear how long the Horizon Project has been active." Clay looked over at me. "But yes, observing Asher and how he handles things like the Stabilizers could be a strong indication of how far things have progressed. As well as what he can remember from his time in the Clinic."

"What about Agent Todd?" I remembered her scheming smile. "She seemed pretty confident she would get Asher back."

"I'm not worried about her." Clay stared out over the garden. "The Breakpoint has multiple safeguards in place, and in all the years Arc has been around, the Clinic hasn't been able to infiltrate a single compound or outpost."

His logic-proven dismissal did very little to alleviate my worries. Although if Agent Todd knew the location of the Breakpoint, I'm pretty sure a Recall Team would've already tried to bust down the door. So, maybe Clay had a point.

"Don't worry, Emma. We've taken several precautions to make sure the Breakpoint stays off the Clinic's radar." He patted my arm. "You need to focus on yourself and healing up."

He was probably right. I was worrying about things that everyone here was prepared for, and—

"Clay." Reed burst out of the dense forest, holding up his phone. "Raine texted. She needs you down in the medical bay. It's urgent."

30

The three of us raced toward the medical wing. My Converses squeaked on the polished concrete floor as we passed one training room after the next. Was it Asher? Had something gone wrong?

We filed into the medical bay and stumbled to a halt. Across the room, Asher was sitting up and alert in his hospital bed. The white T-shirt and gray sweatpants dwarfed his small frame, but were still an improvement over the oversized medical gown from last time.

"There you are." Raine stood by one of the supply cabinets in her light green scrubs with her long hair artfully constructed in a messy bun. She walked over, tablet in hand. Man, anyone who looked this put together at such an early hour surely had dark magic on their side.

Clay glanced around. "Where's Sage?"

"She was here all last night and my shift started about thirty minutes ago." Raine pushed up her glasses on the bridge of her nose. "But I knew you'd want to talk with him the moment he woke up."

Clay nodded. "Good call."

"And there's something else." Raine offered her tablet to Clay, the screen displaying a patient chart. She lowered her voice. "We ran his prints through the system and got a hit."

"You're kidding." Clay scanned the screen.

"He's Flint's kid," Raine said, awe in her voice.

I leaned toward Reed. "Who's Flint?"

"Remember the incident from a few weeks ago that Saylor told you about?" Reed said softly. "When a Recall Team attacked a Striker and his son close to the Breakpoint? Well, Flint was the Striker, and I guess Asher was his son who was captured that day."

Holy crap.

Clay looked up from the tablet, speaking very quietly. "Does he know yet? About his dad?"

Raine lips pressed into a hard line as she shook her head.

"All right." Clay exhaled harshly. "What about any more flare-ups?"

"None so far," Raine said, before they continued into a medical-heavy conversation—half of which had terms that were fiction worthy.

I stepped away as I glanced over at Asher, noting the snow-white bandage wrapping his forearm and the IV attached to his other arm. His eyes were locked on the blanket covering his legs and he fidgeted with the edges. My heart squeezed in a weird combination of sorrow and resentment. But I pushed it down, feeling confident that Asher wouldn't appreciate me feeling sorry for him, even if it came from a good place.

I looked away, trying not to focus too hard on anything in particular. Everything in me wanted to run—go back to the rooftop. Or my room. Or anywhere else. There was really no need for me to be here any—

"I remember you."

My eyes snapped to Asher. "What?"

"I remember you." The black planes of his face scrunched in concentration. "You helped me from the van, I think."

"Ah, yeah." I plastered on a smile as I walked over to his hospital bed. "Me, Decker, and Saylor helped get you out." I stuck out my hand. "I'm Emma."

He tensed, staring at my outstretched hand. "Asher. I would shake your hand, but it's probably not the best idea."

"Oh, right. Pyro-Prints," I said, feeling silly for forgetting.

"Pyro-Prints?" His cheeks tinted.

I winced, holding up my hands. "I meant it as a compliment. If I could do what you can, I'd never need a microwave again."

Asher gazed at his hands. "That's if I can ever control it."

"I'm sure it just takes time and practice. And everyone here will help you."

"If you're not an Igniter, which type are you?"

"Oh, I can't control any of the elements." I adjusted my brace. "I'm only a Halfbreed."

Asher's eyes widened. "Really?"

"Yep. I'm somewhat of an oddity." I smiled.

"I would describe you as more of an anomaly or rarity." Raine popped up beside me, genuine kindness ringing in her tone. "If you had a third eye or something, then I'd classify you as odd."

Asher laughed as I snorted. "Super comforting, thanks."

Raine grinned before looking past me. "Asher, this is Clay Avelino." She gestured to Clay at the foot of his bed. "He's the Breakpoint Captain and would like to talk to you if you're up for it."

Asher peeked over at me as I gave him an encouraging smile, then he nodded at Raine.

"Great, thank you." Raine looked between Reed and me. "Let's give them some privacy."

We headed for the door when Asher said, "Can Emma stay?"

I hesitated.

"Please?" His soft plea cut straight to my heart.

"Sure." I went back and sat on the stool next to his bed. I knew exactly what it felt like to have my entire world turned upside down, so I wasn't just going to abandon him now, especially when he looked so alone.

"All right, then." Clay cleared his throat as Raine and Reed left the room. "Let's start with the day you were ambushed. Can you tell me what happened?"

"I..." Asher struggled to find words.

"Just start small." I remembered what Clay had told me after the Holding-Site-debacle. "Even the smallest details can give Clay insight into the Clinic."

Asher nodded. "I remember leaving the compound. We were heading to the Breakpoint for the weekend, but first we were going to get dinner, and then..." Asher's grip on the blanket tightened. "Everything went fuzzy and then blank."

"That's okay," Clay said gently. "What about after? While you were being held by the Clinic."

"I don't remember," Asher said, a hint of panic in his voice. "Next thing I knew I was being pulled from that van before..." He raised a hand to his neck. "All the pain."

"You're safe now," Clay reassured him before delicately pressing forward. "Do you remember anything before that? Maybe about the facilities? Or anything that was said or done around you?"

Asher shook his head, folding his arms around himself. "Why can't I remember?"

His soft question broke something inside me. What had the Clinic done to him?

"Maybe your mind is still trying to process everything that happened and isn't ready to acknowledge it yet." Clay held up his hands to calm him. "You could still remember. It might just take some time, okay?"

"Okay," Asher said, but it didn't sound like he believed it. "Can I see my dad now?"

My chest hollowed as I looked at Clay's stricken face, wanting nothing more in that moment than to stop time. Stop Asher's world from imploding. Because that's what it would feel like once he found out. Like the entire world had blinked out and you couldn't fathom a way to turn it back on.

Clay's lips moved, but I didn't hear a word. It was like my plug had been pulled from its socket and only a buzzing remained. It wasn't until a heart-piercing cry echoed through the room that everything came back online.

Asher curled in on himself, his face twisted in agony. I resisted the urge to throw my arms around him. I knew what he was going through. The pain was unimaginable, and there was nothing anyone could say or do to diminish it.

"I'm so sorry, Asher." Clay squeezed his shoulder, expression grave.

"Please leave," Asher said hoarsely. When neither of us moved, he added with more force, "*Please.*"

"We'll leave." Clay sounded defeated. "But if you need anything, please let us know."

I followed Clay out into the hall in a daze. We found Raine posted up next to a ladder and construction plastic on the far wall.

"Where's Reed?" Clay asked.

"Tidying things up on the roof." Raine cradled her tablet against her chest. "How did it go?"

"Not well. The news about his father was as devastating as you can imagine." Clay looked back at the medical bay door. "And he remembers nothing from his time at the Clinic."

Raine's delicate brows pinched. "Nothing?"

"I'm afraid so." Clay shrugged. "It could be from all the trauma, so it might still come back, but only time will tell."

"I know it'd be better for Arc if he could remember, but for his sake I'm hoping he doesn't." Raine pushed up her glasses. "But at least he appears to be responding to the Stabilizers. Sage seems optimistic with the response we've seen so far."

"Does that mean the Clinic didn't alter his genetic makeup after all?" I shoved my hands into the front pocket of my adopted sweatshirt.

"That, or the Clinic hasn't progressed as far as we thought with the Horizon Project." Raine tapped her chin. "They might only be at the stage of creating new variants of Elementums in preparation for crossbreeding them."

Clay crossed his arms. "That's definitely a possibility."

If that was true, then maybe I'd been wrong about my mom and she had truly just gotten sick. But then what was her involvement in all this?

"We'll know more in a few days once all the tests on Asher come back," Raine said. "Then we'll have actual data to go from."

"Clay." Decker loomed in the double doors that led to the training wing, tapping his wrist to indicate the time. The T-shirt he wore showcased the inky lines that curved around his biceps.

Clay glanced at his watch. "Damn. I need to get to the third floor for the team meeting." He started down the hall before pointing at Raine. "I'll send Sage down later with a report for you, but in the meantime, keep an eye on Asher, and if you could track down those records I asked you for, that would be great."

Team meeting? Obviously I hadn't been invited—cause duh, not part of the team—but I wondered if it had something to do with my screw-up.

"Of course." Raine opened her tablet again as Clay disappeared with Decker. That's when something she typed caught my eye: *Phoenix file.* As in, the same nickname Commander Herrera had given my mom. Could it be...

The text to Clay I'd seen earlier came back to me: *Don't forget the file I emailed you.* Could it be the same file? Was Clay working on a file about my mom? But I thought he didn't know anything about her. Had he lied to me?

My hand tightened around the fob in the sweatshirt pocket. It was just one more thing to add to the list of secrets being kept from me—and I was getting sick and tired of it.

31

Silence dominated the deserted hallway as I checked over my shoulder for the thousandth time. Thankfully, the security cameras in this area were still being upgraded, so I didn't have to worry about any digital evidence of what I was about to do.

My grip tightened on the fob as I stared at the title on the doorplate in front of me. I'd finally found my target on the loop of offices in the administrative wing. It was across from one of the supply closets I'd investigated on my first day here. Man, that felt like forever ago, but it had only been a week.

I bit down on my lip as I reached out, only to pause. Was I really going to break into Clay's office? All for some file that could *potentially* be about my mom?

Although, was it technically breaking and entering if you had the key? *Yes.* Yes, it was.

Behind the glass sidelight, shadows cloaked the interior of Clay's office, the subtle glow from the high window only allowing me to see the outlines of a bookcase, a few planters, two chairs, and a desk.

My stomach twisted like a pretzel. I could still walk away, pretend I was looking for Clay to return his things. But where would that get me?

I extended the fob the rest of the distance, hitting the small tap sensor above the keypad. The click of the door unlocking was like music to my ears. I wrapped my hand around the metal handle and twisted. As soon as I stepped into the office, the smell of soil greeted me. I decided to leave the door ajar in the hopes that if anyone approached, I'd hear them.

Once my eyes adjusted to the dim lighting, I tiptoed across the carpet to Clay's desk, afraid if I made too much noise something would jump out at me—which was completely dumb. But hey, sometimes your brain doesn't always function logically when stressed.

A computer dominated the desk. Two monitors hooked up to a laptop, to be specific, along with a cup full of pens, two plants, and a face-down picture frame.

Weird.

Had it fallen over? Giving in to my already-active criminal behavior, I lifted the wood frame to find three faces staring out at me. Two I recognized, although they were much younger in the picture than how I knew them now.

On one side, Commander Herrera stood tall and imposing as always, but with a lot less salt-seasoning in his dark hair. Next to him, a scrawny prepubescent Clay repped his signature serious expression—a small comfort to know he had rocked that long before I was around. On the other side of Clay stood a third person I'd never seen before. Dressed in an elegant suit, the man had a sharp stare and perfectly coiffed hair that reminded me of a politician at a campaign rally. But like Commander Herrera, his stance and build were all fighter as he stood confidently with one hand on Clay's smaller shoulder. This dignified delegate had to be Clay's father, which became more and more apparent as I picked up on the slight resemblances. Why would Clay keep a picture of his father and Herrera face down?

I shook myself. That was a puzzle for another day. Right now, my quest concerned the digital vault in front of me. I sat down and wiggled the wireless mouse, waking the two monitors to life. Which was when I was confronted with my first problem: how to get into

Clay's computer. It wasn't like he'd just leave his passcode laying around, and for once there was no sign of my weird pattern-tracking. This was a stupid plan—mainly because there was *no* plan. But regardless, that didn't change where I was or that the login screen was asking for a PIN.

That's when something occurred to me. I still knew the passcode to Clay's phone from when I'd used it to get the address of the Supply Site. Would Clay really use the same passcode twice? Also if I was wrong, would it alert him to the failed attempt? Or worse, wipe his computer or something? Was I really going to take that chance?

But then a tidal wave of betrayal crashed over me as I thought about my first training session and Clay telling me he didn't know anything about my mom. If this Phoenix file was really about my mom, then he had lied to me. Lied straight to my face while he'd been digging into my mom's past all along.

I set my hands to the keyboard and typed in the four digits, holding my breath with each stroke and resulting glow of the keys. A sigh of relief escaped me when the background of a picturesque canyon came into view—and all I could think was Aunt Viv would be so disappointed in Clay. But that wasn't important right now.

I double-clicked the mail icon on the taskbar, and a new window with various columns and sorted rows popped up. I started with the main inbox and found multiple emails from Commander Herrera, but nothing with a file about my mom.

Careful to keep everything the same and all emails that were unread as unread, I hurried onto the different side folders. *BP Field reports. BP Training reports. BP Transfer requests.* I scanned through each of them, but six folders later I still had nothing. It was possible that Clay had saved the file and deleted the email. Would I have to search his entire computer? Would I have time for that?

But I refused to give up just yet. I started on a folder labeled *HP*, only making it one email in when a subject line caught my attention: *Phoenix.*

For a moment, I didn't move—couldn't move. I was frozen in place as goosebumps broke out all over my skin. Then, as if I was moving in slow motion, I clicked on the email.

There was no content in the body of the email, only an attachment. Careful to preview it only in the program itself so as not to leave a timestamp anywhere, I clicked the attachment. The first thing I saw was a photo of an achingly familiar face. My mom must've been around my age when the picture was taken. Her golden-brown waves cascaded down and around her youthful face as bright eyes shined back at me.

I swallowed hard as I read through the information next to and below the image. At the top was a list of stats like age, height, and element—nothing new or groundbreaking there. It wasn't until I reached the bottom that I found what I was searching for under the section labeled *Disappearance*.

Reason for Disappearance: Capture.

It wasn't a new concept. I'd suspected it—but it was an official confirmation that the Clinic had taken my mom. An ocean's worth of emotions flooded me, but I quickly locked them down. That would come later.

Detainment Time Frame: 18 until 20-23 ???

I could help reduce those question marks, because if my calculations were right, my mom had me at twenty-two, so the end of her detainment must've been closer to the twenty-year mark. But that still meant she'd spent two to three years in their clutches.

Detainment Hub: The Crest.

No question marks this time, but more questions on my part. I knew the Detainment Hubs were where the Clinic eventually transferred all its supplies and captive Elementums. But other than that, when it came to the *where* and *how many* Hubs, I was in the dark.

Clinic Project: The Horizon Project.

Again, another thing I'd suspected, but suspecting it and knowing it were two very different things. But I still didn't know what level of experimentation she'd been subjected to.

I moved onto the next two lines—the last two lines in the file, to be exact.

After Detainment: In hiding in California, not with Arcadius.

Death: Attacked by a Recall Team and killed ???

My heart stopped as I read and re-read those words, especially the three question marks at the end. The tiny hairs along the back of my neck stirred at the implication. Was my mom still alive?

The clap of metal on metal rang out in the distance as my head jerked up. Someone was in the administrative wing.

32

My heart accelerated out of control as I closed everything and stood up. I took a hot second to run my shaking hands over the items on the desk. I wasn't completely sure the positioning was correct, but it would have to do.

Without making a sound, I darted for the door. If I was caught sneaking around Clay's office, I'd be *sooo* screwed—nail that coffin shut. And I could officially kiss my goal of continuing to train goodbye.

I peeked around the door frame. The hallway was still blissfully empty. But for how long? I slipped out to the other side, clicking the door shut behind me as quietly as possible. Even so, in the surrounding silence, it sounded as loud as a cannon. Then I stalled out. Right or left?

Right or left?

Left led back to the main hallway on the office loop, and it was most likely the source of the sound. So, that was a no-go. Right led around to the rest of the loop and more importantly the stairs on this side of the Breakpoint. But whoever was in the administrative wing could go around that way. Did I want to take that chance?

Crap.

There was no right answer. It was a loop. Which meant whoever was walking around could come from either direction.

Nausea twisted up my insides as my eyes caught on the door across from me. *The supply closet.* Not letting myself second-guess the idea, I leaped into action. I crossed the polished concrete floor before quietly opening and closing the closet door.

Inside, it was dim, with only a bit of light leaking from the glass sidelight to illuminate the tiny space. It was exactly what I would've expected a supply closet to look like. Racks dominated the walls, supplies lined the shelves, and the air smelled of woodsy pulp and cardboard.

I squeezed behind the first rack of shelves, the thin boxes of pens in front of me creating a mediocre blockade at best. I just hoped the darkened interior was enough to keep me hidden. And at least from this vantage point, I had a full view of the hallway through the sidelight. But what if the unintentional informant never came this way? What if I was stuck waiting in here forever? Eventually I'd need to risk an escape or just accept that I lived here now—mi casa de supply closet, forevermore.

Without warning, someone came into view and halted in front of Clay's office. My heart thundered as I noted the dark slicked-back hair and the inky lines curving around strong biceps. Out of everyone here, it had to be Dirt-Wad? Man, some days life just hated me.

I watched from my hiding spot as Decker typed in a code on the keypad before entering Clay's office. He must have been fetching something for Clay for the team meeting. The one I hadn't been invited to—not that I was bitter. *Nope.* Not at all. Who didn't like being left out?

I wanted to smack myself. This was not the time for a pity party.

A few minutes later, Decker exited the office with Clay's laptop in hand. He shifted the laptop into the crook of his arm before shoving his phone into the front pocket of his tactical pants. Then he glanced around.

I held my breath, not even daring to blink. Afraid it might somehow attract his attention.

He can't see me. He can't see me. He can't see me. I squeezed the metal of the storage rack so hard it bit into my hand.

After what felt like an eternity, Decker strode from view and—I could only hope—out of the administrative wing. My muscles ached as I unfurled myself from the makeshift hidey-hole and tiptoed over to the glass sidelight. I peered out into the empty hallway before cautiously unlatching the door. A burst of cool, conditioned air streamed through the narrow opening as I stood still and listened.

When I didn't hear any incriminating sounds or echoes of footsteps, I crept out into the hallway and raced in the opposite direction, heading for the stairwell around the corner. A muted clang rang out as I cautiously pushed my way through to the other side.

Step after step, I climbed, but my mind stayed back in Clay's office. With that file and my mom's youthful face. What horrors had she gone through with the Horizon Project and at the hands of the Clinic? Where was the Crest Detainment Hub? How had she escaped it?

Clearly, no one here at Arc had helped her; otherwise they wouldn't be digging into it now. But once again, it seemed I was coming away with more questions than answers. Specifically, one fundamental question that haunted me above all the others.

Had my mom been killed by a Recall Team, or was she still alive?

***

With everyone still occupied in the meeting, the allure of a hot cup-of-happiness and something more than a granola bar drove me to a booth at Breaking Grounds. Well, that, and a certain promise I hoped to cash in on.

A steaming cup of herbal tea sat next to my open sketchbook as I doodled aimlessly. All around me in the bustling café was the clatter of plates and the chatter of people. I hadn't seen Cathleen yet. There was a chance she wasn't even working today, but I held out hope.

However, as the minutes ticked by, my hope of chatting with her depleted. Much like the fresh fruit and grilled cheese I'd ordered—because love comes in many forms: shredded, sliced, melted.

I fiddled with my pen as my mind spun back to those three question marks. Hope rose like a wildfire at the thought that my mom could still be alive, burning through me with an unstoppable intensity. But that was dangerous. If it wasn't true, it would destroy me all over again. Not to mention that it meant she was in the hands of the Clinic—*again*. I'd only spent one night in their grip—a blip, a flash—while she potentially had been there this whole time...

Bile climbed up my throat. For the past nine years, I'd been out in the world laughing, smiling and worrying about trivial things. As painful as it was to admit, I had moved on. Sure, it had taken a while, but I had. I'd kept living while she potentially had been suffering.

The leather booth suddenly transformed into the foam padding of a hospital bed. My skin prickled from unwanted injections, and glass walls closed in all around me—

I shook myself, pushing down the terrible feeling of helplessness. I gripped my sketchbook to remind myself where I was—or more accurately where I wasn't. As my pulse resettled, a flash of movement caught my attention and a plate with a cupcake appeared in front of me.

"Hope you don't mind, dear. But you looked in need of a treat." Today Grandma-Moxie's bob of auburn hair was pinned back from her face and she wore a beautiful green dress that accentuated her worried eyes. Eyes that were currently scanning me, and I knew what she was seeing—the healing bruises and scratches from my encounter with Hurricane-Griffin.

"Red velvet was one of Anna's favorites," Cathleen said, her accent making *favorites* sound more as *favawrites*. "I'm hoping she passed that on to you."

My heart squeezed at the thought, but this connection was the whole reason I had come here. "Thank you," I said, though I didn't touch the cupcake. I couldn't stomach a high dose of sugar right now. "I was hoping to run into you."

"To continue our chat?" Cathleen asked, not missing a thing.

My face warmed—busted. I didn't want her to feel used.

"Good." Cathleen seemed unfazed as she slid into the booth across from me. "I was hoping for that as well."

I smiled in relief as I quickly organized my thoughts. I needed to phrase my questions carefully. As the Commander's wife, there was a good chance Cathleen knew about Clay's assignment, but I didn't want to accidentally tip her off that I knew about it—or had seen it.

"Last time, you mentioned my mom went missing." I caught my hand halfway to my neck. "Do you know what happened?"

Cathleen took a breath and settled herself. "Anna was stationed as a Rookie at the Breakpoint, and everything seemed to be going well for her." She smiled fondly. "Not surprising, being the beautiful spark that she was. But then one day she ventured out from the outpost and was never seen again. At the time, no one knew exactly what had happened. But there was a theory."

I glanced around to make sure no one was eavesdropping. "The Clinic?"

"I see you're picking up on the ins and outs around here." Cathleen's eyes gleamed with sadness behind her glasses. "Yes, whenever an Elementum goes missing, usually the Clinic is to blame. We assumed your mother was captured and transferred to one of the Detainment Hubs." Her voice filled with anguish. "The worst part is we rarely discover what becomes of those who are captured. It's unimaginable for the loved ones left behind, never finding closure."

I swallowed hard. "Is there no way of finding these Hubs?"

Cathleen looked over sharply. "If you think tracking down any of those Hubs will gain you insight about your mother, you'd best erase that from your mind." She pinned me with a fierce stare. "It wouldn't do Anna any favors. Or Viv, for that matter. Those horrible facilities are nothing but trouble."

That was easy for her to say. But if there was a chance my mom was alive—even a miniscule one—I had to find out everything I could about the Crest and the Horizon Project. And to do that, it was becoming clear that I needed to figure out a way to stay in Arc.

Cathleen rested a warm hand on top of mine. "You know who would be a good person to ask?" She held my gaze. "Viv. She probably knows the most about what happened to Anna."

Fantastic.

One more thing to pry out of my aunt when she got back—whenever that would be. Since the Holding-Site-debacle, I hadn't received any updates about Aunt Viv's group. I wondered if she'd heard about all the trouble I'd caused yet. With my luck lately, she most definitely had. And if I still had Flipper, I'd be hearing about how grounded I was. So, bright side?

Cathleen squeezed my hand. "I know it's hard being thrust into this world and not knowing what's up or down." She shook her head with a chuckle. "You should've seen me dealing with all of this after meeting Toni."

It struck me then that Cathleen could probably relate to what I was going through more than anyone else at the Breakpoint, what with her being a Neutral in the Elementum world, and more importantly going through the Arc Council approval process. If I wanted to stay, that was the major hurdle I needed to clear.

I leaned forward. "How did you two meet?"

"We first met in New York City about..." Cathleen paused in thought, *New York* sounding more like *Nuw Yawrk*. "Wow, I guess it's been over twenty-five years."

More puzzle pieces clicked together. There must have been another Arc outpost and compound out there—maybe the same one Saylor had been transferred from after her parents were killed by the Clinic. That would make sense. But that also meant there must be a Clinic facility in or near New York City. Was it the Crest?

"Toni used to frequent the little bakery my family owned in Brooklyn," she continued. "It wasn't until a couple months in that I realized it had nothing to do with the cannolis." She laughed, pushing up the flowy sleeves of her dress. "From the first moment I saw him, I knew there was something different about him. Something special. It didn't take long after our first date for our relationship to progress."

Her eyes shone with love. It was comforting to know that through all the darkness and anguish the Clinic caused, there were still bright parts, too.

"Was it difficult entering the Elementum world as a Neutral? Did you have to go through the Arc Council approval process?" I asked, picturing an interrogation room with only a table and two chairs.

"Yes, I did." Cathleen nodded. "A smaller sector handles those decisions. Only major issues are brought before the entire council."

I guess me and my aunt's futures didn't count as major issues.

"You should see that as a good thing," Cathleen added, reading my face. "Fewer politics and all that." Then she sighed. "But I won't lie, it wasn't easy. There was definitely some resistance to me joining Arc, and there will always be certain... *challenges* that, as Neutrals, we'll face."

"What do you mean?"

"Of course there's the fight with the Clinic, which causes its own issues since we can't fight to the extent an Elementum can." Cathleen stared at her hands as if caught in a memory. "But also there are certain groups within Arc that have specific, well, let's just say *expectations* for who an Elementum should end up with."

My stomach dipped. "Only other Elementums?"

"Yes. Unfortunately, those old-fashioned prejudices run deep in certain lines of Elementums."

Old-fashioned? Archaic sounded more accurate. How could anyone reasonably put such harsh restrictions over something as fluid as who someone wanted to be with?

"Thankfully, Igniters tend to be more open-minded about issues like that." Cathleen pushed up her glasses.

Like my mom. Thus, how I'd come to be. But if Igniters weren't the ones, then who?

"Unlike Terras?" I asked, hope rising for some stupid reason.

"Terras are known for their regimented ways, but the Hydros are the worst. Their pride about being the first Elementum created knows no bounds. Oh, but listen to me, I shouldn't be spreading rumors. Toni would be so upset if he knew." Cathleen waved a dismissive hand. "Ignore my petty gossip. Not all Hydros are like that."

I sank back against the booth. Like a certain Hale-Storm? Maybe that was the real reason Saylor had tried to warn me off—and why Kaden and Raine had stayed friends even when they weren't dating. Because it was *expected* for them to end up together. And what about Saylor? Was that why she wouldn't admit to crushing on Decker?

No, no way. I couldn't imagine Saylor putting up with any of that crap.

"Oh, shoot." Cathleen straightened, looking past my shoulder. "Time really got away from me."

I followed her gaze to the back entrance of the café. Kaden stood there in jeans and a maroon T-shirt, a black baseball hat with a blue and maroon "A" logo pulled low over his stony features. He gave Cathleen a nod.

Nervous energy crashed over me at the sight of him. I hadn't seen Kaden since the Holding-Site-debacle, and I still needed to apologize and thank him for helping me. But every time I tried to draft up the words, nothing seemed right.

"Thank you for letting me bend your ear." Cathleen reached out, squeezing my hand again. "Hopefully we can do it again soon."

"Anytime," I said, hoping my enthusiasm showed through.

Cathleen shuffled out of the booth just as two figures descended on our table.

"What's shakin', bacon?" Saylor's braids swished around her black crop top as she stopped at the end of the table. Her gear rings and red plaid skirt completed the edgy punk look she was rocking. "Oh, bacon. That sounds so good right now."

"Who has bacon?" Reed came up next to her. It was hard to tell which had more smudges of dirt, his gray pullover or his dark green joggers.

"Soon you will, dear." Cathleen ushered them toward the booth. "Sit, sit. I'll put in the order once I get back."

"Score." Saylor took a seat with Reed not far behind.

With that, Cathleen disappeared through the back entrance with Kaden. I guess my apology and gratitude would have to wait.

I turned to the Dynamic-Duo, noticing Saylor's eyes were riveted on my untouched cupcake. But maybe I could check off another apology on my list. "Trade ya?"

"Anything." Saylor's eyes never left her target. "A kidney? My first born?"

"Forgiveness." I wiggled the plate. "For destroying your phone and getting you suspended."

"Easy. That was already a done deal." She reached forward. "Although the joke would've been on you cause I'm never having kids."

I smiled as she peeled off the cupcake wrapper. It felt better knowing she wasn't holding a grudge.

"Oh, Emma, before I forget." Reed swiped a finger full of frosting off Saylor's cupcake, resulting in a quick smack on his arm. "Ow."

Saylor pointed an orange-tipped fingernail at him. "Paws off the goods."

Reed grinned before turning back to me. "Clay is looking for you."

"Why?" My heart pounded like a snare drum. There was no way Clay could know about my little office venture, right?

"Not sure." Reed shrugged. "But he said something about his fob."

33

Sweat dripped down my face while the burn in my thighs was a surprising comfort as I finished the ladder course arranged around Training Room A. After I'd missed a few days of training, it was nice to be back at it, and I was relieved that I wasn't hurting. Mostly. Barely... *Fine.* It was manageable—but also a welcomed struggle compared to being cooped up in my room over-analyzing everything.

After I'd left the Dynamic-Duo at Breaking Grounds the other day, I found Clay in the medical wing. He'd only wanted his fob back and had seemed unaware of my earlier B&E. But I used the opportunity to leverage his fob and sweatshirt in exchange for keeping our training sessions going. Thankfully, he agreed, but only if I gave myself one more day to recover.

The downside to that? It allowed the potent sting of betrayal to inch in like the tide, building and building until it fully engulfed me—and wouldn't recede.

"Remember, this is supposed to be a light training day," Clay said, "so take a breather and grab some water."

His casual tone set my teeth on edge. Further proof that I probably shouldn't be training with Captain-Judas today—or interacting with anyone, for that matter.

As I grabbed my water bottle from the sidelines, I felt like there were a million jitterbugs dancing under my skin. It was most likely from everything finally rising to the surface, and not just the lies and betrayal over the Phoenix file—but I couldn't help but blame Clay for it all. I was on edge, and unfortunately he was a convenient outlet—even though I suspected he wasn't the only one keeping secrets.

Saylor and Reed had told me the team meeting was just a standard check-in for Clay to reiterate the list of protocols that had been disregarded the previous week. But I couldn't fight the feeling that they were hiding something. And Cathleen's comments about Neuts not being fully accepted into the fold didn't help—which was why I'd held off on telling them about the Phoenix file.

"Strength training," Clay announced after picking up the ladder course. "And with your wrist, we'll keep it a leg day."

I set down my water bottle and readjusted my brace before taking a calming breath. But the sting on my shoulder from a tiny sand missile only stirred up the storm inside me.

Oh, goodie. The sand bombs were back. Apparently, my pass only applied to arms today.

"Let's go, Cross," Clay called. "Lunges."

I crinkled my way across the vinyl mats, begrudgingly accepting my role as a moving target. If this was what it took to keep training, then I'd suck it up and be Captain-Judas's personal bull's-eye. Because I needed to keep training. If I wanted to find out if my mom was still alive, then I had to survive this world, and training was the best route to achieve that.

I got to work on the lunges, taking several passes on the strain-and-suffering runway as Clay moved along the periphery. His impeccable aim was in fine form today.

Cathleen had said Terras were known for their regimented ways. It was an apt description of Captain-Hard-Ass, with his disciplined personality and orderly tendencies. Decker, too, with his militant and rigid nature. Also, Reed, who loved following the rules—unless Saylor was involved, of course. How had I never noticed these similarities? And what about the other types of Elementums?

Thwack.

"Keep aware, Cross," Clay said as the sting on my shoulder faded.

I gritted my teeth but finished my last pass. My legs trembled with the final ups and downs before I collapsed onto the mats. Man, this was rough.

"Done already?" Clay stared down at me.

"How about we switch?" Irritation chipped at my skin as I wiped the sweat from my face. "I'll pelt you with sand bombs for a while and you do the lunges. Sound like a plan? Great, I think so too."

"You realize I've already been through this training, right?" Clay sent me an arched expression. "You're not even getting the full vicinity drill."

"What?" I sat up.

Clay crossed his arms. "Usually the Trainee is tasked with utilizing their own abilities to defend themselves during these drills."

"You mean target practice?"

"Hilarious." Clay shook his head. "Remember, this training is meant to help you pinpoint threats by honing your instincts in a strained environment. You see, everyone has an innate instinct for certain environmental stimuli but most people try to repress it. They wave it off as just a funny feeling, but in fact it's the body's way of perceiving potential threats. In the case of Elementums, we're hard-wired to have these primal instincts heightened."

My pulse sped up. "And you think because I'm a Halfbreed mine are heightened as well."

Clay nodded. "Not as much as a full-blooded Elementum, but more than a Neutral. If we can train you to call these instincts forward rather than repress them, it will go a long way to help you protect yourself—and not only against Recall Agents but Enforcers too." He hesitated. "Potentially."

I felt his reaction down to my soul. He wasn't wrong. How could I ever hope to survive more than five minutes against an Enforcer? And the truth was I'd already proven that I couldn't—with Griffin. If Kaden hadn't shown up, I would've been recaptured, no question about it. I wasn't dogging myself. I had managed to escape my glass cage, but I had to be realistic about the category-five hurricane Griffin had brought to the table.

"Let's just take this one step at a time." Clay must've read the frustration on my face.

I grunted.

"What's with the attitude today?" He crossed his arms. "You're the one who wanted to get back to training so bad."

"There's no attitude," I lied.

Clay sent me an arched expression.

"We're here to work, right?" I said dryly. "Let's do that."

He stared a little longer before exhaling. "Fine. Let's switch to core exercises."

I held back my groan—*barely*—as I repositioned myself on the mat. Clay gave me instructions and then I set about completing the drills. My abdominal muscles spasmed through each one until I recalled something from my last training session. A pattern? I was pretty sure there'd been a sequence to his sand bomb onslaught, and I believed I was picking up on one today, but there was also something else. In Clay's wake, there was a faint... double shadow? But in reverse. It was like a dull glow that only lasted for the span of a heartbeat—so quick I wasn't sure I'd actually seen it right. *Great.* Had I finally lost it?

As I lifted my upper body in a sit-up, I tracked Clay as best as I could before lowering myself back to the mat. Up, sit. Down, flat. I tried catching a glimpse of his reverse-shadow-glow—

Thwack.

My nose wrinkled in irritation as I returned to my controlled rising and falling, my abs screaming in protest. Every few reps, I noticed Clay moved counter-clockwise a few feet as his reverse-shadow-glow blinked in and out of my eyeline. Was I really seeing this right? Up, sit. Down, flat. If I could just—

Thwack.

I collapsed back onto the mat with a grunt, squeezing my eyes shut as I resisted the urge to throw some sand bombs of my own.

"You keep forgetting to control your breathing." Clay's voice drew closer. "Remember, it will help keep the hesitation and panic at bay."

Yeah, like when Agent Todd had knocked me out from behind. Regulating my breathing had sure helped then—*not*. Doubts swirled to life, latching on like a venomous snake.

"Up, Cross. Or are you taking a nap down there?"

Not deigning to reply to his snarky joke, I approached the on-ramp for the high road—

Thwack.

That's it. I burst to my feet and full-on charged him, which wasn't the greatest strategy. Especially since he had a good fifty or more pounds on me and I had no real offensive training, but too late. With shameful ease, Clay blocked my assault and spun me away. Undeterred, I pivoted and swung at him again. In no time flat, he had me neutralized, flipping me onto my back with a yelp. Pain radiated down my spine as the wind was knocked out of me—*pathetic*.

I scowled up at the exposed piping as I considered the validity of three-times-the-charm. In the end, getting my ass handed to me twice in mere seconds was humiliating enough, and I wasn't looking for a three-peat.

"Are you done playing around?" Clay asked, his breathing infuriatingly under control. "Or can we get back to work now?"

"What's the point?" The words tore from my throat. All my energy drained away in a powerful sense of defeat. How could I expect to survive in this world or, more importantly, find answers about my mom, if I couldn't even manage basic training?

Clay looked down at me, his expression filling with what looked like pity. But then a shout sounded out in the hallway, causing both our heads to snap toward the open door. What the hell?

"Where is she?" The shout repeated at a closer range and from a frantic voice I hadn't heard in what felt like forever.

***

I rushed to follow Clay to the medical wing, our footsteps pounding on the concrete floors. A couple rooms down, a door flung open and a familiar golden-haired figure appeared between the jambs before sprinting in my direction. The impact of the hug was jarring.

"Emma-bug," Aunt Viv muffled against my shoulder.

I ignored the cries of my healing body as I sank into my aunt's comforting embrace, letting everything else fall away—the lies, the secrets, everything. My cheek rested against her olive fleece. Instantly, I was eight years old again, when a hug from my aunt could shield me from all the world's problems.

"I raced back as soon as I could." Aunt Viv pulled back, her hand hovering over the abrasion along my temple. "Are you okay? Are you hurt anywhere else I can't see?"

"Nothing major, just some bumps and bruises." I lifted my left arm for show-and-tell. "And a sprained wrist."

As Aunt Viv inspected my braced wrist for herself, Clay jumped in. "I wasn't expecting your group back for another couple of hours."

He knew they were coming?

"Is Commander Herrera with you?" he added.

Down the hall another door opened, answering Clay's question. Commander Herrera stood there with Raine. I forgot how imposing the Commander was in person, but next to string-bean Raine he looked colossal. The flannel and down-to-earth outfit he wore did nothing to lessen the intimidating vibe he threw off.

"Do I want to know?" Herrera stared down Clay as they approached.

Clay straightened, his olive skin paling as he opened his mouth.

"A rhetorical, Avelino." Herrera cut him off.

Wow. Commander Herrera was not in a friendly mood today. Normally, I'd be thankful it wasn't directed at me, but I couldn't let Clay take the heat for something I did—even if he *had* lied straight to my face.

"Clay shouldn't be blamed for my mistake." I stepped forward, trying to keep my voice steady. "And neither should the others. It was all me."

Herrera leveled his powerful stare on me. "As Clay is the Breakpoint Captain and responsible for those within it, we'll have to agree to disagree on how much that blame should be shared."

"And whose fault is that?" Clay said through clenched teeth.

Suddenly, a facedown picture frame came to mind. It had never occurred to me before, but maybe Clay was mad at Commander Herrera. But I couldn't understand why it would be for appointing him as Breakpoint Captain.

"How did this even happen?" Aunt Viv turned her frantic but puzzled stare on me, which quickly transformed into disapproval. "What were you doing out so late? Wandering the streets alone, no less, in a city you don't know. What were you thinking, Emma?"

I tensed in anticipation of the grounding of the millennia. I'd bent the rules before, but nothing like this.

"Let's all just calm down." Herrera looked at each of us before landing on me. "We received Clay's report, but why don't you run us through it? That way we can all be on the same page before moving forward."

I nodded and broke into a rundown of the other night's events. My audience stood in strained silence as I avoided eye contact with Aunt Viv and skirted the subject of the Horizon Project. I wasn't sure if Clay had included it in his report, so I left it up to him whether to share it.

I ended my recap with our return to the Breakpoint and Raine's Typology Detector theories. "So, either it's a software glitch or my genetic makeup has enough Markers to be detectable but not enough to develop abilities." I shrugged. "And that's what happened and where we ended up."

A tense moment passed. Herrera stroked his beard, appearing deep in thought. My aunt's face had drained of color as she gazed at nothing in particular, her arms hanging limply at her sides. I knew I worried her, but Herrera had said they'd read Clay's report—so this couldn't have been new. Or had I included something that Clay had left out of his report?

"Is that even a possibility?" Clay asked. "I thought Markers were always a sign of abilities."

"It's definitely a theory worth looking into," Herrera said. "A good starting point would be the threshold for which those Detectors are calibrated to trigger. Wouldn't you think, Viv?"

With every silent second that passed, unease took root in my chest, quickly spreading like a toxic weed.

"Viv?" Herrera asked from what felt like a football field away.

"It shouldn't have," Aunt Viv mumbled.

"What shouldn't have?" I asked, heart thundering so fast I feared it'd burst right through my chest.

"The Detector," Viv murmured. "It shouldn't have gone off. The suppressor wouldn't have allowed it."

34

"Suppressor?" My voice turned hoarse as pressure constricted my chest.

Aunt Viv's head jerked up as if realizing she'd spoken out loud. In an instant, her already ashen skin appeared ten shades paler.

"I need you to listen to me." Aunt Viv gripped my shoulders, her wide eyes locking with mine. "Your mother made me promise to keep you from being dragged into this world."

"What suppressor?" I demanded, ears ringing, audience forgotten.

"She pleaded with me to keep her only child safe," Aunt Viv continued. "She made me promise to do whatever it took."

The buzzing in my ears intensified, mixing with the raw pain swirling inside of me.

"What does that mean, Viv?" Herrera asked, but neither of us responded.

Whatever it took. What the hell did that mean? Had she put suppressors in my food? Drugged me in my sleep? Or put something on...

My chest hollowed as I breathed, "My sun charm necklace."

After a few seconds that took a lifetime, Aunt Viv swallowed hard. "Yes."

The world tilted and my concept of reality shattered for the second time in a little over a week.

"You have to understand," she said urgently, "we did it as a precaution. Your mother didn't want you living life as a target. Especially if the most likely scenario was that you wouldn't develop any abilities, and she—"

"Stop." I broke away from her as denial rose like a swift shield. This couldn't be happening. Couldn't be real.

Clay reached for me, but I yanked away. My skin felt stretched too tight and I struggled to get enough oxygen as I stared at my aunt. Here was the one person I trusted most in this world—but no longer recognized.

"How could you do this?" My throat threatened to seal up. "After everything that happened back home, how could you look me in the eye and continue lying to me?"

Tears gathered in her eyes. "I wanted to tell you. I planned to, but I promised Anna—"

"*You promised me.*" I cried out, the rawness cracking my vocal cords. "No more secrets. Only the truth. Remember? How can I ever trust you again?"

Aunt Viv recoiled as if I had slapped her.

"Okay, now." Herrera held up both arms. "Let's all take a breath."

I felt lightheaded as the hallway swayed slightly, the world around me no longer stable. "I had a right to know the truth." My fists clenched. "About myself."

"You're right. You did," Aunt Viv said, the exhaustion of this life-long secret finally showing. "Your mother thought—"

"Stop blaming my mom for this," I yelled, even though it was my mom who'd given me the necklace in the first place. But logic wasn't my friend right now. "*You're* the one who drugged me."

"But it was *her* idea," Aunt Viv shouted back, her composure cracking. "You think I wanted this? Wanted to parent my sister's only child? When I had no idea how to raise you. You think I wanted that?" She flung her arms out. "You think I wanted *this* life?"

I flinched back, tears clogging my throat.

Shock splashed across Aunt Viv's face as if she couldn't believe what she'd just said. "I'm sorry." She shook her head. "I didn't mean that."

"Yes," I whispered. "You did."

One of the doors to the medical bay clattered open and a small figure in a baggy shirt and sweatpants stumbled out into the hall, overriding everything else. What the hell?

Raine and Clay were the first to jump into action, racing down the hallway toward a staggering and disoriented Asher. The rest of us were not far behind when a wave of heat blasted through the hall, flaring across my skin like a heat lamp on high. Flinching back, I threw up an arm on instinct as if I could block out the radiating inferno.

Asher braced himself against the wall as he shuffled forward, leaving a trail of scorched handprints in his wake.

Not good.

"Don't touch him." Raine held her arms out to ward us off. "Clay, get the welding gloves. I'll grab a sedative."

As they disappeared into the medical bay, we kept a safe distance from Asher—and his Pyro-Prints. What had gone wrong? Only two days ago he'd been fine. Why was he having another flare-up now? Or had it been a false positive, and the Stabilizers weren't actually working on him after all?

Raine and Clay re-emerged from the medical bay, a set of thick gloves on his hands and an EpiPen in hers. They approached Asher cautiously but he let out a delirious groan and frantically backed away from their advances. The air sizzled with heat as the singed IV line swung wildly around his arm. How would they even get close to him? Their advances only seemed to antagonize him more. He was like a wary predator afraid to be caged. At this rate, I was afraid he'd end up hurting himself or someone else in his efforts to get away.

I desperately looked around. Back on Mom's worst days during her fever dreams, it always helped to calm her if she had something to ground herself in the moment. But I didn't know how to do that for Asher... That's when he looked toward me, a flare of recognition lit up his panic-filled eyes.

I stepped forward. "Hey. It's okay."

A surge of heat lashed out at the movement. My body recoiled from the warning, but I couldn't give up.

Aunt Viv made a noise at the back of her throat and reached for me.

"Let me try." I waved her off. "I think I can get through to him."

I was also the reason he was having these elemental flare-ups in the first place. If talking him down was the only way I could help him now, I would accept the risk of the burns.

Commander Herrera stepped forward. "I can't allow that—"

"Let her try." Clay cut him off. "I've seen her get through to him before."

Not waiting any longer, I faced Asher and raised my hands slowly. "It's okay. I won't hurt you, remember?" I echoed the words from our very first encounter. "We all just want to help you. But it's your choice, okay?" I held his gaze. "All of this is your choice."

After a tense moment that felt like a lifetime, Asher nodded.

"Okay." I gestured to Clay and Raine. "Will you please let us help you?"

Another long moment later, Asher nodded again, weaving on his feet.

With that, Clay swooped in with his welding gloves to keep him from losing his balance as Raine carefully delivered the sedative. A relief-filled groan escaped Asher's lips as his body went limp in Clay's arms. Then Clay lowered him gently to the floor, making sure only the gloves touched his skin.

I crouched down next to him. "You're going to be okay," I promised as his eyes drifted shut. But in reality, I didn't know if that was true, did I? I had no clue if he would be okay or not.

"Good job, Emma." Clay stared down at a now resting Asher, exhaustion claiming his innocent features.

"Is this because of the Stabilizers?" I asked. "I thought they were working."

"We did, too." Raine knelt down on Asher's other side and checked his pulse. "But this can happen with new variants devised by the Clinic. We just need time to tweak the Stabilizer formula to match." Her uncertain tone did very little to instill confidence.

"Let's get him back in bed and checked out." Commander Herrera infused a calm steadiness back into the hallway. "Then we'll need to alert Sage to this new development."

As Clay and Raine made their way back to the medical bay with Asher, I couldn't help but wonder if this would be me one day. Without the suppressor I'd been deceived into wearing, would I now require Stabilizers too? And with my Halfbreed-misfit-genes, they might not be able to configure a formula for me. Where would that leave me?

An overwhelming wave of helplessness washed over me as I struggled to process it all. It was too much. I needed to get out of here—needed time and space.

My legs trembled as I backed away.

"Wait, Emma." Aunt Viv reached for me again. "We still need to talk."

"Don't." My voice caught, broke a little. "Stay away from me."

Aunt Viv stopped, hurt clearly written across her face. But I didn't care.

Everything became a blur as my feet moved before I knew what I was doing. Voices called out behind me, but I barely heard them over the thundering of my heart as I walked away.

***

Knocks on my door came and went. I didn't answer them. Didn't even acknowledge them. I didn't trust myself to face anyone at the moment. I was afraid I might have a complete meltdown if I did, and who wanted an audience for that?

I lay in bed and stared at the ceiling, seeing nothing.

Suppressor. The word chased me while I slept. Chased me while I was awake. It hounded me as I pulled the covers closer. How was this possible? How could Aunt Viv—and Mom—do this to me?

Also, what did it mean for me? Could I have abilities that were suppressed? And more importantly, was I now a walking time bomb? Ticking down until the lack of a Stabilizer went off and I was the one wandering the halls burning things down—or whatever it was that I could potentially do.

None of it felt real. And I struggled to face it. So, instead I simply sank deeper into my covers and drifted off as my world collapsed all around me.

35

My open sketchbook rested against my propped-up legs. My leather-bound happy place—or rather, what had once been my happy place. Right now? Not so much.

Earlier I'd been chased awake by nightmares of shrouded soldiers, blood-stained ice, and a blazing hydrant of flames hurtling toward me. Then I'd struggled to fall back asleep, but after two days of hibernating that didn't happen. And when unrelenting boredom had hit, I'd reached for my sketchbook, hoping for an ink-filled escape. But it never came. The fresh page I'd opened earlier sat untouched, and the pen in my hand unused.

Exhaling harshly, I removed the photograph I'd hidden in the back pocket. It was the main reason I'd grabbed the sketchbook when we fled our home. That, and the smattering of art clippings from my mom's studio that I'd also stored in the back pocket. And sure, it would've sucked to lose my favorite doodle-diary, but I could've replaced it—not the picture in my hand or the art clippings. They were the few things I had left of my mom. Those and the broken necklace on my bedside table. But I still couldn't bring myself to look at it.

Instead, I stared down at the slightly crinkled snapshot. It had been a happy day. One of Mom's good days. Only a ten-minute drive from our house in Carnelian Bay, Kings Beach was a funky little beach town on the North Shore of Lake Tahoe and one of Mom's favorite getaways. We had spent the whole day there, building sandcastles, splashing in the cool water, and soaking up the summer sun.

The picture had been taken toward the end of our beach day. We'd just overloaded on Mom's favorite sprinkled doughnuts—because any hour was doughnut hour. The three sun-kissed faces smiling up at me were a reminder of all the laughs and fun we'd shared that day. On the right, Aunt Viv stood with her straw hat and green cover-up, her tablet gripped down at her side. Sandwiched in the middle, a younger version of myself stood in a pineapple one-piece with the biggest smile on my face. I looked so carefree—unaware of all the lies and secrets to come.

I felt like I didn't know myself anymore. And to be honest, I felt like I didn't know my mom either. The person I thought I'd known was an illusion that kept shifting like quicksand, and now what remained was a stranger.

I swallowed down the prickly cactus stuck in my throat as I focused on the last face in the picture. Mom sported her paint-splattered white crop top, jean shorts, and a high bun of golden-brown hair. Her smile distracted from the exhaustion under her eyes, while the day's fresh suntan helped disguise the injection points marking her body.

For the millionth time, I questioned if it was possible that she was still alive? She had been so sick during those last few months that it hadn't been hard to believe the illness had gotten her in the end. But if a Recall Team had recaptured her, then the Clinic probably had the technology and proper treatments to save her.

The image grew blurry as I slid the picture carefully back home and set my sketchbook aside. Then I finally looked at my once precious keepsake on the bedside table. I didn't want to believe that the suppressor had been my mom's idea, but I couldn't deny the logic. Ever since she had placed the thing around my neck, I'd rarely taken it off. It had come to feel like a critical part of myself. And both my mom and my aunt had known that, and had used that against me.

Cautiously I picked up the broken chain, the sun charm dangling in the air. Turning it around, I examined the achingly familiar gold charm from a new perspective. That's when I spotted the tiny pinholes, one at each of the sun's points. I'd always assumed they were just how the charm had been made, but now I wondered if this was how the suppressor worked.

I set the necklace back on the side table. I should just throw it away. Get rid of it. It wasn't like I'd ever wear the thing again. But as soon as I had the thought, the walls of the sparse dorm room closed in all around me.

Instead, I launched myself from the bed in desperate need of a change of scenery. I threw on a pair of running shorts and my favorite fleece sweatshirt, relieved to find it wasn't a full-blown struggle anymore. With all the snoozing I'd done, my healing wrist and body were doing much better, which was good news for my checkup tomorrow.

I snagged my fob before heading for the door. Wonderful silence greeted me in the hallway, but halfway to the stairs, the cool concrete registered under my bare feet. Right, shoes. Sighing, I glanced back, but continued on—already gone too far.

I entered the stairwell with no specific destination in mind, just knowing that if I stayed in my room any longer, I'd go mental. I only hoped I didn't run into anyone along the way to wherever I ended up. Looking up, I thought of the peaceful rooftop jungle. The idea of fresh air sounded rejuvenating, but shorts didn't seem like appropriate outerwear for a nighttime stroll.

Down it was. I took the concrete steps one at a time, passing the mysterious third floor before pausing at the training wing door. The yoga studio called to me. I could go for a calming stretch right now. I fobbed the sensor and opened the door, only to freeze. Aunt Viv's voice funneled through the open slot in the door. Out of everyone at the Breakpoint, it had to be *her* on the other side of that door?

I definitely wasn't ready for a showdown with my aunt right now. I didn't think I could handle any more hits. I turned around, only to pause. *Up or down?*

The roof garden was still a no-go. The common room was, well, *common*. Breaking Grounds was closed at this hour, and even if it wasn't I was pretty sure they had a shoe policy and, you know, a purchase requirement. I could—

Aunt Viv's muffled voice grew closer.

Crap.

I descended the stairs quickly, my bare feet slapping off the concrete treads. At the first-floor landing, I stopped to listen just as the training wing door clanged open.

"—it's not looking good." Commander Herrera's voice boomed into the stairwell. "I've sent Sage to the compound to dig deeper into this and to keep things discreet, but honestly I'm not sure how much it'll help."

"Arc hasn't come across any updated Stabilizers from the Clinic?" Aunt Viv asked, drawing closer.

I didn't stop to think as I went down farther, moving as silently as I could before reaching the lowest level. I looked back up the stairs and held my breath.

"There's been no chatter of any," Herrera said. "We're searching for a miracle needle in the Clinical haystack, and time isn't exactly on Asher's side."

Footfalls descended for a tense moment.

"You think the kid's terminal then?" Aunt Viv asked.

"It's looking more and more likely." Herrera sounded defeated. "But there's still a chance Nova can find a lead on that tablet. Once we know more, we'll—"

The clap of a door above cut off their conversation, and silence consumed the stairwell.

Asher was terminal?

It would've been a kindness to leave him there.

Decker's words came back to haunt me. Maybe this was why Agent Todd had felt so confident about getting Asher back. If Arc couldn't figure out the proper Stabilizer formula, would they have to turn him back over to the Clinic if they wanted to save him?

My blood ran cold, as I probably didn't want to know that answer. As I placed my foot on the first step to head back up, I realized I had nowhere to go—wasn't that a perfect metaphor for my life right now.

I debated about my options when the tickling aroma of chlorine made me pause.

36

I stepped out of the stairwell and into the impressive aquatic center, the sound of lapping water greeting me. Wood-slat benches lined the perimeter, along with sleek towel stations and patches of greenery climbing the high concrete walls, while three aquatic areas occupied the large space. The first included a splash pad with multiple nozzles on the blue rubber surface. The second consisted of a shallow pool with two walk-in edges and legit sand coating the bottom. The third was an Olympic-sized swimming pool. Lights glowed from the tiled edges as black and white lane lines split the water.

A body glided along the surface of the far lane, executing an effortless freestyle as a fractured compass tattoo shifted in and out of the water.

So much for finding a solitary sanctuary.

I should leave—preferably before Kaden noticed me. Not only was I not good company, there was still a high chance of my emotions exploding everywhere right now.

But the idea of sitting in my room for another minute kept my bare feet glued to the floor. At least here, the only other person in the vicinity had his head bobbing in and out of the water, so there was that. I walked over and sat down on the edge of the pool a couple of lanes away. Hugging one knee to my chest, I rested my chin on it and dipped the other leg into the brisk water. The gentle surge against my calf made me miss the ocean. Miss home. But that part of my life was over, wasn't it?

With the Clinic still after us, it was clear we wouldn't be going back to Point Reyes. And I didn't know if I ever would. Maybe years from now, but not anytime soon. Claire would be long gone and probably have forgotten about me by then... But I couldn't dwell on that. I needed to focus on the future. My non-suppressor future—whatever that meant. I wondered if I would start lighting things on fire or accidentally burn whoever I touched like Asher had. I sent up a silent prayer hoping that never happened.

Of course, there was always the possibility that even without the suppressor I wouldn't develop any abilities, and I was freaking out over nothing. Well, not *nothing*, but—

"Here for a late-night swim?" Kaden's deep voice startled me. "If so, you're not really dressed for the occasion."

He floated in the next lane over, his arms thrown over the plastic rings. His dark hair dripped water onto his broad shoulders, and when he pulled off his goggles, rings marked the edges of his eyes.

Butterflies swarmed in my stomach. I still had no words for either an apology or my gratitude. Or at least none that seemed adequate.

"Not here to swim." I hugged my knee closer. "Just needed an escape from my room."

"You sure?" Kaden pushed his wet hair back. "I could probably find some floaties somewhere."

"I know how to swim, you jackass." Yep, such good company.

"Did you know it only takes three inches of water for someone to drown?" Kaden messed with the goggles in his bionic hand. "Just three inches. That's all it takes." He shrugged. "Always thought that was interesting."

"Good to know." I removed my leg from the water. My room had to be better than this, and clearly he wasn't in a receptive mood either.

I started to get up when Kaden said, "Trade?"

I sank back down on the pool edge.

"How's your wrist doing?" He twisted his around. "Mine's feeling just fine."

My lips tipped up for the first time in two days as I stuck my leg back into the water. "That's not a fair trade."

"How do you know? I could've hurt my wrist since the last time we saw each other." He grinned, but it didn't fully reach his eyes.

My stomach dipped. I didn't miss the playful glint those sea-blue depths usually held or the fact that he hadn't called me Firefly once since the Holding-Site-debacle. I absolutely did not miss either of those things. *Nope.* Not at all.

"It's better. I have a checkup tomorrow afternoon." I adjusted my brace. "Real trade? How's your forearm and back?"

"I might have some scars, but nothing I'm not used to." Kaden lifted his forearm, showing me where the ice shards from Hurricane-Griffin had struck. The faint pink skin looked much better, like miraculously so—that nifty Elementum healing at work—which made me think of his jawline. What had caused those scars? And why hadn't they healed like these? But it felt too personal to ask.

"Can I offer an altered trade?" I swished my leg through the water.

"Intriguing." Kaden lounged against the lane line. "Altered how?"

"All you have to do is listen." I snuggled deeper into my fleece.

Kaden sent me an arched expression.

"I wanted to say thank you for helping me the other night at the Holding Site, and I'm sorry for what Griffin said about your brother," I said, catching my hand halfway to my neck. "I just needed to tell you that, since I never got the chance earlier. So, thank you and I'm sorry." This was probably a good time to make my exit. "I'll leave you to your workout. I didn't mean to—"

"I'm sorry, too." Kaden locked eyes with me. "For what your aunt did. That was messed up."

My body tensed. How did... *Oh, right*. Raine had been in the audience for that particular life-altering event. She must have told him.

"Yeah." I glanced away. "I'm still processing it all."

Kaden nodded. "Are you going to do the blood panel?"

The blood panel. How could I have forgotten? I mean, sure, there'd been a lot going on, but still.

I shook my head. "I don't know."

"Why wouldn't you?" He tossed his goggles onto the tiled edge of the pool. "Are you afraid because of what happened to your mother? Or is it something else?"

My cheeks heated, remembering he had witnessed my minor freakout and must've put two and two together. "It's not so much that. Although, I guess that's easy to say when I'm not facing down a needle." I rubbed the crook of my arm. "And it'd be nice to know what to expect regarding abilities when the suppressor fully wears off. But I just... I don't know if I'm ready to know. Which is silly, isn't it? Knowing or not knowing won't change the facts."

"That's true." Kaden kicked his legs under the water. "But it's probably the emotional connection that's scaring you."

My brows pinched. "What do you mean?"

He shrugged. "It seems like you've built some sort of scale up inside your head, and now you're afraid to measure yourself against it."

Well, crap. Was he right? Was I afraid? Afraid to see that even after everything, I still didn't belong here. Because if I was really being honest with myself, I *did* want to belong here. And sure, the main reason had to do with my mom and finding out if she was still alive, but it was more than that. I couldn't fight this feeling that this was somehow the piece I'd been missing in my life all these years. The reason I'd always struggled to fit in.

But it felt like too much to hope for—and too crushing if it wasn't true.

"Whether you do the blood panel, or even have abilities or not," Kaden continued, "only you can control how it will affect you emotionally and how you move forward."

Not going to lie, being the one in control sounded nice. But I wasn't sure I had the strength to face it all just yet.

"What was it like when you first developed abilities?" I unclasped my knee and lowered it to the tiled edge in a half butterfly pose. "Was it difficult to control?"

"It was difficult to control at first." Kaden stared out over the lanes. "The genetic alterations the Clinic makes to create an Elementum are tied to the hormonal and molecular changes the body goes through at puberty. So, every time my emotions or hormones spiked, I lashed out with ice. At one point, my Handler had to isolate me completely because he was afraid I might accidentally hurt my family. But eventually I got the hang of it." His jaw flexed, making his scars stand out. "The Clinic made sure of it."

A shudder went through me. "The Clinic held your whole family?"

Kaden shook his head. "Just me and my brother. My parents weren't allowed into the Summit, only to the Holding Sites to visit us from time to time."

No wonder his brother meant so much to him; they'd gone through hell together. But if his parents weren't held by the Clinic, did that mean...

"Your parents are Neutrals?" If so, that meant he hadn't always been a part of this world.

"They were." Kaden nodded, staring out across the lanes. The soft sorrow in his voice made me want to wrap my arms around him—but again, too personal. "When I was fourteen, Arc extracted us during one of our Holding Site visits, but my mom got caught in the crossfire and was killed. We ended up losing my dad not long after that."

My heart sank. He must have lost his brother about two years later then. And now he was all alone.

"I sometimes forget you're new to all this," Kaden said, clearly done talking about that subject. "It's..."

"Annoying?" I offered up.

"Refreshing." His lips tipped up slightly.

Could've been worse. I was like mountain air. Or toothpaste. "Well, if you need another dose, the Summit is one of the Detainment Hubs, right? What are the others?"

"Yes, it's one of three." Kaden lifted the lane line and glided into my lane. "The Summit is concealed within the Rockies here in Colorado. The Pinnacle, or the Pin, is hidden deep in the Catskills in New York. And the Crest is the founding facility and the only Hub that Arc doesn't know the precise location, but we're pretty sure it's somewhere near the original site in Silicon Valley." He leaned back against the tiled edge next to my submerged leg. "Supposedly it's where the Clinic performs their highly experimental studies."

That made sense with my mom somehow being involved in the Horizon Project. But what didn't? Silicon Valley was only a few hours away from Point Reyes. Why would Aunt Viv choose to live so close? It seemed extremely risky... unless she'd always believed Mom was still alive and was being detained there. Maybe Aunt Viv was the reason for the three question marks at the end of the Phoenix file.

"It's rumored that the Crest holds information damning enough to take down the entire Clinic," Kaden added, gliding a hand over the water. "But that feels like a pipe dream."

After everything I'd learned and my brief experience in that glass cage, I could understand why he felt that way. It seemed like an unbeatable fight.

"If you know where the other two Hubs are, why not infiltrate them?"

"All the Hubs are highly secure, remote facilities. Protected by the best security systems and divisions of expertly trained Enforcers. It'd basically be a suicide mission."

Facing off with one Enforcer had been challenging enough—and would have been downright impossible if Kaden hadn't shown up. I couldn't imagine facing an entire division.

"All these questions," he said, "makes me wonder if you're thinking about sticking around."

"I don't think I get a vote." I gripped the pool edge. "Although, that could change if I end up having abilities, right? They wouldn't kick out an untrained Halfbreed, would they?" My chest rose and fell rapidly—too rapidly. "Oh, crap. What if they do? And I can't control the abilities I have? Most Elementums learn when they're younger, right? What if I can't figure it out? And will I need to take Stabilizers now? What if they can't formulate one because of my weird Halfbreed genetics? Will I have to keep using the suppressor to—"

"Breathe, Firefly." Kaden reached up and gripped my chin gently, our eyes locking. "Just breathe."

I inhaled deep a few times as the calloused hand against my skin helped ground me back to the tiled edge.

"There you go." Water dripped down his outstretched arm. "Don't worry, we'll figure this out."

"We will?" I breathed.

Kaden dropped his hold. "Of course. Everyone here at the Breakpoint will help you out."

My stupid heart stumbled. *Right*, not just him. That made more sense.

"Of course," I repeated lamely, plastering on a smile. "All my new friends."

"Plus, you can't be any worse than Saylor when she started out. I heard she flooded her room multiple times."

I narrowed my stare. "Helpful."

Kaden shrugged, a smirk finally lighting up his eyes.

"At least Saylor will help me if I accidentally light something on fire. She'd probably volunteer as my own personal fire extinguisher." Which might not be a bad idea. Or I could just start carrying one around.

"I'm wounded, Firefly. You make it sound like I'm not even allowed to apply for the job." Kaden placed a hand over his bare chest. "I've always dreamed of being a personal fire extinguisher."

"Uh-huh, sure." I waved a dismissive hand. "You'd probably sit back with a bowl of popcorn and say *let it burn*."

"That sounds an awful lot like a challenge." Kaden grinned. "I guess I'll just have to prove my skills."

My muscles locked up. "What are y—"

One second I was perched on the edge of the pool, and the next a soft, rubbery hand grabbed my uninjured arm and yanked me forward. I hit the brisk surface with a yelp. Water rushed up all around us as we both plummeted under. When we reached the bottom, I pushed off of a solid chest and propelled myself back up, resurfacing with a fit of coughs.

Kaden emerged a moment later, shaking his head like a dog. Water went flying as I treaded water, glaring daggers at him.

"See? Putting fires out already." Kaden let out a full-body laugh, accompanied by a heart-wrenching smile—one that could steal hearts and never give them back. "Firefly, you look—"

I splashed water at him. "If you say a drowned rat, you'll regret it."

Kaden chuckled. "What I was going to say before I was so rudely splashed, is you—"

"Rudely splashed?" Laughter burst from me as I sent another wave of water at him, which he effortlessly blocked. "You're the one who pulled me into the pool. Or has all that chlorine affected your brain?"

Kaden gently grasped my unbraced wrist, stopping the onslaught of water and pulling me closer. He wrapped an arm around the small of my back to help keep me afloat as that minty cologne enveloped me. "You really should choose your fights more carefully." He ran his thumb over the center of my captured wrist, sending shivers down my spine. "Picking a fight with a Hydro in a pool? Not the smartest idea."

"Probably not." I tried not to focus on how little space there was between us or the heat rolling off his body. I wanted to physically push back from the building intensity while simultaneously wanting to climb closer. It was the oddest sensation.

Then Kaden released my wrist. And I'm not sure what came over me next. Maybe it had something to do with my life basically imploding? But my hand had a mind of its own. I reached up and slid my hand around the nape of his neck, drawing his head down and closing the small distance between us. The soft contact of our lips meeting jolted my system until I realized Kaden was... just floating there as if he was in shock.

I pulled back, hitting an unyielding arm. My heart fluttered like an ensnared hummingbird. "I'm not sure what that was."

A blistering heat consumed me as I fully considered the advantages of drowning when Kaden reacted. His hand tangled into my wet hair, and he captured my lips with his own. He pulled me closer while my legs unconsciously wrapped around his waist, eradicating what little space remained.

Underneath my palm, Kaden's body hummed with confined power, eliciting a gasp from me. He seized the opportunity by tilting his head and deepening the kiss, causing all thoughts to evaporate like fog being claimed by the sun.

Vaguely I felt him move us through the water before being pressed back against the pool wall. The tile bit into my back. But I didn't care as I nipped at his lower lip, earning a deep growl from the back of his throat. My hand slid into his wet, silky hair as the frenzied kiss began to slow, transforming into something different—something softer. The sweetness of it all flowed through me like nothing else I'd ever experienced before, which was a little frightening.

Softly releasing my lips, Kaden skimmed his nose across my cheek and the world slowly came back online. A cold sensation dotted my temple, followed shortly by another. My eyes blinked open. Was that snow?

Tiny white crystals drifted down, turning the aquatic center into a winter wonderland. Mesmerized, I reached out and caught a few flakes on my palm. But then I caught sight of Kaden's shoulder. A faint glow surrounded his profile. It was the same one I'd seen around Clay at our last training session, but this time it was accompanied by a... warm, low-level hum that flared out from my chest. I wasn't sure if this was just an escalation of my pattern-tracking or maybe it was an ability coming through. Wouldn't that be just my luck. Others could create a firestorm while I got stuck with heartburn.

Then I looked up at Kaden and the relevance of it all faded away. His face locked down right before my eyes, making my heart stall. In an effortless move, he lifted me up and onto the pool edge.

"I can't do this." His jaw flexed. "Not with you. I'm sorry."

Ice blasted my chest as I searched his gaze only to find genuine honesty shining back at me. Emotion clogged my throat and the blistering heat from earlier returned with a vengeance. Was this really happening?

"I'm truly sorry." Kaden pushed back from the pool wall. "I think you should go."

Too shocked and embarrassed to do anything else, that's exactly what I did. I left, not caring that I was completely soaked as my numb feet carried me away.

37

The eucalyptus-and-citrus scent of the medical bay helped to calm my racing mind. I adjusted my position on the exam table, the paper crinkling under the tactical pants that I'd paired with my *bee kind* tank top.

I hadn't seen anyone yet, which was odd. Usually I saw one person here or there, if not more, but not today. Where was everyone? Although it was probably for the best. It gave me a chance to compose myself. I wasn't sure which was worse: facing down the panic-inducing needle or facing Raine after last night's unexpected swim.

After leaving a trail of water back to my room, I'd spent the night struggling to process that I'd actually kissed Kaden. That he'd kissed me back—and then he'd shut it all down spectacularly.

I cringed as his rejection crashed back into me. There were boatloads of potential reasons behind it—possibly dating Raine, the Hydros-only-dated-Hydros thing, me being a temporary transplant here. The list went on and on. But what did it matter? It wouldn't change anything. The sincerity in his eyes said as much.

And honestly? It had only been one kiss—which was the most frustrating part. *One kiss.* That had felt, sure, incredible. I could admit that to myself. But the fact that my emotions were all out of whack due to one kiss was crazy. Unacceptable. And, unfortunately, hard to change.

Because that's how emotions worked, wasn't it? They weren't always logical or negotiable.

"Hey, you're already here." Raine startled me as she strode over to the set of cabinets in the corner. Her light green scrubs rustled with her movements while her long blonde ponytail swished behind her. "Let me grab my stuff and we can get started."

I plastered on a smile. "I was hoping to do the blood panel too, if the offer is still good?"

"Of course." She smiled, removing a pressure cuff and stethoscope from a drawer. "I'll get the supplies for that then."

As she disappeared through the door, I exhaled an unsteady breath. The inside of my arm tingled in nervous anticipation, but the needle pricking would be worth it. Worth facing my fears. Worth getting some answers. Because Kaden had been right last night: Only I could control how all this would affect me emotionally and how I would move forward. And moving forward, I already knew I needed to stay at Arc to find answers about my mom. But to do that I needed to arm myself with proof that I belonged, and a blood panel showing I had abilities seemed like a surefire way.

Raine returned with a caddy full of vials, cotton balls, and nightmares. "How's everything been healing so far?"

"Good, I think." I diverted my eyes, afraid if I looked too long at the caddy, I'd lose my nerve. "But I guess we'll find out."

"True." Raine set her supplies on the counter next to me. "I'll do a quick vitals check and examine your wrist first, then we can do the bloodwork."

She got busy checking my temperature, heart, and blood pressure. Then she poked around the scab on my temple. "This is healing up really nicely."

I tried my best to sit still. "The ointment really helped."

"I know, right? That stuff is magic." Raine pushed her glasses up the bridge of her nose. "All right, let's see the wrist."

My stomach dipped as I released the damp straps. I had tried my best to dry the soaked brace, but it seemed the wet nylon was determined to expose my foolishness. I held out my wrist for inspection and spent the next few moments trying to convince myself there was no way Rainy-Day could know about my unexpected swim. Tried to, and epically failed as she twisted and prodded my sprained limb. But in the end, if she knew, she played it super cool. Unfazed. Secure. Which for some reason bothered me even more—okay, *fine*, I knew the reason. But none of that mattered now.

"Your wrist is mending really well, too." Raine's delicate brows pinched. "Like surprisingly so."

"I've been taking the recovery seriously." I tucked a strand of hair behind my ear as her frown deepened. "Or maybe it wasn't as sprained as we originally thought."

"That's possible," she said, but it didn't sound like she believed it. "Well, the good news is you should be safe to ease back into normal activities as long as you continue wearing the brace while it finishes healing, especially during training. That one is non-negotiable."

I strapped the brace back on, relieved to be one step closer to removing the daily reminder of my screwup.

"Now for the fun part." Raine retrieved the caddy full of nightmares.

Not exactly the word I would've used, but I let that go as I reminded myself it would be worth it.

"Just let me know when it's over." I looked anywhere else. The last thing I needed right now was to add passing out to my list of accomplishments lately. *Worth it. Worth it. Worth it.* But as I felt a cold swipe at the crook of my arm and the tightening of a tourniquet, I started hyperventilating.

"You okay?" Raine asked from what sounded like a room away.

"Yeah." I gave her a thumbs up for good measure—because I was a dork—and focused instead on what I'd overheard in the stairwell last night. "How's Asher?"

Raine hesitated. "He's stable right now."

I swallowed hard. "Have there been any more flare-ups?"

"A few," she said, but her tone told me it had been more than a few.

"He'll continue to have more unless we can find a proper Stabilizer or formulate one, right?" I tried to ignore the biting sting that flared along my arm. "How long does he have?"

Raine avoided my gaze. "I'm not really supposed to discuss it."

"Please, I need to know. I'm the one who took him from that van. I'm the reason he's..." *Dying.* "In this mess."

To my surprise, she answered. "At his age, Asher requires a weekly dosage, and without the proper Stabilizer, he's declining rapidly. We're keeping him under sedation to help with the strain on his body. But he can only withstand this for a few more days, a week tops."

My stomach twisted. A few days was a blink. A flash. A mere multitude of hours.

"There's still a chance," Raine assured me while also seeming to convince herself. "And you're the reason he's free from the Clinic and their dangerous experiments." She squeezed my other arm. "When you're weighing everything out, don't forget that part. It counts for a lot."

I nodded, even though it felt hollow.

Not long after, Raine taped a cotton ball to the bend of my arm before carrying the vials over to the counter.

"How long will it take to get the results?" I flexed my pin-cushioned arm.

"We have all the lab equipment here." Raine pulled a Sharpie from the drawer, marking up the labels. "And since we're still on fall break, it should only take a few days."

Funny how, in that context, a few days seemed like an eternity now, but it was the same amount of time Asher was fighting against.

Raine handed me a small packet of crackers. "They'll help keep you from fainting."

"Thanks." I popped open the airplane-sized bag and diligently ate the salty-sweet snack. I reflected on the fact that I'd actually made it through the blood draw—and didn't pass out. So, bright side?

Raine started collecting her equipment. "So, you were with Kaden?"

"What?" I jolted in my seat, the remaining crackers jumping in the bag. I weighed the risk of fainting if I bolted from the room right now. The flutter that filled my head confirmed that the risk was high.

"Before the agent found you the other night, you were with him, right?" Raine said.

Right. She meant before the Holding Site. "Yeah."

"Raine." A muffled voice sounded out in the hallway.

Raine set down the stethoscope and opened the door to find Clay searching the wing. "Clay, what's wrong?"

"I needed—" Clay stopped short when he spotted me. "Sorry. I didn't realize you were busy."

"We were just finishing up." Raine adjusted her glasses. "What did you need?"

With a glance at me, Clay continued. "Herrera wants to speak with you."

Raine straightened. "Is this about Nova cracking the Clinic tablet?"

My spine straightened at this newsflash. Then my eyes narrowed as I wondered why she was saying this in front of me.

Clay nodded. "Can you head to the third floor when you're through?"

"I'll check on Asher first"—Raine snagged the caddy—"then head up for prep."

Prep for what? Did it have anything to do with the information Nova retrieved from the tablet?

Raine headed for the door, only to stop and point at me. "Finish those crackers and give it fifteen minutes before you go anywhere, okay? And remember your brace."

My grip tightened on the bag. "Sure."

With that, Raine disappeared with my caddy full of answers.

"Good to see you out and about." Clay walked over to me. "You doing okay?"

I plucked out another cracker. "I'm all right."

But Clay didn't appear convinced, which was fair because, hey, he had witnessed what happened. Well, at least one half of the double whammy I'd been slapped with recently.

"Listen, Emma." He rubbed the back of his neck. "I know I wouldn't be your first choice, but if you ever need someone to talk to, I could, you know, be there in the room."

"Wow." I reached out a hand. "Do you think you're going to make it?"

Clay's brows snapped together. "What do you mean?"

"Because that looked painful." I couldn't stop my grin.

"Forget it." He glanced at the hallway, cheeks tinting.

I probably shouldn't have pressed his buttons like that, especially when he was only trying to help, but it felt nice to joke with him again.

"Thank you, Clay." I caught his arm. "Truly. I'm just not ready to talk about it yet." Which was true. I wasn't ready to airtime that emotional-raging-storm. But it reminded me of the emblem I needed to share. I dug into my pocket and pulled out a folded piece of paper. "But I do have something else for you."

With a curious look, Clay took it. "Where did you get this?"

Normally, I would've found his astonished expression hilarious, but the anxious energy humming inside me made that impossible. "I saw that emblem on the doctor's tablet at the Holding Site. It had the label 'Horizon Project' under it. I thought maybe it could be the project emblem."

"It's a possibility," he said, "but we'll need to dig a little deeper before we officially add it to the list." He held up the sketch. "Is it cool if I keep this?"

"Sure." I nodded, the original still safely tucked away in my room. "Do you think it will help with the search for Asher's Stabilizers?"

Clay slid the sketch into his pocket. "Maybe. I'll have Nova look into it now that she's back." He cleared his throat, glancing away. Was his face flushed? What was that about? "I need to get back—"

"To prep?" I suggested. "What are you prepping for?"

Clay hesitated.

"I know I've messed up and you're still upset with me—rightfully so." My heart rate accelerated. "But if this has anything to do with the information from the tablet I stole, then I've earned the right to know."

For a long moment, Clay stared at the hallway. "Meet me at my office in an hour."

38

I glanced down the silent hallway for the hundredth time while I waited, a charge of static electricity buzzing under my skin. It was probably the stress from the whole suppressor-surprise thing. That, or maybe an aftereffect of the bloodwork.

My mind still buzzed with Raine's question about me being out with Kaden the other night. Why had she brought it up? *Not* that I should care. Kaden had proven as much when he'd shut things down last night.

I peered across the corridor. The door plate of the too-familiar office gleamed in the fluorescent lights, forming an uneasy knot of guilt in my stomach. I wondered why we were meeting here. Did it have something to do with the Clinic tablet? Or was it something else?

"Over here."

I jumped at the sound of Clay's voice before spotting him coming around the corner. He wore his three-banded tactical gear and his face was set in hard lines as he gave me a beckoning wave. I followed him around the corner and to the stairwell. Apparently, this wasn't about anything in his office. But then, what were we doing?

We started climbing. His back was tense, making me think that bending the rules wasn't in Captain-Hard-Ass's comfort zone—*at all*. When we paused on the third-floor landing and he retracted his fob, I felt like we were seconds away from stealing the Commander's car and going for a joyride. Were we really going to the mysterious third floor?

"Come on." Clay ushered me through the door.

The hallway beyond was like any other in the Breakpoint—concrete floors, exposed ceilings, and brick walls—except this one had stretches of glass splitting the brick walls like showroom windows. At the first set of windows, I found a server room on one side. Banks of data towers were lined up like dominos as intricate patterns of lights flickered with productivity. Man, if Aunt Viv was here, she'd have a nerd-gasm.

Strike that. On the other side, the sea of high-tech computers was the thing of geek-tastic dreams. Aunt Viv would completely freak out over it all.

I winced at the thought. I really needed to stop avoiding her. I'd been successful at it so far, but it wouldn't last. And it couldn't, not if I wanted answers.

At the next stretch of glass, I discovered what appeared to be a lab. Microscopes, scales, beakers, and other various instruments were spread throughout the interior. This must have been the lab Raine had referred to, and somewhere in this cutting-edge labyrinth were vials of my blood waiting to be tested.

A shiver cascaded over my body before I scrambled after Clay, my running shoes squeaking on the concrete. I caught up to him just as he fobbed himself into one of the far display rooms, and I stalled out.

Holy war rooms.

It suddenly became clear what they were prepping for.

"This is the armory." Clay led the way into the large space.

Racks and glass safes lined the perimeter, each filled with supplies and weapons. There were some I recognized—or that were pretty self-explanatory—but I had no clue what many of them were or what they did. But based on the geometric Arc symbols etched into the frames of certain safes and racks, it was easy to guess which Elementums belonged to which equipment and sources.

I approached the massive center island. "Why are we here?"

"That's something I would like to know as well." Commander Herrera's authoritative voice echoed behind us, causing my spine to straighten.

Crap.

Well, this was a short-lived field trip.

"Emma deserves to be involved," Clay said.

Herrera's brows shot skyward—which made two of us.

"With the prep anyway," he added. "This is only possible because of her quick thinking."

My chest warmed at the vote of confidence.

"Is that so?" Herrera crossed his arms over his barrel chest, the four silver bands on the sleeve of his tactical gear standing out with the motion.

"As Team Lead for this mission, I get to decide who's involved." Clay widened his stance as if he was going into battle. "I'll personally double-check all her work."

After a tense moment, Herrera nodded, a glint of what appeared to be respect shining in his eyes. "Make sure you do."

With one last nod in my direction, Herrera strode from the room, leaving me stunned—but also a little disappointed that he wasn't there to talk to me about the Arc Council's decision. Another reason to stop avoiding Aunt Viv.

I breathed deep. "Thanks for that."

Clay shrugged. "It was only the truth. But that's if you still want to help out. It's completely your choice."

I looked around the armory. "What exactly am I helping prep for?"

"An infiltration mission." Clay picked up a piece of paper showing a map with two starred locations. "Thanks to the information Nova salvaged from the tablet that didn't get corrupted, we have a lead on another Clinic site."

I studied the map. "Why are there two locations marked?"

"Nova found two," Clay said. "But based on today's scouting, it looks like only one of them is active. The good news is it appears to be a Supply Site."

"So, you think the Stabilizers for Asher could be there?" Was this the chance Raine had referred to earlier?

"It looks promising. Especially now that we know what to look for."

"What do you mean?"

"The Clinic usually labels their vials with the project emblems, so the one you gave me earlier can help us identify the right Stabilizers faster." Clay stared intently at the map before adding quietly, "If they're there at all."

Any hope I had deflated like a punctured balloon. Clay was right; there was a chance the proper Stabilizers weren't even being held there. Would the team try the other site? Or would they rely on Sage to formulate a treatment in time?

"What about the other site?" I swallowed hard. "Will you investigate it?"

"There's too slim a chance that anything was left there." Clay tapped one of the starred locations. "This is our best bet."

But if Asher's life was on the line, a slim chance was still a chance.

"Trainee cuties, reporting for duty." Saylor gave Clay a mock salute as she and Reed sauntered into the armory. Like Clay, they were both clothed head to toe in tactical gear—only they were the band-less Trainee version. It seemed like everyone at the Breakpoint was going.

My nervous energy returned with a vengeance. I hadn't seen the Dynamic-Duo since our last visit to Breaking Grounds when all the secrets between us had started.

Clay arched a brow. "May I remind you both that you're still on suspension. The only reason you're being permitted to join tonight's mission is because of the shortage of team members."

Saylor fell silent.

"We completely understand." Reed ushered her over to a rack of tactical belts.

"What's the rush, then?" I looked over at Clay. If they didn't have enough team members, why not wait? Not that I didn't believe in Saylor or Reed, but they were still only Trainees.

"The Clinic will consider the Holding Site the tablet was stolen from to be compromised and potentially halt the others in the area for a time." Clay returned the map to its identical stack before turning to me. "Thus, the accelerated timeframe."

Maybe that was why the other site Nova had found was no longer active. What if the Clinic was already shutting this one down? I resisted the impulse to push them all out the door. Every second that ticked by was wasted time that the Clinic could be shutting down that site.

"Let's get you started on some tasks," Clay said. For the next few minutes, he went over what I needed to do, which mainly involved counting out and organizing medical supplies. I focused on every detail as if I would be tested on it later.

"I need to go check on some things. If you complete your tasks, feel free to help out Saylor or Reed." Clay sent a hard look to the Dynamic-Duo before adding, "I'll be back to review *everyone's* work in a little bit."

Then he slipped out the door, leaving the three of us alone in a room that totally required adult supervision.

After a tense moment, I asked, "So, was this what you guys were hiding?"

"Not the whole time." Reed looked remorseful as he laid out several tactical belts on the island. "But Clay ordered us to keep the information between team members only."

"We wanted to tell you." Saylor fidgeted with her gear rings. "But he threatened further suspension, and—"

"It's cool." I smiled at them. "Water under the bridge."

Saylor returned my smile.

"How are you holding up?" Reed asked, concern filling his eyes.

Right. News around the Breakpoint was like a secret in a sorority—uncontainable.

"Honestly, I'm still trying to process it all." I lined up the rolls of gauze.

"Understandable." Reed nodded. "What your aunt did was jacked up."

"Super jacked up." Saylor shook her head, making her ponytail of sunset-tipped braids sway. "Who knew that was even possible?"

My brows pinched. "What do you mean?"

"Arc doesn't have suppressors in their arsenal." Reed shrugged. "Although, I guess that makes sense considering we're not about limiting others like the Clinic."

"Heinous, conniving bastards." Saylor leaned her elbows on the counter. "Oh, but hey, look at it this way, now your opportunities for Say-and-ReRe-time have increased exponentially." She spread her arms wide. "Like possibly endlessly."

Reed looked skyward as if he were praying for understanding.

"What?" Saylor sent him a confused look.

I smiled, appreciating her unique way of looking at the positive. "Well, hopefully that happens regardless of whether I develop abilities."

"Hear, hear!" Saylor lifted a belt like she was making a toast.

With a shared laugh, we got back on track with prepping while also catching up on everything. *Well,* almost everything. I left out a certain late-night swim—too embarrassed to utter the words out loud—but filled them in on the Phoenix file and what I'd learned about Asher. Unfortunately, like me they had more questions than answers, but it was great getting back on the same page as them.

The evening slipped away, and soon the team started to gather, a buzz of anticipation in the air. Raine was the first to pop in and double-check all the medical gear. Only she could make a tactical outfit look like it belonged on the cover of a magazine, the single forest-green threaded band around her sleeve signaling her Rookie medic role. I spent the next few minutes showing her everything I had laid out, and I was doing fine until Clay returned with a certain Hale-Storm in tow.

Crap.

My pulse accelerated as I kept my eyes trained on the supplies in front of me, resisting the impulse to dive behind the island. I knew I'd have to face Kaden eventually, but that didn't mean I was ready to do it now.

"Thanks for the help," Raine said.

"Of course." I forced a smile.

"Now, if you don't mind packing it all into this?" She offered me a black backpack with forest-green accents. "Oh, and this too." She slid a worn leather tool roll across the counter.

"Wow." I genuinely smiled, touching the soft leather. "This reminds me of a case I used to have, but lost in a move—but of course, it held sketching pens, not medical tools."

"Well, I'm glad for its current occupants. I'd be useless with the pen and paper stuff." A smile lit her face and she glanced over at Kaden. "Just please be careful with it. It was a special gift."

My stomach hollowed. "Sure."

"Great, then we should be good to go." Raine nodded before leaving me to pack. As she passed Kaden on her way out, she gave his arm a light squeeze.

A hot, sticky sensation climbed up my throat as I swallowed back a curse. This was trouble. Not the gesture itself, that was innocent enough. No, what really bothered me was how hyper-aware of it I'd been. Shaking myself, I refocused on packing Rainy-Day's backpack. It was the healthier option compared to obsessing over special gifts and simple gestures that I had no business focusing on.

Suddenly, I caught the smell of mint as a box of Band-Aids and a can of antiseptic spray landed on the counter next to me.

"Don't forget these." Kaden's deep voice sent an unwelcome tingle traveling through my system. "No personal first aid kit is complete without them."

"Can't have that," I said dryly, but then I snagged the box and can to pack—not wanting to be completely childish. And because the reason for all the medical supplies was not lost on me. Raine had said it earlier: *Even the toughest of us need protecting.* What if one of them got hurt? The Clinic was capable of inflicting a lot of harm.

I let out a sigh. "Although, I'm kind of hoping no one will need these supplies tonight."

"Don't sell those little adhesive strips short." Kaden tapped the box. "I can always get creative and turn them into a makeshift weapon."

"Or use the spray like it's Clinic-Be-Gone." I jiggled the can of antiseptic spray.

His lips tilted up in a small grin, but it looked off.

An awkward silence took over. I grabbed the gauze rolls, feeling trapped between wanting to help out and regretting all my life choices lately.

"Listen, Emma." Kaden lowered his voice. "We should talk about last night."

My blood pumped like I was running a marathon—one I hadn't trained for or could handle right now. Much like the impending topic he wanted to discuss, but thankfully, Decker strolled into the room. *Wow.* If that wasn't a sign of dark times, I didn't know what was.

"Please tell me the Neut isn't coming with us." Decker spat the word like it tasted foul.

My fists clenched. I was pretty sure Dirt-Wad had already heard the news that was going around but was choosing to use the potentially-no-longer-accurate term, anyway. *Yep,* dark times indeed.

"Decker," Clay warned from across the island. "Emma won't be joining us. She'll be staying here with Asher and her aunt. Now, is Herrera ready for us?"

Jaw clenched, Decker nodded before pulling out his phone and stalking across the hall. Through the glass, I spotted Commander Herrera leaning over another impressive central island. But this one had a massive glowing screen in the middle that displayed a map.

Kaden turned back to me. "I—"

"You should get over there." I cut him off, jacking my thumb at the adjacent strategy room. "We'll talk later." *Like in fifty years.*

Doubt filled Kaden's eyes. "Okay. Later, then."

He prowled from the room as one by one the others followed him into the neighboring room while I stayed glued in place. Clearly this was a team-members-only meeting. So, here I was, stuck on my side of the glass looking in—yet another metaphor for my life. The urge to join and fight alongside them hit me hard. It was a foolish feeling, even I knew that, but it spread like a wildfire nonetheless—powerful and out of my control.

"Hey, Emma-bug," Aunt Viv said tentatively as she entered the armory. "Can we talk?"

39

Aunt Viv stood next to the massive center island wearing skinny jeans and her *my code is better than your code* T-shirt. She looked exactly the same since the last time I'd seen her. Which, for some reason, shocked me to my core. After the monumental bombshell, I expected her to look... I don't know, different. But maybe that was because I felt different.

"I know you're still upset," she said, her eyes seeking mine.

"No shit." I laughed without humor. If I'd cursed like that a few weeks ago, she would've gone ballistic. Now? Uncertainty clouded her features, which was smart considering the emotions that were rushing back to me. It was like I was back in that medical wing hallway again, the foundation of my life evaporating out from under me.

"I would be upset too if the tables were turned," she added. "But we need to talk."

Yes, we did. I recognized that. But doing so while I was in a rage wouldn't help anyone.

"I know what we did was wrong, keeping all this from you." Aunt Viv glanced down, her lips thinning. "It was a tough situation for everyone involved, with intricate decisions that sometimes require time and experience to understand. But if you give me a chance, I think you'll find we had our reasons."

I was so sick of hearing these kinds of excuses. *It's too complicated. You don't understand the Elementum world.* Well, that's because I'd never been given the chance to. What about *my* chance?

"That won't make it right, I know that, but there's—" Aunt Viv peeked over at the others across the hallway before lowering her voice. "There's a great deal about this world that you don't understand."

"Because of you," I whispered harshly.

"And your mother." There was no heat behind her words. "I'm not trying to lay the blame solely on her, because we both know that's not true and I'm done with the lying."

I wanted to believe her, almost desperately so. Like a compulsion to find a harbor in this endless storm.

"When we were younger, Anna was captured by the Clinic. And as the years passed, we assumed the worst." She swallowed hard. "*I* assumed the worst. So, when she finally contacted me, I was just so relieved to find out that she was still alive that I think... Looking back now, I think I allowed it to cloud my judgment."

Aunt Viv's gaze was lost in the past. "After we moved to Carnelian Bay, Anna made me swear to keep you away from all this. And for right or for wrong, I did." She shook her head. "Then she got sick."

I balled my fists. "But it wasn't from cancer, was it? It was from not having the proper Stabilizers."

"Whatever the Clinic subjected her to made it so that she no longer responded to the Igniter Stabilizers." Tears formed in her eyes. "I tried to convince her to come back to Arc. That it was actually the safest place for all of us. But she... she wouldn't go back."

"Why?" I asked, even though the sinking feeling inside my chest told me I already knew the answer.

"Anna would've given anything for you to have a normal life." Aunt Viv's voice turned hoarse. "And in a way, she did. She knew that without the proper Stabilizers she would only get sicker, and that the longer we stayed in one place, the greater the chances were that the Clinic would find us. She knew the risks but chose to stay."

For me. To give me a home. A normal life.

A wave of nausea rolled through me.

She looked away. "It wasn't till close to the end that I found out about her intentions with the necklace and the suppressor oil."

"Dispersing from the pinholes at the sun charm's points."

"Yes, the oil was released in small daily doses so that it could be absorbed by your skin." Aunt Viv tapped her chest. "It was another sacrifice Anna was willing to make that I didn't agree with."

"Then why did you go through with it?" I asked, swallowing down the unpeeled pineapple lodged in my throat. "Why keep all the lies going?"

"I've wondered that myself a million times. I wanted to tell you. I planned to. But every time I tried," her voice wavered, "it felt like a betrayal to Anna and everything she tried to protect you from. It was the one thing she fought so hard for and entrusted to me after she was gone."

On a deeper level, I knew their protection only came from a place of love. But that didn't mean I agreed with how they'd gone about it. Or make the aftermath any easier to deal with.

"So, you betrayed me instead." I threw her own words at her. "Using the sentimental value of my mom's gift against me and drugging me in the process."

"You weren't the only one being drugged." Aunt Viv flung out her arms.

I frowned at her. "What do you mean?"

"With a limited supply of Stabilizers, I was forced to alternate between the two." Her jaw clenched. "The suppressor oil allowed me to go longer without the Stabilizers, but it was a trade-off. It severely weakened my abilities and was the reason I had to rely on my lighter when the Recall Team attacked us back home."

"That still doesn't excuse what you did." I crossed my arms, hugging myself tight.

"And if I could go back and do it differently, I would." Aunt Viv grasped my arms. "You are my niece and I love you, but I'm not perfect. And I've only ever wanted the best for you. Please believe me on that."

My throat threatened to close. They were simple words, but I hadn't realized until now how much I'd needed to hear them. But they didn't magically wipe away all the pain and lies or the fact that she had basically drugged me—*for years*.

I simply nodded, unable to utter the words *I believe you and I love you too*. Not yet, at least. There was still too much left that needed healing.

Hurt filled Aunt Viv's face; clearly that wasn't the response she had hoped for. "I understand I'll need to earn your forgiveness, but we'll find our way through this, like we always have." She squeezed my arms before stepping back. "Especially once we get back on the road tomorrow."

"What?" I straightened.

"Now that you know what's going on, it'll make it so much easier to hide this time." She continued, seeming lost in thought. "I can find another consulting job and you can finish your GED. We can even figure out a way for you to go to college. It'll have to be online, of course, but—"

"We can't leave."

Aunt Viv frowned. "Of course, we can."

Everything suddenly felt like it was slipping away: the search for answers about my mom and whether she was still alive, all the training I still needed to do, and all the new friends I didn't want to lose. I didn't want to leave it all behind—*not again*. And what if the team didn't find the Stabilizers for Asher? I couldn't just leave him without knowing if he would be okay.

"I want to stay." I held onto the island for stability. "Don't you? Isn't this your chance at a do-over?"

Aunt Viv flinched, no doubt remembering her *you think I wanted this life?* statement. "Emma, you don't belong here."

It was my turn to flinch, but I stood my ground. "I fit in here more than anywhere else we've been. Also, I'm almost eighteen." I threw the age-of-independence at her. "So, if I don't want to go, you can't make me."

"It's not safe for you here." Her voice lowered as she glanced across the hall. "Anna told me a long time ago that there was someone in Arc who couldn't be trusted. That's how she was captured by the Clinic in the first place."

"What?" I looked across the way. "Who?"

"Someone higher up—so, no one who's here right now," she assured me. "Only she didn't know who, but that's one of the reasons she wouldn't risk going back, especially since she had you to consider. As her daughter—and a Halfbreed—you'd be a prize for the Clinic."

Thanks to Raine's little geek-out about my genes, I fully understood how much the Clinic would relish the opportunity to study me. But if my mom had been willing to risk capture for me, then how could I not do the same?

I squared my shoulders as I geared up for the question I needed to ask—even if I wasn't ready for the answer. "Tell me the truth: Is Mom still alive? Was she really killed by that Recall Team? Or was she recaptured?"

Aunt Viv's eyes widened with shock. "Why do you..."

"No more secrets, remember?"

She hesitated before uttering four words that could potentially change my life forever. "I honestly don't know."

The walls of the armory closed in, and my heart pulsed somewhere in my throat. "Then how can you want to leave when—"

The door opened across the hall as the Breakpoint team finished their meeting.

Aunt Viv fixed her determined stare on me. "You are my top priority. I can't go chasing after theories when we have no proof. Especially since Anna entrusted your safety to me. I won't fail her again." Then her voice hardened. "And until you are eighteen, I'm still your legal guardian and I make the decisions."

"Hey, Viv." Nova popped into the doorway wearing standard Arc tactical gear. The three copper-threaded bands that wrapped her sleeve signifying her Tech Ops Lead status. "I need to get you set up in the command center now."

"Understood." Aunt Viv looked back at me and whispered, "Be ready to leave first thing tomorrow."

40

I walked into the medical bay as knots twisted in my stomach. *Tomorrow*. Less than twelve hours, but it felt like only a heartbeat away. How could Aunt Viv expect me to just leave like this? Without knowing if Asher would okay, or if my mom was still alive—all because we didn't have proof.

If Aunt Viv wanted proof, I'd find it for her. Or at least make sure all of Asher's options had been explored.

I took in Asher's small frame wrapped in a medical gown again. He lay sedated on one of the patient beds with his head slightly raised. I was surprised he'd been left alone, but I supposed Raine wouldn't be gone long. The mission was time sensitive—they'd get in, grab, and get out.

After the team left the Breakpoint and Aunt Viv was set to give remote tech-aid, I took the opportunity to *prep* too, snagging a map, a backpack, and an Arc-Armor device for myself. If I was going to infiltrate another Clinic site, even an inactive one, I was going to be as prepared as possible. I just wished I'd had time to change out of my *bee kind* tank top into full tactical gear, but there was no time to waste, so the tactical pants I had on would have to do.

At the supply cabinets, I set the backpack down and adjusted my brace before taking inventory of what was available.

"Emma?"

Thrown off by Asher's soft voice, I straightened from my crouch. He was still laying on the hospital bed, but this time his eyes were open.

"Hey." I walked over. "How are you feeling?"

Less combustible, I hoped. I glanced around, wondering if there was any way to contact Raine. A pocket-sized plastic case sat on the side table with the Igniter symbol on the front and two vials on the inside. Was that the latest Stabilizer formula for Asher?

"I feel fuzzy," Asher said groggily.

"That's understandable." I smiled. "It's probably the sedat—"

Darkness seized the medical bay. One second the lights were on, and the next everything was pitched into shadows. What the hell?

"E-Emma, what's happening?"

"I don't know." A trickle of unease swirled to life.

Then the soft glow of what must be battery-powered lights sprang to life. They were spaced throughout the medical bay and helped fight back the shadows on the supply cabinets, IV poles, oxygen tanks, and hospital beds.

A small sound escaped from Asher.

"Hey, hey." I squeezed his shoulder. "Don't worry. It's probably just a city issue, not just the Breakpo—"

The floor shuddered beneath us as a low rumble sounded out in the distance. Maybe that had come from the street below. Or maybe it was the team returning early with, you know, a *bang*. Or maybe I'd just imagined—

Another eruption rattled the Breakpoint, causing me to tense. The resounding boom was louder this time. I half-expected the building to collapse all around us—definitely not imaginary.

Fear clawed down my spine as a deep primal instinct told me it was something much, much worse. I scanned the darkened medical bay. What should I do? Besides whoever was making all that noise, there were only three of us at the Breakpoint right now, and Aunt Viv was still up on the third floor—

Shit.

That was a floor my fob didn't have access to. We could try to make it up there and knock on the door until my aunt let us in... but also risk getting someone else's attention—hard pass. And based on the blast from below, heading downstairs was also a no-go.

One thing I did know was if it truly was a Recall Team making all that noise, the first place they'd expect to find Asher was right here in the medical wing. Darting to the other side, I quickly detached his IV line at one of the juncture points. I just hoped whatever was leaking all over the floor was something he could do without for now.

Asher pushed his blankets aside and swung his legs off the bed. His haunted eyes fixed on me as I helped him to stand and we shuffled to the door. I held my breath before inching around the edge of the frame and peering into the darkness.

As my eyes adjusted, I picked out the familiar elements of the hallway—concrete floors, exposed ceilings, and brick walls. It was mercifully empty. We'd head for the closest stairwell. After that? The residential floors? But one step at a time.

I directed us toward the double doors that led to the training wing. One panel was propped open, and I could barely make out the weight room door on the other side. With Asher velcroed to my side, we slowly navigated our way through and down the hall, but at this pace I wasn't even sure we'd make it to the stairwell, let alone the residential floors.

Crap.

And even if we did make it up there, what would we do then? Barricade ourselves in—*That's it!*

Not stopping to think, I led us into one of the training rooms. In the moonlight that leaked from the high windows, I spotted the profiles of the metal training bins, water station, and towel hamper—*score*. Sending up a silent thank you to whoever had identically stocked these rooms, I guided us over to the side and leaned Asher against the wall. Next, I quickly rearranged the bin order before reaching into the hamper and pulling out a few layers of crumpled towels.

"I know this isn't ideal." I glanced at Asher. "But it's just in case."

Understanding flared in his eyes as he shuffled closer and reached for the edge of the hamper. I helped him up and in, swiftly replacing the towels to create a layer of camouflage. I just hoped the smell wasn't too bad as I took off my Arc-Armor and placed it on him. Then I grabbed the last towel.

"W-what about you?" Asher asked, lips trembling.

The way his agonized eyes shimmered with unsplit tears nearly broke me. And left no doubt that he knew who was behind the blackout and the explosion down below. Knew who was making their way up here this very second.

"I'll be right back." I forced a smile, even as panic pulsed through me. "But if I'm not, don't make a sound no matter what you hear. And if it comes to it, use the Igniter bin next to you to defend yourself, okay?"

Asher nodded. "Okay."

I wanted to tell him it would be all right, but I just couldn't bring myself to say those words. We both knew it might not be.

I settled the last towel in place, Asher vanishing into a sea of microfiber. Then I launched myself into motion without looking back. Because I couldn't look back. I needed to focus on the task at hand. That's what Clay would have instructed me to do: *Keep aware but focused.*

I headed toward the soft red glow of the stairwell exit sign that must have also been battery-powered. Every step sounded like a marching band to my ears. At the end of the hallway, I got to work scouring the wall. That button had to be here somewhere—*yes*. I leapt forward and pressed my target, engaging the hidden fortress before gripping the sturdy handle, only to hesitate. Was this the right thing to do? Even if we somehow survived this, it was still possible that the team wouldn't find the proper Stabilizers or Arc couldn't formulate one.

What if I just left the shield doors open and let the Clinic recapture Asher? They could give him the proper treatments so he'd survive.

But then Asher's terrified face flashed before my eyes, shooting straight to my chest. I hauled the shield door across its track, the reinforced panel sealing shut with a soft clank and an impressive series of clicks—no turning back now.

I had to protect Asher and stop the Clinic from recapturing him. Pivoting, I moved forward, because that's what I had to do at this point—move forward. And get to the other shield door. Passing one training room after the next, I raced back the other way, debating whether stealth or speed was the better strategy before settling on something in between. I'd never realized how long this hallway was until now.

How had the Clinic found the Breakpoint? Wasn't it supposed to be off their radar? Unless... A heart-wrenching thought occurred to me. Unless the Clinic had somehow tracked the stolen tablet here. Was this all my fault—*no*. I couldn't think like that right now. It wouldn't do any good.

Finally the double doors to the medical wing appeared out of the darkness. I slowed to a stop, unsure of what caused me to halt, but suddenly the tiny hairs on the back of my neck rose on high alert. Then, movement captured my attention.

From the shadows, a form stepped out from one of the treatment rooms. The man was dressed in all black and equipped with tactical gear. A handgun was trained in front of him as he disappeared into the room across the hall. I wasn't sure if his weapon would discharge tranquilizer darts or actual bullets, but neither was optimal for me.

In a panic, I chose the closest doorway and dashed inside. I found myself in the weight room and flattened myself against the wall, trying to blend in with the brick—which was ridiculous. Sweat dampened my forehead as I strained to listen, but I couldn't hear anything over my own heartbeat. What the hell should I do?

I'd only seen one agent, but I wasn't dumb enough to think there weren't more. If I could somehow trick him into heading the other way, then maybe I could still get the shield door closed. But how?

That's when I spotted the rack of weights under the soft glow of the moonlight. Surging to the side, I crept behind what looked like a jungle-gym-from-hell and over to the rack. After choosing the lightest dumbbell I could find, I crept back to the door, staying close to the wall. If I could throw the weight far enough down the hall, it might give me enough time to—

Heavy boots sounded on the concrete.

Pressure clamped my chest as I pressed back against the wall, ending up slightly concealed by the jungle gym. The urge to curse and cry hit me hard as I clutched the dumbbell with clammy palms. If I was going to transform into some kick-ass Halfbreed Igniter, now would definitely be the time.

Inhaling deeply the way Clay had instructed me, I planted my feet and kept my eye on the mirrors lining the perimeter, preparing to swing for the fences. Attacking the agent wasn't the best strategy—given my sheer lack of offensive training—but I refused to go out without a fight.

A heartbeat later, a dark figure drifted soundlessly through the doorway, gun still taking the lead. As the agent proceeded farther into the room, I gripped the weight tighter. I only had one chance. I needed to wait for the right moment.

Three more steps. Two more. One.

I struck, catching him upside the head with the dumbbell. With a grunt of surprise, the agent toppled sideways as his weapon clattered to the floor and out of sight. The crack of his head meeting the concrete was a sound that would probably plague me for the rest of my life.

Chest rising and falling rapidly, I stared down at him in shock. His shallow breathing was the only sign he was still alive. All the while a little voice in my head screamed at me to get moving, get to the shield door.

I started to back away, when it occurred to me to grab the stun gun from the agent's tactical belt—his unconscious body having no need for it anymore. I clutched it at my side before backing away on shaky legs, unable to look away.

A powerful hand clamped around my arm. "You have something of ours, Sweetheart."

41

*G**riffin*. A wave of raw fear engulfed me as the situation just climbed from problematic to impossible.

He tightened his vice grip. "Now, let's play nice—"

I hit the button on the slim device before slamming the crackling end of the stun gun into Griffin's exposed forearm. A hiss of volts connected with flesh as he opened his mouth in a silent scream. His hold weakened and he pitched forward to his knees. I tore away, blindly bumping into one of the machines.

Without warning, razor-sharp pain exploded along my cheek, sending me tripping over something in the darkness. I landed arms-first on the concrete. My braced wrist screamed in protest as I lost my grip on the stun gun—my only weapon.

With a groan, I rolled onto my back as a metallic taste coated my mouth. Griffin stalked forward, his icy blond hair acting like a beacon in the darkness. As I scooted backward, I realized what I'd tripped over—the unconscious agent.

I expected Griffin to step over the agent but was struck silent when a warm, low-level hum I'd felt before flared out from my chest, and he raised his faintly glowing arm. With a wave of his arm, he whipped the agent across the room on a surge of air as if he was trash. The agent smashed into one of the mirrors, fracturing it on impact before crashing to the floor. If the agent had been breathing earlier, he probably wasn't anymore. Weren't they on the same team?

I scrambled to move, but Griffin was faster. One second I was struggling to stand, and the next I was lifted clean off the floor by the throat. I clawed at Griffin's hand, my oxygen supply cut off.

"Did you get yourself partially neutralized again?" Griffin tilted his head. "Makes my job easier, especially since there's no ice prince here to save you this time."

This was it. I would be taken, drugged, and dissected like a lab rat.

"Where's Asher?" Griffin pressed. "Just hand him over. We both know he needs the Clinic's help."

My heart faltered because I couldn't deny that he was right.

"Let my niece go." Aunt Viv's voice echoed into the room.

Griffin turned, surveying the newcomer. "Who am I to deny a lady?"

A second later, I was sailing backward before the backs of my legs crashed into a workout bench and my shoulder smacked off the concrete. I descended into a fit of coughs, my pain receptors firing off like firecrackers.

A battle cry burst from Aunt Viv as my chest flared up. A fire hydrant of flames shot through the air like a torpedo. When Griffin stepped forward, the humming in my chest spiked. Aunt Viv's flames hit an invisible barrier before spreading out like a blazing shield. Several machines around him caught fire, the smell of burnt plastic and rubber saturating the air.

Aunt Viv crouched next to me, helping me to my feet. "Are you okay?"

"Yeah." I straightened, stifling a cry from the unwelcomed movement.

"How cute." Griffin snuffed out the blaze with a predatory grin.

Aunt Viv stepped in front of me, creating a barrier between me and Griffin. My aunt was a badass, no question about it. Like everyone else here at the Breakpoint, she was a trained fighter—a living weapon. But Griffin was a Boosted Enforcer, and she'd been taking suppressor oil to keep us hidden.

"What's cute is how blind you must be." Aunt Viv widened her stance.

Griffin blinked. "What?"

"Who does the Clinic have on the hook for you? A sibling? A parent?"

He stiffened.

"His father," I blurted, remembering Agent Todd's comments from the Holding Site.

"Ah, father it is." Aunt Viv shifted away from me and made her way through the maze of machines. "Let me guess: the Clinic threatened to bankrupt him? Or he was already so far in debt that they promised to wipe it clean in exchange for experimenting on you? Or maybe—"

"He's sick," I continued connecting dots for her.

Griffin's harsh features sharpened on me, his jaw setting like granite.

"Even better," Aunt Viv said. "And I imagine they promised to treat him, right?"

"Shut up," Griffin barked.

"Be honest with yourself," Aunt Viv said. "When was the last time you saw him? And I mean actually laid eyes on him?"

"I said shut up!" Griffin's glowing profile flickered in and out of my vision as the air pressure in the room intensified.

"The Clinic can't be trusted," Aunt Viv continued, undeterred. "All they do is lie and manipulate, making false promises to use your deepest desperations against you. But make no mistake, once they get you on the hook, they cut loose ends." A low current of fury infused the air as my chest flared. "Deep down, you already know your father is gone."

Griffin exploded, turning the weight room into a raging wind tunnel before a blast of air hurtled toward Aunt Viv. Quick as a rattlesnake, she rolled and fired off a streaming blaze in retaliation, holding her copper lighter in a softly glowing hand. In seconds, Griffin raised an invisible wall of wind right before the river of flames slammed into it. The heat being thrown off was like a furnace on high, the air sizzling with power.

Shrinking back, I sidestepped the leg press as the war of wind and fire continued. I was just trying to stay out of the way. The last thing I wanted to do was draw Griffin's attention—or worse, distract my aunt.

Aunt Viv lobbed a molten orb at Griffin, skimming his thigh. A bellow of pain echoed off the mirrors as Hurricane-Griffin escalated to a category five, rattling the fitness machines and lifting smaller pieces of equipment in the gusting force. Dodging a flying medicine ball, I hit the deck and covered my head. My fingers grazed something in the process.

The agent's gun.

Up close, I could now see that the weapon didn't look normal. Sections of transparent slots circled the barrel, displaying a row of tiny, purple-tipped darts. The same ones from—

A spine-chilling cry split the air, jerking my head up. My heart stopped as I spotted something protruding from my aunt's shoulder right before she crumpled to the ground.

"Aunt Viv!" I cried out.

The gale-force winds died down as Griffin stalked toward her, turning my blood to ice.

No, no, no.

Peeling myself off the floor, I curled my fingers around the tranq gun, the lightweight metal cold in my palm. I lined myself up behind Griffin and raised the weapon as a tremor coursed through my outstretched arm—not the best sign, but I buried that red flag deep down.

"Don't worry," Griffin sneered, his focus purely on Aunt Viv. "Deep down, you already know you're gone."

I aimed for the biggest target—his back—and squeezed the trigger. I didn't hear the gun go off with all the adrenaline thundering through me, but my hand jumped from the force. Griffin jerked and swayed on his feet before falling to his knees. A purple-tipped dart protruded from his upper shoulder.

In a daze, I scrambled over to my aunt and dropped down next to her. A scorched metal bar jutted from her shoulder, making my world tilt.

"Aunt Viv." My vocal cords cracked, hands frozen in a hover.

I struggled with what to do, gazing wildly around the room as if a medic would magically appear. All I saw was Griffin, holding the dart he'd just ripped from his back. I assumed those darts were designed to knock out a full-grown Elementum, but I wasn't planning to stick around to find out.

"Aunt Viv." I pleaded, her eyes were closed and her breathing was labored. "I need you to get up."

The request went unanswered as a knot of emotion clogged my throat. But I knew what I had to do as I gripped her under the arms. I cringed at the groan she released.

"I'm sorry," I breathed as I hauled her out of the room.

Out in the hall, my hands slipped and struggled to hold on. I blamed it on my braced wrist and the stress sweat—and *only* that. I refused to believe it could be anything else, especially not the dark substance trailing behind us as I dragged the only family I had left. Crossing the threshold of the medical bay, I carefully lowered her to the ground, studying her pale face in the soft glow of the battery-powered lights.

"I'll be right back," I promised before racing back into the hallway. Relieved to find it still empty, I beelined it for the disguised button on the wall, activating the shield door and sliding the reinforced panel into place.

As the locks triggered, I hoped Asher stayed hidden and that I could beg for his forgiveness later. There was a good chance Griffin had been knocked out from the dart, but with Aunt Viv hurt I wasn't willing to take that risk.

I sprinted back into the medical bay, heading straight for the supply cabinets. *Gauze.* I needed lots of gauze. Ripping open door after door, I searched through the gloves, cotton swabs, and antiseptic sprays, leaving bloody handprints on the pristine laminate as I went. Eventually I gathered enough gauze packages and I dropped to my knees beside Aunt Viv. I tried not to pay attention to the expanding dark pool under her impaled shoulder. I knew better than to remove the metal bar myself. It could unleash an even worse string of injuries.

Instead, I tore open the packaging and pressed the bundles of gauze around the wound. But I wasn't a medic. Aunt Viv needed Raine. Sage. Somebody with more experience than me. But it was possible no one was coming. With the power out, the team might not even know about the Breakpoint's breach. And even if they did, they might not make it back in time. What if no one came?

I looked down at my hands; the once snowy-white bandages were now a deep crimson. Pure dread dug in as I struggled to catch my breath. There was so much blood.

"Emma—" A bout of wet coughs seized Aunt Viv's next words as her copper lighter clattered to the floor.

"No, save your energy," I said, my voice full of gravel. "There will be time to talk later."

There had to be.

I fumbled to open more gauze as my blood-soaked hands kept slipping on the packaging. This couldn't be real. It had to be a nightmare.

"I'm sorry." Aunt Viv gripped my wrist as I pressed more bandages to the drenched pile, each of her breaths wheezing in and out. "I failed... you."

"No, you didn't." I shook my head fiercely as liquid warmth seeped through my fingers. "Never."

"I love you, but I... failed you." Aunt Viv coughed, spraying little red dots onto her lips. "Anna and I... failed you. We tried, but... this life is a curse." Her glazed eyes searched mine as she rambled. "Anna... at the Clinic... but had to save you."

"Just hold on a little longer, okay?"

"Too much risk... being a Crossbreed."

In slow motion, her arm fell to her stomach as the air rattled from her lungs. Then, her chest stilled. No movement up or down. Her eyes stared fixed at the ceiling. For a few seconds, I couldn't move. Couldn't process what my heart already knew.

"Hold on." I pressed the wet bandages frantically to her wound as tears streamed down my cheeks. "Aunt Viv, please hold on. You have to hold on."

There was no response as tremors racked my body. I couldn't go through this—*not again*.

"Please." My voice cracked as the world blurred. "Please don't leave me."

Then something cracked deep inside me, and I screamed. Screamed until my vocal cords gave out. Screamed until nothing mattered anymore and the world faded from focus.

At some point, a distant banging reached my attention, but I was strangely numb. Like my internal capacity had hit its limit, and everything was obscured and muted.

The sound repeated, only louder this time, resonating through the room as if something metallic had been struck—hard.

The shield door.

My gaze flew to the open door as reality trickled back in. Apparently, the tranquilizer hadn't worked on Griffin, but would he really be able to get through it? Saylor and Reed had said only an impressive amount of force could reopen it, but at the moment it sounded possible.

As the banging reverberated through the hallway, I swallowed hard, my throat feeling like I swallowed a cactus. I wanted nothing more than to stay rooted in place and wallow next to—*no*. I shoved down that tidal wave of emotion before I lost it again. I couldn't leave Asher high and dry like that. And I couldn't let Aunt Viv's sacrifice be for nothing. Because there was a genuine threat on the other side of that door, and I could only see two options.

Give up or fight.

Nails biting into my bloodstained palms, I thought back to everything I'd learned over the past two weeks. I could fully admit I was no match for a trained Elementum—let alone a Boosted Enforcer. So, what could I do? What skills did I have?

As I looked down at my aunt, I racked my brain. There had to be something I could do, some way I could fight against Griffin like my aunt. Then a plan formed, if that's what I could even call it. But it was better than nothing.

The banging intensified. I steeled myself and rose on shaky legs before maneuvering my aunt's body to the far corner, careful not to bump her into anything. I refused to think that it didn't matter anymore or that she wouldn't feel it if I did.

Anger rose up inside me and I latched onto it, using it to fuel me for what I had to do next. My aunt's lighter: check. Antiseptic spray: check. Willing my hands to remain steady, I drew the emblem I remembered onto Asher's Stabilizer case before tossing the Sharpie onto the counter. This might fail, but I—

A violent crash echoed in the hallway and dust plumed through the open door, followed by the sound of heavy footfalls. Determination settled deep in my bones.

I had to try.

42

"Oh, *Sweethearrrt*." Griffin's voice drifted out of the shadows. "Come out, come out, wherever you are."

I clutched my little arsenal as a spike of fear shot down my spine. But that was quickly replaced by a burning rage when I spotted my bloodstained hands, the crimson skin a fierce reminder that it was him or me.

Him or me.

When Griffin stalked through the door, I didn't hesitate. I flicked my aunt's copper lighter and hit the nozzle of the antiseptic spray. Flames erupted into the air as my makeshift flamethrower struck its target, resulting in a howl of pain.

I released the nozzle and shifted positions, not taking any chances of Hurricane-Griffin blasting the flames back at me. The goal was to inflict whatever damage I could, while also staying one step ahead of his attacks with my weird heartburn ability-tracking—or what I was pretty sure was my escalated pattern-tracking.

Griffin whipped around and stretched out a softly flickering arm. I darted sideways, my chest humming in light pulses as I kept aligned with his smoking back, avoiding his attack. Or what I assumed was supposed to be an attack—but only a slight breeze came out. What the hell?

I looked past the scorched shirt and really inspected Griffin. He appeared the same—icy hair, lethal gear, Control Band—but his veins… There was something seriously wrong with them. Under the pale skin encasing his forearms, the spiderweb of blood vessels were inky black, like they were circulating sludge. Was it the tranquilizer? Or was it from blasting through the shield door? Maybe he had overloaded his own system—*didn't matter.*

I raised the lighter and antiseptic spray, aiming for Griffin's legs. The blaze shot out, catching him in the thigh just above where my aunt had hit him. Bellowing, Griffin pivoted away before charging me like a linebacker. His hand clamped around my wrist as he wrenched me forward, jerking his knee up at the same time. Sharp pain exploded across my ribs, causing me to lose my grip on the antiseptic spray as my knees cracked off the concrete. I clutched my side, agony stealing my next breath.

"What'd I say about playing nice?" Griffin's grip tightened.

Blinking back tears, I was now at eye level with his charred thigh. The pungent smell of roasted flesh made my stomach curdle. I punched my free fist forward and hit the irritated skin with a war cry, freeing everything festering inside me. A shocked howl echoed off the supply cabinets as Griffin jerked back, swinging me around like a merry-go-round and launching me right at one of the hospital beds.

I caught myself, but not before my hip slammed into the footboard, eliciting a yelp. I stumbled backward, ignoring the flares of pain as Griffin limped after me with a blinking, black-veined arm. But again, only a light breeze stirred the room.

"Technical difficulties?" I staggered away.

"Only a slight hindrance. Nothing the extra Boosters can't remedy." His tone dripped with menace.

So, the Boosters must have been counteracting the tranquilizer and turning his veins into an oil-coated roadmap. But more importantly, I now knew there was a ticking clock on Griffin's rebooting abilities. If I wanted to strike, it needed to be while we were on more even ground.

"All you need to concern yourself with is leading me to Asher," Griffin said as we circled each other. "Has he struggled without his Stabilizers yet?"

My chest hollowed but I didn't say a word.

"He has, hasn't he?" Griffin's predatory smile said he knew he'd hit the mark. "You should just hand him over. It'll be easier that way."

"Do you even know what happens to the Elementums you help capture?" I asked, sounding braver than I felt. "Or is it *easier* not knowing how the Clinic uses them like lab rats? Easier than fighting them, right?"

"You don't know what you're talking about." Griffin's face filled with hostility at his own words being thrown back at him.

"Why have you stopped fighting them? Because it's truly easier? Or because you think my aunt was right?"

Griffin drew up short, fists clenching.

"You do, don't you?" I tightened my hold on Aunt Viv's lighter for strength. "You think it's possible that the Clinic got rid of your father."

"Shut up," Griffin snarled, head shaking.

"If that's true, why would you still work for the Clinic?" I weighed my words carefully. "Why would you help people who have absolutely no respect for you? Who keep you restrained and believe that you're expendable."

Griffin frowned, jaw tightening.

"What do you think the Clinic will do once they create a new and improved replacement for you?" I pressed on. "You really think they'll just let you walk away?"

"I'm not being replaced, and my dad isn't gone." Griffin's profile flickered with confined power just waiting to be unleashed. Like the pressurized calm before the storm.

"It's already happening. Why do you think your Handler is so focused on Asher?" I thought of Agent Todd's obsession. "She wants to trade up by being *his* Handler. Only issue is she doesn't have the bluff of holding his father over him. If the Clinic is willing to get rid of another Elementum like Asher's father, what makes you think your father is safe?"

My chest started to hum and the surrounding air crackled and thinned like a water bottle heading for higher altitude. "And yet here you are, helping them take Asher away from the little he has left. Just like they did to *you*." I waved a hand in his direction. "But you don't have to do that. This is your chance to do the right thing and make up for all the terrible things the Clinic made you do."

Griffin's stance loosened and the air pressure dropped off, allowing my lungs to relax. Maybe I was finally getting through to h—

Blinding pain burst across the side of my head, taking me to my knees. I didn't even feel the impact of the concrete as stars exploded behind my eyelids. A fist coiled into my hair, hauling me up by the roots. I cried out in pain as I stumbled to my feet, head cranking at an uncomfortable angle.

"I've been praying for this little reunion." Agent Todd wrenched my hair back as reactive tears welled up in my eyes. "You won't slip through my fingers this time, and neither will my golden ticket. Now, where is he?"

"He's not here," I ground out as I flailed like a cat being held by the scruff.

"Liar." Agent Todd pressed something solid into my side, sending a bolt of fear down my spine and freezing me in place.

Not good.

"I see someone went crazy with the Boosters." Agent Todd mocked Griffin. "We need to get to Asher before the others do. I'm not letting anyone else get face time with the Director when it's rightfully mine. Now, where are the other assets? We need to interrogate them too."

Mouth setting into a hard line, Griffin glanced to the far side of the room.

"You buffoon," Agent Todd scolded as she looked toward Aunt Viv. Acid climbed up my throat that she was even breathing in the same direction. "The orders were to take them all alive. This will cost you, Griffin. You can expect another delay in treatments because of your insubordination."

The color drained from Griffin's face.

Then Agent Todd wrenched my head back farther. "Now, where is Asher? Even you must realize he needs his Stabilizer before it's too late and this is all ruined."

Ruined?

"You mean by his death?" I bit out in disgust before pointing to the side of Griffin. "You can go to hell because we already found his Stabilizer."

On the side table next to Asher's empty hospital bed sat the pocket-sized plastic case with the two vials, but instead of the Igniter symbol on the front, now the Horizon Project emblem was drawn in its place. I had hoped to use the tactic against Griffin to get information, but this might work too. I just hoped my replica looked official enough from a distance.

"He's already on his way to a different location," I lied.

"That's impossible." Agent Todd tensed behind me, unconsciously lowering her gun-filled hand to her tactical belt. Clipped to the side of it was a similar pocket-sized case. Was that the real Horizon Project Stabilizer?

"How did you get that?" Agent Todd shoved the gun against my side again.

My ribs cried out in protest, but I directed my attention to Griffin. "*See?*"

"See what?" Agent Todd pressed the gun harder.

Pure panic clawed at my throat as the self-preservation part of my brain screamed at me to shut up. But this was my opportunity. I had to take the risk. For Asher.

"You and your father mean nothing to her." I locked eyes with Griffin. "You're nothing but a stepping stone."

Agent Todd yanked my head back. "Shut it."

"Are you trying to replace me with Asher?" Griffin asked her as a stunned moment passed.

"What are you spouting off about, you idiot?" Agent Todd dismissed him.

"Are you?" Griffin stood firm.

"Silence," Agent Todd snapped, her voice pitching higher. "You know what happens if you don't do your goddamn job."

"Answer me!" Griffin erupted like a volcano.

"Remember your place, Enforcer." Agent Todd leveled her gun at Griffin, the patches of purple darts along the barrel a slight comfort, but not enough to calm the panic still rooted in my chest. "I won't miss out on this opportunity just because of you."

"I'm the only reason you have this opportunity in the first place." Griffin's face turned deadly. "Without me, you'd still be stuck in that same position with no signs of a promotion."

"Don't push me, you fool." Agent Todd jerked her weapon for emphasis. "I will neutralize you, and if I do, a Booster won't help you this time."

"The higher-ups know what you are," Griffin continued, despite the livid agent behind me. "They can smell the desperation and failure wafting off you like a disease. Especially after you've backstabbed and sold out everyone you've ever worked with, including *me*." He took a step forward. "I've been your fall guy for every damned mistake you've made, but the joke's on you. You've dug your own grave with your career."

"No, the real joke is that was your father!" Agent Todd shouted, superiority coating every syllable. "You really thought the higher-ups care about one pitiful dying man?"

My chest hummed with the low current of rage that permeated the air as Griffin's profile started to glow.

"You're the fool if you truly bought that." Agent Todd laughed. "The truth is your father died sad and alone, stuck in a grave of his own making. Crying out for an inattentive son who never came."

Everything happened in a flash. Relying on my years of defensive training and the vast improvements thanks to Clay, I kicked back and slammed my heel into Agent Todd's shin. A raw howl pierced the air as the hold on my hair loosened. I seized my opportunity, painfully ripping free, but I didn't go far. I reached for her tactical belt, latching onto the small case as I struggled to get it free.

"You little bitch." Agent Todd grabbed at me as a pulse of pure power contorted the air.

Griffin released an agonized scream as he stepped forward, lifting a glowing, black-veined arm. An alarming rumble shook the room right before the humming in my chest spiked to uncharted levels, alerting me to the impending attack. Acute terror barreled through me as I wrenched the case free.

Then Griffin detonated.

A gale-force wind surged out in all directions, mowing down everything in its path like a tornado. Including me. It whipped me right off my feet.

In midair, time seemed to suspend as medical debris flew every which way and I was tossed like a ragdoll. I had a vague sense of fiery explosions going off in the distance before a blast of hot wind assailed me, the brutal pressure building against every inch of my body.

Hurtling to the floor, I lost my next breath from the impact as pain lit up my system. And then, the world blinked out until there was nothing.

Until I was nothing.

43

Fog surrounded me, smothering everything in a brisk blanket. When had it blown in? It must have sprung up from the ocean, which wasn't a complete shock, considering Northern California was notorious for it, but I couldn't remember how I'd gotten stuck out in it.

No wait, that wasn't right... I struggled to recall anything, but my brain felt like a balloon lost in the clouds—untethered. I could only feel the bone-deep cold that surrounded me. A distant part of me recognized that might not be a good thing.

Confusion sharpened my hazy thoughts as I realized my eyes were actually closed—and super-glued shut. With colossal strength, I pried them open, blinking back the exhaustion that racked my body. I was lying on a hard floor staring up at a shadowy ceiling as an odd ringing buzzed in my ears.

As I eased my head to the side, a war zone came into focus. Patient beds were scattered haphazardly and medical supplies littered the floor. Some had been scorched while others were still ablaze. Following the streams of smoke and falling ash, several of the overhead light covers were missing or barely hanging in there. The light tubes inside were completely fried—either burnt black or exploded. But it was the substantial hole in the floor above that really captured my fuzzy attention. Chunks of concrete dangled from cords of rebar as smoke wafted through the darkened void overhead. How...

I winced. A piercing pain throbbed behind my eyes and wetness pooled beneath my nose. I reached up with a weak hand, my fingertips returning red. Given my surroundings, a nosebleed wasn't that bad. But I had a feeling more serious issues awaited me just under the icy blanket that currently numbed my body.

I lowered my hand, my fingers grazing something solid. It turned out to be a pocket-sized plastic case. Spiderwebbed cracks covered the exterior, but the two little vials on the inside were intact.

Weird.

I gritted my teeth and tried to get up. But a biting pain arced across my lower stomach as I sucked in a sharp gasp. All right, moving wasn't pleasant—good to know. Careful to keep still, I looked down to find a slender metal rod sticking out of my stomach like a three-inch flagpole.

Holy hell.

Bile climbed up my throat as my vision swam. I was afraid I might pass out. But I couldn't let that happen before finding help.

That's when I heard it. A steady drumming pierced the wooziness. What the hell? Around me, things crackled and snapped like a campfire, but I couldn't locate the culprit as it grew louder, closer. Then a tall figure strode through the door—but not just any tall figure...

An angel.

Brain filled with cotton balls and feathers, I took in the stunning newcomer. He appeared to be a year or two older than me and was dressed all in black. An avenging angel, with golden hair like a halo. The powerful build of his arms and shoulders suggested he was a fighter, but I wasn't sure yet whether that was in my best interest.

In the flickering firelight, his eyes locked with mine, and a heartbeat later he was crouched down next to me. His features even more striking up close as he reached out a hand—

Warning bells fired off as panic seized my chest and I pulled away, groaning at the agonizing effort.

"Hey, hey. It's okay." The angel's deep voice broke through my hysteria, concern lining his handsome face. "I'm with Arc, too."

With Arc, too? Foggy information trickled back in—the Breakpoint, Elementums, Arcadius. But I wasn't with Arc, and I felt compelled to correct him. I didn't want him to get in trouble for believing I was.

My lips parted to speak, but my vocal cords were stuffed with fuzziers.

"It's okay. You're safe now," he assured me before hitting some sort of communicator on his shoulder.

Head packed with too much cotton, I couldn't track the words exchanged. All I could do was watch him. I should probably be embarrassed for my blatant stare—well, that's if this wasn't all a dream, which seemed like a strong contender.

Amber eyes focused back on me, reminding me of warm honey—ensnaring everything in their path. "Only a little longer. Then we'll get you out of here, okay?"

The angel's words triggered an important memory.

"Asher." My throat felt raw, each word scraping like sandpaper.

"What was that?" He leaned closer.

"Asher needs... this." I pushed the case of vials at him. "Hidden... in a training room."

He examined the case before firing off more instructions into his communicator. Good. That was good. I tried to keep my eyes open, but it was a losing game. Which was okay. This was all just a dream anyway.

A sting pulsed across my temple, and my eyes flew open.

"Sorry." The angel brushed back strands of my hair and pressed a piece of gauze against my temple. His warm hand was a vast contrast to the icy blanket that weighed me down.

"Hey, hey. Stay with me," he coaxed, his eyes capturing mine. "I know you're tired and hurting, but I need you to stay awake a little longer, okay?"

I nodded. Or at least I thought I did. I wasn't entirely sure what was moving—my head or the rest of the room.

The angel was speaking again, or rather his mouth was moving, but no words registered. It was like the key components of my sound system had come unplugged. Falling ash dotted his golden hair, swirling through the air like snow.

My chest pinched inexplicably as a wave of exhaustion crashed over me. Unable to fight the rising tide, the floating cinders were the last thing I saw before the fog rolled back in. And then, I faded out amidst the swirling air and ashes.

***

The sunshine warmed my skin as the balmy water enveloped me in a comforting hug and I floated along. I'd been to this beach before. I knew I had. I'd played in the frothy waves, walked barefoot in the golden sand, and been happy here. I just couldn't put my finger on the when and where.

But one thing I did know, despite all the haziness—I was finally warm. The gentle waves soothed me as the sunbaked air filled my lungs, smelling faintly of eucalyptus and mint. Which admittedly was a little weird considering I was at a beach, but I was too comfy to care.

At some point, murmuring voices and a soft beeping reached me over the warm tide, beckoning me from a vast distance. I wanted to tell them to quiet down and let me enjoy the peacefulness, but my brain latched onto the low rumbles like a life preserver that kept me from drifting out to sea.

"...holding up?" A composed voice broke through the haze.

"Stable," a clipped voice responded at a closer distance.

Both sounded familiar. But like with the beach, the specifics were lost to the tide.

"No signs of waking?" It was the composed voice, making me think of a sergeant or captain for some odd reason.

"Not yet," the second one said, his frosty voice fighting off exhaustion.

A long pause ensued, stretching out so long that I feared they'd left.

"I heard about Peyton being caught on the security cameras before the explosion," Captain-Composed said, breaching the silence.

Frosty-Fighter grunted.

"Don't beat yourself up." Captain-Composed drifted closer. "He made his own choices."

"Yeah," Frosty-Fighter said in defeat. "It proves my theory that he's somehow connected to the Horizon Project. I just don't know how yet."

The Horizon Project? Recognition flared as the soft beeping in the background increased. How did I know that name?

"It also proves how far they're willing to go to retrieve the kid," Captain-Composed said.

"At least they failed on that front," Frosty-Fighter said, though his tone lacked any triumph.

"And they showed their hand." Captain-Composed lowered his voice. "If they risked infiltrating the Breakpoint only for him, then he's got to be pretty damn important to the Director." He paused. "We'll have to discuss this more soon. Until then, Herrera needs us to be extra vigilant while our unexpected guests are in town."

"Understood," Frosty-Fighter said quietly.

But unlike him, I was having a hard time understanding. The words drifted into one ear while the meaning drifted right out the other.

"Update me if anything changes." Captain-Composed wandered farther away. "They're clearing out the last parts of the Breakpoint right now and just gave the okay to remove the bodies. I need to be there when they do." He released a sigh. "Why don't you send out for a shift change and go get some rest. You look like hell."

"Aw, you say the sweetest things." Frosty-Fighter's voice dripped with sarcasm.

Captain-Composed snorted. "I'll be back later to check in."

Another long pause followed as the warm tide rolled back in, returning me to the beach.

"Come on, Firefly," Frosty-Fighter pleaded, breaking through once more. "Wake up."

Firefly... Only one person called me that.

I fought to comply with his request, but it proved impossible. The rising tide was too enticing, too calming. Everything floated away.

44

Eventually a soft beeping and low whispers in the distance lured me into consciousness. As I pried my eyes open, I found myself lying on a comfy bed, propped up by a mound of pillows. Which was good considering my body felt like it had been put through a meat grinder. And there was this sluggish warmth that floated just under my skin.

In the soft glow from the hallway, the darkened room gradually came into focus. I spotted a side table and chair beside me, two other chairs across the way, a large window with the curtains drawn, and an organized network of medical equipment that included an IV attached to the top of my hand—which must have been the influencer of the warm-and-fuzzies currently flowing through my system. Also, maybe the reason my medical anxieties were dormant. Man, whatever they were pumping through my IV was definitely doing the trick.

All in all, I knew I was in some kind of patient room—the medical equipment and rails along the bed dead giveaways—but I didn't recognize the uncluttered but comfortable room. Where was I? And why was I hooked up to an IV?

When I took a deep breath, pain lanced across my ribs and lower stomach. All right, pain meds only went so far—duly noted. I took stock of myself as I twitched all my fingers and toes. Despite the acute discomfort along my ribs, the bandages across my temple and lower stomach, and the brace on my left wrist, everything felt intact. But why was I—

Images broke through the mental fog. The medical bay. Agent Todd. Hurricane-Griffin. And Aunt Viv... I saw my aunt lying motionless on the concrete floor, surrounded by a pool of her own blood, her eyes lifeless and devoid of emotion.

This life is a curse.

Guilt formed knots in my stomach as raw pain sliced through me. I felt like I was the curse. I was alive and breathing, while my aunt... wasn't. And never would be again.

I buried my face in my hands and curled in on myself, ignoring the throbbing pain the position caused. Tears poured out in uncontrollable surges, the heartache and anguish threatening to devour me whole.

Suddenly a pair of strong arms pulled me against a warm, hard chest. A fierce round of shivers pulsed across my skin as a minty cologne surrounded me.

Kaden.

I pressed my hands tighter to my face and sank further into his arms. His solid embrace was the only thing keeping me tethered to the world.

"I couldn't save her," I muffled into my hands. "I couldn't fight him."

Kaden made a sound at the back of his throat. "You can't think like that. None of this was your fault."

But that wasn't true, was it? I had unblocked that damn firewall. I'd attracted the Clinic's attention. And I had caused us to end up here, where I'd condemned my suppressor-hindered aunt into the path of Griffin.

"But it is." My voice gave out, but I didn't care. I was too stuck in my festering spiral, and if the void at the center of my chest was any indication, there were no signs of stopping it. No chances of piecing myself back together. Because there was no fixing this. No changing what had happened—*what I'd caused.*

Kaden pulled back, tugging at my hands. "Hey, look at me."

My blurry vision connected with eyes the color of the sea.

"I know where you're going with this. Trust me, I've been exactly where you are. But I need you to hear me when I say this," Kaden said softly, concern sculpting his face. "What happened to your aunt is not your fault. I should've ended things at that Holding Site. Those bastards at the Clinic are the ones who attacked the Breakpoint. They're the ones who caught us all off guard." He squeezed my unbraced wrist. "Anyone would've struggled in a situation like that."

I wasn't so sure about that. Kaden wouldn't have been cowering on the concrete floor between the weight machines while someone else fought for him.

"And against all those odds, you survived," he continued. "That's what matters. It's what your aunt would've wanted."

Another blast of crushing pain speared my chest. How I even had any tears left to cry was a mystery, but that didn't seem to matter. The second floodgate opened as Kaden simply stayed there and held me.

Eventually my achy and swollen eyes gave up as I sucked down a few shallow breaths. I sat back, feeling depleted and numb. Seeming to sense I needed space, Kaden moved to the empty chair next to me, a resigned understanding pouring off him.

I wiped at my eyes. "I'm sorry for all that."

"Don't be." His voice sounded off.

In the soft light, his face appeared paler than normal, making his scars stand out. He was still dressed in his tactical gear, which made me wonder how long I'd been out for. His midnight hair was disheveled, as if maybe he'd run his hand through it numerous times, but even in that state of ruffled disarray he was still so painfully striking.

I cleared my throat, the action cutting like knives. "Even for using you as my own personal tissue?"

"Even for that." A small grin played at Kaden's lips, but it seemed amiss—broken. "How are you feeling? Any pain? I can grab a medic."

I shook my head, settling into the mound of pillows. My body felt like a ten-ton weight. Too absorbed in my devastation, I hadn't noticed but the warm, low-level hum was back. But instead of pulsing out to all my limbs like it had when I'd faced off with Griffin, it only buzzed lightly in the center of my chest. Was I sensing Kaden's abilities? But that didn't make sense. He wasn't using any from what I could see. Or was it a fresh wave of medications kicking in?

"You sure you don't need a medic?" Kaden sounded doubtful.

"I'm okay." I absently reached for my neckline, only to let my hand fall lamely back into my lap—old habits and all that. "What happened? Is everyone else okay?" I looked around the unfamiliar room. "And where are we?"

He leaned back. "Storm Point."

"Storm what?"

"Storm Point," he repeated, a more normal smirk gracing his face—one that usually drove me up the wall, but after everything, it was a surprising comfort. "This is one of Arc's compounds. It's hidden along the Front Range and is the primary facility the Breakpoint acts as an outpost for."

This must have been the compound where Aunt Viv, Nova, and Commander Herrera had disappeared to. Did this mean that the Arc Council had cleared me? Although it seemed no one else knew of Aunt Viv's plan to leave.

"As for everyone else," he continued, "we're all fine. Worried about you, but otherwise fine. The mission was a complete bust. But that's not important right now." He shook his head. "We found a second tracker implanted in Asher. They placed it in his neck under the Control Collar so we missed it in the initial screening. It eventually got past the jammers and that's how the Clinic located the Breakpoint. It's just another example of how the Clinic keeps finding new ways to stay a hundred steps ahead of us." He stared across the room. "But it was safely removed and Asher is doing much better."

Holy crap.

Asher. I'd forgotten about him. How awful did that make me?

"Did he get his Stabilizers?" I asked, vaguely remembering giving them to an angel... unless that had really been a dream.

"He did, thanks to you." Kaden's voice filled with what sounded like awe. "And now the lab here has what they need to analyze and recreate it, so he'll be in the clear soon."

I had more questions, but I put a mental bookmark down to revisit them later when I had more energy to work with.

Kaden leaned forward, bracing his arms on his knees as our eyes locked. We didn't speak for several moments, but words bubbled up in the silence between us. Things that needed to be said to clear the air. But this wasn't the time—*soon though*.

I looked away, adjusting my IV line so it wouldn't get tangled.

"I have something for you." Kaden reached into his pocket, pulling out two small objects. One he kept in his grip, while the other he placed on the side table next to me. About the size of a golf ball, the small orb had a coal-black shell with a flattened bottom, while on top it had a milky center dotted with a single wick.

My heart clenched. I'd seen this type of candle before—roughly every year for the past nine years, to be exact.

"It's an Igniter tradition, so I've never done this before." He gestured at the candle. "But I'm told it's their way of paying tribute to a life lost. Igniting the candle signifies that their memory will burn on, even as the—"

"Spark sets them free," I finished for him, throat constricting. "We did this for my mom, but I... I didn't know what it truly meant back then."

Or that my mom might still be alive. Aunt Viv had suggested as much with her last words. I wondered if she'd truly meant it or if I'd only heard what I wanted to hear.

"I thought you might want to light one for your aunt." Kaden held out his bionic hand without meeting my eyes.

"How?" I whispered, extending my shaky hand and picking up my aunt's copper lighter.

"It was found next to you before they brought you in. I thought you'd want to use it for this." He pointed at the candle. "For whenever you're ready."

Then he rose from his chair, unfurling his body with an envious grace. It wasn't hard to see why Kaden was so special. And it had nothing to do with his good looks or being a badass Hydro. It had everything to do with the considerate gestures like this. They set him apart and made it hard not to be drawn to him.

"Thank you." I tightened my grip on the lighter.

With a nod, he strode from the room, giving me the privacy to say goodbye.

After several breaths and an unknown amount of time, I flicked the lighter and held it over the wick. In seconds, a small flame sparked to life, burning bright in the darkened room.

I settled back, holding Aunt Viv's lighter to my chest. There were still so many messy emotions to wade through. I could feel them just under the surface waiting to engulf me. But right now, I would honor my aunt and let the flickering flame set us both free.

45

"At least the bruises on your face are fading." Saylor lounged against the pillows next to me.

"*Saylor*." Reed looked heavenward from his seat next to the large window.

"What?" Saylor sent him a confused look. "That's a good thing."

The curtains were open now, revealing golden-tipped leaves swaying against the blue sky. The courtyard below was surrounded by the other wings of the Storm Point medical facility, which appeared to be built into the side of a mountain, creating an interesting canyon effect.

My lips tipped up at her honesty. It still felt odd to smile after everything that had happened, but I kept trying to convince myself that Aunt Viv would've wanted me to find happiness, even if she wasn't here to share it with me. The past couple of days had been like that. Taking it all step by step. Persuading and negotiating with myself to keep going, despite that all the arguments rang hollow. But it was the only strategy I could cobble together to survive the ghost land I was currently living in.

Saylor and Reed's visits helped. They gave me other things to think about and helped ground me back into the land of the living. As did all my other visitors. Everyone from the Breakpoint team had stopped by, including Decker—who was shockingly reserved, which I guessed was his version of a get-well gift. Even Commander Herrera and Clay had made time to check in on me while they were dealing with their own aftermath.

After the Clinic's infiltration, the Breakpoint had been stripped of all evidence and information and then abandoned. Now Herrera and Clay were working on finding and setting up a new outpost site.

My gaze drifted to the copper lighter on my bedside table, making me think of my other regular visitor. So far during my recovery, a certain Hale-Storm had frequently taken up residence in the chair beside me. But I didn't allow myself to read too much into it. I knew it only had to do with his guilt over not finishing things with Griffin when he'd had the chance, nothing more.

"Emma? Hello?"

"I'm sorry, what?" I snapped back to reality, glancing between Saylor and Reed.

Crap.

"I did it again, didn't I?" I cringed, pushing up the sleeves of my favorite fleece. Over the past few days, I kept unintentionally retreating into the abyss of my own thoughts, lost to either the nothingness or the chaos—my subconscious's twisted version of roulette.

"It's cool." Reed sent my pillow-pal a judgy stare. "Saylor was only complaining about our field session getting cut short and going back to class at the academy."

"Oh, come on." Saylor threw up her arms. "Being stuck behind one of those stupid wooden desks? It's tragic."

I couldn't imagine Saylor making it through an entire lesson plan. She seemed more like a learn-on-the-move type of girl—a rushing river rather than a calm sea.

"And you wonder why I never invite you to yoga?" Reed's tone dripped with sarcasm.

"That's different." Saylor waved a dismissive hand.

"Is it, though?" Reed arched his brows.

A knock sounded at the door and Clay appeared, the warm, low-level hum flaring within my chest. "Mind if we break up the party?" His Captain's attire radiated a professional energy as he entered the room with Kaden in tow.

"Not at all." Reed rose from his chair. "We have some errands to run, anyway."

"Always the responsible one," Saylor grumbled before reluctantly getting up.

After we exchanged hugs and they promised a future visit, the Dynamic-Duo disappeared. Clay took the chair next to me, while Kaden posted up next to the large window, his Rookie Striker gear only adding to the official-business vibe.

Clay leaned forward. "How are you holding up?"

"Less discomfort. It's getting easier to move around." I shifted against the pillows. "But I don't think that's what you're really here to discuss."

"You're right, it's not." Clay rubbed the back of his neck. "Commander Herrera wanted to be here personally, but with everything going on he hopes you'll forgive him for sending me instead."

My pulse picked up. "Sending you to do what?"

"After discussions with Commander Herrera and your aunt last week, the Arc Council has decided to offer you a training position here at Storm Point." Clay braced his elbows on his knees. "Herrera is still sorting out the details, and it'll be a difficult road getting you up to speed with the other Trainees, but if you're interested, the spot is yours."

Holy crap.

All I could do was stare at him. There'd been this small part of me that had been terrified they would kick me out as soon as I recovered. So, this was a vastly better alternative, but—*it's not safe for you here*—Aunt Viv had said there was someone higher up in Arc that couldn't be trusted. But where else could I go?

Even given the risks, I found myself wanting to stay. Then again, I'd realized something in between receiving a beatdown from Griffin and his explosive end. A moment of clarity that my mom and aunt had been right... But they had also been wrong. I might never fully fit into this world, even with my Halfbreed blood—or due to it, depending on how you looked at it—but that didn't mean I didn't have anything at stake here. My mom. My Aunt Viv. And now, myself.

This was my fight, too.

And it was my choice whether I let others' fears keep me from finding where I belonged or who I truly was—

"*Wait*. What if I don't have any abilities?" I blurted. "Will I be kicked out?"

"No one is kicking you out. You have a place here either way," Clay assured me. "But you do have abilities."

"What?" I straightened, which pulled on my incision. "I thought the explosion destroyed my blood sample and all the lab equipment?"

"It did." Clay held up a hand to calm me. "But there's been a new development thanks to Nova and the security camera stationed outside the training wing entrance. You see, all the cameras were configured to switch to battery power if the power ever went out, and the one positioned there captured a flare of heat through the medical bay door right before the explosion knocked the camera out. It was a heat shield, and it was wrapped around you."

Stunned, all I could do was sit back against the pillows. *I had abilities.* It felt surreal even repeating it in my head. I mean, I always knew this was a possibility—it was the reason I'd faced down the blood draw in the first place—but actually having it confirmed was something altogether different.

"A heat shield?" I tested out the words. Had I really summoned a heat shield without knowing it? Then again, there had been a lot going on at that particular moment.

"You must've instinctively triggered it when Griffin went full-on tsunami," Kaden said, speaking for the first time.

And even though I knew Griffin was dead—the oxygen tanks setting off behind him hadn't given him a chance—that still didn't stop the involuntary spike of fear that went through me at the mention of his name.

"We believe it's how you escaped the explosion with only relatively minor injuries," Clay added. "The stress and fear of the situation must've pushed your abilities past the remaining suppressants in your system. Since waking up, you might've noticed an influx of odd sensations."

"Is that why I've been feeling this, um"—I looked down at my hands—"I'm not quite sure how to describe it, but it's like—"

"A low-level hum when you're around other Elementums?" Kaden approached the foot of the bed.

"Exactly. I felt it when I faced off with Griffin, and then again when I woke up, but it was pretty faint. That's until Commander Herrera visited and it changed." I looked over at Clay. "The hum was still there, but there was this additional... sensation? It reminded me of cinnamon, that's the only way I can describe it."

When only silence answered me, I got nervous. Had I done something wrong already?

"Well, this is certainly a unique development." Clay cleared his throat. "But cinnamon sensation aside, it makes sense that Herrera triggered the highest reaction. As a full-blooded Igniter, he's the closest typology to yours. You see, what you're picking up on is our genetic Power Signatures." He tapped the center of his chest, reminding me of my conversation with Saylor and the need for the Arc-Armor devices.

"It's called Tracing." Kaden gripped the footboard, glancing over at Clay. "And it's considered a fairly high-level ability."

"It's interesting that as a Halfbreed you're able to do it." Clay sounded deep in thought. "But we knew this might take time and some trial and error before we determined which abilities you've acquired."

Fantastic.

Something to look forward to. A nerve-racking lottery of my Halfbreed abilities.

"What about Stabilizers? Isn't there a chance I'll need them now that the suppressor is wearing off?" That question had been banging around in the back of my head ever since the whole suppressor-surprise thing. Would Arc be able to formulate one for my weird-Halfbreed-genetics? Or would I go all blazing-beast-mode like Asher had and become terminal? My blood ran cold at that prospect. After everything, would I end up back on the suppressor oil?

"That's definitely a possibility." Clay sat back. "Unfortunately, that's also going to take some time to figure out, but the good news is we know what signs to look out for, and with your age, the timeline should be a little more gracious than Asher's was."

Super comforting.

"Has the lab been able to analyze and recreate Asher's Stabilizers yet?" I asked, needing something positive to focus on.

"Yes." Clay smiled. "And the results are better than we could have expected."

"What do you mean?"

"Asher's only an enhanced variant of an Igniter," Kaden explained. "Meaning the Clinic hasn't developed the Horizon Project as far as we'd feared."

Clay nodded. "But that doesn't mean we can take our foot off the gas. Based on all the intel we've gathered, it's clear this project is a high priority for the Clinic." He turned his serious gaze to Kaden. "They're breaking all the rules on this one, which means they could make some costly mistakes."

"This could be the key to finally taking them down." Kaden's tone was filled with determination.

And it could be the key to finding my mom. But I kept that to myself. Clay didn't know I'd seen the Phoenix file on his computer. And even though there were still questions that needed answering, I knew where I needed to keep digging: the Horizon Project.

"It's possible." Clay sounded less optimistic. "But we'll all need to work together on this if we're going to make any headway." He glanced at Kaden before landing on me, and faltering. "Well, that's if you're interested in the training position. I know you've been through a lot and if you need time—"

"I'm interested," I interjected.

"You sure?" Clay asked. "You don't have to answer me now."

"This is my fight, too." My eyes never wavered from Clay's. "It always was, even when I didn't know it."

Plus, I had my own fight. Not only did I need to find out if my mom was still alive, but I also wanted justice for what had happened to my Aunt Viv. This? This was personal.

"All right, then," Clay said with a look I almost thought was pride. "I'll touch base with Herrera and we'll get all the details sorted out." He clasped his hands. "Also, I'm afraid there will be some mandatory consequences and assignments for breaking protocol over the past two weeks. I hope you understand, but with your aunt gone, it falls on us to determine what those penalties will be."

At the mention of Aunt Viv, the deep void of loss threatened to devour me all over again. It was always creeping along the edges, just waiting to be triggered.

"I understand." I swallowed hard. And I did. Atonement was more than fair after everything I'd caused.

Clay nodded and rose from his chair, giving my shoulder a squeeze. "I'm glad you're choosing to stay." He pivoted and shared a look with

Kaden. "Don't forget the meeting with our New York visitors." He glanced at his watch. "Thirty minutes."

Kaden crossed his arms. "Seared into my brain."

Clay grunted and strode from the room, leaving me alone with Kaden who looked strung tight as a wire. Did it have something to do with me staying? Or the meeting Clay had mentioned?

"You can go, too." I plastered on a smile, refusing to let him use me to ease his guilty conscience. "I'm sure you have other things to do, and I feel confident there aren't any Enforcers lurking around."

"You can never be too careful." Kaden strolled over to his usual chair, the low-level minty hum—or his Power Signature—intensifying with his every step. "Plus, me and this chair are finally getting to know each other."

"Seriously, you can go." I gripped the blanket covering my legs.

"And miss out on my time with this nonexistent back support? Or this padding that feels like paper?" He wiggled in his chair a little. "Not likely."

I couldn't stop the snort as he kicked up his booted feet onto the edge of the bed. He crossed his ankles and lounged back like a snow leopard surveying his territory. In that moment he could have almost passed for any other teenage guy—*almost*. But it was his scars that set him apart. The physical ones, yes, but also the unseen ones that churned deep within those sea-blue eyes—and rang similar to mine. Maybe that's why we kept gravitating toward each other. But whereas his first instinct was to build a fortress between himself and that kind of distraction, I found myself running in circles unsure of how or if I wanted to slow down.

Neither was healthy. And right now, that's what I needed—some self-care. I needed to focus on finding my mom and figuring out how I fit into this world, not burying myself in some kind of escape.

Our eyes locked as a strained silence stretched out between us, the unspoken words from the other night climbing to the tip of my tongue. Then I ripped off the Band-Aid. "We should talk."

46

"We'll talk." Kaden's jaw tightened. "Once you're all healed up."

"No, now would be best," I said, shoring myself up. Plus, waiting for later wouldn't change the outcome.

Kaden lowered his feet and sat up. "Listen Emma, I'm not—"

"I think we should be friends." I cut him off, beating him to the knockout punch and saving some dignity. "I really like hanging out with you, and I don't want that to change just because of my stupid mistake. And I truly mean that. What happened the other night in the pool is all on me." I placed a hand over my chest. "I guess I was looking for some kind of escape from, well, *everything*, and that wasn't fair." I slowed my rambling roll as I tried to gauge his reaction.

"Friends?" Kaden repeated, sounding doubtful.

"Yeah." I caught my hand halfway to my neck. "I need friends here to help me navigate this new world, and I'm hoping that includes you."

A long moment passed as Kaden's gaze focused on somewhere in front of him. "What if I'm okay with it only being an escape?"

My heartbeat faltered and then accelerated as I considered what he was offering. Did I want to do the casual thing? The spine-tingling memory of Kaden's lips on mine said I did.

But also I was tired of things being temporary. In my experience, it was only a road to heartache and loss. And with my new training position here at Storm Point, this was my chance to establish something more permanent. Did I really want to complicate that with whatever this would be?

"I don't think that's the best idea." I hesitated, searching for the right words. "With everything I'm dealing with right now and needing to figure out my abilities, I'm in no shape to deal with anything else."

Kaden nodded absently, not meeting my eye. "Friends, then."

My smile felt hollow. "Good."

That's when I picked up on a new Trace. The low-level cinnamon hum pulsed through me, announcing the tall blond Igniter who stalked through the door.

"Hale, you're not hassling the patient, are you?" a hazily familiar voice said.

Holy crap.

"You're real," I blurted.

The angel halted, tilting his head. "Last time I checked."

I'd been so convinced he was a dream, but no, there he was. His golden hair still reminded me of a halo even pushed back from his tan, handsome face. The black gear he had on molded to his fighter's build and was similar to Kaden's, except his had two gold-threaded bands, one wrapping each sleeve. What rank did those mean?

"But if you need reassurance"—a wicked grin transformed the angel's face—"I'll let you pinch me wherever you want."

My cheeks heated.

"Back off, Talon." Kaden rose, the one called Talon ending up being the slightly taller of the two. "Or I'll be doing a lot more than pinching."

"Well, aren't you in rare fighting form today, Snowflake." Talon chuckled deeply, reclining against the wall. "Did I hit a nerve?"

"That does seem to be your specialty." Kaden stared him down.

"What can I say?" Talon shrugged, amber eyes locking with mine. "I'm talented."

Kaden's jaw flexed. "What do you want, Talon?"

Talon's gaze never wavered from mine. "What a loaded question."

My flush deepened as Kaden looked seconds away from throwing the other Elementum through the window or... My next breath came out in a visible puff.

Talon shook his head at Kaden. "Pretty sure freezing a patient is considered a no-no."

"Let's take it down a notch, shall we?" I said, finally finding my vocal cords.

Neither backed down from their intense stares, but at least the room temperature returned to normal.

"Great, so glad we all agree." I turned my attention to Talon and added with sincerity. "Thank you for helping me the other night. I would've been in real trouble if you hadn't."

"You're very welcome, Angel."

"What?" I squeaked.

"That's what you called me the first time we met." Talon grinned. "So, I figured I'd return the gesture. It's way more accurate in your case anyway."

Oh, goodie. That had been real too.

"Sorry about that." I cleared my throat, resisting the urge to jump out the window myself. "I'm pretty sure the head injury was to blame."

"Why are you here, Talon?" Kaden clenched his fists—both flesh and bionic.

"I came to retrieve you. The Command General would like a word before the meeting."

Suddenly a few dots connected. These must be the visitors from New York that Clay had mentioned earlier. And why did the leader of the Command—or the big gun as Saylor called him—want to talk with Kaden?

"Of course, he does." Kaden rumbled low.

Talon turned to me. "And I guess I'll be seeing you for training soon."

"What?" Kaden and I harmonized in confusion.

"I won't ruin all the surprises, cause, you know, spoilers. I'll leave the rest for Commander Herrera to explain," Talon said, amusement dancing in his eyes. "And now that I've succeeded as messenger boy, I'll see you at the meeting, Hale." He leveled his gaze on me. "I'll see you on the mats, Angel."

Then he strolled from the room, leaving both of us stunned. What the hell just happened?

"Who was that?" I asked, stomach knotting like a pretzel.

"That was Talon Sparks." Kaden stared at the exit like he wanted to freeze it shut. "He's an Igniter who recently joined the Breaker assholes."

Well, wasn't that a different take on the high-ranking division of Breakers.

"Why wouldn't Clay have mentioned him training me earlier? Or do you think Talon was just messing with us?"

"Clay would've. As for Talon, he likes messing around, but not with stuff like that."

My mind raced. Him training me? A Breaker? It had to be a mistake. There was no way they'd stick him with me unless they were punishing him. *No*. No way. Not again.

"Don't worry." Kaden faced me. "We'll get this sorted out."

"All right." I swallowed hard, settling back against the pillows. "And let me know if Sparky gives you any more trouble. I can sick Saylor on him if necessary."

He chuckled half-heartedly. "I wouldn't wish that even on my worst enemies, but thanks."

"Hey, what are friends for?"

Kaden looked away as the muscle along his jaw flexed, making his scars stand out.

Time. We just needed time to adjust—or at least that's what I hoped.

"I should go." Kaden ran a hand through his midnight hair. "You going to be okay?"

I waved a dismissive hand. "I don't need a babysitter, remember?"

"If you were a fan of history, you would know it proves otherwise."

"Funny."

Then an unreadable expression crossed his face before transforming into lopsided grin—as if an undisclosed decision had been made. "I could alert the medics." He jacked his thumb toward the hallway as he backed away. "Or find some bubble wrap. Or maybe flood the room with those pesky little packing peanuts. You know, for your own safety."

"How about I bubble wrap your mouth?" I smirked at his stupidly handsome face. "You know, for your own safety."

"I think you'd miss my mouth if you did that." Kaden squeezed my foot through the blanket as he passed.

"Never." I denied as my foolish little heart jumped at the movement. Maybe this whole friend thing would be harder than I thought.

Kaden grinned as his sea-blue eyes locked with mine. "It's pronounced *always*, Firefly."

The Elementum Series: Book 2

For an exclusive first look at the next installment in the Elementum series, check out the link below:

ABOUT THE AUTHOR

Margaret Mantor is an author, architect, and avid science fantasy romance reader. She lives in Colorado with her husband and corgi, Karl. When she isn't writing, she is sketching, pampering her little burnt-toast-loaf, and cheering on her talented ceramic artist husband.

After years of adventuring in worlds in her head, she took the leap and put keystrokes to paper space. *Air and Ashes* is her debut novel, and a dream come true. Explore more of the Elementum world at: www.margaretmantor.com.

REVIEW, SHARE + CONNECT

Thank you for taking a chance on me and *Air and Ashes*. As a new author, it truly means more to me than I could ever put into words.

Review.

If you enjoyed this story and wouldn't mind sharing your opinion, please consider leaving a review. I'd love to hear from you!

Share.

If you feel moved by the book gods, please share this book with anyone who would like to enter the Elementum world and join the fight against the Clinic.

Connect.

Find me online:

ACKNOWLEDGEMENTS

First, a special thanks to you, the reader. Without your support, none of this would be possible. I thank you from the bottom of my heart for taking a chance on me and Emma's story.

Thank you to my team of editors, Savannah, Michelle, and Samantha. You each hacked and cleaved at this story in different ways, but without you, it wouldn't be as fierce and fiery as it is today.

To my beta readers Alexia, Bailey, Eva, Josh, Kara, Kristen, Lisa, Marissa, Meg, and Ryan. Thank you for your valuable feedback, time, and for sticking with me while I figured this whole writing thing out. Hope you're excited for round two.

To my friends and family. Thank you for your endless support and for not calling me crazy (even if you thought it—it's cool, I thought it too) when I announced I was writing a book. I'm beyond lucky to have all of you in my corner.

To my parents, who always encouraged me to go after my dreams, but also taught me the meaning of hard work and how to logically accomplish my goals. You shaped the person and author I am today.

Air and Ashes was a pipe dream. A world that for so long I thought would only live in my head. And that would've remained true, if it wasn't for the unrivaled support and love of my husband, Will. I love adventuring through life with you.

Last, to Karl—my little burnt-toast-loaf, my silly-corgi-bean—you know all my plot twists, but I know they're always safe with you. Thanks for being the best writing buddy I could ever ask for.

www.ingramcontent.com/pod-product-compliance
Lightning Source LLC
Chambersburg PA
CBHW022016310726
48972CB00006B/1680